Jack Reacher – a hero for our time

'**Clint Eastwood**, **Mel Gibson** and **Bruce Willis** all rolled into one, a **superman** for our time' *Irish Times*

'Thinking girl's beefcake'
The Times

'TOUGH-BUT-FAIR'
Mirror

'ONE OF THE GREAT **ANTIHEROES**'
Independent

'**Admired** by his male readers and **lusted** after by his female ones'
Daily Express

'Arms the size of **Popeye's**'
Independent

'The lonest of **lone wolves**... **too cool** for school'
San Francisco Chronicle

'Part-**Robin Hood**, part-**gorilla**'
Sunday Times

'One of the truly memorable **tough-guy heroes**' Jeffery Deaver

'This is Jack **Reacher** for pity's sake, he'll **eat you** for breakfast!' *Los Angeles Times*

Have you read them all?

The Jack Reacher thrillers by Lee Child – in the order in which they first appeared.

KILLING FLOOR

Jack Reacher gets off a bus in a small town in Georgia. And is thrown into the county jail, for a murder he didn't commit.

DIE TRYING

Reacher is locked in a van with a woman claiming to be FBI. And ferried right across America into a brand new country.

TRIPWIRE

Reacher is digging swimming pools in Key West when a detective comes round asking questions. Then the detective turns up dead.

THE VISITOR

Two naked women found dead in a bath filled with paint. Both victims of a man just like Reacher.

ECHO BURNING

In the heat of Texas, Reacher meets a young woman whose husband is in jail. When he is released, he will kill her.

WITHOUT FAIL

A Washington woman asks Reacher for help. Her job? Protecting the Vice-President.

PERSUADER

A kidnapping in Boston. A cop dies. Has Reacher lost his sense of right and wrong?

THE ENEMY
Back in Reacher's army days, a general is
found dead on his watch.

ONE SHOT
A lone sniper shoots five people dead in a heartland city.
But the accused guy says, 'Get Reacher'.

THE HARD WAY
A coffee on a busy New York street leads to a shoot-out
three thousand miles away in the Norfolk countryside.

BAD LUCK AND TROUBLE
One of Reacher's buddies has shown up dead in the California
desert, and Reacher must put his old army unit back together.

NOTHING TO LOSE
Reacher crosses the line between a town called
Hope and one named despair.

GONE TOMORROW
On the New York subway, Reacher counts
down the twelve tell-tale signs of a suicide bomber.

61 HOURS
In freezing South Dakota, Reacher hitches
a lift on a bus heading for trouble.

WORTH DYING FOR
Reacher runs into a clan that's terrifying the Nebraska locals,
but it's the unsolved case of a missing child that he can't let go.

THE AFFAIR
Six months before the events in *Killing Floor*,
Major Jack Reacher of the US Military Police goes
undercover in Mississippi, to investigate a murder.

A WANTED MAN

A freshly-busted nose makes it difficult for Reacher
to hitch a ride. When at last he's picked up by two
men and a woman, it soon becomes clear
they have something to hide . . .

JACK REACHER: ONE SHOT

Lee Child

BANTAM BOOKS

LONDON · TORONTO · SYDNEY · AUCKLAND · JOHANNESBURG

TRANSWORLD PUBLISHERS
61–63 Uxbridge Road, London W5 5SA
A Random House Group Company
www.transworldbooks.co.uk

JACK REACHER: ONE SHOT
A BANTAM BOOK: 9780857501189
9780857501196

First published in Great Britain as *ONE SHOT*
in 2005 by Bantam Press
an imprint of Transworld Publishers
Bantam edition published 2006
Bantam edition reissued 2011
Bantam edition reissued as *JACK REACHER: ONE SHOT* 2012

Addresses for Random House Group Ltd companies outside the UK
can be found at: www.randomhouse.co.uk
The Random House Group Ltd Reg. No. 954009

The Random House Group Limited supports The Forest Stewardship
Council (FSC®), the leading international forest-certification organization.
Our books carrying the FSC label are printed on FSC®-certified paper.
FSC is the only forest-certification scheme endorsed by the leading
environmental organizations, including Greenpeace. Our paper procurement
policy can be found at www.randomhouse.co.uk/environment

Typeset in 11/13½pt Times by
Kestrel Data, Exeter, Devon.
Printed and bound by
CPI Group (UK) Ltd, Croydon, CR0 4YY.

2 4 6 8 10 9 7 5 3 1

MIX
Paper from
responsible sources
FSC
www.fsc.org   FSC® C016897

For Maggie Griffin
Jack Reacher's first and best friend in America

ONE

Friday. Five o'clock in the afternoon. Maybe the hardest time to move unobserved through a city. Or, maybe the easiest. Because at five o'clock on a Friday nobody pays attention to anything. Except the road ahead.

The man with the rifle drove north. Not fast, not slow. Not drawing attention. Not standing out. He was in a light-coloured minivan that had seen better days. He was alone behind the wheel. He was wearing a light-coloured raincoat and the kind of shapeless light-coloured beanie hat that old guys wear on the golf course when the sun is out or the rain is falling. The hat had a two-tone red band all round it. It was pulled down low. The coat was buttoned up high. The man was wearing sunglasses, even though the van had dark windows and the sky was cloudy. And he was wearing gloves, even though winter was three months away and the weather wasn't cold.

Traffic slowed to a crawl where First Street started up a hill. Then it stopped completely where two lanes became one because the black-top was torn up for construction. There was construction all over town. Driving had been a nightmare for a year. Holes in the road, gravel trucks, concrete trucks, blacktop spreaders. The man with the rifle lifted his hand off the wheel. Pulled back his cuff. Checked his watch.

Eleven minutes.

Be patient.

He took his foot off the brake and crawled ahead. Then he stopped again where the roadway narrowed and the sidewalks widened where the downtown shopping district started. There were big stores to the left and the right, each one set a little higher than the last, because of the hill. The wide sidewalks gave plenty of space for shoppers to stroll. There were cast-iron flag poles and cast-iron lamp posts all lined up like sentries between the people and the cars. The people had more space than the cars. Traffic was very slow. He checked his watch again.

Eight minutes.

Be patient.

A hundred yards later the prosperity faded a little. The congestion eased. First Street opened out and became slightly shabby again. There were bars and dollar stores. Then a parking garage on the left. Then yet more construction, where the parking garage was being extended. Then further ahead the street was blocked by a low wall. Behind it was a windy pedestrian plaza with an ornamental pool and a fountain. On the plaza's left, the old city library. On its right, a new office building. Behind it, a black glass tower. First Street turned an abrupt right angle in front of the plaza's boundary wall and ran away west, past

12

untidy rear entrances and loading docks and then on under the raised state highway.

But the man in the minivan slowed before he hit the turn in front of the plaza and made a left and entered the parking garage. He drove straight up the ramp. There was no barrier, because each space had its own parking meter. Therefore there was no cashier, no witness, no ticket, no paper trail. The man in the minivan knew all that. He wound round the ramps to the second level and headed for the far back corner of the structure. Left the van idling in the aisle for a moment and slipped out of the seat and moved an orange traffic cone from the space he wanted. It was the last one in the old part of the building, right next to where the new part was being added on.

He drove the van into the space and shut it down. Sat still for a moment. The garage was quiet. It was completely full with silent cars. The space he had protected with the traffic cone had been the last one available. The garage was always packed. He knew that. That was why they were extending it. They were doubling its size. It was used by shoppers. That was why it was quiet. Nobody in their right mind would try to leave at five o'clock. Not into the rush hour traffic. Not with the construction delays. Either they would get out by four or wait until six.

The man in the minivan checked his watch.

Four minutes.

Easy.

He opened the driver's door and slid out. Took a quarter from his pocket and put it in the meter. Twisted the handle hard and heard the coin fall and saw the clockwork give him an hour in exchange. There was no other sound. Nothing in the air except the smell of parked automobiles. Gasoline, rubber, cold exhaust.

He stood still next to the van. On his feet he had a pair of old desert boots. Khaki suede, single eyelets, white crepe soles, made by Clarks of England, much favoured by Special Forces soldiers. An iconic design, unchanged in maybe sixty years.

He glanced back at the parking meter. Fifty-nine minutes. He wouldn't need fifty-nine minutes. He opened the minivan's sliding rear door and leaned inside and unfolded a blanket and revealed the rifle. It was a Springfield M1A Super Match autoloader, American walnut stock, heavy premium barrel, ten shot box magazine, chambered for the .308. It was the exact commercial equivalent of the M14 self-loading sniper rifle that the American military had used during his long-ago years in the service. It was a fine weapon. Maybe not quite as accurate with the first cold shot as a top-of-the-line bolt gun, but it would do. It would do just fine. He wasn't going to be looking at extraordinary distances. It was loaded with Lake City M852s. His favourite custom cartridges. Special Lake City Match brass, Federal powder, Sierra Matchking 168-grain hollow point boat tail bullets. The load was better than the gun, probably. A slight mismatch.

He listened to the silence and lifted the rifle off the rear bench. Carried it away with him to where the old part of the garage finished and the new part began. There was a half-inch trench between the old concrete and the new. Like a demarcation line. He guessed it was an expansion joint. For the summer heat. He guessed they were going to fill it with soft tar. Directly above it there was yellow and black *Caution Do Not Enter* tape strung between two pillars. He dropped to one knee and slid under it. Stood up again and walked on into the raw new construction.

Parts of the new concrete floor were trowelled smooth and parts were rough, still waiting for a final surface. There were wooden planks laid here and there as walkways. There were haphazard piles of paper cement sacks, some full, some empty. There were more open expansion joints. There were strings of bare light bulbs, turned off. Empty wheelbarrows, crushed soda cans, spools of cable, unexplained lengths of lumber, piles of crushed stone, silent concrete mixers. There was grey cement dust everywhere, as fine as talc, and the smell of damp lime.

The man with the rifle walked on in the darkness until he came close to the new northeast corner. Then he stopped and put his back tight against a raw concrete pillar and stood still. Inched to his right with his head turned until he could see where he was. He was about eight feet from the garage's new perimeter wall. Looking due north. The wall was about waist-high. It was unfinished. It had bolts cast into it to take lengths of metal barrier to stop cars hitting the concrete. There were receptacles cast into the floor to take the new parking meter posts.

The man with the rifle inched forward and

turned a little until he felt the corner of the pillar between his shoulder blades. He turned his head again. Now he was looking north and east. Directly into the public plaza. The ornamental pool was a long narrow rectangle running away from him. It was maybe eighty feet by twenty. It was like a large tank of water, just sitting there. Like a big above-ground lap pool. It was bounded by four waist-high brick walls. The water lapped against their inner faces. His line of sight ran on an exact diagonal from its near front corner to its far back corner. The water looked to be about three feet deep. The fountain splashed right in the centre of the pool. He could hear it, and he could hear slow traffic on the street, and the shuffle of feet below him. The front wall of the pool was about three feet behind the wall that separated the plaza from First Street. The two low walls ran close together and parallel for twenty feet, east to west, with just the width of a narrow walkway between them.

He was on the garage's second level but the way First Street ran uphill meant the plaza was much less than one storey below him. There was a definite downward angle, but it was shallow. On the right of the plaza he could see the new office building's door. It was a shabby place. It had been built and it hadn't rented. He knew that. So to preserve some kind of credibility for the new downtown the state had filled it with government offices. The Department of Motor Vehicles was in there, and a joint Army–Navy–Air Force–Marine Corps recruiting office. Maybe Social Security was in there. Maybe the Internal

Revenue Service. The man with the rifle wasn't really sure. And he didn't really care.

He dropped to his knees and then to his stomach. The low crawl was a sniper's principal mode of movement. In his years in the service he had low crawled a million miles. Knees and elbows and belly. Standard tactical doctrine was for the sniper and his spotter to detach from the company a thousand yards out and crawl into position. In training he had sometimes taken many hours to do it, to avoid the observer's binoculars. But this time he had only eight feet to cover. And as far as he knew there were no binoculars on him.

He reached the base of the wall and lay flat on the ground, pressed up tight against the raw concrete. Then he squirmed up into a sitting position. Then he knelt. He folded his right leg tight underneath him. He planted his left foot flat and his left shin vertical. He propped his left elbow on his left knee. Raised the rifle. Rested the end of the forestock on the top of the low concrete wall. Sawed it gently back and forth until it felt good and solid. *Supported kneeling*, the training manual called it. It was a good position. Second only to lying prone with a bipod, in his experience. He breathed in, breathed out. *One shot, one kill.* That was the sniper's credo. To succeed required control and stillness and calm. He breathed in, breathed out. Felt himself relax. Felt himself come home.

Ready.
Infiltration successful.
Now wait until the time is right.

*   *   *

He waited about seven minutes, keeping still, breathing low, clearing his mind. He looked at the library on his left. Above it and behind it a spur of the raised highway curled in on stilts, like it was embracing the big old limestone building, cradling it, protecting it from harm. Then it straightened a little and passed behind the black glass tower. It was about level with the fourth storey back there. The tower itself had the NBC peacock on a monolith near its main entrance, but the man with the rifle was sure that a small network affiliate didn't occupy the whole building. Probably not more than a single floor. The rest of the space was probably one-man law firms or CPAs or real estate offices or insurance brokers or investment managers. Or empty.

People were coming out of the new building on the right. People who had been getting new licences or turning in old plates or joining the army or hassling with federal bureaucracy. There were a lot of people. The government offices were closing. Five o'clock, on a Friday. The people came out the doors and walked right to left directly in front of him, funnelling into single file as they entered the narrow space and passed the short end of the ornamental pool between the two low walls. Like ducks in a shooting gallery. One after the other. *A target-rich environment*. The range was about a hundred feet. Approximately. Certainly less than thirty-five yards. *Very close*.

He waited.

Some of the people trailed their fingers in the

18

water as they walked. The walls were just the right height for that. The man with the rifle could see bright copper pennies on the black tile under the water. They swam and rippled where the fountain disturbed the surface.

He watched. He waited.

The stream of people thickened up. Now there were so many of them coming all at once that they had to pause and group and shuffle and wait to get into single file to pass between the two low walls. Just like the traffic had snarled at the bottom of First Street. A bottleneck. *After you. No, after you.* It made the people slow. Now they were *slow* ducks in a shooting gallery.

The man with the rifle breathed in, and breathed out, and waited.

Then he stopped waiting.

He pulled the trigger, and kept on pulling.

His first shot hit a man in the head and killed him instantly. The gunshot was loud and there was a supersonic *crack* from the bullet and a puff of pink mist from the head and the guy went straight down like a puppet with the strings cut.

A kill with the first cold shot.

Excellent.

He worked fast, left to right. The second shot hit the next man in the head. Same result as the first, exactly. The third shot hit a woman in the head. Same result. Three shots in maybe two seconds. Three targets down. Absolute surprise. No reaction for a split second. Then chaos broke out. Pandemonium. Panic. There were twelve people caught in the narrow space between the plaza wall and the pool wall. Three were already down. The remaining nine ran. Four ran forward and five spun away from the corpses and ran back. Those five collided with the press of people still moving their way. There were sudden loud screams. There was a solid stalled mass of panicked humanity, right in front of the man with the rifle. Range, less than thirty-five yards. Very close.

His fourth head shot killed a man in a suit. His fifth missed completely. The Sierra Matchking passed close to a woman's shoulder and hissed straight into the ornamental pool and disappeared. He ignored it and moved the Springfield's muzzle a fraction and his sixth shot caught a guy on the bridge of his nose and blew his head apart.

The man with the rifle stopped firing.

He ducked low behind the garage wall and crawled backwards three feet. He could smell burnt powder and over the ringing in his ears he could hear women screaming and feet pounding and the crunch of panicked fender benders on the street below. *Don't worry, little people*, he thought. *It's over now. I'm out of here.* He lay on his front and swept his spent shell cases into a pile. The bright Lake City brass shone right there in front of him. He scooped five of them into his gloved hands but the sixth rolled away and fell into an unfinished expansion joint. Just dropped right down into the tiny nine-inch-deep, half-inch-wide trench. He heard a quiet metallic sound as it hit bottom.

Decision?

Leave it, surely.

No time.

He jammed the five cases he had in his raincoat pocket and crawled backwards on his toes and his fingers and his belly. He lay still for a moment and listened to the screaming. Then he came to his knees and stood up. Turned round and walked back the same way he had come, fast but in control, over the rough concrete, along the walkway planks, through the dark and the dust, under the yellow and black tape. Back to his minivan.

The rear door was still open. He rewrapped the warm rifle in its blanket and slid the door shut on it. Got in the front and started the engine. Glanced through the windshield at the parking meter. He had forty-four minutes left on it. He backed out and headed for the exit ramp. Drove down it and out the unmanned exit and made a right and another right into the tangle of streets behind the department stores. He had passed under the raised highway before he heard the first sirens. He breathed out. The sirens were heading east, and he was heading west.

Good work, he thought. *Covert infiltration, six shots fired, five targets down, successful exfiltration, as cool as the other side of the pillow*.

Then he smiled suddenly. Long-term military records show that a modern army scores one enemy fatality for every fifteen thousand combat rounds expended by its infantry. But for its specialist snipers, the result is better. Way better. Twelve and a half *thousand* times better, as a matter of fact. A modern army scores one enemy fatality for every one-point-two combat rounds expended by a sniper. And one for one-point-two happened to be the same batting average as five for six. Exactly the same average. Simple arithmetic. So even after all those years a trained military sniper had scored exactly what his old instructors would have expected. They would have been very pleased about that.

But his old instructors had trained snipers for the battlefield, not for urban crime. With urban crime, factors unknown on the battlefield kick in fast. Those factors tend to modify the definition of *successful exfiltration*. In this particular case, the media reacted fastest. Not surprisingly, since the shootings took place right in front of the local NBC affiliate's window. Two things happened even before a dozen panicked bystanders all hit 911 on their cell phones simultaneously. First, every minicam in the NBC office starting rolling. The cameras were grabbed up and switched on and pointed at the windows. Second, a local news anchor called Ann Yanni started rehearsing what she knew would be her very first network breaking-news report. She was sick and scared and badly shaken, but she knew an opportunity when she saw it. So she started drafting, in her head. She knew that words set agendas, and the words that came to her first were *sniper* and *senseless* and *slaying*. The alliteration was purely instinctive. So was the banality. But *slaying* was how she saw it. And *slaying* was a great word. It communicated the randomness, the wantonness, the savagery, the ferocity. It was a motiveless and impersonal word. It was exactly the right word for the story. At the same time she knew it wouldn't work for the caption below the pictures. *Massacre*

would be better there. *Friday Night Massacre*?
Rush Hour Massacre? She ran for the door and
hoped her graphics guy would come up with
something along those lines unbidden.

Also not present on the battlefield is urban law
enforcement. The dozen simultaneous 911 cell
phone calls lit up the emergency switchboard like
a Christmas tree and the local police and fire
departments were rolling within forty seconds.
Everything was despatched, all of them with
lights popping and sirens blaring. Every black-
and-white, every available detective, every crime
scene technician, every fire engine, every
paramedic, every ambulance. Initially there was
complete mayhem. The 911 calls had been
panicked and incoherent. But crimes were plainly
involved, and they were clearly serious, so the
Serious Crimes Squad's lead detective was given
temporary command. He was a high-quality
twenty-year PD veteran who had come all the
way up from patrolman. His name was Emerson.
He was blasting through slow traffic, dodging
construction, hopelessly, desperately, with no way
of knowing what had happened. Robbery, drugs,
gang fight, terrorism, he had no hard information.
None at all. But he was calm. Comparatively. His
heart rate was holding below a hundred and fifty.
He had an open channel with the 911 despatcher,
desperate to hear more as he drove.

'New guy on a cell phone now,' the despatcher
screamed.

'Who?' Emerson screamed back.

'Marine Corps, from the recruiting office.'

23

'Was he a witness?'

'No, he was inside. But he's outside now.'

Emerson clamped his teeth. He knew he wasn't going to be first-on-scene. Not even close. He knew he was leading from the rear. So he needed eyes. Now. *A Marine? He'll do.*

'OK,' he said. 'Patch the Marine through.'

There were loud clicks and electronic sounds and then Emerson heard a new acoustic. Outdoors, distant screaming, the splash of water. *The fountain*, he thought.

'Who is this?' he asked.

A voice came back, calm but rushed, loud and breathy, pressed close to a cell phone mouthpiece.

'This is Kelly,' it said. 'First Sergeant, United States Marine Corps. Who am I speaking with?'

'Emerson, PD. I'm in traffic, about ten minutes out. What have we got?'

'Five KIA,' the Marine said.

'Five dead?'

'Affirmative.'

Shit. 'Injured?'

'None that I can see.'

'Five dead and no injured?'

'Affirmative,' the Marine said again.

Emerson said nothing. He had seen shootings in public places. He had seen dead people. But he had never seen *only* dead people. Public-place shootings always produced injured along with the dead. Usually in a one-to-one ratio, at least.

'You sure about no injured?' he said.

'That's definitive, sir,' the Marine said.

'Who are the DOAs?'

24

'Civilians. Four males, one female.'

'Shit.'

'Roger that, sir,' the Marine said.

'Where were you?'

'In the recruiting office.'

'What did you see?'

'Nothing.'

'What did you hear?'

'Incoming gunfire, six rounds.'

'Handguns?'

'Long gun, I think. Just one of them.'

'A *rifle*?'

'An autoloader, I think. It fired fast, but it wasn't on full automatic. The KIAs are all hit in the head.'

A sniper, Emerson thought. *Shit. A crazy man with an assault weapon.*

'Has he gone now?' he said.

'No further firing, sir.'

'He might still be there.'

'It's a possibility, sir. People have taken cover. Most of them are in the library now.'

'Where are you?'

'Head down behind the plaza wall, sir. I've got a few people with me.'

'Where was *he*?'

'Can't say for sure. Maybe in the parking garage. The new part. People were pointing at it. There may have been some muzzle flash. And that's the only major structure directly facing the KIAs.'

A warren, Emerson thought. *A damn rat's nest.*

'The TV people are here,' the Marine said.

Shit, Emerson thought.

'Are you in uniform?' he asked.

'Full dress, sir. For the recruiting office.'

'OK, do your best to keep order until my guys get there.'

'Roger that, sir.'

Then the line went dead and Emerson heard his despatcher's breathing again. *TV people and a crazy man with a rifle*, he thought. *Shit, shit, shit. Pressure and scrutiny and second-guessing, like every other place that ever had TV people and a crazy man with a rifle.* He hit the switch that gave him the all-cars radio net.

'All units, listen up,' he said. 'This was a lone nutcase with a long gun. Probably an automatic weapon. Indiscriminate firing in a public place. Possibly from the new part of the parking garage. So either he's still in there, or he's already in the wind. If he left, it was either on foot or in a vehicle. So all units that are more than ten blocks out, stop now and lock down a perimeter. Nobody enters or exits, OK? No vehicles, no pedestrians, nobody under any circumstances. All units that are closer than ten blocks, proceed inward with extreme caution. But do not let him get away. *Do not* miss him. This is a must-win, people. We need this guy *today*, before CNN gets all over us.'

The man in the minivan thumbed the button on the remote on the visor and the garage door rumbled upward. He drove inside and thumbed the button again and the door came down after him. He shut the engine off and sat still for a moment. Then he got out of the van and walked through the mud room and on into the kitchen. He patted the dog and turned on the television.

Paramedics in full body armour went in through the back of the library. Two of them stayed inside to check for injuries among the sheltering crowd. Four of them came out the front and ran crouched through the plaza and ducked behind the wall. They crawled towards the bodies and confirmed they were all DOA. Then they stayed right there. Flat on the ground and immobile next to the corpses. *No unnecessary exposure until the garage has been searched*, Emerson had said.

Emerson double-parked two blocks from the plaza and told a uniformed sergeant to direct the search of the parking garage, from the top down, from the southwest corner. The uniforms cleared the fourth level, and then the third. Then the second. Then the first. The old part was problematical. It was badly lit and full of parked cars, and every car represented a potential hiding place. A guy could be inside one, or under one, or behind one. But they didn't find anybody. They had no real problem with the new construction. It wasn't lit at all, but there were no parked cars in that part. The patrolmen simply came down the stairwell and swept each level in turn with flash-light beams.

Nobody there.

The sergeant relaxed and called it in.

'Good work,' Emerson said.

And it was good work. The fact that they searched from the southwest corner outward left the northeast corner entirely untouched. Nothing was disturbed. So by good luck or good judgement the PD had turned in an immaculate performance in the first phase of what would eventually be seen as an immaculate investigation from beginning to end.

By seven o'clock in the evening it was going dark and Ann Yanni had been on the air eleven times. Three of them network, eight of them local. Personally she was a little disappointed with that ratio. She was sensitive to a little scepticism coming her way from the network editorial offices. *If it bleeds, it leads*, was any news organization's credo, but this bleeding was way out there, far from New York or LA. It wasn't happening in some manicured suburb of Washington D.C. It had a tinge of weirdo-from-the-heartland about it. There was no real possibility that anyone *important* would walk through this guy's cross hairs. So it was not really prime time stuff. And in truth Ann didn't have much to offer. None of the victims was identified yet. None of the *slain*. The local PD was holding its cards close to its chest until families had been notified individually. So she had no heartwarming background stories to share. She wasn't sure which of the male victims had been family men. Or churchgoers. She didn't know if the woman had been a mother or a wife. She didn't have much to offer in the way of visuals, either. Just a gathering crowd held five blocks back by police barricades, and a static long shot down the greyness of First Street, and occasional close-ups of the parking garage, which was where everyone seemed to assume the sniper had been.

By eight o'clock Emerson had made a lot of progress. His guys had taken hundreds of statements. Marine Corps First Sergeant Kelly was still sure he had heard six shots. Emerson was inclined to believe him. Marines could be trusted on stuff like that, presumably. Then some other guy mentioned his cell phone must have been open the whole time, connected to another guy's voice mail. The cellular company retrieved the recording and six gunshots were faintly audible on it. But the medical examiners had counted only five entry wounds in the five DOAs. Therefore there was a bullet missing. Three other witnesses were vague, but they all reported seeing a small plume of water kick out of the ornamental pool.

Emerson ordered the pool to be drained.

The fire department handled it. They set up floodlights and switched off the fountain and used a pumping engine to dump the water into the city storm drains. They figured there were maybe eighty thousand gallons of water to move, and that the job would be complete in an hour.

Meanwhile crime scene technicians had used drinking straws and laser pointers to estimate the fatal trajectories. They figured the most reliable evidence would come from the first victim. Presumably he was walking purposefully right to left across the plaza when the first shot came in. After that, it was possible the subsequent victims were twisting or turning or moving in other

29

unpredictable ways. So they based their conclusions solely on the first guy. His head was a mess, but it seemed pretty clear the bullet had travelled slightly high to low and left to right as it passed through. One tech stood upright on the spot and another held a drinking straw against the side of his head at the correct angle and held it steady. Then the first guy ducked out of the way and a third fired a laser pointer through the straw. It put a tiny red spot on the northeast corner of the parking garage extension, second level. Witnesses had claimed they had seen muzzle flashes up there. Now science had confirmed their statements.

Emerson sent his crime scene people into the garage and told them they had all the time they needed. But he told them not to come back with nothing.

Ann Yanni left the black glass tower at eight thirty and took a camera crew down to the barricades five blocks away. She figured she might be able to identify some of the victims by a process of elimination. People whose relatives hadn't come home for dinner might be gathering there, desperate for information. She shot twenty minutes of tape. She got no specific information at all. Instead she got twenty minutes of crying and wailing and sheer stunned incredulity. The whole city was in pain and in shock. She started out secretly proud that she was in the middle of everything, and she ended up with tears in her eyes and sick to her stomach.

*　　　*　　　*

30

The parking garage was where the case was broken. It was a bonanza. A treasure trove. A patrolman three blocks away had taken a witness statement from a regular user of the garage saying that the last space on the second level had been blocked off with an orange traffic cone. Because of it, the witness had been forced to leave the garage and park elsewhere. He had been pissed about it. A guy from the city said the cone hadn't been there officially. No way. Couldn't have been. No reason for it. So the cone was bagged for evidence and taken away. Then the city guy said there were discreet security cameras at the entrance and the exit, wired to a video recorder in a maintenance closet. The tape was extracted and taken away. Then the city guy said the new extension was stalled for funding and hadn't been worked on for two weeks. So anything in there less than two weeks old wasn't anything to do with him.

The crime scene technicians started at the yellow and black *Caution Do Not Enter* tape. The first thing they found was a scuff of blue cotton material on the rough concrete directly underneath it. Just a peach-fuzz of barely visible fibre. Like a guy had dropped to one knee to squirm underneath, and had left a little of his blue jeans behind. They photographed the scuff and then picked it up whole with an adhesive sheet of clear plastic. Then they brought in klieg lights and angled them low across the floor. Across the two-week-old cement dust. They saw perfect footprints. *Really* perfect footprints. The lead tech called Emerson on his Motorola.

'He was wearing weird shoes,' he said.

'What kind of weird shoes?'

'You ever heard of crêpe? It's a kind of crude rubber. Almost raw. Very grippy. It picks everything up. If we find this guy, we're going to find crêpe-soled shoes with cement dust all over the soles. Also, we're going to find a dog in his house.'

'A dog?'

'We've got dog hair here, picked up by the crêpe rubber, earlier. And then scraped off again where the concrete's rough. And carpet fibres. Probably from his rugs at home and in his car.'

'Keep going,' Emerson said.

At ten to nine Emerson briefed his Chief of Police for a press conference. He held nothing back. It was the Chief's decision what to talk about and what to conceal.

'Six shots fired and five people dead,' Emerson said. 'All head shots. I'm betting on a trained shooter. Probably ex-military.'

'Or a hunter?' the Chief said.

'Big difference between shooting deer and shooting people. The technique might be the same, but the emotion isn't.'

'Were we right to keep this away from the FBI?'

'It wasn't terrorism. It was a lone nut. We've seen them before.'

'I want to be able to sound confident about bringing this one in.'

'I know,' Emerson said.

'So how confident can I sound?'

'So far we've got good stuff, but not great stuff.'

The Chief nodded, and said nothing.

At nine o'clock exactly Emerson took a call from the pathologist. His staff had X-rayed all five heads. Massive tissue damage, entry and exit wounds, no lodged bullets.

'Hollow points,' the pathologist said. 'All of them through and through.'

Emerson turned and looked at the ornamental pool. *Six bullets in there*, he thought. Five through-and-throughs, and one miss. The pool was finally empty by nine fifteen. The fire department hoses started sucking air. All that was left was a quarter-inch of scummy grit, and a lot of trash. Emerson had the lights re-angled and sent twelve recruits from the Academy over the walls, six from one end and six from the other.

The crime scene techs in the parking garage extension logged forty-eight footprints going and forty-four coming back. The perp had been confident but wary on the way in, and striding longer on the way out. In a hurry. The footprints were size eleven. They found fibres on the last pillar before the northeast corner. Mercerized cotton, at a guess, from a pale-coloured raincoat, at shoulder-blade height, like the guy had pressed his back against the raw concrete and then slid round it for a look out into the plaza. They found major dust disturbance on the floor between the pillar and the perimeter wall. Plus more blue fibres and more raincoat fibres, and tiny crumbs of crêpe rubber, pale in colour, and old.

'He low-crawled,' the lead tech said. 'Knees and elbows on the way there, and knees, *toes* and elbows coming backwards. We ever find his shoes, they're going to be all scraped up at the front.'

They found where he must have sat up and then knelt. Directly in front of that position, they saw varnish scrapings on the lip of the wall.

'He rested his gun there,' the lead tech said. 'Sawed it back and forth, to get it steady.'

He lined himself up and aimed his gaze over the varnish scrapings, like he was aiming a rifle. What he saw in front of him was Emerson, pacing in front of the empty ornamental pool, less than thirty-five yards away.

The Academy recruits spent thirty minutes in the empty pool and came out with a lot of miscellaneous junk, nearly eight dollars in pennies, and six bullets. Five of them were just misshapen blobs of lead, but one of them looked absolutely brand new. It was a boat tail hollow point, beautifully cast, almost certainly a .308. Emerson called his lead crime scene tech up in the garage.

'I need you down here,' he said.

'No, I need you up here,' the tech replied.

Emerson got up to the second level and found all the techs crouched in a low huddle with their flashlight beams pointing down into a narrow crack in the concrete.

'Expansion joint,' the lead tech said. 'And look what fell in it.'

Emerson shouldered his way in and looked down and saw the gleam of brass.

'A cartridge case,' he said.

'The guy took the others with him. But this one got away.'

'Fingerprints?' Emerson asked.

'We can hope,' the tech said. 'Not too many people wear gloves when they load their magazines.'

'How do we get it out of there?'

The tech stood up and used his flashlight beam to locate an electrical box on the ceiling. There was one close by, new, with unconnected cables spooling out like fronds. He looked on the floor directly underneath and found a rat's nest of discarded trimmings. He chose an eighteen-inch length of ground wire. He cleaned it and bent it into an L-shape. It was stiff and heavy. Probably overspecified for the kind of fluorescent ceiling fixtures he guessed the garage was going to use. Maybe that was why the project was stalled for funding. Maybe the city was spending money in all the wrong places.

He jiggled the wire down into the open joint and slid it along until the end went neatly into the empty cartridge case. Then he lifted it out very carefully, so as not to scratch it. He dropped it straight into a plastic evidence bag.

'Meet at the station,' Emerson said. 'In one hour. I'll scare up a DA.'

He walked away, on a route exactly parallel to the trail of footprints. Then he stopped, next to the empty parking bay.

'Empty the meter,' he called. 'Print all the quarters.'

'Why?' the tech called back. 'You think the guy paid?'

'I want to cover all the bases.'

'You'd have to be crazy to pay for parking just before you blow five people away.'

'You don't blow five people away *unless* you're crazy.'

The tech shrugged. Empty the meter? But he guessed it was the kind of insight detectives were paid for, so he just dialled his cell phone and asked the city liaison guy to come on back again.

Someone from the District Attorney's office always got involved at this point because the responsibility for prosecution rested squarely on the DA's shoulders. It wasn't the PD that won or lost in court. It was the DA. So the DA's office made its own evaluation of the evidence. Did they have a case? Was the case weak or strong? It was like an audition. Like a trial before a trial. This time, because of the magnitude, Emerson was performing in front of the DA himself. The big cheese, the actual guy who had to run for election. And re-election.

They made it a three-man conference in Emerson's office. Emerson, and the lead crime scene tech, and the DA. The DA was called Rodin, which was a contraction of a Russian name that had been a whole lot longer before his great-grandparents came to America. He was fifty years old, lean and fit, and very cautious. His office had an outstanding victory percentage, but that was mostly due to the fact that he wouldn't prosecute anything less than a total certainty. Anything less than a total certainty, and he gave up early and blamed the cops. At least that was how it seemed to Emerson.

'I need seriously good news,' Rodin said. 'The whole city is freaking out.'

'We know exactly how it went down,' Emerson told him. 'We can trace it every step of the way.'

'You know who it was?' Rodin asked.

'Not yet. Right now he's still John Doe.'

'So walk me through it.'

'We've got monochrome security videotape of a light-coloured minivan entering the garage eleven minutes before the event. Can't see the plates for mud and dirt, and the camera angle isn't great. But it's probably a Dodge Caravan, not new, with aftermarket tinted windows. And we're also looking through old tapes right now because it's clear he entered the garage at some previous time and illegally blocked off a particular space with a traffic cone stolen earlier from a city construction site.'

'Can we prove stolen?'

'OK, obtained,' Emerson said.

'Maybe he works for the city construction depart-ment.'

'Maybe.'

'You think the cone came from the work on First Street?'

'There's construction all over town.'

'First Street would be closest.'

'I don't really care where the cone came from.'

Rodin nodded. 'So, he reserved himself a parking space?'

Emerson nodded in turn. 'Right where the new construction starts. Therefore the cone would have looked plausible. We have a witness who saw it in place at least an hour before. And the cone has fingerprints on it. Lots of them. The right thumb and index finger match prints on a quarter we took out of the parking meter.'

'He paid to park?'

'Evidently.'

Rodin paused.

'Won't stand up,' he said. 'Defence will claim he could have placed the cone for an innocent reason. You know, selfish, but innocent. And the quarter could have been in the meter for days.'

Emerson smiled. *Cops think like cops, and lawyers think like lawyers.*

'There's more,' he said. 'He parked, and then he walked through the new construction. At various points he left trace evidence behind, from his shoes and his clothing. And he'll have picked trace evidence up, in the form of cement dust, mostly. Probably a lot of it.'

Rodin shook his head. 'Ties him to the scene sometime during the last two weeks. That's all. Not specific enough.'

'We've got a three-way lock on his weapon,' Emerson said.

That got Rodin's attention.

'He missed with one shot,' Emerson said. 'It went into the pool. And you know what? That's exactly how ballistics labs test-fire a gun. They fire into a long tank of water. The water slows

38

and stops the bullet with absolutely no damage at all. So we've got a pristine bullet with all the lands and grooves we need to tie it to an individual rifle.'

'Can you find the individual rifle?'

'We've got varnish scrapings from where he steadied it on the wall.'

'That's good.'

'You bet it is. We find the rifle and we'll match the varnish and the scratches. It's as good as DNA.'

'Are you going to find the rifle?'

'We found a shell case. It's got tool marks on it from the ejector mechanism. So we've got a bullet *and* a case. Together they tie the weapon to the crime. The scratches tie the weapon to the garage location. The garage location ties the crime to the guy who left the trace evidence behind.'

Rodin said nothing. Emerson knew he was thinking about the trial. Technical evidence was sometimes a hard sell. It lacked a human dimension.

'The shell case has got fingerprints on it,' he said. 'From when he loaded the magazine. Same thumb and index finger as on the quarter in the parking meter and on the traffic cone. So we can tie the crime to the gun, and the gun to the ammo, and the ammo to the guy who used it. See? It all connects. The guy, the gun, the crime. It's a total slam dunk.'

'The videotape shows the minivan leaving?'

'Ninety seconds after the first 911 call came in.'

'Who is he?'

'We'll know just as soon as the fingerprint databases get back to us.'

'If he's in the databases.'

'I think he was a military shooter,' Emerson said. 'All military personnel are in the databases. So it's just a matter of time.'

It was a matter of forty-nine minutes. A desk guy knocked and entered. He was carrying a sheaf of paper. The paper listed a name, an address, and a history. Plus supplementary information from all over the system. Including a driver's licence photo. Emerson took the paper and glanced through it once. Then again. Then he smiled. Exactly six hours after the first shot was fired, the situation was nailed down tight. *A must-win.*

'His name is James Barr,' Emerson said.

Silence in the office.

'He's forty-one years old. He lives twenty minutes from here. He served in the U.S. Army. Honourable discharge fourteen years ago. Infantry specialist, which I'm betting means a sniper. DMV says he drives a six-year-old Dodge Caravan, beige.'

He slid the papers across his desk to Rodin. Rodin picked them up and scanned them through, once, twice, carefully. Emerson watched his eyes. Saw him thinking *the guy, the gun, the crime.* It was like watching a Vegas slot machine line up three cherries. *Bing bing bing! A total certainty.*

'James Barr,' Rodin said, like he was savouring the sound of the words. He separated out the DL picture and gazed at it. 'James Barr, welcome to a shitload of trouble, sir.'

'Amen to that,' Emerson said, waiting for a compliment.

40

'I'll get the warrants,' Rodin said. 'Arrest, and searches on his house and car. Judges will be lining up to sign them.'

He left and Emerson called the Chief of Police with the good news. The Chief said he would schedule an eight o'clock press conference for the next morning. He said he wanted Emerson there, front and centre. Emerson took that as all the compliment he was going to get, even though he didn't much like the press.

The warrants were ready within an hour, but the arrest took three hours to set up. First, unmarked surveillance confirmed Barr was home. His place was an unremarkable one-storey ranch. Not immaculate, not falling down. Old paint on the siding, fresh blacktop on the driveway. Lights were on and a television set was playing in what was probably the living room. Barr himself was spotted briefly, in a lighted window. He seemed to be alone. Then he seemed to go to bed. Lights went off and the house went quiet. So then there was a pause. It was standard operating procedure to plan carefully for the takedown of an armed man inside a building. The PD SWAT team took charge. They used zoning maps from the city offices and came up with the usual kind of thing. Covert encirclement, overwhelming force on standby front and rear, sudden violent assault on the front and rear doors simultaneously. Emerson was detailed to make the actual arrest, wearing full body armour and a borrowed helmet. An assistant DA would be alongside him, to monitor the legality of the process. Nobody wanted to give a defence attorney anything to chew on later. A paramedic team would be instantly available. Two K9 officers would go along, because of the crime scene investigator's theory about the dog in the house. Altogether thirty-eight men were involved, and they were all tired. Most of them had been working nineteen hours straight. Their regular watches, plus overtime. So there was a lot of nervous tension in the air. People figured that nobody owned just one automatic weapon. If a guy had one, he had more. Maybe full-auto machine guns. Maybe grenades or bombs.

But in the event the arrest was a walk in the park. James Barr barely even woke up. They broke down his doors at three in the morning and found him asleep, alone in bed. He stayed asleep with fifteen armed men in his bedroom aiming fifteen submachine guns and fifteen flashlight beams at him. He stirred a little when the SWAT commander threw his blankets and pillows to the floor, searching for concealed weapons. He had none. He opened his eyes. Mumbled something that sounded like *What?* and then went back to sleep, curling up on the flat mattress, hugging himself against the sudden cold. He was a large man, with white skin and black hair that was going grey all over his body. His pyjamas were too small for him. He looked slack, and a little older than his forty-one years.

His dog was an old mutt that woke up reluctantly and staggered in from the kitchen. The K9 team captured it immediately and took it straight out to their truck. Emerson took his helmet off and pushed his way through the crowd in the tiny bedroom. Saw a three-quarters-full pint of Jack Daniel's on the night table, next to an orange prescription bottle that was also three-quarters full. He bent to look at it. Sleeping pills. Legal. Recently prescribed, to someone called Rosemary Barr. The label said: *Rosemary Barr. Take one for sleeplessness.*

'Who's Rosemary Barr?' the assistant DA asked. 'Is he married?'

Emerson glanced round the room. 'Doesn't look like it.'

'Suicide attempt?' the SWAT commander asked.

Emerson shook his head. 'He'd have swallowed them all. Plus the whole pint of JD. So I guess Mr Barr had trouble getting off to sleep tonight, that's all. After a very busy and productive day.'

The air in the room was stale. It smelled of dirty sheets and an unwashed body.

'We need to be careful here,' the assistant DA said. 'He's impaired right now. His lawyer is going to say he's not fully capable of understanding Miranda. So we can't let him say anything. And if he does say something, we can't listen.'

Emerson called for the paramedics. Told them to check Barr out, to make sure he wasn't faking, and to make sure he wasn't about to die on them. They fussed around for a few minutes, listened to his heart, checked his pulse, read the prescription label. Then they pronounced him reasonably fit and healthy, but fast asleep.

'Psychopath,' the SWAT commander said. 'No conscience at all.'

'Are we even sure this is the right guy?' the assistant DA asked.

Emerson found a pair of suit trousers folded over a chair and checked the pockets. Came out with a small wallet. Found the driver's licence. The name was right, and the address was right. And the photograph was right.

'This is the right guy,' he said.

'We can't let him say anything,' the ADA said again. 'We need to keep this kosher.'

'I'm going to Mirandize him anyway,' Emerson said. 'Make a mental note, people.'

He shook Barr by the shoulder and got half-opened eyes in response. Then he recited the Miranda warning. The right to remain silent, the right to a lawyer. Barr tried to focus, but didn't succeed. Then he went back to sleep.

'OK, take him in,' Emerson said.

They wrapped him in a blanket and two cops dragged him out of the house and into a car. A paramedic and the ADA rode with him. Emerson stayed in the house and started the search. He found the scuffed blue jeans in the bedroom closet. The crêpe-soled shoes were placed neatly on the floor below them. They were dusty. The raincoat was in the hall closet. The beige Dodge Caravan was in the garage. The scratched rifle was in the basement. It was one of several resting on a rack bolted to the wall. On a bench underneath it were five nine-millimetre handguns. And boxes of ammunition, including a half-empty box of Lake City M852 168-grain boat tail hollow point .308s. Next to the boxes were glass jars with empty cartridge cases in them. Ready for

44

recycling, Emerson thought. Ready for hand-loading. The jar nearest the front of the bench held just five of them. Lake City brass. The jar's lid was still off, like the five latest cases had been dumped in there recently and in a hurry. Emerson bent down and sniffed. The air in the jar smelled of gunpowder. Cold and old, but not very.

Emerson left James Barr's house at four in the morning, replaced by forensic specialists who would go through the whole place with a fine-toothed comb. He checked with his desk sergeant and confirmed that Barr was sleeping peaccfully, in a cell on his own with round-the-clock medical supervision. Then he went home and caught a two-hour nap before showering and dressing for thc press conference.

The press conference killed the story stone dead. A story needs the guy to be *still out there*. A story needs the guy roaming, sullen, hidden, shadowy, dangerous. It needs fear. It needs to make every-day chores exposed and hazardous, like pumping gas or visiting the mall or walking to church. So to hear that the guy was found and arrested even before the start of the second news cycle was a disaster for Ann Yanni. Immediately she knew what the network offices were going to think. *No legs, over and done with, history. Yesterday's news*, literally. *Probably wasn't much of anything anyway. Just some inbred heartland weirdo too dumb to stay free through the night. Probably sleeps with his cousin and drinks Colt 45.* Nothing sinister there. She would get one more network breaking-news spot to recap the crime and report the arrest, and that would be it. Back to obscurity.

So Yanni was disappointed, but she hid it well. She asked questions and made her tone admiring. About halfway through she started putting together a new theme. A new narrative. People would have to admit the police work had been pretty impressive. And this perp *wasn't* a weirdo. Not necessarily. So a serious bad guy had been caught by an even more serious police department. Right out there in the heartland. Something that had taken considerable time on the coasts in previous famous cases. Could she sell it? She started drafting titles in the back of her mind. *America's Fastest*? Like a play on *Finest*?

The Chief yielded the floor to Emerson after about ten minutes. Emerson filled in full details on the perp's identity and his history. He kept it dry. *Just the facts, ma'am.* He outlined the investigation. He answered questions. He didn't boast. Ann Yanni thought that he felt the cops had been lucky. That they had been given much more to go on than they usually got.

Then Rodin stepped up. He made it sound like the PD had been involved in some early minor skirmishing and that the real work was about to begin. His office would review everything and make the necessary determinations. And yes, Ms Yanni, because he thought the circumstances warranted it, certainly he would seek the death penalty for James Barr.

*   *   *

James Barr woke up in his cell with a chemical hangover at nine o'clock, Saturday morning. He was immediately fingerprinted and re-Mirandized once, and then twice. The right to remain silent, the right to a lawyer. He chose to remain silent. Not many people do. Not many people can. The urge to talk is usually overwhelming. But James Barr beat it. He just clamped his mouth shut and kept it that way. Plenty of people tried to talk to him, but he didn't answer. Not once. Not a word. Emerson was relaxed about it. Truth was, Emerson didn't really want Barr to say anything. He preferred to line up all the evidence, scrutinize it, test it, polish it, and to get to a point where he could anticipate a conviction *without* a confession. Confessions were so vulnerable to defence accusations of coercion or confusion that he had learned to run away from them. They were icing on the cake. Literally the *last* thing he wanted to hear, not the first. Not like on the TV cop shows, where relentless interrogation was a kind of performance art. So he just stayed out of the loop and let his forensics people complete their slow, patient work.

James Barr's sister was younger than him and unmarried and living in a rented downtown condo. Her name was Rosemary. Like the rest of the city's population, she was sick and shocked and stunned. She had seen the news Friday night. And she caught it again Saturday morning. She heard a police detective say her brother's name. At first she thought it was a mistake. That she had misheard. But the guy kept on saying it.

James Barr, James Barr, James Barr. She burst into tears. First tears of confusion, then tears of horror, then tears of fury.

Then she forced herself to calm down, and got busy.

She worked as a secretary in an eight-man law firm. Like most firms in small heartland cities, hers did a little bit of everything. And it treated its employees fairly well. The salary wasn't spectacular, but there were intangibles to compensate. One was a full package of benefits. Another was being called a paralegal instead of a secretary. Another was a promise that the firm would handle legal matters for its employees and their families free, gratis, and for nothing. Mostly that was about wills and probate and divorce, and insurance company hassles after fender benders. It wasn't about defending adult siblings who were wrongly accused in notorious urban sniper slayings. She knew that. But she felt she had to give it a try. Because she knew her brother, and she knew he couldn't be guilty.

She called the partner she worked for, at home. He was mostly a tax guy, so he called the firm's criminal litigator. The litigator called the managing partner, who called a meeting of all the partners. They held it over lunch at the country club. From the start the agenda was about how to turn down Rosemary Barr's request in the most tactful way possible. A defence to a crime of this nature wasn't the sort of thing they were equipped to handle. Or *inclined* to handle. There were public relations implications. There was immediate agreement on that point. But

48

they were a loyal bunch, and Rosemary Barr
was a good employee who had worked many
years for them. They knew she had no money,
because they did her taxes. They assumed her
brother had no money either. But the Constitu-
tion guaranteed competent counsel, and they
didn't have a very high opinion of public
defenders. So they were caught in a genuine
ethical dilemma.

The litigator resolved it. His name was David
Chapman. He was a hardscrabble veteran who
knew Rodin over at the DA's office. He knew
him pretty well. It would have been impossible
for him not to, really. They were two of a kind,
raised in the same neighbourhood and working
in the same business, albeit on opposite sides. So
Chapman went to the smoking room and used his
cell phone to call the DA at home. The two
lawyers had a full and frank discussion. Then
Chapman came back to the lunch table.

'It's a slam dunk,' he said. 'Ms Barr's brother is
guilty all to hell and gone. Rodin's case is going to
read like a textbook. Hell, it's probably going
to *be* a textbook one day. He's got every kind of
evidence there is. There's not a chink of daylight
anywhere.'

'Was he levelling with you?' the managing
partner asked.

'There's no bullshitting between old buddies,'
Chapman said.

'So?'

'All we would have to do is plead in mitigation.
If we can get the lethal injection reduced to life
without, there's a big win right there. That's all

49

Ms Barr has a right to expect. Or her damn brother, with all due respect.'

'How much involvement?' the managing partner asked.

'Sentencing phase only. Because he'll have to plead guilty.'

'You happy to handle it?'

'Under the circumstances.'

'How many hours will it cost us?'

'Not many. There's practically nothing we can do.'

'What grounds for mitigation?'

'He's a Gulf War vet, I believe. So there's probably chemical stuff going on. Or some kind of delayed post-traumatic thing. Maybe we could get Rodin to agree beforehand. We could get it done over lunch.'

The managing partner nodded. Turned to the tax guy. 'Tell your secretary we'll do everything in our power to help her brother in his hour of need.'

Barr was moved from the police station lockup to the county jail before either his sister or Chapman got a chance to see him. His blanket and pyjamas were taken away and he was issued with paper underwear, an orange jumpsuit, and a pair of rubber shower sandals. The county jail wasn't a pleasant place to be. It smelled bad and it was noisy. It was radically overcrowded and the social and ethnic tensions that were kept in control on the street were left to rage unchecked inside. Men were stacked three to a cell and the guards were shorthanded. New guys were called fish, and they were left to fend for themselves.

But Barr had been in the army, so the culture shock for him was a little less than it might have been. He survived as a fish for two hours, and then he was escorted to an interview room. He was told there was a lawyer waiting there for him. He found a table and two chairs bolted to the floor in a windowless cubicle. In one of the chairs was a guy he vaguely recognized from somewhere. On the table was a pocket tape recorder. Like a Walkman.

'My name is David Chapman,' the guy in the chair said. 'I'm a criminal defence attorney. A lawyer. Your sister works at my firm. She asked us to help you out.'

Barr said nothing.

'So here I am,' Chapman said.

Barr said nothing.

'I'm recording this conversation,' Chapman said. 'Putting it on tape. I take it that's OK with you?'

Barr said nothing.

'I think we met once,' Chapman said. 'Our Christmas party one year?'

Barr said nothing.

Chapman waited.

'Have the charges been explained to you?' he asked.

Barr said nothing.

'The charges are very serious,' Chapman said.

Barr stayed quiet.

'I can't help you if you won't help yourself,' Chapman said.

Barr just stared at him. Just sat still and quiet

for several long minutes. Then he leaned forward towards the tape machine and spoke for the first time since the previous afternoon.

He said, 'They got the wrong guy.'

'They got the wrong guy,' Barr said again.

'So tell me about the right guy,' Chapman said immediately. He was a good courtroom tactician. He knew how to get a rhythm going. Question, answer, question, answer. That was how to get a person to open up. They fell into the rhythm, and it all came out.

But Barr just retreated back into silence.

'Let's be clear about this,' Chapman said.

Barr didn't answer.

'Are you *denying* it?' Chapman asked him.

Barr said nothing.

'Are you?'

No response.

'The evidence is all there,' Chapman said. 'It's just about overwhelming, I'm afraid. You can't play dumb now. We need to talk about *why* you did it. That's what's going to help us here.'

Barr said nothing.

'You want me to help you?' Chapman said. 'Or not?'

Barr said nothing.

'Maybe it was your old wartime experience,' Chapman said. 'Or post-traumatic stress. Or some kind of mental impairment. We need to focus on the reason.'

Barr said nothing.

'Denying it is not smart,' Chapman said. 'The evidence is right there.'

Barr said nothing.

'Denying it is not an option,' Chapman said.

'Get Jack Reacher for me,' Barr said.

'Who?'

'Jack Reacher.'

'Who's he? A friend?'

Barr said nothing.

'Someone you know?' Chapman said.

Barr said nothing.

'Someone you used to know?'

'Just get him for me.'

'Where is he? *Who* is he?'

Barr said nothing.

'Is Jack Reacher a doctor?' Chapman asked.

'A doctor?' Barr repeated.

'Is he a doctor?' Chapman asked.

But Barr didn't speak again. He just got up from the table and walked to the cubicle's door and pounded on it until the jailer opened it up and led him back to his overcrowded cell.

Chapman arranged to meet Rosemary Barr and the firm's investigator at his law offices. The investigator was a retired cop shared by most of the city's law firms. They all had him on retainer. He was a private detective, with a licence. His name was Franklin. He was nothing like a private eye in a TV show. He did all his work at a desk, with phone books and computer databases. He didn't go out, didn't wear a gun, didn't own a hat. But he had no equal as a fact-checker or a skip-tracer and he still had plenty of friends in the PD.

'The evidence is rock solid,' he said. 'That's what I'm hearing. Emerson was in charge and he's pretty reliable. So is Rodin, really, but for a different reason. Emerson's a stiff and Rodin is a coward. Neither one of them would be saying what they're saying unless the evidence was there.'

'I just can't believe he did it,' Rosemary Barr said.

'Well, certainly he seems to be denying it,' Chapman said. 'As far as I can understand him. And he's asking for someone called Jack Reacher. Someone he knows or used to know. You ever heard that name? You know who he is?'

Rosemary Barr just shook her head. Chapman wrote the name *Jack Reacher* on a sheet of paper and slid it across to Franklin. 'My guess is he may be a psychiatrist. Mr Barr brought the name up right after I told him how strong the evidence is. So maybe this Reacher guy is someone who can help us out with the mitigation. Maybe he treated Mr Barr in the past.'

'My brother never saw a psychiatrist,' Rosemary Barr said.

'To your certain knowledge?'

'Never.'

'How long has he been in town?'

'Fourteen years. Since the army.'

'Were you close?'

'We lived in the same house.'

'His house?'

Rosemary Barr nodded.

'But you don't live there any more.'

Rosemary Barr looked away.

'No,' she said. 'I moved out.'

'Might your brother have seen a shrink after you moved out?'

'He would have told me.'

'OK, what about before? In the service?'

Rosemary Barr said nothing. Chapman turned back to Franklin.

'So maybe Reacher was his army doctor,' he said. 'Maybe he has information about an old trauma. He could be very helpful.'

Franklin accepted the sheet of paper.

'In which case I'll find him,' he said.

'We shouldn't be talking about mitigation anyway,' Rosemary Barr said. 'We should be talking about reasonable doubt. About *innocence*.'

'The evidence is very strong,' Chapman said. 'He used his own gun.'

Franklin spent three hours failing to find Jack Reacher. First he trawled through psychiatric associations. No hits. Then he searched the Internet for Gulf War support groups. No trace. He tried Lexis-Nexis and all the news organizations. Nothing. Then he started back at the beginning and accessed the National Personnel Record Center's database. It listed all current and former military. He found Jack Reacher's name in there easily enough. Reacher had entered the service in 1984 and there was an honourable discharge in 1997. James Barr himself had signed up in 1985 and mustered out in 1991. So there was a six-year overlap. But Reacher had been no kind of doctor. No kind of a psychiatrist. He had been a military cop. An officer. A major. Maybe a high-level investigator. Barr had finished as a lowly Specialist E-4. Infantry, not military police. So what was the point of contact between a military police major and an infantry E-4? Something helpful, obviously, or Barr wouldn't have mentioned the name. But what?

At the end of three hours Franklin figured he would never find out, because Reacher fell off the radar after 1997. Completely and totally. There was no trace of him anywhere. He was still alive, according to the Social Security Administration. He wasn't in prison, according to the NCIC. But he had disappeared. He had no credit rating. He wasn't listed as title holder to any real estate, or automobiles, or boats. He had no debts. No liens. No address. No phone number. No warrants outstanding, no judgements entered. He wasn't a husband. Wasn't a father. He was a ghost.

James Barr spent the same three hours in serious trouble. It started when he stepped out of his cell. He turned right to walk down to the pay phones. The corridor was narrow. He bumped into another guy, shoulder to shoulder. Then he made a bad mistake. He took his eyes off the floor and glanced at the other guy and apologized.

A bad mistake, because a fish can't make eye contact with another prisoner. Not without implying disrespect. It was a prison thing. He didn't understand.

The guy he made eye contact with was a Mexican. He had gang tattoos, but Barr didn't recognize them. Another bad mistake. He should have put his gaze back on the floor and moved on and hoped for the best. But he didn't.

Instead, he said, 'Excuse me.'

Then he raised his eyebrows and half smiled in a self-deprecating way, like he was saying, *This is some place, right?*

Bad mistake. Familiarity, and a presumption of intimacy.

'What are you looking at?' the Mexican said.

At that point, James Barr understood completely. *What are you looking at?* That was pretty much a standard opener. Barrack rooms, bar rooms, street corners, dark alleys, it was not a phrase you wanted to hear.

'Nothing,' he said, and realized he had made the situation much worse.

'You calling me nothing?'

Barr put his eyes back on the floor and moved on, but it was way too late. He felt the Mexican's stare on his back and gave up on the pay phone idea. The phones were in a dead-end lobby and he didn't want to feel trapped. So he walked a long counterclockwise circuit and headed back to his cell. He got there OK. Didn't look at anyone, didn't speak. He lay down on his bunk. About two hours later, he felt OK. He guessed he could handle a little macho bluster. And he was bigger than the Mexican. He was bigger than two Mexicans.

He wanted to call his sister. He wanted to know she was OK.

He set off for the pay phones again.

He got there unmolested. It was a small space. There were four phones on the wall, four men talking, four lines of other men waiting behind them. Noise, shuffling feet, crazed laughter, impatience, frustration, sour air, the smell of sweat and dirty hair and stale urine. Just a normal prison scene, according to James Barr's preconceptions.

Then it wasn't a normal scene.

The men in front of him vanished. Just disappeared. They just melted out of sight. Those on the phone hung up mid-sentence and ducked back past him. Those waiting in line peeled away. In half a second the lobby went from being full and noisy to being deserted and silent.

James Barr turned round.

He saw the Mexican with the tattoos. The Mexican had a knife in his hand and twelve friends behind him. The knife was a plastic toothbrush handle wrapped with tape and sharpened to a point, like a stiletto. The friends were all stocky little guys, all with the same tattoos. They all had cropped hair with intricate patterns shaved across their skulls.

'Wait,' Barr said.

But the Mexicans didn't wait, and eight minutes later Barr was in a coma. He was found some time after that, on the floor, beaten pulpy, with multiple stab wounds and a cracked skull and severe subdural bleeding. Afterwards, jail talk said he had had it coming. He had disrespected the Latinos. But jail talk said he hadn't gone quietly. There was a hint of admiration. The Mexicans had suffered a little. But not nearly as much as James Barr. He was medevacked to the city hospital and sewn up and operated on to relieve pressure from a swollen brain. Then he was dumped in a secure intensive care unit, comatose. The doctors weren't sure when he would wake up again. Maybe in a day. Maybe in a week. Maybe in a month. Maybe never. The doctors didn't really know, and they didn't really care. They were all local residents.

The warden at the jail called late at night and told Emerson. Then Emerson called and told Rodin. Then Rodin called and told Chapman. Then Chapman called and told Franklin.

'So what happens now?' Franklin asked him.

'Nothing,' Chapman said. 'It's on ice. You can't try a guy in a coma.'

'What about when he wakes up?'

'If he's OK, then they'll go ahead, I guess.'

'What if he isn't?'

'Then they won't. Can't try a vegetable.'

'So what do we do now?'

'Nothing,' Chapman said. 'We weren't taking it very seriously anyhow. Barr's guilty all to hell and gone, and there's nothing much anyone can do for him.'

Franklin called and told Rosemary Barr, because he wasn't sure if anyone else would have taken the trouble. He found out that nobody else had. So he broke the news himself. Rosemary Barr didn't have much of an outward reaction. She just went very quiet. It was like she was on emotional overload.

'I guess I should go to the hospital,' she said.

'If you want,' Franklin said.

'He's innocent, you know. This is so unfair.'

'Did you see him yesterday?'

'You mean, can I alibi him?'

'Can you?'

'No,' Rosemary Barr said. 'I can't. I don't know where he was yesterday. Or what he was doing.'

'Are there places he goes regularly? Movies, bars, anything like that?'

'Not really.'

'Friends he hangs with?'

'I'm not sure.'

'Girlfriends?'

'Not for a long time.'

'Other family he visits?'

'There's just the two of us. Him and me.'

Franklin said nothing. There was a long, distracted pause.

'What happens now?' Rosemary Barr asked.

'I don't know exactly.'

'Did you find that person he mentioned?'

'Jack Reacher? No, I'm afraid not. No trace.'

'Will you keep on looking?'

'There's really nothing more I can do.'

'OK,' Rosemary Barr said. 'Then we'll have to manage without him.'

But even as they spoke, on the phone late at night on the Saturday, Jack Reacher was on his way to them.

TWO

Reacher was on his way to them because of a woman. He had spent Friday night in South Beach, Miami, in a salsa club, with a dancer from a cruise ship. The boat was Norwegian, and so was the girl. Reacher guessed she was too tall for ballet, but she was the right size for everything else. They met on the beach in the afternoon. Reacher was working on his tan. He felt better brown. He didn't know what she was working on. But he felt her shadow fall across his face and opened his eyes to find her staring at him. Or maybe at his scars. The browner he got, the more they stood out, white and wicked and obvious. She was pale, in a black bikini. A *small* black bikini. He pegged her for a dancer long before she told him. It was in the way she held herself.

They ended up having a late dinner together and then going out to the club. South Beach salsa wouldn't have been Reacher's first choice, but her company made it worthwhile. She was fun to be with. And she was a great dancer, obviously. Full of energy. She wore him out. At four in the morning she took him back to her hotel, eager to wear him out some more. Her hotel was a small Art Deco place near the ocean. Clearly the cruise line treated its people well. Certainly it was a much more romantic destination than Reacher's own motel. And much closer.

And it had cable television, which Reacher's place didn't. He woke at eight on Saturday morning when he heard the dancer in the shower. He turned on the TV and went looking for ESPN. He wanted Friday night's American League highlights. He never found them. He clicked his way through successive channels and then stopped dead on CNN because he heard the chief of an Indiana police department say a name he knew: *James Barr*. The picture was of a press conference. Small room, harsh light. Top of the screen was a caption that said: *Courtesy NBC*. There was a banner across the bottom that said: *Friday Night Massacre*. The police chief said the name again, *James Barr*, and then he introduced a homicide detective called Emerson. Emerson looked tired. Emerson said the name for a third time: *James Barr*. Then, like he anticipated the exact question in Reacher's mind, he ran through a brief biography: *Forty-one years old, local Indiana resident, U.S. Army infantry specialist from 1985 to 1991, Gulf War veteran, never married, currently unemployed.*

Reacher watched the screen. Emerson seemed like a concise type of a guy. He was brief. No bullshit. He finished his statement and in response to a reporter's question declined to specify what if anything James Barr had said during interrogation. Then he introduced a district attorney. This guy's name was Rodin, and he wasn't concise. Wasn't brief. He used plenty of bullshit. He spent ten minutes claiming Emerson's credit for himself. Reacher knew how *that* worked. He had been a cop of sorts for thirteen years. Cops bust their tails, and prosecutors bask in the glory. Rodin said *James Barr* a few more times and then said the state was maybe looking to fry him.

For what?

Reacher waited.

A local anchor called Ann Yanni came on. She recapped the events of the night before. Sniper slaying. Senseless slaughter. An automatic weapon. A parking garage. A public plaza. Commuters on their way home after a long working week. Five dead. A suspect in custody, but a city still grieving.

Reacher thought it was Yanni who was grieving. Emerson's success had cut her story short. She signed off and CNN went to political news. Reacher turned the TV off. The dancer came out of the bathroom. She was pink and fragrant. And naked. She had left her towels inside.

'What shall we do today?' she said, with a wide Norwegian smile.

'I'm going to Indiana,' Reacher said.

He walked north in the heat to the Miami bus depot. Then he leafed through a greasy timetable and planned a route. It wasn't going to be an easy trip. Miami to Jacksonville would be the first leg. Then Jacksonville to New Orleans. Then New Orleans to St Louis. Then St Louis to Indianapolis. Then a local bus, presumably, south into the heartland. Five separate destinations. Arrival and departure times were not well integrated. Beginning to end, it was going to take more than forty-eight hours. He was tempted to fly or rent a car, but he was short of money and he liked buses better and he figured nothing much was going to happen on the weekend anyway.

What happened on the weekend was that Rosemary Barr called her firm's investigator back. She figured Franklin would have a semi-independent point of view. She got him at home, ten o'clock in the morning on the Sunday.

'I think I should hire different lawyers,' she said.

Franklin said nothing.

'David Chapman thinks he's guilty,' Rosemary said. 'Doesn't he? So he's already given up.'

'I can't comment,' Franklin said. 'He's one of my employers.'

Now Rosemary Barr said nothing.

'How was the hospital?' Franklin asked.

'Awful. He's in intensive care with a bunch of prison deadbeats. They've got him handcuffed to the bed. He's in a *coma*, for God's sake. How do they think he's going to escape?'

'What's the legal position?'

'He was arrested but not arraigned. He's in a kind of limbo. They're assuming he wouldn't have gotten bail.'

'They're probably right.'

'So they claim under the circumstances it's like he actually *didn't* get bail. So he's *theirs*. He's in the system. Like a twilight zone.'

'What would you like to happen?'

'He shouldn't be in handcuffs. And he should be in a VA hospital at least. But that won't happen until I find a lawyer who's prepared to help him.'

Franklin paused. 'How do you explain all the evidence?'

'I know my brother.'

'You moved out, right?'

'For other reasons. Not because he's a homicidal maniac.'

'He blocked off a parking space,' Franklin said. 'He premeditated this thing.'

'You think he's guilty too.'

'I work with what I've got. And what I've got doesn't look good.'

Rosemary Barr said nothing.

'I'm sorry,' Franklin said.

'Can you recommend another lawyer?'

'Can you make that decision? Do you have a power of attorney?'

'I think it's implied. He's in a coma. I'm his next of kin.'

'How much money have you got?'

'Not much.'

'How much has *he* got?'

'There's some equity in his house.'

'It won't look good. It'll be like a kick in the teeth for the firm you work for.'

'I can't worry about that.'

'You could lose everything, including your job.'

'I'll lose it anyway, unless I help James. If he's convicted, they'll let me go. I'll be notorious. By association. An embarrassment.'

'He had your sleeping pills,' Franklin said.

'I gave them to him. He doesn't have insurance.'

'Why did he need them?'

'He has trouble sleeping.'

Franklin said nothing.

'You think he's guilty,' Rosemary said.

'The evidence is overwhelming,' Franklin said.

'David Chapman isn't really trying, is he?'

'You have to consider the possibility that David Chapman is right.'

'Who should I call?'

Franklin paused.

'Try Helen Rodin,' he said.

'Rodin?'

'She's the DA's daughter.'

'I don't know her.'

'She's downtown. She just hung out her shingle. She's new and she's keen.'

'Is it ethical?'

'No law against it.'

'It would be father against daughter.'

'It was going to be Chapman, and Chapman knows Rodin a lot better than his daughter does, probably. She's been away for a long time.'

'Where?'

'College, law school, clerking for a judge in D.C.'

'Is she any good?'

'I think she's going to be.'

Rosemary Barr called Helen Rodin on her office number. It was like a test. Someone new and keen should be at the office on a Sunday.

Helen Rodin was at the office on a Sunday. She

answered the call sitting at her desk. Her desk was secondhand and it sat proudly in a mostly empty two-room suite in the same black glass tower that had NBC as the second-floor tenant. The suite was rented cheap through one of the business subsidies that the city was throwing around like confetti. The idea was to kick-start the rejuvenated downtown area and clean up later with healthy tax revenues.

Rosemary Barr didn't have to tell Helen Rodin about the case because the whole thing had happened right outside Helen Rodin's new office window. She had seen some of it for herself, and she had followed the rest on the news afterwards. She had caught all of Ann Yanni's TV appearances. She recognized her, from the building's lobby, and the elevator.

'Will you help my brother?' Rosemary Barr asked.

Helen Rodin paused. The smart answer would be *no way*. She knew that. Like *no way, forget about it, are you out of your mind?* Two reasons. One, she knew a major clash with her father was inevitable at some point, but did she need it *now*? And two, she knew that a new lawyer's early cases defined her. Paths were taken that led down fixed routes. To end up as a when-all-else-fails criminal defence attorney would be OK, she guessed, all things considered. But to start out by taking a case that had offended the whole city would be a marketing disaster. The shootings weren't being seen as a *crime*. They were being seen as an *atrocity*. Against humanity, against the whole community, against the rejuvenation efforts downtown, against the whole idea of being from Indiana. It was like LA or New York or Baltimore had come to the heartland, and to be the person who tried to excuse it or explain it away would be a fatal mistake. Like a mark of Cain. It would follow her the rest of her life.

'Can we sue the jail?' Rosemary Barr asked. 'For letting him get hurt?'

Helen Rodin paused again. Another good reason to say no. *An unrealistic client.*

'Maybe later,' she said. 'Right now he wouldn't generate much sympathy as a plaintiff. And it's hard to prove damages, if he's heading for death row anyway.'

'Then I can't pay you much,' Rosemary Barr said. 'I don't have money.'

Helen Rodin paused for a third time. *Another* good reason to say no. It was a little early in her career to be contemplating pro bono work.

But. But. But.

The accused deserved representation. The Bill of Rights said so. And he was innocent until proven guilty. And if the evidence was as bad as her father said it was, then the whole thing would be little more than a supervisory process. She would verify the case against him, independently. Then she would advise him to plead guilty. Then she would watch his back as her father fed him through the machine. That was all. It could be seen as honest dues-paying. A constitutional chore. She hoped.

'OK,' she said.

'He's innocent,' Rosemary Barr said. 'I'm sure of it.'

They always are, Helen Rodin thought.

'OK,' she said again. Then she told her new client to meet her in her office at seven the next morning. It was like a test. A sister who really believed in her brother's innocence would show up for an early appointment.

Rosemary Barr showed up right on time, at seven o'clock on Monday morning. Franklin was there, too. He believed in Helen Rodin and was prepared to defer his bills until he saw which way the wind was blowing. Helen Rodin herself had already been at her desk for an hour. She had informed David Chapman of the change in representation on Sunday afternoon and had obtained his audiotape of his initial interview with James Barr. Chapman had been happy to hand it over and wash his hands. She had played the tape to herself a dozen times Sunday night and a dozen more that morning. It was all anyone had of James Barr. Maybe all anyone was ever going to get. So she had listened to it carefully, and she had drawn some early conclusions from it.

'Listen,' she said.

She had the tape cued up and ready in an old-fashioned machine the size of a shoe box. She pressed play and they all heard a hiss and breathing and room sounds and then David Chapman's voice: *I can't help you if you won't help yourself.* There was a long pause, full of more hiss, and then James Barr spoke: *They got the wrong guy. They got the wrong guy*, he said again. Then Helen watched the tape counter numbers and spooled forward to Chapman saying: *Denying it is not an option.* Then Barr's voice came through: *Get Jack Reacher for me.* Helen spooled onward to Chapman's question: *Is he a doctor?* Then there was nothing on the tape except the sound of Barr beating on the interview room door.

'OK,' Helen said. 'I think he really believes he didn't do it. He claims as much, and then he gets frustrated and terminates the interview when Chapman doesn't take him seriously. That's clear, isn't it?'

'He *didn't* do it,' Rosemary Barr said.

'I spoke with my father yesterday,' Helen Rodin said. 'The evidence is all there, Ms Barr. He did it, I'm afraid. You need to accept that a sister maybe can't know her brother as well as she'd like. Or if she once did, that he changed for some reason.'

There was a long silence.

'Is your father telling you the truth about the evidence?' Rosemary asked.

'He has to,' Helen said. 'We're going to see it all anyway. There's the discovery process. We're going to take depositions. There would be no sense in him bluffing at this point.'

Nobody spoke.

'But we can still help your brother,' Helen said, in the silence. 'He believes he didn't do it. I'm sure of that, after listening to the tape. Therefore he's delusional now. Or at least he was, on Saturday. Therefore perhaps he was delusional on Friday, too.'

'How does that help him?' Rosemary Barr asked. 'It's still admitting he did it.'

'The consequences will be different. If he re-covers. Time and treatment in an institution will be a lot better than time and *no* treatment in a maximum security prison.'

'You want to have him declared insane?'

Helen nodded. 'A medical defence is our best shot. And if we establish it right now it might improve the way they handle him before the trial.'

'He might die. That's what the doctors said. I don't want him to die a criminal. I want to clear his name.'

'He hasn't been tried yet. He hasn't been con-victed. He's still an innocent man in the eyes of the law.'

'That's not the same.'

'No,' Helen said. 'I guess it isn't.'

There was another long silence.

'Let's meet back here at ten thirty,' Helen said. 'We'll thrash out a strategy. If we're aiming for a change of hospitals, we should try for it sooner rather than later.'

'We need to find this Jack Reacher person,' Rosemary Barr said.

Helen nodded. 'I gave his name to Emerson and my father.'

'Why?'

'Because Emerson's people cleared your brother's house out. They might have found an address or a phone number. And my father needed to know because we want this guy on our witness list, not the prosecution's. Because he might be able to help us.'

'He might be an alibi.'

'Maybe an old army buddy, at best.'

'I don't see how,' Franklin said. 'They were different ranks and different branches.'

'We need to find him,' Rosemary Barr said. 'James asked for him, didn't he? That has to mean something.'

Helen nodded again. 'I'd certainly like to find him. He might have something for us. Some exculpatory information, possibly. Or at least he might be a link to something we can use.'

'He's out of circulation,' Franklin said.

He was two hours away, in the back of a bus out of Indianapolis. The trip had been slow, but pleasant enough. He had spent Saturday night in New Orleans, in a motel near the bus depot. He had spent Sunday night in Indianapolis. So he had slept and fed himself and showered. But mostly he had rocked and swayed and dozed on buses, watching the passing scenes, observing the chaos of America, and surfing along on the memory of the Norwegian. His life was like that. It was a mosaic of fragments. Details and contexts would fade and be inaccurately recalled, but the feelings and the experiences would weave over time into a tapestry equally full of good times and bad. He didn't know yet exactly where the Norwegian would fall. At that point he thought of her as a missed opportunity. But she would have sailed away soon anyway. Or he would have. CNN's intervention had shortened things, but maybe only by a fraction.

The bus was doing 55 on Route 37, heading south. It stopped in Bloomington. Six people got out. One of them left the Indianapolis paper behind. Reacher picked it up and checked the sports. The Yankees were still ahead in the East. Then he flipped to the front and checked the news. He saw the headline: *Sniper Suspect Hurt in Jail Attack*. He read the first three paragraphs: *Brain injury. Coma. Uncertain prognosis.* The journalist seemed torn between condemning the Indiana Board of Corrections for its lawless prisons and applauding Barr's attackers for doing their civic duty.

This might complicate things, Reacher thought.

The later paragraphs carried a reprise of the original crime story, plus updated background, plus new facts. Reacher read them all. Barr's sister had moved out of his house some months before the incident. The journalist seemed to think that was either a cause or an effect of Barr's evident instability. Or both.

The bus moved out of Bloomington. Reacher folded the paper and propped his head against the window and watched the road. It was a black ribbon, wet with recent rain, and it unspooled beside him with the centre line flashing by like an urgent Morse Code message. Reacher wasn't sure what it was saying to him. He couldn't read it.

The bus pulled into a covered depot and Reacher came out into the daylight and found himself five blocks west of where a raised highway curled round behind an old stone building. Indiana lime-stone, he guessed. The real thing. It would be a bank, he thought, or a courthouse, or maybe a library. There was a black glass tower beyond it.

73

The air was OK. It was colder than Miami but he was still far enough south for winter to feel safely distant. He wasn't going to have to refresh his wardrobe because of weather. He was in white chino pants and a bright yellow canvas shirt. Both were three days old. He figured he would get another day out of them. Then he would buy replacements, cheap. He had brown boat shoes on his feet. No socks. He felt he was dressed for the boardwalk and thought he must look a little out of place in the city.

He checked his watch. Nine twenty in the morning. He stood on the sidewalk in the diesel fumes and stretched and looked around. The city was one of those heartland places that are neither large nor small, neither new nor old. It wasn't booming and it wasn't decrepit. There was probably some history. Probably some corn and soybean trading. Maybe tobacco. Maybe livestock. There was probably a river, or a railhead. Maybe some manufacturing. There was a small downtown area. He could see it ahead of him, east of where he stood. Taller structures, some stone, some brick, some billboards. He figured the black glass tower would be the flagship building. No reason to build it anyplace else than the heart of downtown.

He walked towards it. There was a lot of construction under way. Repairs, renewals, holes in the road, gravel piles, fresh concrete, heavy trucks moving slowly. He crossed in front of one and hit a side street and came out along the north side of a half-finished parking garage extension. He recalled Ann Yanni's fevered breaking-news

74

recap and glanced up at it and then away from it to a public square. There was an empty ornamental pool with a fountain spout sticking up forlornly in the centre. There was a narrow walkway between the pool itself and a low wall. The walkway was decorated with makeshift funeral tributes. There were flowers, with their stems wrapped in aluminium foil. Photographs under plastic, and small stuffed animals, and candles. There was a dusting of leftover sand. The sand had soaked up the blood, he guessed. Fire engines carry boxes of sand, for accidents and crime scenes. And stainless steel shovels, for removal of body parts. He glanced back at the parking garage. Less than thirty-five yards, he thought. Very close.

He stood still. The plaza was silent. The whole city was quiet. It felt stunned, like a limb briefly paralysed after a massive bruising blow. The plaza was the epicentre. It was where the blow had landed. It was like a black hole, with emotion compressed into it too tight to escape.

He walked on. The old limestone building was a library. *That's OK*, he thought. *Librarians are nice people. They tell you things, if you ask them.* He asked for the DA's office. A sad and subdued woman at the checkout desk gave him directions. It wasn't a long walk. It wasn't a big city. He walked east past a new office building that had signs for the DMV and a military recruitment centre. Behind it was a block of off-brand stores and then a new courthouse building. It was a plain flat-roof off-the-shelf design dressed up with mahogany doors and etched glass. It could have been a church, from some weird denomination with a generous but strapped congregation.

He avoided the main public entrance. He circled the block until he came to the office wing. He found a door labelled *District Attorney*. Below it on a scparate brass plate he found Rodin's name. *An elected official*, he thought. *They use a separate plate to make it cheaper when the guy changes every few Novembers*. Rodin's initials were *A. A.* He had a law degree.

Reacher went in through the door and spoke to a receptionist at a counter. Asked to see A. A. Rodin himself. 'About what?' the receptionist asked, quietly, but politely. She was middle-aged, well cared for, well turned out, wearing a clean white blouse. She looked like she had worked behind a desk all her life. A practised bureaucrat. But stressed. She looked like she was carrying all the town's recent troubles on her shoulders.

'About James Barr,' Reacher said.

'Are you a reporter?' the receptionist asked.

'No,' Reacher said.

'May I tell Mr Rodin's office your connection to the case?'

'I knew James Barr in the army.'

'That must have been some time ago.'

'A long time ago,' Reacher said.

'May I have your name?'

'Jack Reacher.'

The receptionist dialled a phone and spoke. Reacher guessed she was speaking to a secretary, because both he and Rodin were referred to in the third person, like abstractions. *Can he see a Mr Reacher about the case?* Not the Barr case.

Just *the case*. The conversation continued. Then the receptionist covered the phone by clamping it to her chest, below her collar bone, above her left breast.

'Do you have information?' she asked.

The secretary upstairs can hear your heart beating, Reacher thought.

'Yes,' he said. 'Information.'

'From the army?' she asked.

Reacher nodded. The receptionist put the phone back to her face and continued the conversation. It was a long one. Mr A. A. Rodin had an efficient pair of gatekeepers. That was clear. No way of getting past them without some kind of an urgent and legitimate reason. That was clear, too. Reacher checked his watch. Nine forty in the morning. But there was no rush, under the circumstances. Barr was in a coma. Tomorrow would do it. Or the next day. Or maybe he could get to Rodin through the cop, if need be. What was his name? Emerson?

The receptionist hung up the phone.

'Please go straight up,' she said. 'Mr Rodin is on the third floor.'

I'm honoured, Reacher thought. The receptionist wrote his name on a visitor pass and slipped it into a plastic sleeve. He clipped it on his shirt and headed for the elevator. Rode it to the third floor. The third floor had low ceilings and internal corridors lit by fluorescent tubes. There were three doors made of painted fibreboard that were closed and one set of double doors made of polished wood that were open. Behind those was a secretary at a desk. The

77

second gatekeeper. She was younger than the downstairs lady, but presumably more senior.

'Mr Reacher?' she asked.

He nodded and she came out from behind her desk and led him to where the windowed offices started. The third door they came to was labelled *A. A. Rodin.*

'What's the *A. A.* for?' Reacher asked.

'I'm sure Mr Rodin will tell you if he wants to,' the secretary said.

She knocked on the door and Reacher heard a baritone reply from inside. Then she opened the door and stood aside for Reacher to go in past her.

'Thanks,' he said.

'You're most welcome,' she said.

Reacher went in. Rodin was already on his feet behind his desk, ready to welcome his visitor, full of reflexive courtesy. Reacher recognized him from the TV. He was a guy of about fifty, fairly lean, fairly fit, grey hair cut short. In person he looked smaller. He was maybe an inch under six feet and a pound under two hundred. He was dressed in a summer-weight suit, dark blue. He had a blue shirt on, and a blue tie. His eyes were blue. Blue was his colour, no doubt about it. He was immaculately shaved and wearing cologne. He was a very squared away guy, no question. *As opposed to me*, Reacher thought. It was like a study in contrasts. Next to Rodin, Reacher was an unkempt giant. He was six inches taller and fifty pounds heavier. His hair was two inches longer and his clothes were a thousand dollars cheaper.

'Mr Reacher?' Rodin said.

78

Reacher nodded. The office was government-basic, but neat. It was cool and quiet. No real view from the window. Just the flat roofs of the off-brand stores and the DMV office, with all the duct work showing. The black glass tower was visible in the distance. There was a weak sun in the sky. At right angles to the window there was a trophy wall behind the desk, with college degree certificates and photographs of Rodin with politicians. There were framed newspaper headlines reporting guilty verdicts in seven different cases. On another wall was a photograph of a blonde girl wearing a mortar board and a gown and holding a degree scroll. She was pretty. Reacher looked at her for a moment longer than he needed to.

'That's my daughter,' Rodin said. 'She's a lawyer too.'

'Is she?' Reacher said.

'She just opened her own office here in town.'

There was nothing in his tone. Reacher wasn't sure whether he was proud, or disapproving.

'You're due to meet with her, I think,' Rodin said.

'Am I?' Reacher said. 'Why?'

'She's defending James Barr.'

'Your daughter? Is that ethical?'

'There's no law against it. It might not be sensible, but it's not unethical.'

He said *sensible* with emphasis, hinting at a number of meanings. Not smart to defend a notorious case, not smart for a daughter to take on her father, not smart for *anyone* to take on A. A. Rodin. He sounded like a very competitive guy.

'She put your name on her provisional witness list,' he said.

'Why?'

'She thinks you have information.'

'Where did she get my name?'

'I don't know.'

'From the Pentagon?'

Rodin shrugged. 'I'm not sure. But she got it from somewhere. Therefore people have been looking for you.'

'Is that why I got in here?'

Rodin nodded.

'Yes, it is,' he said. 'That's exactly why. Generally I don't encourage walk-ins.'

'Your staff seems to be on board with that policy.'

'I certainly hope so,' Rodin said. 'Sit down, please.'

Reacher sat in the visitor chair and Rodin sat behind his desk. The window was on Reacher's left and Rodin's right. Neither man had the light in his eyes. It was an equitable furniture arrangement. Different from some prosecutors' offices Reacher had known.

'Coffee?' Rodin asked.

'Please,' Reacher said.

Rodin made a call and asked for coffee.

'Naturally I'm interested in why you came to see me first,' he said. 'The prosecution, I mean, rather than the defence.'

'I wanted your personal opinion,' Reacher said.

'On what?'

'On how strong a case you've got against James Barr.'

Rodin didn't answer immediately. There was a short silence and then there was a knock at the door and the secretary came in with coffee. She had a silver tray with the works on it. A cafetière, two cups, two saucers, a sugar bowl, a tiny pitcher of cream, two silver spoons. The cups were fine china. *Not government issue*, Reacher thought. *Rodin likes his coffee done right*. The secretary put the tray on the edge of the desk, so that it was exactly halfway between the desk chair and the visitor chair.

'Thanks,' Reacher said.

'You're most welcome,' she said, and left the room.

'Help yourself,' Rodin said. 'Please.'

Reacher pushed the plunger down and poured himself a cup, no cream, no sugar. It smelled dark and strong. Coffee, done right.

'The case against James Barr is exceptionally good,' Rodin said.

'Eyewitnesses?' Reacher asked.

'No,' Rodin said. 'But eyewitness testimony can be of random value. I'm almost glad we don't have eyewitnesses. Because what we've got instead is exceptional physical evidence. And science doesn't lie. It doesn't get confused.'

'Exceptional?' Reacher said.

'A complete rock-solid evidence trail that ties the man to the crime.'

'How solid?'

'As good as it gets. The best I've ever seen. I'm completely confident.'

'I've heard prosecutors say that before.'

'Not this one, Mr Reacher. I'm a very cautious

81

man. I don't prosecute capital cases unless I'm certain of the outcome.'

'Keeping score?'

Rodin gestured above and behind him at his trophy wall.

'Seven for seven,' he said. 'One hundred per cent.'

'In how long?'

'In three years. James Barr will make it eight for eight. If he ever wakes up.'

'Suppose he wakes up damaged?'

'If he wakes up with any brain function at all, he's going to trial. What he did here can't be forgiven.'

'OK,' Reacher said.

'OK what?'

'You've told me what I wanted to know.'

'You said you had information. From the army.'

'I'll keep it to myself for now.'

'You were a military policeman, am I right?'

'Thirteen years,' Reacher said.

'And you knew James Barr?'

'Briefly.'

'Tell me about him.'

'Not yet.'

'Mr Reacher, if you have exculpatory information, or anything to add at all, you really need to tell me now.'

'Do I?'

'I'll get it anyway. My daughter will submit it. She'll be looking for a plea bargain.'

'What does the *A. A.* stand for?'

'Excuse me?'

'Your initials.'

'Aleksei Alekseivitch. My family came from Russia. But a long time ago. Before the October Revolution.'

'But they keep up traditions.'

'As you can see.'

'What do people call you?'

'Alex, of course.'

Reacher stood up. 'Well, thanks for your time, Alex. And the coffee.'

'Are you going to see my daughter now?'

'Is there any point? You seem pretty sure of yourself.'

Rodin smiled an indulgent smile.

'It's a matter of procedure,' he said. 'I'm an officer of the court, and you're on a witness list. I'm obliged to point out that you're obliged to go. Anything less would be unethical.'

'Where is she?'

'In the glass tower you can see from the window.'

'OK,' Reacher said. 'I guess I could drop by.'

'I still need whatever information you have,' Rodin said.

Reacher shook his head.

'No,' he said. 'You really don't.'

He returned his visitor pass to the woman at the reception desk and headed back to the public plaza. Stood in the cold sun and turned a complete circle, getting a sense of the place. All cities are the same, and all cities are different. They all have colours. Some are grey. This one was brown. Reacher guessed the brick was made from local clay and had carried the colour of old farmland into the façades. Even the stone was flecked with tan, like it carried deposits of iron. There were accents of dark red here and there, like old barns. It was a warm place, not busy, but it was surviving. It would rebound after the tragedy. There was progress and optimism and dynamism. All the new construction proved it. There were work zones and raw concrete kerbs everywhere. Lots of planning, lots of rebuilding. Lots of hope.

The new parking garage extension anchored the north end of the downtown strip. It suggested commercial expansion. It was south and slightly west of the kill zone. Very close. Directly west and maybe twice as distant was a length of the raised highway. It ran free and clear through a curve for maybe thirty yards before curling in behind the library. Then it straightened a little and passed behind the black glass tower. The tower was due north of the plaza. It had an NBC sign near the door, on a black granite slab. Ann Yanni's workplace, Reacher guessed, as well as Rodin's daughter's. East of the plaza was the office building with the DMV and the recruiting office. That was where the victims had come from. They had spilled out the door. What had Ann Yanni said? At the end of a long working week? They had hustled west across the plaza towards their parked cars or the bus depot and had stumbled into a nightmare. The narrow walkway would have slowed them down and lined them up. Like shooting fish in a barrel.

Reacher walked the length of the empty ornamental pool to the revolving door at the base of the tower. He went in and checked the lobby for a directory. There was a glassed-in board made of ridged black felt with press-in white letters. NBC was on the second floor. Some of the other suites were empty and Reacher guessed the rest changed hands fast enough to make it worth holding on to the press-in letter system. *Law Offices of Helen Rodin* was listed on four. The letters were a little misaligned and the spacing was off. *Rockefeller Center it ain't*, Reacher thought.

He waited for the elevator in a queue of two, him and a pretty blonde woman. He looked at her and she looked at him. She got out on two and he realized it was Ann Yanni. He recognized her from the broadcast. Then he figured all he needed to do was meet Emerson from the local PD and he would have brought the whole breaking-news tableau to life.

He found Helen Rodin's suite. It was at the front of the building. Her windows were going to overlook the plaza. He knocked. Heard a muffled reply and went in. There was an empty reception room with a secretary's desk. The desk was unoccupied. It was secondhand, but not recently used. *No secretary yet*, Reacher thought. *Early days*.

He knocked on the inner office door. Heard the same voice make a second reply. He went in and found Helen Rodin at another secondhand desk. He recognized her from her father's photograph. But face to face she looked even better. She was probably no more than thirty, quite tall, lightly built. Slim, in an athletic sort of a way. Not anorexic. Either she ran or she played soccer or she had been very lucky with her metabolism. She had long blond hair and her father's blue eyes. There was intelligence behind them. She was dressed all in black, in a trouser suit with a tight stretch top under the coat. *Lycra*, Reacher thought. *Can't beat it.*

'Hello,' she said.

'I'm Jack Reacher,' he said.

She stared at him. 'You're kidding. Are you really?'

He nodded. 'Always have been, always will be.'

'Unbelievable.'

'Not really. Everybody's somebody.'

'I mean, how did you know to come? We couldn't find you.'

'I saw it on the TV. Ann Yanni, Saturday morning.'

'Well, thank God for TV,' she said. 'And thank God you're here.'

'I was in Miami,' he said. 'With a dancer.'

'A dancer?'

'She was Norwegian,' he said.

He walked to the window and looked out. He was four storeys up and the main shopping street ran away directly south, down a hill, emphasizing his elevation. The ornamental pool was placed with its long axis exactly lined up with the street. The pool was *on* the street, really, except they had blocked the street off to make the plaza. Someone returning from a long spell away would be surprised to find a big tank of water where once there had been roadway. The pool was much longer and narrower than it had looked from ground level. It looked sad and empty, with just a thin layer of mud and scum on the black tile. Beyond it and slightly to the right was the new parking structure. It was slightly downhill from the plaza. Maybe half a storey's difference.

'Were you here?' Reacher asked. 'When it happened?'

'Yes, I was,' Helen Rodin said quietly.

'Did you see it?'

'Not at first. I heard the first three gunshots. They came very fast. The first, and then a tiny pause, and then the next two. Then another pause, a little longer, but just a split second, really. I stood up in time for the last three. Horrible.'

Reacher nodded. *Brave girl*, he thought. *She hears gunshots, and she stands up. She doesn't dive under the desk*. Then he thought: *The first, and then a tiny pause*. That was the sound of a skilled rifleman watching where his first cold shot went. So many variables. The cold barrel, the range, the wind, the zeroing, the sighting-in.

'Did you see people die?' he asked.

'Two of them,' she said, behind him. 'It was awful.'

'Three shots and two people?'

'He missed once. Either the fourth or the fifth shot, they're not sure. They found the bullet in the pool. That's why it's empty. They drained it.'

Reacher said nothing.

'The bullet is part of the evidence,' Helen said. 'It ties the rifle to the crime.'

'Did you know any of the dead people?'

'No. They were just people, I guess. In the wrong place at the wrong time.'

Reacher said nothing.

'I saw flames from the gun,' Helen said. 'Way over there, in the shadows, in the dark. Little spits of flame.'

'Muzzle flashes,' Reacher said.

He turned back from the window. She held out her hand.

'I'm Helen Rodin,' she said. 'I'm sorry, I should have introduced myself properly.'

Reacher took her hand. It was warm and firm.

'Just Helen?' he said. 'Not Helena Alekseyovna or something?'

She stared at him again. 'How the hell did you know that?'

'I met your dad,' he said, and let go of her hand.

'Did you?' she said. 'Where?'

'In his office, just now.'

'You went to *his* office? Today?'

'I just left there.'

'Why did you go to *his* office? You're *my* witness. He shouldn't have seen you.'

'He was very keen to talk.'

'What did you tell him?'

'Nothing. I asked questions instead.'

'What questions?'

'I wanted to know how strong his case was. Against James Barr.'

'I'm representing James Barr. And you're a defence witness. You should have been talking to me, not him.'

Reacher said nothing.

'Unfortunately the case against James Barr is very strong,' she said.

'How did you get my name?' Reacher asked.

'From James Barr, of course,' she said. 'How else?'

'From *Barr*? I don't believe it.'

'Well, listen,' she said.

She turned away to the desk and pressed a key on an old-fashioned cassette player. Reacher heard a voice he didn't recognize say: *Denying it is not an option.* Helen touched the pause key and kept her finger on it.

'His first lawyer,' she said. 'We changed representation yesterday.'

'How? He was in a coma yesterday.'

'Technically my client is James Barr's sister. His next of kin.'

Then she let go of the pause key and Reacher heard room sounds and hiss and then a voice he hadn't heard for fourteen years. It was exactly how he remembered it. It was low, and tense, and raspy. It was the voice of a man who rarely spoke. It said: *Get Jack Reacher for me.*

He stood there, stunned.

Helen Rodin pressed the stop key.

'See?' she said.

Then she checked her watch.

'Ten thirty,' she said. 'Stick around and join in the client conference.'

She unveiled him like a conjurer on a stage. Like a rabbit out of a hat. First in was a guy Reacher immediately took for an ex-cop. He was introduced as Franklin, a contract investigator who worked for lawyers. They shook hands.

'You're a hard man to find,' Franklin said.

'Wrong,' Reacher said. 'I'm an impossible man to find.'

'Want to tell me why?' There were instant questions in Franklin's eyes. A cop's questions. Like, *how much use is this guy going to be as a witness? What is he? A felon? A fugitive? Will he have credibility on the stand?*

'Just a hobby,' Reacher said. 'Just a personal choice.'

'So you're cool?'

'You could skate on me.'

Then a woman came in. She was in her mid- to late thirties, probably, dressed for an office, and stressed and sleepless. But behind the agitation she wasn't unappealing. She looked like a kind and decent person. Even pretty. But she was clearly James Barr's sister. Reacher knew that even before they were introduced. She had the same colouring and a softer, feminized, fourteen-years-older version of the same face.

'I'm Rosemary Barr,' she said. 'I'm so glad you found us. It feels providential. Now I really feel we're getting somewhere.'

Reacher said nothing at all.

The law offices of Helen Rodin didn't run to a conference room. Reacher figured that would come later. Maybe. If she prospered. So all four people crowded into the inner office. Helen sat at her desk. Franklin perched on a corner of it. Reacher leaned on the window sill. Rosemary Barr paced, nervously. If there had been a rug, she would have worn holes in it.

'OK,' Helen said. 'Defence strategy. At the minimum we want to pursue a medical plea. But

90

we'll aim higher than that. How high we eventually get will depend on a number of factors. In which connection, first, I'm sure we all want to hear what Mr Reacher has to say.'

'I don't think you do,' Reacher said.

'Do what?'

'Want to hear what I've got to say.'

'Why wouldn't we?'

'Because you jumped to the wrong conclusion.'

'Which is?'

'Why do you think I went to see your father first?'

'I don't know.'

'Because I didn't come here to help James Barr.'

Nobody spoke.

'I came here to bury him,' Reacher said.

They all stared.

'But why?' Rosemary Barr asked.

'Because he's done this before. And once was enough.'

THREE

Reacher moved and propped his back against the window reveal and turned sideways so that he could see the plaza. And so that he couldn't see his audience.

'Is this a privileged conversation?' he asked.

'Yes,' Helen Rodin said. 'It is. It's a client conference. It's automatically protected. Nothing we say here can be repeated.'

'Is it ethical for you to hear bad news, legally?'

There was a long silence.

'Are you going to give evidence for the prosecution?' Helen Rodin asked.

'I don't think I'll have to, under the circumstances. But I will if necessary.'

'Then we would hear the bad news anyway. We would take a deposition from you before the trial. To guarantee no more surprises.'

More silence.

'James Barr was a sniper,' Reacher said. 'Not the best the army ever had, and not the worst. Just a good, competent rifleman. Average in almost every way.'

Then he paused and turned his head and

92

looked down to his left. At the cheap new building with the recruitment office in it. Army, Navy, Air Force, Marine Corps.

'Four types of people join the military,' he said. 'First, for people like me, it's a family trade. Second, there are patriots, eager to serve their country. Third, there are people who just need a job. And fourth, there are people who want to kill other people. The military is the only place where it's legal to do that. James Barr was the fourth type. Deep down he thought it would be fun to kill.'

Rosemary Barr looked away. Nobody spoke.

'But he never got the chance,' Reacher said. 'I was a very thorough investigator when I was an MP, and I learned all about him. I studied him. He trained for five years. I went through his log books. Some weeks he fired two thousand rounds. All of them at paper targets or silhouettes. I counted a career total of nearly a quarter-million rounds fired, and not one of them at the enemy. He didn't go to Panama in 1989. We had a very big army back then, and we required only a very small force, so most guys missed out. It burned him up. Then Desert Shield happened, in 1990. He went to Saudi. But he wasn't in Desert Storm, in 1991. They made it a mostly armoured campaign. James Barr sat it out in Saudi, cleaning sand out of his rifle, firing two thousand training rounds a week. Then after Desert Storm was over, they sent him to Kuwait City for the clean-up.'

'What happened there?' Rosemary Barr asked.

'He snapped,' Reacher said. 'That's what happened there. The Soviets had collapsed. Iraq was back in its box. He looked ahead and saw that war was over. He had trained nearly six years and had never fired his gun in anger and was never going to. A lot of his training had been about visualization. About seeing himself putting the reticle on the medulla oblongata, where the spinal cord broadens at the base of the brain. About breathing slow and squeezing the trigger. About the split second pause while the bullet flies. About seeing the puff of pink mist from the back of the head. He had visualized all of that. Many times. But he had never seen it. Not once. He had never seen the pink mist. And he really wanted to.'

Silence in the room.

'So he went out one day, alone,' Reacher said. 'In Kuwait City. He set up and waited. Then he shot and killed four people coming out of an apartment building.'

Helen Rodin was staring at him.

'He fired from a parking garage,' Reacher said. 'Second level. It was directly opposite the apartment building's door. The victims were American noncoms, as it happened. They had weekend passes, and they were in street clothes.'

Rosemary Barr was shaking her head.

'This can't be true,' she said. 'It just *can't* be. He wouldn't do it. And if he did, he'd have gone to prison. But he got an honourable discharge instead. Right after the Gulf. And a campaign medal. So it can't have happened. It can't possibly be true.'

'That's exactly why I'm here,' Reacher said. 'There was a serious problem. Remember the

94

sequence of events. We had four dead guys, and we worked from there. In the end I followed the trail all the way to your brother. But it was a very tough trail. We took all kinds of wrong turns. And along one of them we found stuff out about the four dead guys. Stuff we really didn't want to know. Because they had been doing things they shouldn't have been doing.'

'What things?' Helen Rodin asked.

'Kuwait City was a hell of a place. Full of rich Arabs. Even the poor ones had Rolexes and Rolls-Royces and marble bathrooms with solid gold faucets. A lot of them had fled temporarily, for the duration. But they had left all their stuff behind. And some of them had left their families behind. Their wives and daughters.'

'And?'

'Our four dead noncoms had been doing the conquering army thing, just like the Iraqis before them. That's how they saw it, I guess. We saw it as rape and armed robbery. As it happened they had left quite a trail that day, inside that building. And other buildings, on other days. We found enough loot in their footlockers to start another branch of Tiffany's. Watches, diamonds, all kinds of portable stuff. And underwear. We figured they used the underwear to keep count of the wives and daughters.'

'So what happened?'

'It got political, inevitably. It went up the chain of command. The Gulf was supposed to be a big shiny success for us. It was supposed to be a hundred per cent wonderful and a hundred per cent squeaky clean. And the Kuwaitis were our

95

allies, and so on and so forth. So ultimately we were told to cover for the four guys. We were told to bury the story. Which we did. Which also meant letting James Barr walk, unfortunately. Because whispers had gotten out and we knew his lawyer would have used them. We were afraid of blackmail, basically. If we took Barr to trial, his lawyer would have countered with a justifiable homicide claim. He would have said Barr had been standing up for the honour of the army, in a rough and ready sort of a way. All the beans would have spilled in the process. We were told not to risk that. So our hands were tied. It was a stalemate.'

'Maybe it *was* justifiable homicide,' Rosemary Barr said. 'Maybe James really did know all along.'

'Ma'am, he didn't know. I'm very sorry, but he didn't. He was never near any of those guys before. Didn't know them from Adam. Didn't say anything to me about them when I caught up to him. He hadn't been in KC long. Not long enough to know anything. He was just killing people. For fun. He confessed to that, to me personally, before any of the other stuff ever came to light.'

Silence in the room.

'So we hushed it up and mustered him out,' Reacher said. 'We said his four guys had been killed by Palestinians, which was plausible in Kuwait City in 1991, just. I was mildly pissed about the whole thing. It wasn't the worst situation I had ever seen, but it wasn't the nicest, either. James Barr got away with murder, by sheer luck. So I went to see him before he left and I told him to justify his great good fortune by never stepping out of line again, not ever, the whole rest of his life. I told him if he ever did, I would come find him and make him sorry.'

Silence in the room. It lasted minutes.

'So here I am,' Reacher said.

'This must be classified information,' Helen Rodin said. 'I mean, surely it can't ever be *used*. There would be a huge scandal.'

Reacher nodded. 'It's highly classified. It's sealed inside the Pentagon. That's why I asked if this conversation was privileged.'

'You'd get in big trouble if you talked about it.'

'I've been in big trouble before. I came here to find out if I needed to get in big trouble again. As it happens, I don't think I do. I think your father can put James Barr away without my help. But my help is always available if he needs it.'

Then Helen understood.

'You're here to pressure me,' she said. 'Aren't you? You're telling me if I try too hard, you'll cut me off at the knees.'

'I'm here to keep my promise,' Reacher said. 'To James Barr.'

He closed the door and left them there, three silent and disappointed people in a room. Then he rode down in the elevator. Ann Yanni got in again on two. He wondered for a moment if she spent all day riding the elevators, hoping to be recognized. Hoping to be asked for an autograph. He ignored her. Got out with her in the lobby and just headed for the door.

He stood for a moment in the plaza. Deciding.

James Barr's medical condition was the complicating factor. He didn't want to stick around until the guy woke up. If that happened at all, it might take weeks. And Reacher was not a guy who liked to stick around. He liked to be on the move. Two days in one place was about his limit. But he was stuck for alternatives. He couldn't hint at anything to Alex Rodin. Couldn't give him a call-me-if-you-need-me number. For one thing, he didn't have a phone. For another, a guy as squared away and cautious as Alex Rodin was would worry away at the hint until something began to unravel. He would make the link to the Pentagon easily enough. Reacher had even asked *did she get my name from the Pentagon?* That had been a careless mistake. So Alex Rodin would put two and two together, eventually. He would figure *there's something extra here, and I can find out what it is from the Pentagon.* The Pentagon would stonewall him, of course. But Rodin wouldn't like being stonewalled. He would go to the media. Ann Yanni, probably. She would be ready for another network story. And at bottom Rodin would be insecure enough about losing the case to simply *have* to know. He wouldn't give up on it.

And Reacher didn't want the story out there. Not unless it was absolutely necessary. Gulf War vets had it hard enough, with the chemical stuff and the uranium poisoning. All they had going for them was the conflict's spotless just-war reputation. They didn't need defaming by association with people like Barr and his victims. People would say *hey, they were all doing it.* And they weren't all doing it, in Reacher's experience. That had been a good army. So he didn't want the story out there, unless it was absolutely necessary, and he wanted to judge that for himself.

So, no hints to Alex Rodin. No call-me contingencies.

So . . . what, exactly?

He decided to stick around for twenty-four hours. Maybe there would be a clearer prognosis on Barr's condition after that. Maybe somehow he could check with Emerson and get a better feel for the evidence. Then maybe he could feel OK about leaving things with Alex Rodin's office, on a kind of forensic autopilot. If there were problems down the road maybe he would read about them in a newspaper somewhere, far in the future, on a beach or in a bar, and then he could come all the way back again.

So, twenty-four hours in a small heartland city.

He decided to go see if there was a river.

There was a river. It was a broad, slow body of water that moved west to east through an area south of downtown. Some tributary that fed the mighty Ohio, he guessed. Its north bank was straightened and strengthened with massive stone blocks along a three-hundred-yard stretch. The blocks might have weighed fifty tons each. They were immaculately chiselled and expertly fitted. They made a quayside. A wharf. They had tall fat iron mushrooms set into them, to tie off ropes. Stone paving slabs made the wharf thirty feet deep. All along its length were tall wooden sheds, open on the river side, open on the street side.

The street was made of cobbles. A hundred years ago there would have been huge river barges tied up and unloading. There would have been swarms of men at work. There would have been horses and carts clattering on the cobbles. But now there was nothing. Just absolute stillness, and the slow drift of the water. Scabs of rust on the iron mushrooms, clumps of weeds between the stones.

Some of the sheds still had faded names on them. *McGinty Dry Goods. Allentown Seed Company. Parker Supply.* Reacher strolled the three hundred yards and looked at all of them. They were still standing, strong and square. Ripe for renovation, he guessed. A city that put an ornamental pool with a fountain in a public plaza would spruce up the waterfront. It was inevitable. There was construction all over town. It would move south. They would give someone tax breaks to open a riverside café. Maybe a bar. Maybe with live music, Thursday through Saturday. Maybe with a little museum laying out the history of the river trade.

He turned to walk back and came face to face with Helen Rodin.

'You're not such a hard man to find,' she said.

'Evidently,' he said.

'Tourists always come to the docks.'

She was carrying a lawyer-size briefcase.

'Can I buy you lunch?' she said.

She walked him back north to the edge of the new gentrification. In the space of a single dug-up block the city changed from old and worn to

100

new and repainted. Stores changed from dusty mom-and-pop places with displays of vacuum cleaner bags and washing machine hoses to new establishments showing off spotlit hundred-dollar dresses. And shoes, and four-dollar lattes, and things made of titanium. They walked past a few such places and then Helen Rodin led him into an eatery. It was the kind of place he had seen before. It was the kind of place he usually avoided. White walls, some exposed brick, engine-turned aluminium tables and chairs, weird salad combinations. Random ingredients thrown together, and called inventive.

She led him to a table in the far back corner. An energetic kid came by with menus. Helen Rodin ordered something with oranges and walnuts and Gorgonzola cheese. With a cup of herbal tea. Reacher gave up on reading his menu and ordered the same thing as her, but with coffee, regular, black.

'This is my favourite place in town,' Helen said.

He nodded. He believed her. She looked right at home. The long straight hair, the black clothes. The youthful glow. He was older and came from a different time and a different place.

'I need you to explain something,' she said.

She bent down and opened her briefcase. Came out with the old tape player. Placed it carefully on the table. Pressed play. Reacher heard James Barr's first lawyer say: *Denying it is not an option.* Then he heard Barr say: *Get Jack Reacher for me.*

'You already played that for me,' he said.

'But why would he say it?' Helen asked.

'That's what you want me to explain?'

101

She nodded.

'I can't,' he said.

'Logically you're the last person he should have asked for.'

'I agree.'

'Could he have been in any doubt about how you felt? Fourteen years ago?'

'I don't think so. I made myself pretty clear.'

'Then why would he ask for you now?'

Reacher didn't answer. The food came, and they started eating. Oranges, walnuts, Gorgonzola cheese, all kinds of leaves and lettuces, and a raspberry vinaigrette. It wasn't too bad. And the coffee was OK.

'Play me the whole tape,' he said.

She put her fork down and pressed the rewind key. Kept her hand there, one fingertip on each key, like a pianist. She had long fingers. No rings. Polished nails, neatly trimmed. She pressed play and picked up her fork again. Reacher heard no sound for a moment until the blank leader cleared the tape head. Then he heard a prison acoustic. Echoes, distant metallic clattering. A man breathing. Then he heard a door open and the thump of another man sitting down. No scraping of chair legs on concrete. A prison chair, bolted to the floor. The lawyer started talking. He was old and bored. He didn't want to be there. He knew Barr was guilty. He made banal small talk for a while. Grew frustrated with Barr's silence. Then he said, full of exasperation: *I can't help you if you won't help yourself.* There was a long, long pause, and then Barr's voice came through, agitated, close to the microphone: *They got the wrong guy*. He said it again. Then the lawyer started up again, not believing him, saying the evidence was all there, looking for a reason behind an indisputable fact. Then Barr asked for Reacher, twice, and the lawyer asked if Reacher was a doctor, twice. Then Barr got up and walked out. There was the sound of hammering on a locked door, and then nothing more.

Helen Rodin pressed the stop key.

'So why?' she asked. 'Why say he didn't do it and then call for a guy who knows for sure he did it before?'

Reacher just shrugged his shoulders and said nothing. But he saw in Helen's eyes that she had an answer.

'You know something,' she said. 'Maybe you don't know you know it. But there's got to be something there. Something he thinks can help him.'

'Does it matter? He's in a coma. He might never wake up.'

'It matters a lot. He could get better treatment.'

'I don't know anything.'

'Are you sure? Was there a psychiatric evaluation made back then?'

'It never got that far.'

'Did he claim insanity?'

'No, he claimed a perfect score. Four for four.'

'Did you think he was nuts?'

'That's a big word. Was it nuts to shoot four people for fun? Of course it was. Was *he* nuts, legally? I'm sure he wasn't.'

'You must know something, Reacher,' Helen

said. 'It must be way down in there. You've got to dredge it up.'

He kept quiet for a moment.

'Have you actually seen the evidence?' he asked.

'I've seen a summary.'

'How bad is it?'

'It's terrible. There's no question he did it. This is about mitigation, nothing more. And his state of mind. I can't let them execute an insane person.'

'So wait until he wakes up. Run some tests.'

'They won't count. He could wake up like a fruitcake and the prosecution will say that was caused by the blow to the head in the jailhouse fight. They'll say he was perfectly sane at the time of the crime.'

'Is your dad a fair man?'

'He lives to win.'

'Like father, like daughter?'

She paused.

'Somewhat,' she said.

Reacher finished up his salad. Chased the last walnut round with his fork and then gave up and used his fingers instead.

'What's on your mind?' Helen asked.

'Just a minor detail,' he said. 'Fourteen years ago it was a very tough case with barely adequate forensics. And he confessed. This time the forensics seem to be a total slam dunk. But he's denying it.'

'What does that mean?'

'I don't know.'

'So think about what you *do* know,' Helen said. 'Please. You must know something. You have to ask yourself, why did he come up with your name? There has to be a reason.'

Reacher said nothing. The kid who had served them came back and took their plates away. Reacher pointed at his coffee cup and the kid made another trip and refilled it. Reacher cradled it in his hands and smelled the steam.

'May I ask you a personal question?' Helen Rodin said to him.

'Depends how personal,' Reacher said.

'Why were you so untraceable? Normally guys like Franklin can find anybody.'

'Maybe he's not as good as you think.'

'He's probably better than I think.'

'Not everyone is traceable.'

'I agree. But you don't look like you belong in that category.'

'I was in the machine,' Reacher said. 'My whole life. Then the machine coughed and spat me out. So I thought, OK, if I'm out, I'm out. All the way out. I was a little angry and it was probably an immature reaction. But I got used to it.'

'Like a game?'

'Like an addiction,' Reacher said. 'I'm addicted to being out.'

The kid brought the check. Helen Rodin paid. Then she put her tape player back in her briefcase and she and Reacher left together. They walked north, past the construction at the bottom of First Street. She was heading to her office and he was going to look for a hotel.

A man called Grigor Linsky watched them walk. He was slumped low in a car parked on the kerb. He knew where to wait. He knew where she ate, when she had company.

105

FOUR

Reacher checked into a downtown hotel called the Metropole Palace, two blocks east of First Street, about level with the main shopping strip. He paid cash up front for one night only and used the name Jimmy Reese. He had cycled through all the presidents and vice presidents long ago and was now using second basemen from the Yankees' non-championship years. Jimmy Reese had played pretty well during part of 1930 and pretty badly during part of 1931. He had come from nowhere and moved on to St Louis for part of 1932. Then he had quit. He had died in California, aged 93. But now he was back, with a single room and a bath in the Metropole Palace, for one night only, due to check out the next morning before eleven o'clock.

The Metropole was a sad, half-empty, faded old place. But it had once been grand. Reacher could see that. He could picture the corn traders a hundred years ago, walking up the hill from the river wharf and staying the night. He guessed the lobby had once looked like a western saloon, but now it was thinly made over with modernist touches. There was a refurbished elevator. The rooms had swipe cards instead of keys. But he guessed the building hadn't really changed very much. His room was certainly old-fashioned and gloomy. The mattress felt like a part of the original inventory.

He lay down on it and put his hands behind his head. Thought back more than fourteen years to Kuwait City. All cities have colours, and KC was white. White stucco, white-painted concrete, white marble. Skies burned white by the sun. Men in white robes. The parking garage James Barr had used was white, and the apartment building opposite was white. Because of the glare the four dead guys had all been wearing aviator shades. All four men had been hit in the head, but none of the shades had broken. They had just fallen off. All four bullets had been recovered, and they broke the case. They were match-grade 168-grain jacketed boat tails. Not hollow points, because of the Geneva Convention. They were an American sniper's bullets, either Army or Marines. If Barr had used a battle rifle or a sub-machine gun or a sidearm, Reacher would have got nowhere. Every firearm in theatre except the sniper rifles used standard NATO rounds, which would have cast the net way too wide, because just about all of NATO was in country. But Barr's whole purpose had been to use his own specialist weapon, just for once, this time for real. And in the process, his four thirteen-cent bullets had nailed him.

But it had been a tough, tough case. Maybe Reacher's finest ever. He had used logic, deduction, paperwork, footwork, intuition, and ultimately elimination. At the end of the trail was James Barr, a man who had finally seen the pink mist and was strangely at peace with his capture.

He had confessed.

The confession was voluntary, fast, and complete. Reacher never laid a hand on him. Barr talked quite freely about the experience. Then he asked questions about the investigation, like he was fascinated by the process. Clearly he had not expected to be caught. Not in a million years. He was simultaneously aggrieved and admiring. He had even acted a little sympathetic when the political snafu eventually broke him loose. Like he was sorry that Reacher's fine efforts had come to nothing.

Fourteen years later he had not confessed.

There was another difference between this time and the last time, too. But Reacher couldn't pin it down. Something to do with how hot Kuwait City had been.

Grigor Linsky used his cell phone and called the Zec. The Zec was the man he worked for. It wasn't just Zec. It was *the* Zec. It was a question of respect. The Zec was eighty years old, but he still broke arms if he smelled disrespect. He was like an old bull. He still had his strength and his attitude. He was eighty years old *because of* his strength and his attitude. Without them he would have died at age twenty. Or later, at thirty, which was about when he went insane and his real name finally slipped his mind.

'The lawyer went back to her office,' Linsky said. 'Reacher turned east off First Street. I laid back and didn't follow him. But he turned away from the bus depot. Therefore we can assume he's staying in town. My guess is he checked into the Metropole Palace. There's nothing else in that direction.'

The Zec made no reply.

'Should we do anything?' Linsky asked.

'How long is he here for?'

'That depends. Clearly he's on a mission of mercy.'

The Zec said nothing.

'Should we do anything?' Linsky asked again.

There was a pause. Cellular static, and an old man breathing.

'We should maybe distract him,' the Zec said. 'Or discourage him. I'm told he was a soldier. Therefore he will probably maintain a predictable pattern of behaviour. If he's at the Metropole, he won't stay in tonight. Not there. No fun for a soldier. He'll go out somewhere. Probably alone. So there could be an incident. Use your imagination. Make it a big scenario. Don't use our own people. And make it look natural.'

'Damage?'

'Broken bones, at least. Maybe he gets a head injury. Maybe he winds up in the coma ward along with his buddy James Barr.'

'What about the lawyer?'

'Leave her alone. For now. We'll open that can of worms later. If we need to.'

Helen Rodin spent an hour at her desk. She took three calls. The first was from Franklin. He was bailing out.

'I'm sorry, but you're going to lose,' he said. 'And I've got a business to run. I can't put in unbilled hours on this any more.'

'Nobody likes hopeless cases,' Helen said, diplomatically. She was going to need him again, in the future. No point in holding his feet to the fire.

'Not pro bono hopeless cases,' Franklin said.

'If I get a budget, will you come back on board?'

'Sure,' Franklin said. 'Just call me.'

Then they hung up, all proprieties observed, their relationship preserved. The next call came ten minutes later. It was from her father, who sounded full of concern.

'You shouldn't have taken this case, you know,' he said.

'It wasn't like I was spoiled for choice,' Helen said.

'Losing might be winning, if you know what I mean.'

'Winning might be winning, too.'

'No, winning will be losing. You need to understand that.'

'Did you ever set out to lose a case?' she asked.

Her father said nothing. Then he went fishing.

'Did Jack Reacher find you?' he asked, meaning: *Should I be worried?*

'He found me,' she said, keeping her voice light.

'Was he interesting?' Meaning: *Should I be very worried?*

'He's certainly given me something to think about.'

'Well, should we discuss it?' Meaning: *Please, tell me.*

'I'm sure we will soon. When the time is right.'

They small-talked for a minute more and arranged to meet for dinner. He tried again: *Please, tell me.* She didn't. Then they hung up. Helen smiled. She hadn't lied. Hadn't even really bluffed. But she felt she had participated. The law was a game, and like any game it had a psychological component.

The third call was from Rosemary Barr at the hospital.

'James is waking up,' she said. 'He coughed up his breathing tube. He's coming out of the coma.'

'Is he talking?'

'The doctors say he might be tomorrow.'

'Will he remember anything?'

'The doctors say it's possible.'

An hour later Reacher left the Metropole. He stayed east of First Street and headed north towards the off-brand stores he had seen near the courthouse. He wanted clothes. Something local. Maybe not a set of bib overalls, but certainly something more generic than his Miami gear. Because he figured he might head to Seattle next. For the coffee. And he couldn't walk around Seattle in a bright yellow shirt.

He found a store and bought a pair of pants that the label called taupe and he called olive drab. He found a flannel shirt almost the same colour. Plus underwear. And he invested in a pair of socks. He changed in the cubicle and threw his old stuff away in the store's own trash bin. Forty bucks, for what he hoped would be four days' wear. Extravagant, but it was worth ten bucks a day to him not to carry a bag.

He came out and walked west towards the afternoon sun. The shirt was too thick for the weather, but he could regulate it by rolling up the sleeves and opening a second button. It was OK. It would be fine for Seattle.

He came out into the plaza and saw that the fountain had been restarted. It was refilling the pool, very slowly. The mud on the bottom was an inch deep and moving in slow swirls. Some people were standing and watching it. Others were walking. But nobody was using the short route past the memorial tributes, where Barr's victims had died. Maybe nobody would ever again. Instead everyone was looping the long way round, past the NBC sign. Instinctively, respectfully, fearfully, Reacher wasn't sure.

He picked his way among the flowers and sat on the low wall, with the sound of the fountain behind him, and the parking garage in front of him. One shoulder was warmed by the sun and the other was cool in the shade. He could feel the leftover sand under his feet. He looked to his left and watched the DMV building's door. Looked to his right and watched the cars on the raised highway. They tracked through the curve, high up in the air, one after the other, single file, in a single lane. There weren't many of them. Traffic up there was light, even though First Street itself was already building up to the afternoon rush hour. Then he looked to his left again and saw Helen Rodin sitting down beside him. She was out of breath.

'I was wrong,' she said. 'You *are* a hard man to find.'

'But you triumphed none the less,' he said.

'Only because I saw you from my window. I ran all the way down, hoping you wouldn't wander off. That was a half-hour after calling all the hotels in town and being told you aren't registered anywhere.'

'What hotels don't know won't hurt them.'

'James Barr is waking up. He might be talking tomorrow.'

'Or he might not.'

'You know much about head injuries?'

'Only the ones I cause.'

'I want you to do something for me.'

'Like what?' he asked.

'You can help me,' she said. 'With something important.'

'Can I?'

'And you can help yourself.'

He said nothing.

'I want you to be my evidence analyst,' she said.

'You've got Franklin for that.'

She shook her head. 'Franklin's too close to his old PD buddies. He won't be critical enough. He won't want to tear into them.'

'And I will? I want Barr to go down, remember.'

'Exactly. That's exactly why you should do it. You want to confirm that they've got an unbreakable case. Then you can leave town and be happy.'

'Would I tell you if I found a hole?'

'I'd see it in your eyes. And I'd know from what you did next. If you go, it's a strong case. If you stay around, it's weak.'

'Franklin quit, didn't he?'

She paused, and then she nodded. 'This case is a loser, all ways around. I'm doing it pro bono. Because nobody else will. But Franklin's got a business to run.'

'So he won't do it for free, but I will?'

'You *need* to do it. I think you're already planning to do it. That's why you went to see my father first. He's confident, for sure. You saw that. But you still want a peek at the data. You were a thorough investigator. You said so yourself. You're a perfectionist. You want to be able to leave town knowing everything is buttoned down tight, according to your own standards.'

Reacher said nothing.

'This gets you a real good look,' she said. 'It's their constitutional obligation. They have to show us everything. The defence gets a full discovery process.'

Reacher said nothing.

'You've got no choice,' she said. 'They're not going to show you anything otherwise. They don't show stuff to strangers off the street.'

A real good look. Leave town and be happy. No choice.

'OK,' Reacher said.

She pointed. 'Walk four blocks west and one block south. The PD is right there. I'll go upstairs and call Emerson.'

'We're doing this now?'

'James Barr is waking up. I need this stuff out

114

of the way early. I'm going to be spending most of tomorrow trying to find a psychiatrist who will work for free. A medical plea is still our best bet.'

Reacher walked four blocks west and one block south. It took him under the raised highway and brought him to a corner. The PD had the whole block. Their building occupied most of it and there was an L-shaped parking lot on the rest of it for their vehicles. There were black-and-whites slotted in at angles, and unmarked detective cars, and a crime scene van, and a SWAT truck. The building itself was made of glazed tan brick. It had a flat roof with big HVAC ducts all over it. There were bars on all the windows. Razor wire here and there round the perimeter.

He went inside and got directions and found Emerson waiting for him behind his desk. Reacher recognized him from his TV spot on Saturday morning. Same guy, pale, quiet, competent, not big, not small. In person he looked like he had been a cop since birth. Since the moment of conception, maybe. It was in his pores. In his DNA. He was wearing grey flannel pants and a white short-sleeved shirt. Open neck. No tie. There was a tweed jacket on the back of his chair. His face and his body were a little shapeless, like he had been moulded by constant pressures.

'Welcome to Indiana,' he said.

Reacher said nothing.

'I mean it,' Emerson said. 'Really. We love it when old friends of the accused show up to tear our work to shreds.'

'I'm here for his lawyer,' Reacher said. 'Not as a friend.'

Emerson nodded.

'I'll give you the background myself,' he said. 'Then my crime scene guy will walk you through the particulars. You can see absolutely anything you want and you can ask absolutely anything you want.'

Reacher smiled. He had been a cop of sorts himself for thirteen long years, on a tough beat, and he knew the language and all its dialects. He knew the tone and he understood the nuances. And the way Emerson spoke told him things. It told him that despite the initial hostility this was a guy secretly happy to meet with a critic. Because he knew for sure he had a solid gold slam-dunk case.

'You knew James Barr pretty well, am I right?' Emerson asked.

'Did you?' Reacher asked back.

Emerson shook his head. 'Never met him. There were no warning signs.'

'Was his rifle legal?'

Emerson nodded. 'It was registered and un-modified. As were all his other guns.'

'Did he hunt?'

Emerson shook his head again. 'He wasn't an NRA member and he didn't belong to a gun club. We never saw him out in the hills. He was never in trouble. He was just a low-profile citizen. A *no*-profile citizen, really. No warning signs at all.'

'You seen this kind of thing before?'

'Too many times. If you include the District of Columbia then Indiana is tied for sixteenth

116

place out of fifty-one in terms of homicide deaths per capita. Worse than New York, worse than California. This town isn't the worst in the state, but it's not the best, either. So we've seen it all before, and sometimes there are signs, and sometimes there aren't, but either way around we know what we're doing.'

'I spoke with Alex Rodin,' Reacher said. 'He's impressed.'

'He should be. We performed well. Your old buddy was toast six hours after the first shot. It was a textbook case, beginning to end.'

'No doubts at all?'

'Put it this way. I wrote it up Saturday morning and I haven't given it a whole lot of thought since then. It's a done deal. About the best done deal I ever saw, and I've seen a lot.'

'So is there any point in me walking through it?'

'Sure there is. I've got a crime scene guy desperate to show off. He's a good man, and he deserves his moment in the sun.'

Emerson walked Reacher to the lab and introduced him as a lawyer's scout, not as James Barr's friend. Which helped a little with the atmosphere. Then he left him there. The crime scene guy was a serious forty-year-old called Bellantonio. His name was more exuberant than he was. He was tall, dark, thin, and stooped. He could have been a mortician. And he suspected James Barr was going to plead guilty. He thought he wasn't going to get his day in court. That was clear. He had laid out the evidence chain in a logical sequence on long tables in a sealed police garage bay, just so that he could give visitors the performance he would never give a jury.

The tables were white canteen-style trestles and they ran all the way round the perimeter of the bay. Above them was a horizontal line of cork boards with hundreds of printed sheets of paper pinned to them. The sheets were cased in plastic page protectors and they related to the specific items found directly below. Trapped tight in the square made by the tables was James Barr's beige Dodge Caravan. The bay was clean and brightly lit with harsh fluorescent tubes and the minivan looked huge and alien in there. It was old and dirty and smelled of gasoline and oil and rubber. The sliding rear door was open and Bellantonio had rigged a light to shine in on the carpet.

'This all looks good,' Reacher said.

'Best crime scene I ever worked,' Bellantonio said.

'So walk me through it.'

Bellantonio started with the traffic cone. It was sitting there on a square of butcher paper, looking large and odd and out of place. Reacher saw the print powder on it, read the notes above it. Barr had handled it, that was for sure. He had clamped his right hand round it, near the top, where it was narrow. More than once. There were fingerprints and palm prints. The match was a laugher. There were way more comparison points than any court would demand.

Same for the quarter from the parking meter, same for the shell case. Bellantonio showed Reacher laser-printed stills from the parking

118

garage video, showing the minivan coming in just before the event and going out again just after it. He showed him the interior of the Dodge, showed him the automotive carpet fibres recovered from the raw new concrete, showed him the dog hairs, showed him the denim fibres and the raincoat threads. Showed him a square of rug taken from Barr's house, showed him the matching fibres found at the scene. Showed him the desert boots, showed him how crêpe rubber was the best transfer mechanism going. Showed him how the tiny crumbs of rubber found at the scene matched new scuffs on the shoes' toes. Showed him the cement dust tracked back into Barr's house and recovered from the garage and the basement and the kitchen and the living room and the bedroom. Showed him a comparison sample taken from the parking garage and a lab report that proved it was the same.

Reacher scanned the transcripts from the 911 calls and the radio chatter between the squad cars. Then he glanced through the crime scene protocol. The initial sweep by the uniformed officers, the forensic examination by Bellantonio's own people, Emerson's inspiration with the parking meter. Then he read the arrest report. It was printed out and pinned up along with everything else. The SWAT tactics, the sleeping suspect, the ID from the driver's licence from the wallet in the trouser pocket. The paramedics' tests. The capture of the dog by the K9 officers. The clothes in the closet. The shoes. The guns in the basement. He read the witness reports. A Marine recruiter had heard six shots. A cell phone company had provided a recording. There was a graph attached. A grey smear of sound, with six sharp spikes. Left to right, they were arrayed in a pattern that matched what Helen Rodin had said she had heard. *One, two-three, pause, four-five-six.* The graph's vertical axis represented volume. The shots had been faint but clear on the recording. The horizontal axis represented the time base. Six shots in less than four seconds. Four seconds that had changed a city. For a spell, at least.

Reacher looked at the rifle. It was heat-sealed into a clear plastic sleeve. He read the report pinned above it. A Springfield M1A Super Match, ten shot box magazine, four cartridges still in it. Barr's prints all over it. Scratches on the forestock matching varnish scrapings found at the scene. The intact bullet recovered from the pool. A ballistics lab report matching the bullet to the barrel. Another report matching the shell case to the ejector. Slam dunk. Case closed.

'OK, enough,' Reacher said.

'It's good, isn't it?' Bellantonio said.

'Best I ever saw,' Reacher said.

'Better than a hundred eyewitnesses.'

Reacher smiled. Crime scene techs loved to say that.

'Anything you're not happy with?' he asked.

'I love it all,' Bellantonio said.

Reacher glanced at his reflection in the Dodge's tinted window. The black glass made his new shirt look grey.

'Why did he leave the traffic cone behind?' he said. 'He could have pitched it into the back of the van, easy as anything.'

120

Bellantonio said nothing.

'And why did he pay to park?' Reacher asked.

'I'm forensics,' Bellantonio said. 'Not psychology.'

Then Emerson came back in and stood there, waiting to accept Reacher's surrender. Reacher gave it up, no hesitation. He shook their hands and congratulated them on a well-worked case.

He walked back, one block north and four blocks east, under the raised highway, heading for the black glass tower. It was after five o'clock and the sun was on his back. He arrived at the plaza and saw that the fountain was still going and the pool had filled another inch. He went in past the NBC sign and rode up in the elevator. Ann Yanni didn't show. Maybe she was preparing for the six o'clock news.

He found Helen Rodin at her secondhand desk.

'Watch my eyes,' he said.

She watched them.

'Pick your own cliché,' he said. 'It's a cast-iron, solid gold slam dunk. It's Willie Mays under a fly ball.'

She said nothing.

'See any doubt in my eyes?' he asked.

'No,' she said. 'I don't.'

'So start calling psychiatrists. If that's what you really want to do.'

'He deserves representation, Reacher.'

'He stepped out of line.'

'We can't just lynch him.'

Reacher paused. Then he nodded. 'The shrink should think about the parking meter. I mean,

121

who pays for ten minutes even if they're *not* shooting people? It strikes me as weird. It's so law-abiding, isn't it? It kind of puts the whole event into a law-abiding envelope. Maybe he really was nuts this time. You know, confused about what he was doing.'

Helen Rodin made a note. 'I'll be sure to mention it.'

'You want to get some dinner?'

'We're on opposite sides.'

'We had lunch.'

'Only because I wanted something from you.'

'We can still be civilized.'

She shook her head. 'I'm having dinner with my father.'

'He's on the opposite side.'

'He's my father.'

Reacher said nothing.

'Were the cops OK?' she asked.

Reacher nodded. 'They were courteous enough.'

'They can't have been very pleased to see you. They don't understand why you're really here.'

'They don't need to worry. They've got a great case.'

'It's not over until the fat lady sings.'

'She's been singing since Friday at five. Pretty loud.'

'Maybe we could have a drink after dinner,' she said. 'If I can get away in time. There's a sports bar six blocks north of here. Monday night, it's about the only place in town. I'll drop by and see if you're there. But I can't promise anything.'

'Neither can I,' Reacher said. 'Maybe I'll be at the hospital, unplugging James Barr's life support.'

*   *   *

He rode down in the elevator and found Rosemary Barr waiting for him in the lobby. He guessed she had just got back from the hospital and had called upstairs and Helen Rodin had told her he was on his way down. So she had waited. She was pacing nervously, side to side, crossing and recrossing the route between the elevator bank and the street door.

'Can we talk?' she asked.

'Outside,' he said.

He led her through the door and across the plaza to the south wall of the pool. It was still filling, slowly. The fountain splashed and tinkled. He sat where he had sat before, with the funeral tributes at his feet. Rosemary Barr stood in front of him, facing him, very close, her eyes on his, not looking down at the flowers and the candles and the photographs.

'You need to keep an open mind,' she said.

'Do I?' he said.

'James wanted you here, therefore he can't be guilty.'

'That's a leap.'

'It's logical,' she said.

'I just saw the evidence,' he said. 'More than enough for anyone.'

'I'm not going to argue about fourteen years ago.'

'You can't.'

'But he's innocent now.'

Reacher said nothing.

'I understand how you feel,' Rosemary said. 'You think he let you down.'

'He did.'

'But suppose he didn't? Suppose he met your conditions and this is all a mistake? How would you feel then? What would you do for him? If you're ready to stand up against him don't you think you should be equally ready to stand up *for* him?'

'That's too hypothetical for me.'

'It's not hypothetical. I'm just asking, if you're proved wrong, if he didn't do it, will you put the same energy into helping him?'

'If I'm proved wrong he won't need my help.'

'Will you?'

'Yes,' Reacher said, because it was an easy promise to make.

'So you need to keep an open mind.'

'Why did you move out?'

She paused. 'He was angry all the time. It was no fun living with him.'

'Angry at what?'

'At everything.'

'So maybe it's you who should keep an open mind.'

'I could have made up a reason. But I didn't. I told you the truth. I don't want to hide anything. I need you to trust me. I need to make you believe. He's an unhappy man, maybe even disturbed. But he didn't do *this*.'

Reacher said nothing.

'Will you keep an open mind?' she asked.

Reacher didn't answer. Just shrugged and walked away.

*   *   *

He didn't go to the hospital. Didn't unplug James Barr's machines. He went to the sports bar instead, after a shower back at the Metropole Palace. The six blocks north of the black glass tower took him under the highway again and out into a hinterland. Gentrification had a boundary to the south, as he had seen, and now he saw it had a boundary to the north, too. The bar was a little way beyond it. It was in a plain square building that could have started out as anything. Maybe a feed store, maybe an automobile showroom, maybe a pool hall. It had a flat roof and bricked-up windows and moss growing where blocked rainwater gutters had spilled.

Inside it was better, but generic. It was like every other sports bar he had ever been in. It was one tall room with black-painted air conditioning ducts pinned to the ceiling. It had three dozen TV screens hanging from the walls and the roof. It had all the usual sports bar stuff all over the place. Signed uniform jerseys framed under glass, football helmets displayed on shelves, hockey sticks, basketballs, baseballs, old game-day programmes. The waiting staff was all female, all of them in cheerleader-style uniforms. The bar staff was male and dressed in striped umpire uniforms.

The TVs were all tuned to football. Inevitable, Reacher guessed, on a Monday night. Some of the screens were regular TVs, and some were plasmas, and some were projectors. The same event was displayed dozens of times, all with slightly different colour and focus, some big, some small, some bright, some dim. There were

125

plenty of people in there, but Reacher got a table to himself. In a corner, which he liked. A hard-worked waitress ran over to him and he ordered beer and a cheeseburger. He didn't look at the menu. Sports bars always had beer and cheese-burgers.

He ate his meal and drank his beer and watched the game. Time passed and the place filled up and got more and more crowded and noisy but nobody came to share his table. Reacher had that kind of effect on people. He sat there alone, in a bubble of quiet, with a message plainly displayed: *Stay away from me.*

Then someone ignored the message and came to join him. It was partly his own fault. He looked away from the screen and saw a girl hovering nearby. She was juggling a bottle of beer and a full plate of tacos. She was quite a sight. She had waved red hair and a red gingham shirt open at the neck and tied off at the navel. She had tight pants on that looked like denim but had to be Spandex. She had the whole hourglass thing going, big time. And she was in shiny lizard-skin boots. Open the encyclopedia to *C* for *Country Girl* and her picture was going to be right there staring back at you. She looked too young for the beer. But she was past puberty. That was for damn sure. Her shirt buttons were straining. And there was no visible panty line under the Spandex. Reacher looked at her for a second too long, and she took it as an invitation.

'Can I share your table?' she asked, from a yard away.

'Help yourself,' he said.

She sat down. Not opposite him, but in the chair next to him.

'Thanks,' she said.

She drank from her bottle and kept her eyes on him. Green eyes, bright, wide open. She half turned towards him and arched the small of her back. Her shirt was open three buttons. Maybe a 34D, Reacher figured, in a push-up bra. He could see the edge of it. White lace.

She leaned close, because of the noise.

'Do you like it?' she asked.

'Like what?' he said.

'Football,' she said.

'A bit,' he said.

'Did you play?'

Did you, not *do you*. She made him feel old.

'You're certainly big enough,' she said.

'I tried out for Army,' he said. 'When I was at West Point.'

'Did you make the team?'

'Only once.'

'Were you injured?'

'I was too violent.'

She half smiled, not sure if he was joking.

'Want a taco?' she said.

'I just ate.'

'I'm Sandy,' she said.

So was I, he thought. *Friday, on the beach.*

'What's your name?' she asked.

'Jimmy Reese,' he said.

He saw a flash of surprise in her eyes. He didn't know why. Maybe she had had a boyfriend called Jimmy Reese. Or maybe she was a serious fan of the New York Yankees.

127

'I'm pleased to meet you, Jimmy Reese,' she said.

'Likewise,' he said, and turned back to the game.

'You're new in town, aren't you?' she said.

'Usually,' he said.

'I was wondering,' she said. 'If you only like football a bit, maybe you would like to take me somewhere else.'

'Like where?'

'Like somewhere quieter. Maybe somewhere a little lonelier.'

He said nothing.

'I've got a car,' she said.

'You old enough to drive?'

'I'm old enough to do lots of things. And I'm pretty good at some of them.'

Reacher said nothing. She moved on her chair. Pushed it out from the table a little way. Turned towards him and looked down.

'Do you like these pants?' she asked.

'I think they suit you very well.'

'I do too. Only problem is, they're too tight to wear anything underneath.'

'We all have our cross to bear.'

'Do you think they're too revealing?'

'They're opaque. That usually does it for me.'

'Imagine peeling them off.'

'I can't. I doubt if I would have gotten them on.'

The green eyes narrowed. 'Are you a queer?'

'Are you a hooker?'

'No *way*. I work at the auto parts store.'

Then she paused and seemed to think again. She reconsidered. She came up with a better answer. Which was to jump up from her chair and scream and slap his face. It was a loud scream and a loud slap and everyone turned to look.

'He called me a *whore*,' she screamed. 'He called me a damn *whore*!'

Chairs scraped and guys stood up fast. Big guys, in jeans and work boots and plaid shirts. Country boys. Five of them, all the same.

The girl smiled in triumph.

'Those are my brothers,' she said.

Reacher said nothing.

'You just called me a whore in front of my *brothers*.'

Five boys, all staring.

'He called me a *whore*,' the girl wailed.

Rule one, be on your feet and ready.

Rule two, show them what they're messing with.

Reacher stood up, slow and easy. Six-five, two-fifty, calm eyes, hands held loose by his sides.

'He called me a *whore*,' the girl wailed again.

Rule three, identify the ringleader.

There were five guys. Any five guys will have one ringleader, two enthusiastic followers, and two reluctant followers. Put the ringleader down, and both of the keen sidekicks, and it's over. The reluctant pair just run for it. So there's no such thing as five-on-one. It never gets worse than three-on-one.

Rule four: The ringleader is the one who moves first.

A big corn-fed twenty-something with a shock of yellow hair and a round red face moved first. He stepped forward a pace and the others fell in behind him in a neat arrowhead formation. Reacher stepped forward a pace of his own to meet them. The downside of a corner table is there's no other way to go except forward.

But that was fine.

Because, rule five: Never back off.

But, rule six: Don't break the furniture.

Break furniture in a bar, and the owner starts thinking about his insurance policy, and insurance companies require police reports, and a patrolman's first instinct is to throw everyone in jail and sort it out later. Which generally means: *Blame it on the stranger.*

'He called me a whore,' the girl said, plaintively. Like her heart was broken. She was standing off to the side, looking at Reacher, looking at the five guys, looking at Reacher. Her head was turning like a spectator at a tennis game.

'Outside,' the big guy said.

'Pay your check first,' Reacher said.

'I'll pay later.'

'You won't be able to.'

'You think?'

'That's the difference between us.'

'What is?'

'I think.'

'You've got a smart mouth, pal.'

'That's the least of your worries.'

'You called my sister a whore.'

'You prefer sleeping with virgins?'

'Get outside, pal, or I'll put you down right here.'

Rule seven: Act, don't react.

'OK,' Reacher said. 'Let's go outside.'

The big guy smiled.

'After you,' Reacher said.

'Stay here, Sandy,' the big guy said.

'I don't mind the sight of blood,' she said.

'I'm sure you love it,' Reacher said. 'One week in four, it makes you feel mighty relieved.'

'*Outside*,' the big guy said. '*Now*.'

He turned round and shooed the others towards the door. They formed up in single file and threaded between the tables. Their boots clattered on the wood. The girl called Sandy tagged after them. Other customers shrank away from them. Reacher put twenty dollars on his table and glanced up at the football game. Someone was winning, someone was losing.

He followed the girl called Sandy. Followed the blue Spandex pants.

They were all waiting for him on the sidewalk. They were all tensed up in a shallow semicircle. There were yellow lamps on poles twenty yards away north and south and another across the street. The lamps gave each guy three shadows. There was neon outside the bar that filled the shadows with pink and blue. The street was empty. And quiet. No traffic. No noise, except sports bar sounds muffled by the door.

The air was soft. Not hot, not cold.

Rule eight: Assess and evaluate.

The big guy was round and smooth and heavy, like a bull seal. Maybe ten years out of high school. An unbroken nose, no scar tissue on his brows, no misshapen knuckles. Therefore, not a boxer. Probably just a linebacker. So he would fight like a wrestler. He would be a guy who wants you on the ground.

So he would start by charging. Head low.

That was Reacher's best guess.

And Reacher was right.

The guy exploded out of the blocks and charged, head low. Straight for Reacher's chest. Looking to drive him backwards and have him stumble and fall. Whereupon the other four could all pile in together and stomp him and kick him to their hearts' content.

Mistake.

Because, rule nine: Don't run head-on into Jack Reacher.

Not when he's expecting it. It's like running into an oak tree.

The big guy charged and Reacher turned slightly sideways and bent his knees a little and timed it just right and drove all his weight up and forward off his back foot and through his shoulder straight into the big guy's face.

Kinetic energy is a wonderful thing.

Reacher had hardly moved at all but the big guy bounced off crazily, stunned, staggering backwards on stiff legs, desperately trying to stay upright, one foot tracing a lazy half-circle in the air, then the other. He came to rest six feet away with his feet firmly planted and his legs wide apart, just like a big dumb capital letter *A*.

Blood on his face.

Now he had a broken nose.

Put the ringleader down.

Reacher stepped in and kicked him in the groin, but left-footed. Right-footed, he would have popped bits of the guy's pelvis out through his nose. *Your big soft heart*, an old army instructor had said. *One day it'll get you killed.*

But not today, Reacher thought. Not here. The big guy went down. He fell on his knees and pitched forward on his face.

Then it got *real* easy.

The next two guys came in together shoulder to shoulder and Reacher dropped the first with a head butt and the second with an elbow to the jaw. They both went straight down and lay still. Then it was over, because the last two guys ran. The last two guys always do. The girl called Sandy ran after them. Not fast. The tight Spandex and the high-heeled boots impeded her. But Reacher let her go. He turned back and kicked her three downed brothers onto their sides. Checked they were still breathing. Checked their hip pockets. Found their wallets. Checked their licences. Then he dropped them and straightened up and turned round because he heard a car pull up behind him at the kerb.

It was a taxi. It was a taxi with Helen Rodin getting out of it.

She threw a bill at the driver and he took off fast, gazing straight ahead, deliberately not looking left or right. Helen Rodin stood still on the sidewalk and stared. Reacher was ten feet away from her, with three neon shadows and three inert forms on the ground behind him.

'What the hell is going on?' she asked.

'You tell me,' he said. 'You live here. You know these damn people.'

'What does that mean? What the hell happened?'

'Let's walk,' he said.

They walked south, fast, and turned a corner

and went east. Then south again. Then they slowed a little.

'You've got blood on your shirt,' Helen Rodin said.

'But not mine,' Reacher said.

'What happened back there?'

'I was in the bar watching the game. Minding my own business. Then some underage red-haired bimbo started coming on to me. I wasn't playing and she got it to where she found a reason to slap me. Then five guys jumped up. She said they were her brothers. We took it out-side.'

'Five guys?'

'Two ran away.'

'After you beat up the first three?'

'I defended myself. That's all. Minimum force.'

'She slapped you?'

'Right in the face.'

'What had you said to her?'

'Doesn't matter what I said to her. It was a set-up. So I'm asking you, is that how people get their kicks around here? Picking on strangers in bars?'

'I need a drink,' Helen Rodin said. 'I came to meet you for a drink.'

Reacher stopped walking. 'So let's go back there.'

'We can't go back there. They might have called the cops. You left three men on the sidewalk.'

He looked back over his shoulder.

'So let's try my hotel,' he said. 'There's a lobby. There might be a bar.'

They walked together in silence, through dark

quiet streets, four blocks south. They stayed
east of the plaza and passed by the courthouse.
Reacher glanced at it.

'How was dinner?' he asked.

'My father was fishing. He still thinks you're
my witness.'

'Did you tell him?'

'I can't tell him. Your information is classified.
Thank God.'

'So you let him stew.'

'He's not stewing. He's totally confident.'

'He should be.'

'So are you leaving tomorrow?'

'You bet I am. This place is weird.'

'Some girl comes on to you, why does that have
to be a big conspiracy?'

Reacher said nothing.

'It's not unheard of,' she said. 'Well, is it? A
bar, the new guy in town all alone, why shouldn't
some girl be interested? You're not exactly repul-
sive, you know.'

Reacher just walked.

'What did you say to her to get slapped?'

'I wasn't showing any interest, she kept on
coming on, I asked her if she was a hooker.
Something like that.'

'A hooker? That'll get you slapped, in Indiana.
And her brothers would hate it.'

'It was a set-up, Helen. Let's be realistic. It's
nice of you to say it, but I'm not the sort of guy
that women chase after. I know that, OK? So it
was a set-up.'

'No woman ever chased you before?'

'She smiled in triumph. Like she had found

135

an opening and *delivered* me. Like she had succeeded at something.'

Helen Rodin said nothing.

'And those guys weren't her brothers,' Reacher said. 'They were all more or less the same age and when I checked their licences they all had different last names.'

'Oh.'

'So it was all staged. Which is weird. There are only two reasons for doing something like that. Fun, or money. A guy in a bar might have a few bucks, but that's not enough. So they staged it for fun. Which is weird. Doubly weird, because why pick on me? They must have known they were going to get their butts kicked.'

'There were five of them. Five guys never think one guy could kick their butts. Especially not in Indiana.'

'Or maybe I was the only stranger in the bar.'

She looked ahead, down the street. 'You're at the Metropole Palace?'

He nodded. 'Me and not too many other people.'

'But I called and they said you weren't registered. I called all the hotels, looking for you this afternoon.'

'I use aliases in hotels.'

'Why on earth?'

'Just a bad habit. Like I told you. It's automatic now.'

They went up the front steps together and in through the heavy brass door. It wasn't late, but the place was quiet. The lobby was deserted. There was a bar in a side room. It was empty, except for a lone barman leaning back against the register.

'Beer,' Helen Rodin said.

'Two,' Reacher said.

They took a table near a curtained window and the guy brought two beers in bottles, two napkins, two chilled glasses, and a bowl of mixed nuts. Reacher signed the check and added his room number.

Helen Rodin smiled. 'So who does the Metropole think you are?'

'Jimmy Reese,' Reacher said.

'Who's he?'

'Wait,' Reacher said.

A flash of surprise in her eyes. He didn't know why.

I'm pleased to meet you, Jimmy Reese.

'The girl was looking for me personally,' he said. 'She wasn't looking for some random lone stranger. She was looking for Jack Reacher specifically.'

'She was?'

He nodded. 'She asked my name. I said Jimmy Reese. It knocked her off balance for a second. She was definitely surprised. Like, *you're not Jimmy Reese, you're Jack Reacher, someone just told me*. She paused, and then she recovered.'

'The first letters are the same. Jimmy Reese, Jack Reacher. People sometimes do that.'

'She was fast,' he said. 'She wasn't as dumb as she looked. Someone pointed her at me, and she wasn't going to be deflected. Jack Reacher was supposed to get worked over tonight, and she was going to make sure it happened.'

'So who were they?'

'Who knows my name?'

137

'The police department. You were just there.'

Reacher said nothing.

'What?' Helen said. 'Were they *cops*? Protecting their case?'

'I'm not here to attack their case.'

'But they don't know that. They think that's exactly why you're here.'

'Their case doesn't need protecting. It's solid gold. And they didn't look like cops.'

'Who else has an interest?'

'Rosemary Barr. She has an interest. She knows my name. And she knows why I'm here.'

'That's ridiculous,' Helen said.

Reacher said nothing.

'That's ridiculous,' Helen said again. 'Rosemary Barr is a mousy little legal secretary. She wouldn't try a thing like that. She wouldn't know *how*. Not in a million years.'

'It was a very amateur attempt.'

'Compared to what? It was five guys. Enough for most people.'

Reacher said nothing.

'Rosemary Barr was at the hospital,' Helen said. 'She went over there after the client conference, and she stayed there most of the afternoon, and I bet she's back there now. Because her brother is waking up. She wants to be with him.'

'A buck gets ten she's got a cell phone.'

'Can't use cell phones near the ICU. They cause interference.'

'A pay phone, then.'

'She's too preoccupied.'

'With saving her brother.'

Helen Rodin said nothing.

138

'She's your client,' Reacher said. 'Are you sure you're impartial?'

'You're not thinking straight. James Barr *asked* for you. He *wanted* you here. Therefore his sister wants you here too. She wants you to stick around long enough to figure out how you can help. And she knows you can help, or why would her brother have asked for you in the first place?'

Reacher said nothing.

'Accept it,' Helen said. 'It wasn't Rosemary Barr. It's in her best interests to have you here, alive and well and thinking.'

Reacher took a long pull on his beer. Then he nodded. 'I was followed to the bar tonight, obviously. From here. Therefore I was followed here, after lunch. If Rosemary went straight to the hospital this morning she didn't have time to set that up.'

'So we're back to someone who thinks you can damage the case. Why not the cops? Cops could follow you anywhere. There's a lot of them and they all have radios.'

'Cops start trouble face to face. They don't get a girl to do it for them.'

'The girl might be a cop too.'

Reacher shook his head. 'Too young. Too vacant. Too much hair.'

Helen took a pen from her purse and wrote something on her cocktail napkin. Slid it across the table.

'My cell phone number,' she said. 'You might need it.'

'I don't think anyone will sue me.'

'I'm not worried about you getting sued. I'm

139

worried about you getting arrested. Even if it wasn't cops actually doing it, they might have gone to the bar anyway. The owner might have called them. Or the hospital might have called them. Those three boys went to the hospital, that's for sure. And the girl definitely knows your alias now. So you might be in trouble. If you are, listen to the Miranda and then call me.'

Reacher smiled. 'Ambulance chasing?'

'Looking out for you.'

Reacher picked up the napkin. Put it in his back pocket.

'OK,' he said. 'Thanks.'

'Are you still going to leave tomorrow?'

'Maybe. Or maybe not. Maybe I'll stick around and think about why someone would use violence to protect a case that's already a hundred per cent watertight.'

Grigor Linsky called the Zec, on his cell phone from his car.

'They failed,' he said. 'I'm very sorry.'

The Zec said nothing, which was worse than a tirade.

'They won't be traced to us,' Linsky said.

'Will you make sure of that?'

'Certainly.'

The Zec said nothing.

'No harm, no foul,' Linsky said.

'Unless it served merely to provoke the soldier,' the Zec said. 'Then there would be harm. Possibly considerable harm. He is James Barr's friend, after all. That fact will have implications.'

Now Linsky said nothing.

'Let him see you one more time,' the Zec said. 'A little additional pressure might help. But after that, don't let him see you again.'

'And then?'

'Then monitor the situation,' the Zec said. 'Make absolutely certain it doesn't turn from bad to worse.'

Reacher saw Helen Rodin into a cab and then went upstairs to his room. He took off his shirt and put it in the bathroom sink and left it to soak in cold water. He didn't want bloodstains on a one-day-old shirt. Three-days-old, maybe. But not a brand new garment.

Questions. There were a lot of questions, but as always the key would be finding the basic question. The fundamental question. Why would someone use violence to protect a case that was already watertight? First question: *Was* the case already watertight? He trawled through the day in his head and heard Alex Rodin say: *It's as good as it gets. The best I've ever seen.* Emerson had said: *It's the best done deal I ever saw.* The mortician-like Bellantonio had said: *It's the best crime scene I ever worked. I love it all.* Those guys all had professional self-interest in play, of course. And pride, and expediency. But Reacher himself had seen Bellantonio's work. And had said: *It's a cast-iron, solid gold slam dunk. It's Willie Mays under a fly ball.*

Was it?

Yes, it was. It was Lou Gehrig with the bases loaded. It was as close to a certainty as human life offers.

But that wasn't the fundamental question.

He rinsed his shirt and wrung it out hard and spread it on the room heater. Turned the heater on high and opened the window. There was no noise outside. Just silence. New York City, it wasn't. It sounded like they rolled up the sidewalks at nine o'clock. *I went to Indiana, but it was closed*. He lay down on the bed. Stretched out. Damp heat came off his shirt and filled the room with the smell of wet cotton.

What was the fundamental question?

Helen Rodin's cassette tape was the fundamental question. James Barr's voice, low, hoarse, frustrated. His demand: *Get Jack Reacher for me*.

Why would he say that?

Who was Jack Reacher, in James Barr's eyes? Fundamentally?

That was the basic question.

The best crime scene I ever worked.

The best I've ever seen.

Why did he pay to park?

Will you keep an open mind?

Get Jack Reacher for me.

Jack Reacher stared at his hotel room ceiling. Five minutes. Ten. Twenty. Then he rolled over one way and pulled the cocktail napkin out of his back pocket. Rolled the other way and dialled the phone. Helen Rodin answered after eight rings. She sounded sleepy. He had woken her up.

'It's Reacher,' he said.

'Are you in trouble?'

'No, but I've got some questions. Is Barr awake yet?'

'No, but he's close. Rosemary went back to the hospital. She left me a message.'

'What was the weather like last Friday at five?'

'The weather? Friday? It was kind of dull. Cloudy.'

'Is that normal?'

'No, not really. It's usually sunny. Or else raining. This time of year it's usually one or the other. More likely sunny.'

'Was it warm or cold?'

'Not cold. But not *hot*. It was comfortable, I guess.'

'What did you wear to work?'

'What is this, a dirty phone call?'

'Just tell me.'

'Same as I wore today. Pant suit.'

'No coat?'

'Didn't need one.'

'Have you got a car?'

'A car? Yes, I've got a car. But I use the bus for work.'

'Use your car tomorrow. I'll meet you at eight o'clock in your office.'

'What's this about?'

'Tomorrow,' he said. 'Eight o'clock. Go back to sleep now.'

He hung up. Rolled off the bed and checked his shirt. It was warm and wet. But it would be dry by morning. He hoped it wouldn't shrink.

FIVE

Reacher woke at six. Took a long cold shower, because the room was hot. But his shirt was dry. It was as stiff as a board, and still the right size. There was no room service. He went out for breakfast. The roads were full of trucks, hauling gravel, hauling fill, mixing concrete, feeding the work zones' appetites. He dodged them and walked south towards the waterfront. Through the gentrification frontier. He found a working-men's diner with a basic menu. He drank coffee and ate eggs. He sat at a window and watched the street for aimless doorway lurkers or men in parked cars. Because if he had been followed the night before it was logical to assume he would be followed again. So he kept his eyes open. But he saw nobody.

Then he walked the length of First Street, north. The sun was up on his right. He used store windows as mirrors and watched his back. Plenty of people were going his way, but none of them was following him. He guessed whoever it was would be waiting for him in the plaza, ready to confirm what he expected to see:

The witness went to the lawyer's office.

The fountain was still going. The pool was nearly half full. The tributes were still there, neatly lined up, another day older, a little more faded, a little more wilted. He figured they would be there for a week or so. Until after the last of the funerals. Then they would be removed, discreetly, maybe in the middle of the night, and the city would move on to the next thing.

He sat for a moment on the NBC monolith, with his back to the tower, like a guy wasting time because he was early. Which he was. It was only seven forty-five. There were other people in the same situation. They stood around, singly or in groups of two or three, smoking last cigarettes, reading the morning news, chilling before the daily grind. Reacher looked first at men on their own with newspapers. That was a pretty traditional surveillance cover. Although in his opinion it was due for replacement with a new exiled-smoker cover. Guys standing near doorways and smoking were the new invisibles. Or guys on cell phones. You could stand there with a Nokia up to your ear for ever and nobody thought twice.

In the end he settled on a guy who was smoking *and* talking on a cell phone. He was a short man of about sixty. Maybe more. A damaged man. There was a permanent lopsided tension in the way he held himself. An old spinal injury, maybe. Or busted ribs that had been badly set, years ago. Whatever it was, it made him look uncomfortable and querulous. He wasn't the type of guy who would happily converse at length. But there he was, on his phone, just talking, aimlessly. He had

145

thin grey hair, recently barbered but not stylishly. He was in a double breasted suit that had been expensively tailored, but not in the United States. It was square and boxy, too heavy for the weather. Polish, maybe. Or Hungarian. Eastern European, certainly. His face was pale and his eyes were dark. They didn't glance Reacher's way, even once.

Reacher checked his watch. Seven fifty-five. He slid off the shiny granite and walked into the tower's lobby.

Grigor Linsky stopped pretending and dialled an actual number on his phone.

'He's here,' he said. 'He just went up.'

'Did he see you?' the Zec asked.

'Yes, I'm sure he did.'

'So make that the last time. Now you stay in the shadows.'

Reacher found Helen Rodin already at her desk. She looked settled in, like she had been there a long time already. She was in the same black suit, but her shirt was different. It was a simple scoop-neck, not tight. It was china blue and matched her eyes exactly. Her hair was tied back in a long pony tail. Her desk was covered with legal books. Some were face down, some were face up. They were all open. She had about eight pages of notes going, on a yellow legal pad. References, case notes, decisions, precedents.

'James Barr is conscious,' she said. 'Rosemary called me at five this morning.'

'Is he talking?'

146

'Only to the doctors. They won't let anyone else near him yet. Not even Rosemary herself.'

'What about the cops?'

'They're waiting. But I'll need to be there first. I can't let him talk to the cops without representation.'

'What is he saying to the doctors?'

'That he doesn't know why he's there. That he doesn't remember anything about Friday. The doctors say that's to be expected. Amnesia is predictable with head injuries, possibly covering several days before the trauma. Several weeks, sometimes.'

'Where does that leave you?'

'With two big problems. First, he might be faking the amnesia. And that's actually very hard to test, either way. So now I'm going to have to find a specialist opinion on *that*, too. And if he isn't faking, we're in a real grey area. If he's sane now, and he was sane before, but he's missing a week, then how can he get a fair trial? He won't be able to participate in his own defence. Not if he hasn't got the slightest idea what anyone is talking about. And the state put him in that position. They let him get hurt. It was their jail. They can't do that and then go ahead and try him.'

'What's your father going to think?'

'He's going to fight it tooth and nail. Obviously. No prosecutor can afford to admit the possibility that amnesia might screw up a trial. Otherwise everyone would jump right on it. Everyone would be looking to get beat up in pre-trial detention. Suddenly nobody would be able to remember anything.'

'It must have happened before.'

Helen nodded. 'It has.'

'So what do the law books say?'

'I'm reading them now. As you can see. Dusky versus the United States, Wilson versus the United States.'

'And?'

'There are lots of ifs and buts.'

Reacher said nothing. Helen looked straight at him.

'It's spinning out of control,' she said. 'Now there'll be a trial about a trial. It's something that might need to go all the way to the Supreme Court. I'm not equipped for that. And I don't *want* that. I don't want to be the lawyer who gets people off on weird technicalities. That's not who I am and it's a label I can't afford right now.'

'So plead him guilty and the hell with it.'

'When you called me last night I thought you were going to walk in here this morning and tell me he's innocent.'

'Dream on,' Reacher said.

She looked away.

'But,' he said.

She looked back. 'There's a but?'

He nodded. 'Unfortunately.'

'What's the but?'

'He's not quite as guilty as I thought he was.'

'How?'

'Get your car and I'll show you.'

They rode down together to a tenants-only underground parking garage. There were NBC broadcast trucks in there and cars and pickups and SUVs of various makes and vintages. There was a new blue Mustang convertible with an NBC sticker in the windshield. Ann Yanni's, probably, Reacher thought. It was right for her. She would drive top-down on her days off and top-up during the working week, to keep her hair OK for the cameras. Or maybe she used a lot of spray.

Helen Rodin's ride was a small dark green sedan so anonymous Reacher didn't know what it was. A Saturn, maybe. It was unwashed and not new. It was a graduate student's car, the sort of thing a person uses until a first salary kicks in and lease payments become affordable. Reacher knew all about lease payments. Baseball on the TV carried a lot of commercials. Every half inning, and every call to the bullpen.

'Where are we going?' Helen asked.

'South,' Reacher said.

He racked his seat back and crunched a whole lot of stuff in the footwell behind him. She had her seat close to the wheel, even though she wasn't a short woman. He ended up looking at her more or less from behind.

'What do you know?' she asked.

'It's not what I know,' he said. 'It's what James Barr knows.'

'About what?'

'About me.'

She came up out of the garage and started south down a street parallel with First. Eight o'clock in the morning, the rush hour traffic was still heavy. Going the opposite way from the afternoon rush, he guessed.

'What does James Barr know about you?' she asked.

'Something that made him want me here,' he said.

'He ought to hate you.'

'I'm sure he does. But he still wanted me here.'

She crawled south, towards the river.

'He never met me before,' Reacher said. 'Never saw me again afterwards. We knew each other for three weeks, more than fourteen years ago.'

'He knew you as an investigator. Someone who broke a tough case.'

'A case he thought couldn't be broken. He watched me do it every step of the way. He had a front row seat. He thought I was an investigative genius.'

'That's why he wanted you here?'

Reacher nodded. 'I spent last night trying to live up to his opinion.'

They crossed the river, on a long iron trestle. The sun was on their left. The wharf was on their right. The slow grey water moved listlessly past it.

'Go west now,' Reacher said.

She made a right and took a two-lane county road. There were bait stores on the riverbank, and shacks selling barbecue and beer and crushed ice.

'But this case was already broken,' she said. 'He knew that.'

'This case was only halfway broken,' Reacher said. 'That's what he knew.'

'Halfway?'

150

Reacher nodded, even though he was behind her.

'There's more to this case than Emerson saw,' he said. 'Barr wanted someone else to understand that. But his first lawyer was lazy. He wasn't very interested. That's why Barr got so frustrated.'

'What more is there?'

'I'll show you.'

'A lot?'

'I think so.'

'So why didn't he just lay out the facts, whatever they are?'

'Because he couldn't. And because nobody would have believed him anyway.'

'Why? What the hell happened here?'

There was a highway cloverleaf ahead, just like he had hoped.

'I'll show you,' he said again. 'Take the highway north.'

She powered the little car through the ramp and merged with the traffic. There was a mixed stream flowing north. Eighteen-wheelers, panel trucks, pickups, cars. The road recrossed the river on a concrete bridge. The wharf was visible to the east, in the distance. The city centre was ahead, on the right. The highway rose gently on its stilts. Helen drove onward, with the roofs of low edge-of-town buildings flashing past on the left and the right.

'Be ready to take the spur that runs behind the library,' Reacher said.

It was going to be a right exit. It was announced well in advance with a sign. The broken line separating the right lane from the centre lane

151

became a solid line. Then the solid line became a narrow wedge. The through traffic was forced away to the left. The exit lane angled slightly right. They stayed in it. The wedge grew wider and was filled in with bold cross-hatched lines. Up ahead were yellow drums. They passed them by, onto the spur that would lead behind the library. Reacher twisted in his seat and checked the rear window. Nobody behind them.

'Go slow,' he said.

Two hundred yards ahead the spur started to curve, behind the library, behind the black glass tower. The roadbed was wide enough for two lanes. But the radius was too tight to make it safe for two lanes to run side by side at high speed into the corner. Traffic engineers had thought better of it. They had advised a gentler trajectory. They had marked out a single lane through the curve. It was a little wider than a normal lane, to allow for misjudgements. It started way on the left and then swung sharply to the right and cut across the apex of the curve at a shallower angle.

'Go real slow now,' Reacher said.

The car slowed. Way up ahead of them on the left was a crescent-moon shape of white cross-hatching. Beginning right next to them on the right was a long thin triangle of white cross-hatching. Just lines of paint on the blacktop, but they shepherded people along and kept them safe.

'Pull over,' Reacher said. 'Here, on the right.'

'Can't stop here,' Helen said.

'Like you had a flat. Just pull over. Right here.'

She braked hard and turned the wheel and

steered onto the cross-hatched no-man's-land on their right. They felt the thick painted lines thumping under the tyres. A juddery little rhythm. It slowed as she slowed.

She stopped.

'Back up a little,' Reacher said.

She backed up, like she was parallel parking against the concrete parapet.

'Now forward a yard,' Reacher said.

She drove forward a yard.

'OK,' he said.

He wound his window down. The traffic lane on their left was clear and smooth, but the cross-hatched no-man's-land they were stopped on was covered with grit and trash and debris blown across it by years of passing vehicles. There were cans and bottles and detached mud flaps and tiny cubes of broken headlight glass and plastic splinters from old fender benders. Far away to the left the through traffic rumbled north on a separate bridge. There was a constant stream over there. But they sat for a whole minute before anyone else came the way they had taken. A lone pickup passed close on their left and rocked them with its slipstream. Then the spur went quiet again.

'Not busy,' Reacher said.

'It never is,' Helen said. 'This doesn't really go anywhere people need to get. It was a total waste of money. But I guess they've always got to be building something.'

'Look down,' Reacher said.

The highway was raised up on tall stilts. The roadbed was maybe forty feet above ground level.

The parapet wall was three feet high. Beyond it, ahead and to their right, was the upper storey of the library building. It had an intricate cornice, carved from limestone, and a slate roof. It felt close enough to touch.

'What?' Helen asked.

Reacher pointed with his thumb, and then leaned way back so she could see across him. Directly to their right was an unobstructed view down into the plaza, with a perfectly straight line of sight along the narrow bottleneck between the end of the ornamental pool and the plaza wall. And beyond it, dead ahead, perfectly aligned, was the door of the DMV office.

'James Barr was a sniper,' Reacher said. 'Not the best, not the worst, but he was one of ours and he trained for more than five years. And training has a purpose. It takes people who aren't necessarily very smart and it makes them *seem* smart by beating some basic tactical awareness into them. Until it becomes instinctive.'

'I don't understand.'

'*This* is where a trained sniper would have fired from. Up here on the highway. Because from here he's got his targets walking directly towards him in a straight line. Single file, into a bottleneck. He sets up with one aiming point and never has to vary it. His targets just walk into it, one after the other. Shooting from the side is much harder. The targets are passing right to left in front of him, relatively quickly, he's got to figure in deflection compensation, he's got to move the rifle after each shot.'

'But he didn't fire from here.'

154

'That's my point. He should have, but he didn't.'

'So?'

'He had a minivan. He should have parked it right where we are now. On this exact spot. He should have climbed through into the back seat and opened the sliding door. He should have fired from inside the minivan, Helen. It had tinted windows. The few cars that passed him wouldn't have seen a thing. He should have fired his six shots, with the much easier aim, and the six cartridge cases would have ejected inside the van, and then he should have shut the door and climbed back into the driver's seat and driven away. It would have been a much better firing position and he would have left nothing at all behind. No physical evidence of any kind, because nothing would have touched anything except his tyres would have touched the road.'

'It's farther away. It's a longer distance to shoot.'

'It's about seventy yards. Barr was reliable at five times that distance. Any military sniper is. With an M1A Super Match, seventy yards is the same thing as point-blank range.'

'Someone would have gotten his plate number. There's always *some* traffic. They would have remembered him being here, afterwards.'

'His plates were covered with mud. Probably on purpose. It would have been a great getaway. In five minutes he would have been five miles away. Much better than threading through the traffic on the surface streets.'

Helen Rodin said nothing.

'And he was expecting it to be sunny,' Reacher said. 'You told me it usually is. Five o'clock in the afternoon, the sun would have been in the west, behind him. He would have been firing out of the sun. That's an absolutely basic preference, for a sniper.'

'Sometimes it rains.'

'That would have been OK too. It would have washed his tyre tracks out of this grit. Either way around, he should have been up here in his van. Every reason in the world says he should have been up here in his van.'

'But he wasn't.'

'Evidently.'

'Why not?'

'We should get back to your office. That's where you need to be now. You've got a lot of strategizing to do.'

Helen Rodin sat down at her desk. Reacher walked to her window and looked out into the plaza. Looked for the damaged man in the boxy suit. Didn't see him.

'What strategizing?' Helen asked. 'Barr made a choice about where to shoot from, that's all, and it wasn't a great choice, according to you, according to some fourteen-year-old military theory that he probably forgot all about the day he quit the service.'

'They don't forget,' Reacher said.

'I'm not convinced.'

'That's why he walked out on Chapman. Chapman wasn't going to be convinced either. That's why he asked for me.'

156

'And you *are* convinced?'

'I'm looking at a situation where a trained sniper passed up an excellent location in favour of a much worse one.'

'He used a parking garage in Kuwait City. You said so yourself.'

'Because that *was* a good location. It was directly in line with the apartment building's door. The four guys were walking directly towards him. They went down like dominoes.'

'This is fourteen years later. He's not as good as he was. That's all.'

'They don't forget,' Reacher said again.

'Whatever, how does it make him less guilty?'

'Because if a person chooses a terrible *B* instead of a great *A*, there has to be a reason for it. And reasons have implications.'

'What was his reason?'

'It had to be a real good one, didn't it? Because he trapped himself inside a building, down at street level, in a congested area, with a much harder shot, in a place whose very nature made it the best crime scene a twenty-year veteran like Emerson has ever seen.'

'OK, tell me why he would do that.'

'Because he was literally going out of his way to leave every last piece of evidence he could.'

She stared at him. 'That's crazy.'

'It was a great crime scene. Everyone was so happy with how great it was they never stopped to realize it was way *too* great. Me included. It was like Crime Scene 101, Helen. It was what they must have given Bellantonio on his first day in college. It was too good to be true, therefore it *wasn't* true. Everything was wrong with it. Like, why would he wear a raincoat? It was warm and it wasn't raining and he was in a car and he was never outside. He wore it so he could scrape unique fibres off it onto the pillar. Why would he wear those stupid shoes? You look at a pair of shoes like that and you just *know* they track every last piece of crap around. Why did he shoot out of the dark? So that people would see his muzzle flash and pinpoint the location so they could go up there afterwards and find all the other clues. Why would he scrape his rifle on the wall? That's a twenty-five-hundred-dollar purchase. Why didn't he take the traffic cone away with him? It would have been easier just to throw it in the back of his van than leave it there.'

'This is crazy,' Helen said.

'Two clinchers,' Reacher said. 'Why did he pay to park? That bothered me from the start. I mean, who *does* that? But he did. And he did it just so he could leave one little extra clue. Nothing else makes any sense. He wanted to leave a quarter in the meter with his prints on it. Just to tie it all in a nice little bow. To connect it with the shell case, which he probably also left there on purpose.'

'It fell in a trench.'

'He could have gotten it out. There was plenty of wire lying around, according to Bellantonio's report. It would have taken a second and a half.'

Helen Rodin paused. 'What's the other clincher?'

'That's easy, once you start looking through the right end of the telescope. He wanted to be looking at the pool from the south, not the west.

That was crucial. He wanted to be looking at it lengthwise, not sideways.'

'Why?'

'Because he didn't miss, Helen. He fired into the pool deliberately. He wanted to put a bullet in the water, down the long diagonal axis, from a low angle, just like a ballistics tank, just so it could be found later, undamaged. Just so it could tie his barrel to the crime. Sideways wouldn't have worked for him. Not enough travel distance through the water. The bullet would have hit the wall too hard. It would have gotten damaged.'

'But why the hell would he do all that?'

Reacher didn't answer.

'Remorse? For fourteen years ago? So he could be found and punished?'

Reacher shook his head. 'He would have confessed as soon as they found him. A remorseful person would have been *wanting* to confess.'

'So why did he do all that?'

'Because he was made to, Helen. Simple as that.'

She stared at him.

'Someone forced him to do it,' Reacher said. 'He was forced to do it and he was forced to take the blame for it. He was told to go home afterwards and wait for the arrest. That's why he took the sleeping pill. He was probably going crazy, sitting there waiting for the shoe to fall.'

Helen Rodin said nothing.

'He was coerced,' Reacher said. 'Believe it. It's the only logical explanation. He wasn't a lone nutcase. That's why he said *They've got the wrong guy*. It was a message. He was hoping someone would pick up on it. He meant they should be looking for the other guy. The guy who made him do it. The guy he feels is more responsible.'

Helen Rodin said nothing.

'The puppet master,' Reacher said.

Reacher checked the plaza again, from the window. The ornamental pool was about two-thirds full. The fountain was splashing merrily. The sun was out. There were no loiterers visible.

Helen Rodin got up from her desk. Just stood there behind it.

'I should be turning cartwheels,' she said.

'He still killed five people.'

'But if the coercion was substantial, it's going to help him.'

Reacher said nothing.

'What do you think it was? A double-dare? Some kind of thrill-seeking?'

'Maybe,' Reacher said. 'But I doubt it. On the face of it James Barr is twenty years too old for double-dares. That's a kid thing. And they'd have done it from the highway, anyway. They would have wanted to survive to do it again.'

'So what was it?'

'Something else entirely. Something real.'

'Should we take it to Emerson?'

'No,' Reacher said.

'I think we should.'

'There are reasons not to.'

'Like?'

'For one, Emerson's got the best done deal he ever saw. He's not going to pick at the seams now. No cop would.'

'So what should we do?'

'We should ask ourselves three basic questions,' Reacher said. 'Like who, and how, and why. It was a transaction. We need to figure out who benefits. Because James Barr certainly didn't.'

'The who was whoever set those guys on you last night. Because he liked the way the transaction was going and he didn't want the boat rocked by some new guy showing up.'

'Correct,' Reacher said.

'So I need to look for that person.'

'You might not want to do that.'

'Why wouldn't I?'

'It might get your client killed,' Reacher said.

'He's in the hospital, guarded night and day.'

'Your client isn't James Barr. It's Rosemary Barr. You need to think about what kind of a threat can have made James Barr do what he did. He was looking at life without parole at best. Getting strapped to the gurney at worst. He knew that, well in advance. He must have. So why would he go along? Why would he walk meekly into all that? It had to have been one hell of an effective threat, Helen. And what's the only thing Barr's got to lose? No wife, no kids, no family at all. Except a sister.'

Helen Rodin said nothing.

'He was told to keep quiet, to the end. Obviously. That's why he asked for me. It was like a coded communication. Because the puppet can't talk about the puppet master, not now, not ever, because the threat is still out there. I think he might be trading his life for his sister's. Which gives you a big problem. If the puppet master sees you poking around, he'll think the puppet talked. That's why you can't go to Emerson.'

'But the puppet didn't talk. You figured it out.'

'We could put an announcement in the paper. Think anyone would believe it?'

'So what should I do?'

'Nothing,' Reacher said. 'There's nothing you can do. Because the more you try to help James Barr, the more likely you are to get Rosemary Barr killed for it.'

Helen Rodin was quiet for a long moment.

'Can we protect her?' she asked.

'No,' Reacher said. 'We can't. There's only two of us. We'd need four guys minimum, and a safe house. That would cost a lot of money.'

Helen Rodin came out from behind her desk. Walked round and stood next to Reacher and gazed out of the window. She put her hands on the sill, lightly, like a pianist's on a keyboard. Then she turned round and leaned against the glass. She was fragrant. Some clean scent a little like soap.

'You could look for him,' she said.

'Could I?' he answered, nothing in his voice.

She nodded. 'He made a mistake. He gave you a reason that's not connected to James Barr. Not directly. He set those boys on you. Therefore you've got a legitimate interest in finding their employer. An independent interest. You could go after him and he wouldn't necessarily conclude that James Barr had talked.'

'I'm not here to help the defence.'

'Then look at it as helping the prosecution. If two people were involved, then two people

162

deserve to go down. Why let the patsy take the fall on his own?'

Reacher said nothing.

'Just look at it as helping me,' Helen said.

Grigor Linsky dialled his cell phone.

'They're back in her office,' he said. 'I can see both of them in the window.'

SIX

Reacher rode the elevator to the top of the black glass tower and found a maintenance stairwell that led to the roof. He came out through a triangular metal hutch next to the water tank and the elevator winding gear. The roof was grey tarpaper covered with gravel. It was fifteen storeys up, which wasn't much in comparison with some cities. But it felt like the highest point in Indiana. He could see the river to the south. South and west, he could see where the raised highway separated. He walked to the northwest corner and wind whipped at him and flattened his shirt against his body and his pants against his legs. Directly below him the highway spur curled round behind the library and the tower and ran away due east. Far beyond it in the distance the state highway carried on north and met a cloverleaf about two miles away in the haze. A long straight road came off the cloverleaf and ran back towards him. He fixed its position in his mind, because that was the road he wanted.

He rode down to the lobby and set out walking. At street level the air was warm and still. He went north and west, which meant he missed the sports bar by a block. The road he wanted came in at a shallow angle south of it and diverted him away. It was straight and wide. Four lanes. Closest to downtown it had small rundown establishments. There was a gun store with heavy mesh on the windows. There was a barbershop with a sign: *Any Style $7*. There was an old-fashioned motor court hotel on a lot that once must have stood on the edge of town. Then there was a raw cross street and beyond it the lots got bigger and the buildings got newer. Fresh commercial territory. No existing leases, nothing to tear down. Once virgin land, now paved over.

He kept on walking and after a mile he passed a fast food drive-through. Then a tyre store. *Four New Radials $99!* Then a lube franchise and a dealership for small cars from Korea. *America's Best Warranty!* He looked ahead, because he figured he was getting close.

Are you a hooker?

No way. I work at the auto parts store.

Not *an* auto parts store. *The* auto parts store. Maybe the only one, or at least the main one. The biggest one. Which in any city is always right there on the same strip as the tyre stores and the auto dealers and the lube shops. Which in any city is always a wide new strip near a highway cloverleaf. Cities are all different, but they're also all the same.

He spent ten minutes hiking past a Ford dealership with about a thousand new pickup trucks lined up shoulder to shoulder with their front wheels up on ramps. Behind them was a giant inflatable gorilla tied down with guy wires. The wires had tinsel bunting attached to them. Beyond the new trucks were old trucks. Trade-ins, Reacher guessed, looking for new homes. Beyond the used lot was a fire road.

And then an auto parts store.

It was a franchise operation, long and low, neat and clean. New blacktop in the lot, urgent messages in the windows. Cheap oil filters, cheap antifreeze, guaranteed brake parts, super duty truck batteries. The parking lot was about a quarter full. There were slammed Hondas with wide pipes and blue headlight bulbs and rubber-band tyres on chrome wheels. There were listing pickup trucks with broken springs. There were tired sedans halfway through their third hundred thousand miles. There were two cars alone together in the end bays. The store staff's cars, Reacher figured. They weren't allowed to park in the prime front-and-centre slots, but they wanted their rides where they could see them through the windows. One was a four-cylinder Chevy, and the other was a small Toyota SUV. The Chevy had chromed silhouettes of reclining women on the mud flaps, which made the Toyota the red-head's car. That was Reacher's conclusion.

He went inside. The air was set very cold and smelled of sharp chemical flavours. There were maybe a half-dozen customers walking around, looking. At the front of the store were racks full of glass and chrome things. Dress-up accessories, Reacher guessed. At the back were racks of things in red cardboard boxes. Clutch plates, brake pads, radiator hoses, stuff like that,

166

he guessed. Parts. He had never put parts on a car. In the army there had been guys to do it for him, and since the army he had never had a vehicle of his own.

Between the glamour stuff and the boring stuff was a service corral made of four counters boxed together. There were registers and computers and thick paper manuals. Behind one of the computers was a tall boy somewhere in his early twenties. Not someone Reacher had seen before. Not one of the five from the sports bar. Just a guy. He looked to be in charge. He was wearing red overalls. A uniform, Reacher guessed, partly practical and partly suggestive of the kind of thing an Indy 500 pit mechanic might wear. Like a symbol. Like an implied promise of fast hands-on help with all kinds of matters automotive. The guy was a manager, Reacher guessed. Not the franchise owner. Not if he drove a four-cylinder Chevy to work. His name was embroidered on the left of his chest: *Gary*. Up close he looked sullen and unhelpful.

'I need to speak with Sandy,' Reacher said to him. 'The redhead.'

'She's in back right now,' the guy called Gary said.

'Shall I go through or do you want to go get her for me?'

'What's this about?'

'Personal.'

'She's here to work.'

'It's a legal matter.'

'You're not a cop.'

'I'm working with a lawyer.'

167

'I need to see some ID.'

'No, Gary, you don't. You need to go get Sandy.'

'I can't. I'm short-staffed today.'

'You could call her on the phone. Or page her.'

The guy called Gary just stood still. Did nothing. Reacher shrugged and bypassed the corral of counters and headed for a door marked *No Admittance*. It would be an office or a lunch room, he guessed. Not a stock room. A place like that, stock was unloaded directly onto the shelves. No hidden inventory. Reacher knew how modern retail worked. He read the papers people left behind on buses and in diner booths.

It was an office, small, maybe ten by ten, dominated by a large white laminate desk with oily hand prints on it. Sandy was sitting behind it, wearing red overalls. Hers looked a whole lot better than Gary's. They were cinched in tight round her waist with a belt. The zipper was open about eight inches. Her name was embroidered on the left, displayed a lot more prominently than Gary's was. Reacher figured that if he owned the franchise he would have Sandy working the counter and Gary in the office, no question.

'We meet again,' he said.

Sandy said nothing. Just looked up at him. She was working with invoices. There was a stack of them on her left, and a stack of them on her right. One of them was in her hand, frozen in mid-air on its journey from one stack to the other. She looked smaller than Reacher remembered, quieter, less energetic, duller. Deflated.

'We need to talk,' he said. 'Don't we?'

'I'm very sorry for what happened,' she said.

'Don't apologize. I wasn't offended. I just want to know how it went down.'

'I don't know how.'

'You do, Sandy. You were there.'

She said nothing. Just placed the invoice on top of the stack to her right, and used her fingers to line it up exactly.

'Who set it up?' Reacher asked.

'I don't know.'

'You must know who told *you* about it.'

'Jeb,' she said.

'Jeb?'

'Jeb Oliver,' she said. 'He works here. We hang out sometimes.'

'Is he here today?'

'No, he didn't show.'

Reacher nodded. The guy called Gary had said: *I'm short-staffed today.*

'Did you see him again last night? Afterwards?'

'No, I just ran for it.'

'Where does he live?'

'I don't know. With his mother somewhere. I don't know him that well.'

'What did he tell you?'

'That I could help with something he had to do.'

'Did it sound like fun?'

'Anything sounds like fun on a Monday night in this town. Watching a barn plank warp sounds like fun.'

'How much did he pay you?'

Sandy didn't answer.

169

'A thing like that, nobody does it for free,' Reacher said.

'Hundred dollars,' she said.

'What about the other four guys?'

'Same for them.'

'Who were they?'

'His buddies.'

'Who came up with the plan? The brothers thing?'

'It was Jeb's idea. You were supposed to start pawing me. Only you didn't.'

'You improvised very well.'

She smiled a little, like it had been a small unscripted success in a life that held very few of them.

'How did you know where to find me?' Reacher asked.

'We were cruising in Jeb's truck. Around and around. Kind of standing by. Then he got word on his cell.'

'Who called him?'

'I don't know.'

'Would his buddies know?'

'I don't think so. Jeb likes to know things that nobody else knows.'

'You want to lend me your car?'

'My car?'

'I need to go find Jeb.'

'I don't know where he lives.'

'You can leave that part to me. But I need wheels.'

'I don't know.'

'I'm old enough to drive,' Reacher said. 'I'm old enough to do lots of things. And I'm pretty good at some of them.'

She half smiled again, because he was using her own line from the night before. She looked away, and then she looked back at him, shy, but curious.

'Was I any good?' she asked. 'You know, last night, with the act?'

'You were great,' he said. 'I was preoccupied, or I would have given up on the football in a heartbeat.'

'How long would you need my car for?'

'How big is this town?'

'Not very.'

'Not very long, then.'

'Is this a big deal?'

'You got a hundred bucks. So did four other guys. That's five hundred right there. My guess is Jeb kept another five for himself. So someone paid a thousand bucks to put me in the hospital. That's a moderately big deal. For me, anyway.'

'I wish I hadn't gotten involved now.'

'It turned out OK.'

'Am I in trouble?'

'Maybe,' Reacher said. 'But maybe not. We could deal. You could lend me your car and I could forget all about you.'

'Promise?'

'No harm, no foul,' Reacher said.

She ducked down and lifted her purse off the floor. Rooted through and came out with a set of keys.

'It's a Toyota,' she said.

'I know,' Reacher said. 'End of the row, next to Gary's Chevy.'

'How did you know that?'

'Intuition,' he said.

171

He took the keys and closed the door on her and headed back to the corral of counters. Gary was ringing some guy up for some unidentifiable purchase. Reacher waited in line behind him. Got to the register inside about two minutes.

'I need Jeb Oliver's address,' he said.

'Why?' Gary said.

'A legal matter.'

'I want to see some ID.'

'You had a criminal conspiracy running out of your store. If I were you, the less I knew about it, the better.'

'I want to see something.'

'What about the inside of an ambulance? That's the next thing you're going to see, Gary, unless you give me Jeb Oliver's address.'

The guy paused a moment. Glanced beyond Reacher's shoulder at the line forming behind him. Apparently decided that he didn't want to start a fight he knew he couldn't win with a whole bunch of people watching. So he opened a drawer and took out a file and copied an address onto a slip of paper torn off the top of a memo pad provided by an oil filter manufacturer.

'North of here,' he said. 'About five miles.'

'Thank you,' Reacher said, and took the slip of paper.

The redhead's Toyota started on the first turn of the key. Reacher let the engine idle and racked the seat back and adjusted the mirror. Clipped his belt and propped the slip of paper against the instrument panel. It meant he couldn't see the tachometer, but he wasn't very interested in whatever information that dial might supply. All he cared about was how much gas was in the tank, and there looked to be more than enough for five miles out and five miles back.

Jeb Oliver's address was nothing more than a house number on a rural route. Easier to find than a road with a name, like Elm Street, or Maple Avenue. In Reacher's experience some towns had more roads named after trees than trees themselves.

He moved out of the parking lot and drove north to the highway cloverleaf. There was the usual forest of signs. He saw the route number he wanted. It was going to be a dogleg, right and then left. East, and then north. The little SUV hummed along OK. It was tall for its width, which made it feel tippy on the turns. But it didn't fall over. It had a small engine that kept itself working hard. The interior smelled of perfume.

The west–east part of the dogleg was some kind of major county road. But after the turn north the blacktop narrowed and the shoulders grew ragged. There was agriculture going on to the left and the right. Some kind of a winter crop was planted in giant circles. Radial irrigation booms turned slowly. The corners where the booms didn't reach were unplanted and stony. Superimposing circles on squares wasted more than twenty-one per cent of every acre, but Reacher figured that might be an efficient trade-off in places where land was plentiful and irrigation hardware wasn't.

He drove four more miles through the fields and passed a half-dozen tracks with mailboxes at the end of them. The mailboxes were painted with numbers and the tracks led away west and east to small swaybacked farm dwellings maybe two hundred yards off the road. He watched the numbers and slowed before he got to the Oliver place. It had a mailbox like all the others, up on a post made out of two figure-eight concrete blocks stacked end on end. The number was daubed in white on a weathered plywood rectangle wired to the concrcte. The track was narrow with two muddy ruts flanking a weedy centre hump. There were sharp tyre tracks in the mud. New treads, wide, aggressive, from a big truck. Not the kind of tyres you bought at the $99-for-four place.

Reacher turned the Toyota in and bumped down the track. At the end of it he could see a clapboard farmhouse with a barn behind it and a clean red pickup truck next to it. The truck was turned nose-out and it had a massive chrome radiator grille. A Dodge Ram, Reacher figured. He parked in front of it and got out. The house and the barn were about a hundred years old and the truck was about a month old. It had the big Hemi motor, and the crew cab, and four wheel drive, and huge tyres. It was probably worth more than the house, which was badly maintained and one winter away from serious trouble. The barn was no better. But it had new iron clasps on the doors, with a bicycle U-lock through them.

There was no sound except for a distant rainfall hiss as the irrigation booms turned slowly in the fields. No activity anywhere. No traffic on the road. No dogs barking. The air was still and full of the sharp smell of fertilizer and earth. Reacher walked to the front door and knocked twice with the flat of his hand. No response. He tried again. No response. He walked round to the back of the house and found a woman sitting on a porch glider. She was a lean and leathery person wearing a faded print dress and holding a pint bottle of something golden in colour. She was probably fifty, but she could have passed for seventy, or forty if she took a bath and got a good night's sleep. She had one foot tucked up underneath her, and was using the other to scoot the glider slowly back and forth. She wasn't wearing shoes.

'What do you want?' she said.

'Jeb,' Reacher said.

'Not here.'

'He's not at work either.'

'I know that.'

'So where is he?'

'How would I know?'

'Are you his mother?'

'Yes, I am. You think I'm hiding him here? Go ahead and check.'

Reacher said nothing. The woman stared at him and rocked the glider, back and forth, back and forth. The bottle rested easy in her lap.

'I insist,' she said. 'I mean it. Search the damn house.'

'I'll take your word for it.'

'Why should you?'

'Because if you invite me to search the house it means he's not in it.'

'Like I said. He's not here.'

'What about the barn?'

'It's locked from the outside. There's only one key and he's got it.'

Reacher said nothing.

'He went away,' the woman said. 'Disappeared.'

'Disappeared?'

'Only temporarily, I hope.'

'Is that his truck?'

The woman nodded. Took a small, delicate sip from her bottle.

'So he walked?' Reacher said.

'He was picked up. By a friend.'

'When?'

'Late last night.'

'To go where?'

'I have no idea.'

'Take a guess.'

The woman shrugged, rocked, sipped.

'Far away, probably,' she said. 'He has friends all over. California, maybe. Or Arizona. Or Texas. Or Mexico.'

'Was this trip planned?' Reacher asked.

The woman wiped the neck of the bottle on the hem of her dress and held it out towards him. He shook his head. Sat down on the porch step. The old wood creaked once under his weight. The glider kept on rocking, back and forth. It was almost silent. Almost, but not quite. There was a small sound from the mechanism that came once at the end of each swing, and a little creak from a porch board as it started its return. Reacher could smell mildew from the cushions, and bourbon from the bottle.

'Cards on the table, whoever the hell you are,' the woman said. 'Jeb got home last night limping.

176

With his nose busted. And I'm figuring you for the guy who bust it.'

'Why?'

'Who else would come looking for him? I'm guessing he started something he couldn't finish.'

Reacher said nothing.

'So he ran,' the woman said. 'The pussy.'

'Did he call someone last night? Or did someone call him?'

'How would I know? He makes a thousand calls a day, he takes a thousand calls a day. His cell phone is the biggest thing in his life. Next to his truck.'

'Did you see who picked him up?'

'Some guy in a car. He waited on the road. Wouldn't come down the track. I didn't see much. It was dark. White lights on the front, red lights on the back, but all cars have those.'

Reacher nodded. He had seen only a single set of tyre marks in the mud, from the big pickup. The car that had waited on the road was probably a sedan, too low-slung to make it down the farm track.

'Did he say how long he would be gone?'

The woman just shook her head.

'Was he scared of something?'

'He was kind of beaten down. Deflated.'

Deflated. Like the redhead in the auto parts store.

'OK,' Reacher said. 'Thanks.'

'You going now?'

'Yes,' Reacher said. He walked back the way he had come, listening to the glider moving, listening to the hiss of irrigation water. He backed

177

the Toyota all the way to the road and swung the wheel and headed south.

He put the Toyota next to the Chevy and headed inside the store. Gary was still behind the register. Reacher ignored him and headed straight for the *No Admittance* door. The redhead was still behind the desk. She was almost through with the invoices. The stack on her right was tall, and the stack on her left had just one sheet of paper in it. She wasn't doing anything with it. She was leaning back in the chair, unwilling to finish, unwilling to get back out to the public. Or to Gary.

Reacher put the car keys on the desk.

'Thanks for the loan,' he said.

'Did you find him?' she asked.

'He's gone.'

She said nothing.

'You look tired,' Reacher said.

She said nothing.

'Like you've got no energy. No sparkle. No enthusiasm.'

'So?'

'Last night you were full of beans.'

'I'm at work now.'

'You were at work last night too. You were getting paid.'

'You said you were going to forget all about that.'

'I am. Have a nice life, Sandy.'

She watched him for a minute.

'You too, Jimmy Reese,' she said.

He turned round and closed the door on her

again and headed out to the daylight. Started walking south, back to town.

There were four people in Helen Rodin's office when he got there. Helen herself, and three strangers. One of them was a guy in an expensive suit. He was sitting in Helen's chair, behind her desk. She was standing next to him, head bent, talking. Some kind of an urgent conference. The other two strangers were standing near the window, like they were waiting, like they were next in line. One was a man, one was a woman. The woman had long dark hair and glasses. The man had no hair and glasses. Both were dressed casually. Both had lapel badges with their names printed large. The woman had *Mary Mason* followed by a bunch of letters that had to be medical. The man had *Warren Niebuhr* with the same bunch of letters. Doctors, Reacher figured, probably psychiatrists. The name badges made them look like they had been dragged out of a convention hall. But they didn't seem unhappy about it.

Helen looked up from her discussion.

'Folks, this is Jack Reacher,' she said. 'My investigator dropped out and Mr Reacher agreed to take over his role.'

News to me, Reacher thought. But he said nothing. Then Helen gestured at the guy in her chair, proudly.

'This is Alan Danuta,' she said. 'He's a lawyer specializing in veterans' issues. From D.C. Probably the best there is.'

'You got here fast,' Reacher said to him.

'I had to,' the guy said back. 'Today is the critical day for Mr Barr.'

'We're all headed for the hospital,' Helen said. 'The doctors say he's ready for us. I was hoping that Alan would consult by phone or e-mail, but he flew right in.'

'Easier for me that way,' Danuta said.

'No, I got lucky,' Helen said. 'And then even luckier, because there's a psychiatric conference in Bloomington all week. Dr Mason and Dr Niebuhr drove straight down.'

'I specialize in memory loss,' Dr Mason said.

'And I specialize in coercion,' Dr Niebuhr said. 'Dependency issues in the criminal mind, and so on.'

'So this is the team,' Helen said.

'What about his sister?' Reacher asked.

'She's already with him.'

'We need to talk.'

'Privately?'

'Just for a moment.'

She made an *excuse me* face to the others and led Reacher into the outer office.

'You get anywhere?' she asked him.

'The bimbo and the four other guys were recruited by a friend of theirs called Jeb Oliver. He paid them a hundred bucks each. I figure he kept another five for his trouble. I went to his house, but he's gone.'

'Where?'

'Nobody knows. He was picked up by a guy in a car.'

'Who is he?'

'He works at the store with the bimbo. But

he's also a small-time dope dealer.'

'Really?'

Reacher nodded. 'There's a barn behind his house with a fancy lock on it. Maybe a meth lab, maybe a store room. He spends a lot of time on his cell phone. He owns a truck that had to cost twice what a store clerk makes in a year. And he lives with his mother.'

'What does that prove?'

'Drug dealers are more likely than anyone else to live with their mothers. I read it in the paper.'

'Why?'

'They've usually got small-time priors. They can't pass the kind of background checks that landlords like to run.'

Helen said nothing.

'They were all hopped up last night,' Reacher said. 'All six of them. Speed, probably, judging by the way the bimbo looked today. She was different. Really down, like an amphetamine hangover.'

'They were doped up? Then you were lucky.'

Reacher shook his head. 'You want to fight with me, your best choice would be aspirin.'

'Where does this get us?'

'Look at it from Jeb Oliver's point of view. He was doing something for somebody. Part work, part favour. Worth a thousand bucks. Had to be for someone higher up on one of his various food chains. And it probably wasn't for the auto parts manager.'

'So you think James Barr was involved with a dope dealer?'

'Not necessarily involved. But maybe coerced by one for some unknown reason.'

'This raises the stakes,' Helen said.

'A little,' Reacher said.

'What should we do?'

'We should go to the hospital. Let Dr Mason find out if Barr is bullshitting about the amnesia. If he is, then the fastest way through all of this is to slap him around until he tells us the truth.'

'What if he isn't bullshitting?'

'Then there are other approaches.'

'Like what?'

'Later,' Reacher said. 'Let's hear what the shrinks have to say first.'

Helen Rodin drove out to the hospital in her Saturn with the lawyer Alan Danuta sitting beside her in the front and Reacher sprawling in the back. Mason and Niebuhr followed her in the Taurus they had rented that morning in Bloomington. The two cars parked side by side in a large visitors' lot and all five people got out and stood for a moment and then headed together towards the building's main entrance.

Grigor Linsky watched them walk. He was fifty feet across the lot, in the Cadillac that Jeb Oliver's mother had seen in the dark the night before. He kept the motor running and dialled his cell phone. The Zec answered on the first ring.

'Yes?' he said.

'The soldier is very good,' Linsky said. 'He's already been out to the boy's house.'

'And?'

'Nothing. The boy is no longer there.'

'Where is the boy?'

'Distributed.'

'Specifically?'

'His head and his hands are in the river. The rest of him is under eight yards of crushed stone in the new First Street roadbed.'

'What's happening now?'

'The soldier and the lawyer are at the hospital. With three others. Another lawyer and two doctors, I think. Specialist counsel and expert witnesses, I imagine.'

'Are we relaxed?'

'We should be. They have to try. That's the system here, as you know. But they won't succeed.'

'Make sure they don't,' the Zec said.

The hospital was on the outer edge of the city and therefore relatively spacious. Clearly there had been no real estate restraints. Just county budget restrictions, Reacher figured, that had limited the building to plain concrete and six storeys. The concrete was painted white inside and out and the storeys were short of headroom. But other than those factors the place looked like any hospital anywhere. And it smelled like any hospital anywhere. Decay, disinfectant, disease. Reacher didn't like hospitals very much. He was following the other four down a long bright corridor that led to an elevator. The two shrinks were leading the way. They seemed pretty much at home. Helen Rodin and Alan Danuta were right behind them. They were side by side, talking. The shrinks reached the elevator bank and Niebuhr hit the button. The little column of people closed up behind him. Then Helen Rodin turned back and stopped Reacher before he caught up with the others. Stepped close and spoke quietly.

'Does the name Eileen Hutton mean anything to you?'

'Why?'

'My father faxed a new witness list. He added her name.'

Reacher said nothing.

'She seems to be from the army,' Helen said. 'Do you know her?'

'Should I?'

Helen came closer and turned away from the others.

'I need to know what she knows,' she said quietly.

This could complicate things, Reacher thought.

'She was the prosecutor,' he said.

'When? Fourteen years ago?'

'Yes.'

'So how much does she know?'

'I think she's at the Pentagon now.'

'How much does she know, Reacher?'

He looked away.

'She knows it all,' he said.

'How? You never got anywhere near a court-room.'

'Even so.'

'How?'

'Because I was sleeping with her.'

She stared at him. 'Tell me you're kidding.'

'I'm not kidding.'

'You told her *everything*?'

184

'We were in a relationship. Naturally I told her everything. We were on the same side.'

'Just two lonely people in the desert.'

'We had a good thing going. Three great months. She was a nice person. Still is, probably. I liked her very much.'

'That's more information than I need, Reacher.'

He said nothing.

'This is *way* out of control now,' Helen said.

'She can't use what she's got. Even less than I can. It's still classified and she's still in the army.'

Helen Rodin said nothing.

'Believe it,' Reacher said.

'Then why is she on the damn list?'

'My fault,' Reacher said. 'I mentioned the Pentagon to your father. When I couldn't understand how my name had come up. He must have poked around. I thought he might.'

'It's over before it starts if she talks.'

'She can't.'

'Maybe she can. Maybe she's going to. Who knows what the hell the military is going to do?'

The elevator bell rang and the small crowd shuffled closer to the doors.

'You're going to have to talk to her,' Helen said. 'She'll be coming here for a deposition. You're going to have to find out what she's going to say.'

'She's probably a one-star general by now. I can't make her tell me anything.'

'Find a way,' Helen said. 'Exploit old memories.'

'Maybe I don't want to. She and I are still on the same side, remember. As far as Specialist E-4 James Barr is concerned.'

Helen Rodin turned away and stepped into the elevator car.

The elevator opened into a sixth-floor lobby that was all blank painted concrete except for a steel-and-wired-glass door that led into a security airlock. Beyond that Reacher could see signs to an ICU, and two isolation wards, one male, one female, and two general wards, and a neonatal facility. Reacher guessed the whole sixth floor had been funded by the state. It wasn't a pleasant place. It was a perfect blend of prison and hospital, and neither thing was a fun ingredient.

A guy in a Board of Corrections uniform met the party at a reception desk. Everyone was searched and everyone signed a liability waiver. Then a doctor showed up and led them to a small waiting area. The doctor was a tired man of about thirty and the waiting area had chairs made of tubular steel and green vinyl. They looked like they had been ripped out of 1950s Chevrolets.

'Barr is awake and reasonably lucid,' the doctor said. 'We're listing him as stable, but that doesn't mean he's a well man. So today we're restricting his visitors to a maximum of two at any one time, and we want them to keep things as brief as possible.'

Reacher saw Helen Rodin smile, and he knew why. The cops would want to come in pairs, and therefore Helen's presence as defence counsel would make three at a time. Which meant that the medical restrictions were handing her a defence-only day.

'His sister is with him right now,' the doctor

said. 'She'd prefer it if you would wait until they've finished their visit before going in.'

The doctor left them there and Helen said, 'I'll go first, on my own. I need to introduce myself and get his consent for the representation. Then Dr Mason should see him, I think. Then we'll decide what to do next based on her conclusions.'

She spoke fast. Reacher realized she was a little nervous. A little tense. All of them were, apart from him. None of them apart from him had ever met James Barr before. Barr had become an unknown destination for each of them, all in separate ways. He was Helen's client, albeit one that she didn't really want. He was an object of study for Mason and Niebuhr. Maybe the subject of future academic papers, even fame and reputation. Maybe he was a condition waiting to be named. *Barr's Syndrome*. Same for Alan Danuta. Maybe to him the whole thing was a Supreme Court precedent waiting to be argued. A textbook chapter. A law school class. *Indiana versus Barr*. *Barr versus the United States*. They were all investing in a man they had never even seen.

They took a green vinyl chair each and settled in. The little lobby smelled of chlorine disinfectant and it was silent. There was no sound at all except for a faint rush of water in pipes and a distant electronic pulse from a machine in another room. Nobody said anything but everyone seemed to know they were in for a long slow process. No point in starting out impatient. Reacher sat opposite Mary Mason and watched her. She was relatively young, for an expert. She seemed warm and open. She had chosen eyeglasses with large frames so that her eyes could be clearly seen. Her eyes looked kind and welcoming, and reassuring. How much of that was bedside manner and how much was for real, Reacher didn't know.

'How do you do this?' he asked her.

'The assessment?' she said. 'I start out assuming it's more likely to be real than fake. A brain injury bad enough for a two-day coma almost always produces amnesia. Those data were settled long ago. Then I just watch the patient. True amnesiacs are very unsettled by their condition. They're disoriented and frightened. You can see them really trying to remember. They want to remember. Fakers show up different. You can see them avoiding the days in question. They look away from them, mentally. Sometimes even physically. There's often some distinctive body language.'

'Kind of subjective,' Reacher said.

Mason nodded. 'It is basically subjective. It's very hard to prove a negative. You can use brain scans to show differing brain activity, but what the scans actually *mean* is still subjective. Hypnotism is sometimes useful, but courts are scared of hypnotism, generally. So yes, I'm in the opinion business, nothing more.'

'Who does the prosecution hire?'

'Someone exactly like me. I've worked both sides of the fence.'

'So it's he said, she said?'

Mason nodded again. 'It's usually about which of us has more letters after her name. That's what juries respond to.'

'You've got a lot of letters.'

'More than most people,' Mason said.

'How much will he have forgotten?'

'Several days, minimum. If the trauma happened Saturday, I'd be very surprised if he remembers anything after Wednesday. Before that there'll be a shadowy period just about as long where he remembers some things and not others. But that's the minimum. I've seen cases where months are missing, sometimes after concussions, not even comas.'

'Will anything come back?'

'From the initial shadowy period, possibly. He might be able to work backwards from the last thing he remembers, through the preceding few days. He might be able to pick out a few previous incidents. Working forward, he'll be much more limited. If he remembers his last lunch, he might eventually get as far as dinner. If he remembers being out at a movie, he might eventually recall driving home. But there'll be a hard boundary somewhere. Typically it would be when he went to sleep on the last day he's aware of.'

'Will he remember fourteen years ago?'

Mason nodded. 'His long term memory should be unimpaired. Different people seem to have different internal definitions of long term, because there seems to be a literal chemical migration from one part of the brain to another, and no two brains are identical. The physical biology isn't well understood. People like to use computer metaphors now, but that's all wrong. It's not about hard drives and random access memory. The brain is entirely organic. It's like throwing a bag of apples down the stairs. Some bruise, some don't. But I would say fourteen years counts as long term for just about anybody.'

The waiting area went quiet. Reacher listened to the distant electronic pulse. It was a sinus rhythm, he guessed, from a machine that was either monitoring a heartbeat, or causing one. It was running at about seventy beats a minute. It was a restful sound. He liked it. Then a door opened halfway down a corridor and Rosemary Barr stepped out of a room. She was showered and her hair was brushed but she looked thin and exhausted and sleepless and ten years older than the day before. She stood still for a moment and then looked right, looked left, and walked slowly towards the waiting area. Helen Rodin got up and went to meet her halfway. They stood together, talking low. Reacher couldn't hear what they were saying. A two-way progress report, he guessed, first medical, and then legal. Then Helen took Rosemary's arm and led her onward to the group. Rosemary looked at the two psychiatrists, at Alan Danuta, at Reacher. She said nothing. Then she walked on alone towards the security desk. Didn't look back.

'Avoidance,' Niebuhr said. 'We're all here to poke and prod at her brother, physically, mentally, legally, metaphorically. That's invasive and un-attractive. And to acknowledge us means to acknowledge her brother's jeopardy.'

'Maybe she's just tired,' Reacher said.

'I'm going in to see him now,' Helen said.

She walked back up the corridor and went into the room Rosemary had come out of. Reacher watched her until he heard the door close. Then he turned back to Niebuhr.

'Seen this kind of thing before?' he asked him.

'Coercion? Have *you* seen it before?'

Reacher smiled. Every psychiatrist he had ever met liked to answer questions with questions. Maybe they were taught to, day one at psychiatry school.

'I've seen it a lot,' he said.

'But?'

'Usually there was more evidence of a dire threat.'

'A threat against the sister isn't dire? You came up with that hypothesis yourself, I believe.'

'She hasn't been kidnapped. She's not a prisoner somewhere. He could have arranged to have her safeguarded. Or told her to get out of town.'

'Exactly,' Niebuhr said. 'We can only conclude that he was instructed not to do any such thing. Evidently he was told to leave her open, and ignorant, and vulnerable. That demonstrates to us how powerful the coercion must have been. And it demonstrated to *him* how powerful it was. And it demonstrated to him how powerless he was in comparison. Every day. He must have been living with deep dread, and helplessness, and guilt for his obedience.'

'Ever seen a rational man afraid enough to do what he did?'

'Yes,' Niebuhr said.

'Me too,' Reacher said. 'Once or twice.'

'The threatener must be a real monster. Although I'd expect to see other factors present,

191

as enhancers, or multipliers. Very likely a recent relationship, some kind of dependency, an infatuation, a desire to please, to impress, to be valued, to be loved.'

'A woman?'

'No, you don't kill people to impress women. That usually has the opposite effect. This will be a man. Seductive, but not in a sexual way. Compelling, somehow.'

'An alpha male and a beta male.'

'Exactly,' Niebuhr said again. 'With any final reluctance resolved by the threat to the sister. Possibly Mr Barr was never entirely sure whether the threat was a joke or for real. But he chose not to test it. Human motivation is very complex. Most people don't really know why they do things.'

'That's for sure.'

'Do you know why you do things?'

'Sometimes,' Reacher said. 'Other times I don't have the faintest idea. Maybe you could tell me.'

'I'm normally very expensive. That's why I can afford to do things like this for nothing.'

'Maybe I could pay you five bucks a week, like rent.'

Niebuhr smiled, uncertainly.

'Uh, no,' he said. 'I don't think so.'

Then the waiting area went quiet again and stayed quiet for ten long minutes. Danuta stretched his legs way out and worked on papers inside an open briefcase that he kept balanced on his knees. Mason had her eyes closed and might have been asleep. Niebuhr stared into space. The three of them were clearly accustomed to waiting. As was Reacher himself. He had been a military cop for thirteen years, and *Hurry Up And Wait* was the real MP motto. Not *Assist, Protect, Defend*. He focused on the distant electronic heartbeat, and passed the time.

Grigor Linsky turned his car round and watched the hospital door in his mirror. Made a bet with himself that nothing would happen for at least sixty minutes. At least sixty, but not more than ninety. Then he rehearsed an order of priority in case they didn't all come out together. Who should he ignore and who should he tail? In the end he decided to stick with whoever acted alone. He figured that was most likely to be the soldier. His guess was the lawyers and the doctors would head back to the office. They were predictable. The soldier wasn't.

Helen Rodin came out of James Barr's room fifteen minutes after she went in. She walked straight back to the waiting area. Everyone looked at her. She looked at Mary Mason.

'Your turn,' she said. Mason stood up and walked away down the corridor. She took nothing with her. No briefcase, no paper, no pen. Reacher watched her until Barr's door closed behind her. Then he leaned back in his chair, in the silence.

'I liked him,' Helen said, to nobody in particular.

'How is he?' Niebuhr asked.

'Weak,' Helen said. 'Smashed up. Like he got hit by a truck.'

'Is he making sense?'

'He's coherent. But he doesn't remember anything. And I don't think he's faking.'

'How far back is he blanking?'

'I can't tell. He remembers listening to a baseball game on the radio. Could have been last week or last month.'

'Or last year,' Reacher said.

'Did he accept your representation?' Danuta asked.

'Verbally,' Helen said. 'He can't sign anything. He's handcuffed to the bed.'

'Did you walk him through the charges and the evidence?'

'I had to,' Helen said. 'He wanted to know why I thought he needed a lawyer.'

'And?'

'He assumes he's guilty.'

There was silence for a moment. Then Alan Danuta closed his briefcase and took it off his knees and put it on the floor. Sat up straight, fast, all in one fluid movement.

'Welcome to the grey areas,' he said. 'This is where good law comes from.'

'Nothing good about it,' Helen said. 'Not so far.'

'We absolutely cannot let him go to trial. The government injured him through its own negligence and now it wants to put him on trial for his life? I don't think so. Not if he can't even remember the day in question. What kind of a defence could he conduct?'

'My father will have kittens.'

'Obviously. We'll have to cut him out. We'll have to go straight to federal court. It's a Bill of

Rights issue anyway. Federal, then Appeals, then the Supremes. That's the process.'

'That's a *long* process.'

Danuta nodded.

'Three years,' he said. 'If we're lucky. The most applicable precedent is Wilson, and that case took three and a half years. Almost four.'

'And we've got no guarantee of winning. We might lose.'

'In which case we'll go to trial down the road and we'll do the best we can.'

'I'm not qualified for this,' Helen said.

'Intellectually? That's not what I heard.'

'Tactically and strategically. And financially.'

'There are veterans' associations that can help with the money. Mr Barr served his country, after all. With honour.'

Helen didn't reply to that. Just glanced Reacher's way. Reacher said nothing. He turned away and stared at the wall. He was thinking *this guy is going to get away with murder again? Twice?*

Alan Danuta moved in his chair.

'There is an alternative,' he said. 'Not very exciting legally, but it's out there.'

'What is it?' Helen asked.

'Give your father the puppet master. Under these circumstances, half a loaf is better than none. And the puppet master is the better half anyway.'

'Would he go for it?'

'You know him better than me, presumably. But he'd be a fool not to go for it. He's looking at a minimum three-year appeals process before he even gets Mr Barr inside a courtroom. And any prosecutor worth his salt wants the bigger fish.'

Helen glanced at Reacher again.

'The puppet master is only a theory,' she said. 'We don't have anything that even remotely resembles evidence.'

'Your choice,' Danuta said. 'But one way or the other, you can't let Barr go to trial.'

'One step at a time,' Helen said. 'Let's see what Dr Mason thinks.'

Dr Mason came back twenty minutes later. Reacher watched her walk. The length of her stride and the look in her eyes and the set of her jaw told him she had arrived at a firm conclusion. There was no uncertainty there. No diffidence, no doubt. None at all. She sat back down and smoothed her skirt across her knees.

'Permanent retrograde amnesia,' she said. 'Completely genuine. As clear a case as I ever saw.'

'Duration?' Niebuhr asked.

'Major League baseball will tell us that,' she said. 'The last thing he remembers is a particular Cardinals game. But my bet would be a week or more, counting backwards from today.'

'Which includes Friday,' Helen said.

'I'm afraid so.'

'OK,' Danuta said. 'There it is.'

'Great,' Helen said. She stood up and the others joined her and they all moved round and ended up facing the exit, either consciously or unconsciously, Reacher wasn't sure. But it was clear that Barr was behind them, literally and figuratively. He had changed from being a man to being a medical specimen and a legal argument.

'You guys go on ahead,' he said.

'You're staying here?' Helen asked.

Reacher nodded.

'I'm going to look in on my old buddy,' he said.

'Why?'

'I haven't seen him for fourteen years.'

Helen stepped away from the others and came close.

'No, why?' she asked quietly.

'Don't worry,' he said. 'I'm not going to switch his machines off.'

'I hope you're not.'

'I can't,' he said. 'I don't have much of an alibi, do I?'

She stood still for a moment. Said nothing. Then she stepped back and joined the others. They all left together. Reacher watched them process out at the security desk and as soon as they were through the steel door and in the elevator lobby he turned round and walked down the corridor to James Barr's door. He didn't knock. Just paused a beat and turned the handle and went inside.

SEVEN

The room was overheated. You could have roasted chickens in it. There was a wide window with white venetian blinds closed against the sun. They glowed and filled the room with soft white light. There was medical equipment piled everywhere. A silent respirator, disconnected. IV stands and heart monitors. Tubes and bags and wires.

Barr was flat on his back in a bed in the middle of the room. No pillow. His head was clamped in a brace. His hair was shaved and he had bandages over the holes they had drilled in his skull. His left shoulder was wrapped in bandages that reached to his elbow. His right shoulder was bare and unmarked. The skin there was pale and thin and marbled. His chest and his sides were bandaged. The bed sheet was folded down at his waist. His arms were straight at his sides and his wrists were handcuffed to the cot rails. He had IV needles taped to the back of his left hand. There was a peg on his right middle finger that was connected by a grey wire to a box. There were red wires leading out from under the

198

bandages on his chest. They led to a machine with a screen. The screen was showing a rolling pattern that reminded Reacher of the cellular company's recording of the gunshots. Sharp peaks, and long troughs. The machine made a muted beep every time a peak hit the screen.

'Who's there?' Barr asked.

His voice was weak and rusty, and slow. And scared.

'Who's there?' he asked again. The way his head was clamped limited his field of vision. His eyes were moving, left and right, up and down.

Reacher stepped closer. Leaned over the bed. Said nothing.

'You,' Barr said.

'Me,' Reacher said.

'Why?'

'You know why.'

Barr's right hand trembled. The motion put a ripple in the wire from the peg. The handcuff moved against the bed rail and made a quiet metallic sound.

'I guess I let you down,' he said.

'I guess you did.'

Reacher watched Barr's eyes, because they were the only part of him that could move. He was incapable of body language. His head was immobile and most of the rest of him was trussed up like a mummy.

'I don't remember anything,' Barr said.

'You sure?'

'It's all blank.'

'You clear on what I'll do to you if you're bullshitting me?'

'I can guess.'

'Triple it,' Reacher said.

'I'm not bullshitting,' Barr said. 'I just can't remember anything.' His voice was quiet, help-less, confused. Not a defence, not a complaint. Not an excuse. Just a statement of fact, like a lament, or a plea, or a cry.

'Tell me about the ballgame,' Reacher said.

'It was on the radio.'

'Not the TV?'

'I prefer the radio,' Barr said. 'For old times' sake. That's how it always was. When I was a kid. The radio, all the way from St Louis. All those miles. Summer evenings, warm weather, the sound of baseball on the radio.'

He went quiet.

'You OK?' Reacher said.

'My head hurts real bad. I think I had an oper-ation.'

Reacher said nothing.

'I don't like baseball on the TV,' Barr said.

'I'm not here to discuss your media preferences.'

'Do you watch baseball on TV?'

'I don't have a TV,' Reacher said.

'Really? You should get one. You can get them for a hundred bucks. Maybe less, for a small one. Look in the Yellow Pages.'

'I don't have a phone. Or a house.'

'Why not? You're not still in the army.'

'How would you know?'

'Nobody's still in the army. Not from back then.'

'Some people are,' Reacher said, thinking about Eileen Hutton.

'Officers,' Barr said. 'Nobody else.'

'I *was* an officer,' Reacher said. 'You're supposed to be able to remember stuff like that.'

'But you weren't like the others. That's what I meant.'

'How was I different?'

'You worked for a living.'

'Tell me about the ballgame.'

'Why don't you have a house? Are you doing OK?'

'You worried about me now?'

'Don't like it when folks aren't doing so well.'

'I'm doing fine,' Reacher said. 'Believe me. You're the one with the problem.'

'Are you a cop now? Here? I never saw you around.'

Reacher shook his head. 'I'm just a citizen.'

'From where?'

'From nowhere. Out in the world.'

'Why are you here?'

Reacher didn't answer.

'Oh,' Barr said. 'To nail me.'

'Tell me about the ballgame.'

'It was the Cubs at the Cardinals,' Barr said. 'Close game. Cards won, bottom ninth, walk-off.'

'Home run?'

'No, an error. A walk, a steal, then a groundout to second put the runner on third, one out. Soft grounder to short, check the runner, throw to first, but the throw went in the dugout and the run scored on the error. The winning run, without a hit in the inning.'

'You remember it pretty well.'

'I follow the Cards. I always have.'

201

'When was this?'

'I don't even know what day it is today.'

Reacher said nothing.

'I can't believe that I did what they say,' Barr said. 'Just can't believe it.'

'Plenty of evidencc,' Reacher said.

'For real?'

'No qucstion.'

Barr closed his eyes.

'How many peoplc?' he asked.

'Five.'

Barr's chest started moving. Tears welled out of his closed eyes. His mouth opened in a ragged oval. He was crying, with his head in a vice.

'Why did I do it?' he said.

'Why did you do it the first time?' Reacher said.

'I was crazy then,' Barr said.

Reacher said nothing.

'No excuses,' Barr said. 'I was a different person then. I thought I'd changed. I was sure I *had*. I was good afterwards. I tried real hard. Fourteen years, reformed.'

Reacher said nothing.

'I would have killed myself,' Barr said. 'You know, back then. Afterwards. I came close, a couple of times. I was so ashamed. Except those four guys from KC turned out to be bad. That was my only consolation. I clung on to it, like redemption.'

'Why do you own all those guns?'

'Couldn't give them up. They were reminders. And they keep me straight. Too easy to stay straight without them.'

202

'Do you ever use them?'

'Occasionally. Not often. Now and then.'

'How?'

'At a range.'

'Where? The cops checked.'

'Not here. I go across the line to Kentucky. There's a range there, cheap.'

'You know the plaza downtown?'

'Sure. I live here.'

'Tell me how you did it.'

'I don't remember doing it.'

'So tell me how you *would* do it. Theoretically. Like a recon briefing.'

'What would the targets be?'

'Pedestrians. Coming out of the DMV building.'

Barr closed his eyes again. 'That's who I shot?'

'Five of them,' Reacher said.

Barr started crying again. Reacher moved away and pulled a chair from against a wall. He turned it round and sat down on it, backwards.

'When?' Barr said.

'Friday afternoon.'

Barr stayed quiet for a long time.

'How did they catch me?' he asked.

'You tell the story.'

'Was it a traffic stop?'

'Why would it be?'

'I would have waited until late. Maybe just after five. Plenty of people then. I would have stopped on the highway behind the library. Where it's raised. Sun in the west, behind me, no reflection off the scope. I would have opened the passenger window and lined it all up and emptied

203

the mag and hit the gas again. Only way to get caught would be if a state trooper pulled me over for speeding and saw the rifle. But I think I would have been aware of that. Wouldn't I? I think I would have hidden the rifle and driven slow. Not fast. Why would I have risked standing out?'

Reacher said nothing.

'What?' Barr said. 'Maybe a trooper stopped to help me right there. Was that it? While I was parked? Maybe he thought I had a flat. Or I was out of gas.'

'Do you own a traffic cone?' Reacher asked.

'A what?'

'A traffic cone.'

Barr started to say no, but then he stopped.

'I guess I've *got* one,' he said. 'Not sure if I own it, exactly. I had my driveway blacktopped. They left a cone on the sidewalk to stop people driving on it. I had to leave it there three days. They never came back for it.'

'So what did you do with it?'

'I put it in the garage.'

'Is it still there?'

'I think so. I'm pretty sure.'

'When was this driveway work done?'

'Start of spring, I think. A few months ago.'

'You got receipts?'

Barr tried to shake his head. Winced at the pressure from the clamp.

'It was a gypsy crew,' he said. 'I think they stole the blacktop from the city. Probably from where they were starting to fix First Street. I paid cash, quick and dirty.'

'You got any friends?'

'A few.'

'Who are they?'

'Just guys. One or two.'

'Any new friends?'

'I don't think so.'

'Women?'

'They don't like me.'

'Tell me about the ballgame.'

'I already did.'

'Where were you? In the car? At home?'

'Home,' Barr said. 'I was eating.'

'You remember that?'

Barr blinked. 'The shrink lady said I should try to remember the circumstances. It might bring more stuff back. I was in the kitchen, eating chicken, cold. With potato chips. I remember that. But that's as far as I can get.'

'Drink? Beer, juice, coffee?'

'I don't remember. I just remember listening to the game. I've got a Bose radio. It's in the kitchen. There's a TV in there too, but I always listen to the game, never watch. Like when I was a kid.'

'How did you feel?'

'Feel?'

'Happy? Sad? Normal?'

Barr went quiet again for a moment.

'The shrink lady asked the same question,' he said. 'I told her normal, but actually I think I was feeling happy. Like something good was on the horizon.'

Reacher said nothing.

'I really blew that call, didn't I?' Barr said.

'Tell me about your sister,' Reacher said.

'She was just here. Before the lawyer came in.'

'How do you feel about her?'

'She's all I've got.'

'How far would you go to protect her?'

'I would do anything,' Barr said.

'What kind of anything?'

'I'll plead guilty if they let me. She'll still have to move, maybe change her name. But I'll spare her what I can. She bought me the radio. For the baseball. Birthday gift.'

Reacher said nothing.

'Why are you here?' Barr asked him.

'To bury you.'

'I deserve it.'

'You didn't fire from the highway. You were in the new parking garage.'

'On First Street?'

'North end.'

'That's insane. Why would I fire from there?'

'You asked your first lawyer to find me. On Saturday.'

'Why would I do that? You ought to be the last person I wanted to see. You know about Kuwait City. Why would I want that brought up?'

'What was the Cards' next game?'

'I don't know.'

'Try to remember. I need to understand the circumstances here.'

'I can't remember,' Barr said. 'There's nothing there. I remember that winning run, and that's all. The announcers were going crazy. You know how they are. They were kind of incredulous. I mean, what a stupid way to lose a ballgame. But it's the

Cubs, right? They were saying they always find some way to lose.'

'What about before the game? Earlier that day?'

'I don't remember.'

'What would you normally be doing?'

'Not much. I don't do much.'

'What happened in the Cardinals' previous game?'

'I don't recall.'

'What's the next to last thing you remember?'

'I'm not sure. The driveway?'

'That was months ago.'

'I remember going out somewhere,' Barr said.

'When?'

'Not sure. Recently.'

'Alone?'

'Maybe with people. I'm not sure. Not sure where, either.'

Reacher said nothing. Just leaned back in his chair and listened to the quiet beep from the heart machine. It was running pretty fast. Both handcuffs were rattling.

'What's in the IVs?' Barr asked.

Reacher squinted against the daylight and read the writing on the bags.

'Antibiotics,' he said.

'Not painkillers?'

'No.'

'I guess they think I don't deserve any.'

Reacher said nothing.

'We go way back, right?' Barr said. 'You and me?'

'Not really,' Reacher said.

'Not like we were friends.'

'You got that right.'

'But we were connected.'

Reacher said nothing.

'Weren't we?' Barr asked.

'In a way,' Reacher said.

'So would you do something for me?' Barr asked. 'As a favour?'

'Like what?' Reacher said.

'Pull the IV needles out of my hand.'

'Why?'

'So I can get an infection and die.'

'No,' Reacher said.

'Why not?'

'Not time yet,' Reacher said.

He stood up and put his chair back against the wall and walked out of the room. He processed out at the security desk and passed through the airlock and rode the elevator down to the street. Helen Rodin's car wasn't in the lot. She was already gone. She hadn't waited for him. So he set out walking, all the way from the edge of town.

He picked his way past ten blocks of construction and went to the library first. It was getting late in the afternoon, but the library was still open. The sad woman at the desk told him where the old newspapers were kept. He started with the previous week's stack of the same Indianapolis paper he had read on the bus. He ignored Sunday, Saturday, and Friday. He started with Thursday, Wednesday, and Tuesday, and he got a hit with the second paper he looked at. The Chicago Cubs had played a three-game series in St Louis starting Tuesday. It was the series opener that had ended the way Barr had described. Tie game in the bottom of the ninth, a walk, a steal, a groundout, an error. The details were right there in Wednesday morning's paper. A walk-off winning run without a hit in the inning. About ten in the evening, Tuesday. Barr had heard the announcers' frenzied screams just sixty-seven hours before he opened fire.

Then Reacher backtracked all the way to the police station. Four blocks west, one block south. He wasn't worried about its opening hours. It had looked like a 24/7 kind of a place to him. He went straight to the reception desk and claimed defence counsel's right to another look at the evidence. The desk guy made a call to Emerson and then pointed Reacher straight to Bellantonio's garage bay.

Bellantonio met him there and unlocked the door. Not much had changed, but Reacher noticed a couple of new additions. New sheets of paper, behind plastic, pinned above and below the original pages on the cork boards, like footnotes or addenda or appendices.

'Updates?' he asked.

'Always,' Bellantonio said. 'We never sleep.'

'So what's new?'

'Animal DNA,' Bellantonio said. 'Exact match of Barr's dog's hair to the scene.'

'Where is the dog now?'

'Put to sleep.'

'That's cold.'

'*That's* cold?'

'The damn dog didn't do anything wrong.'

Bellantonio said nothing.

'What else?' Reacher asked.

'More tests on the fibres, and more ballistics. We're beyond definite on everything. The Lake City ammo is relatively rare, and we've confirmed a purchase by Barr less than a year ago. In Kentucky.'

'He used a range down there.'

Bellantonio nodded. 'We found that out, too.'

'Anything else?'

'The traffic cone came from the city's construction department. We don't know how or when.'

'Anything else?'

'I think that's about it.'

'What about the negatives?'

'The negatives?'

'You're giving me all the good news. What about the questions that didn't get answered?'

'I don't think there were any.'

'You sure about that?'

'I'm sure.'

Reacher glanced round the square of cork boards, one more time, and carefully.

'You play poker?' he asked.

'No.'

'Good decision. You're a terrible liar.'

Bellantonio said nothing.

'You should start worrying,' Reacher said. 'He slides, he's going to sue your ass for the dog.'

'He won't slide,' Bellantonio said.

'No,' Reacher said. 'I don't suppose he will.'

*   *   *

210

Emerson was waiting outside Bellantonio's door. Jacket on, tie off. Frustration in his eyes, the way cops get when they're snagged up in lawyer stuff.

'Did you see him?' he asked. 'At the hospital?'

'He's blank from Tuesday night onward,' Reacher said. 'You've got a battle on your hands.'

'Terrific.'

'You should run safer jails.'

'Rodin will bring experts in.'

'His daughter already did.'

'There are legal precedents.'

'They go both ways, apparently.'

'You *want* to see that piece of shit back on the street?'

'Your screw-up,' Reacher said. 'Not mine.'

'As long as you're happy.'

'Nobody's happy,' Reacher said. 'Not yet.'

He left the police station and walked all the way back to the black glass tower. Helen Rodin was at her desk, studying a sheet of paper. Danuta and Mason and Niebuhr had left. She was alone.

'Rosemary asked her brother about Kuwait City,' she said. 'She told me so, when she came out of his room at the hospital.'

'And?' Reacher said.

'He told her it was all true.'

'Not a fun conversation, probably.'

Helen Rodin shook her head. 'Rosemary is pretty devastated. She says James is, too. He can't believe he did it again. Can't believe he threw fourteen years away.'

Reacher said nothing. Silence in the office.

211

Then Helen showed Reacher the sheet of paper she was reading.

'Eileen Hutton is a brigadier general,' she said.

'Then she's done well,' Reacher said. 'She was a major when I knew her.'

'What were you?'

'A captain.'

'Wasn't that illegal?'

'Technically. For her.'

'She was in the JAG Corps.'

'Lawyers can break the law, same as anyone else.'

'She's still in the JAG Corps.'

'Obviously. They don't retrain them.'

'Based in the Pentagon.'

'That's where they keep the smart people.'

'She'll be here tomorrow.'

Reacher said nothing.

'For her deposition,' Helen said.

Reacher said nothing.

'It's scheduled for four o'clock in the afternoon. Chances are she'll fly down in the morning and check in somewhere. Because she'll have to stay the night in town. Too late for a flight back.'

'You going to ask me to take her out for dinner?'

'No,' Helen said. 'I'm not. I'm going to ask you to take her out for lunch. Before she meets with my father. I need to know in advance what she's here for.'

'They put Barr's dog to sleep,' Reacher said.

'It was old.'

'That doesn't bother you?'

'Should it?'

'The dog didn't do anything to anyone.'

Helen said nothing.

'Which hotel will Hutton use?' Reacher asked.

'I have no idea. You'll have to catch her at the airport.'

'What flight?'

'I don't know that either. But there's nothing direct from D.C. So I expect she'll change planes in Indianapolis. She won't get here before eleven in the morning.'

Reacher said nothing.

'I apologize,' Helen said. 'For telling Danuta we didn't have any evidence for the puppet master. I didn't mean it to sound dismissive.'

'You were right,' Reacher said. 'We didn't have any evidence. At the time.'

She looked at him. 'But?'

'We do now.'

'What?'

'They've been gilding the lily over at the police station. They've got fibres, ballistics, dog DNA, a receipt for the ammunition all the way from some place in Kentucky. They traced the traffic cone to the city. They've got all kinds of stuff.'

'But?' Helen said again.

'But they haven't got James Barr on tape driving in to place the cone in the garage beforehand.'

'Are you sure?'

Reacher nodded. 'They must have looked at the tapes a dozen times by now. If they had found him, they'd have printed the stills and pinned them up for the world to see. But they're not there, which means they didn't find them. Which means James Barr didn't drive in and leave the cone beforehand.'

'Which means someone else did.'

'The puppet master,' Reacher said. 'Or another of his puppets. Sometime after Tuesday night. Barr thinks the cone was still in his garage Tuesday.'

Helen looked at him again. 'Whoever it was must be on the tapes.'

'Correct,' Reacher said.

'But there'll be hundreds of cars.'

'You can narrow it down some. You're looking for a sedan. Something too low-slung to get itself down a farm track.'

'The puppet master really exists, doesn't he?'

'No other explanation for how it went down.'

'Alan Danuta is probably right, you know,' Helen said. 'My father will trade Barr for the puppet master. He'd be a fool not to.'

Reacher said nothing.

'Which means Barr is going to walk,' Helen said. 'You understand that, right? There's no alternative. The prosecution's legal problems are overwhelming.'

Reacher said nothing.

'I'm not happy about it either,' Helen said. 'But for me it's just a PR problem. I can spin my way out of it. At least I hope I can. I can blame it all on the way the jail was run. I can claim that it wasn't *me* who got him off.'

'But?' Reacher said.

'What are you going to do? You came here to bury him and he's going to walk.'

'I don't know what I'm going to do,' Reacher said. 'What choices do I have?'

'Only two that I'm scared of. One, you could give up on helping me find the puppet master. I can't do it alone and Emerson won't even be willing to try.'

'And two?'

'You could settle things with Barr yourself.'

'That's for sure.'

'But you can't do that. You'd go to prison for life if you were lucky.'

'If I got caught.'

'You would get caught. I would know you did it.'

Reacher smiled. 'You'd rat me out?'

'I would have to,' Helen said.

'Not if you were my lawyer. You couldn't say a word.'

'I'm not your lawyer.'

'I could hire you.'

'Rosemary Barr would know too, and she'd rat you out in a heartbeat. And Franklin. He heard you tell the story.'

Reacher nodded.

'I don't know what I'm going to do,' he said again.

'How do we find this guy?'

'Like you said, why would I want to?'

'Because I don't think you're the type who settles for half a loaf.'

Reacher said nothing.

'I think you want the truth,' Helen said. 'I don't think you like it when the wool gets pulled over your eyes. You don't like being played for a sucker.'

Reacher said nothing.

'Plus this whole situation stinks,' Helen said. 'There were six victims here. The five who died and Barr himself.'

'That expands the definition of victimhood a little too far for me.'

'Dr Niebuhr expects we'll find a pre-existing relationship. Probably recent. Some new friend. Wc could go at it that way.'

'Barr told me he doesn't have any new friends,' Reacher said. 'Only has one or two old friends.'

'Was he telling the truth?'

'I think he was.'

'So is Niebuhr wrong?'

'Niebuhr's guessing. He's a shrink. All they do is guess.'

'I could ask Rosemary.'

'Would she know his friends?'

'Probably. They're pretty close.'

'So get a list,' Reacher said.

'Is Dr Mason guessing too?'

'No question. But in her case I think she's guessing right.'

'If Niebuhr's wrong about the friend, what do we do?'

'We go proactive.'

'How?'

'There had to have been a guy following me last night and I know for sure there was one following me this morning. I saw him out there in the plaza. So the next time I see him I'll have a word with him. He'll tell me who he's working for.'

'Just like that?'

'People usually tell me what I want to know.'

'Why?'

'Because I ask them nicely.'

'Don't forget to ask Eileen Hutton nicely.'

'I'll see you around,' Reacher said.

He walked south, beyond his hotel, and found a cheap place to eat dinner. Then he walked north, slowly, through the plaza, past the black glass tower, under the highway spur, all the way back to the sports bar. Altogether he was on the street the best part of an hour, and he saw nobody behind him. No damaged men in odd suits. Nobody at all.

The sports bar was half empty and there was baseball on every screen. He found a corner table and watched the Cardinals play the Astros in Houston. It was a listless late-season game between two teams well out of contention. During the commercial breaks he watched the door. Saw nobody. Tuesday was even quieter than Monday, out there in the heartland.

Grigor Linsky dialled his cell.

'He's back in the sports bar,' he said.

'Did he see you?' the Zec asked.

'No.'

'Why is he in the sports bar again?'

'No reason. He needed a destination, that's all. He paraded around for nearly an hour, trying to make me show myself.'

Silence for a beat.

'Leave him there,' the Zec said. 'Come in and we'll talk.'

*   *   *

217

Alex Rodin called Emerson at home. Emerson was eating a late dinner with his wife and his two daughters, and he wasn't thrilled about taking the call. But he did. He went out to the hallway and sat on the second-to-bottom stair, leaning forward, his elbows on his knees, the phone trapped between his shoulder and his ear.

'We need to do something about this Jack Reacher guy,' Rodin said to him.

'I don't see how he's a huge problem,' Emerson said. 'Maybe he wants to, but he can't make the facts go away. We've got more than we need on Barr.'

'This is not about facts now,' Rodin said. 'It's about the amnesia. It's about how hard the defence is going to push it.'

'That's up to your daughter.'

'He's a bad influence on her. I've been reading the case law. It's a real grey area. The test isn't really about whether Barr remembers the day in question. It's about whether he understands the process, right now, today, and whether we've got enough other stuff on him to convict without his direct testimony.'

'I would say we do.'

'Me too. But Helen needs to swallow that. She needs to agree. But she's got that guy standing over her all the time, turning her head. I know her. She's not going to suck it up until he's out of the picture.'

'I don't see what I can do.'

'I want you to bring him in.'

'I can't,' Emerson said. 'Not without a complaint.'

Rodin went quiet.

'Well, keep an eye on him,' he said. 'He spits on the sidewalk, I want you to bring him in and do something to him.'

'This isn't the Wild West,' Emerson said. 'I can't run him out of town.'

'An arrest might be enough. We need something that breaks the spell. He's pushing Helen where she doesn't want to go. I know her. On her own she'll give Barr up, no question.'

Linsky was in pain on the way back to his car. An hour on his feet was about all he could take. A long time ago the bones in his spine had been methodically cracked with an engineer's ball-peen hammer, one after the other, starting with the coccyx and moving upward through all the lower vertebrae, and not in rapid sequence. Generally one bone had been allowed to heal before the next was broken. When the last had healed, they had started over again. Playing the xylophone, they had called it. Playing scales. Ultimately he had lost count of how many scales they had played on him.

But he never spoke of it. Worse had happened to the Zec.

The Cadillac had a soft seat and it was a relief to get in. It had a quiet motor and a gentle ride and a nice radio. Cadillacs were the kind of thing that made America such a wonderful place, along with the trusting population and the hamstrung police departments. Linsky had spent time in several different countries and there was no question in his mind about which was the most satisfactory. Elsewhere he had walked or run or crawled through dirt or hauled carts and sleds by hand. Now he drove a Cadillac.

He drove it to the Zec's house, which stood eight miles north and west of town, next to his stone-crushing plant. The plant was a forty-year-old industrial facility built on a rich limestone seam that had been discovered under farmland. The house was a big fancy palace built a hundred years ago when the landscape was still unspoiled, for a rich dry goods merchant. It was bourgeois and affected in every way, but it was a comfortable house in the same way that the Cadillac was a comfortable car. Best of all it stood alone in the centre of many acres of flat land. Once there had been beautiful gardens, but the Zec had razed the trees and levelled the shrubberies to create a completely flat and open vista all round. There were no fences, because how could the Zec bear to live another day behind wire? For the same reason there were no extra locks, no bolts, no bars. The openness was the Zec's gift to himself. But it was also excellent security in its own right. There were surveillance cameras. Nobody could approach the house undetected. By day visitors were clearly visible at least two hundred yards away and after dark night-vision enhancement picked them up only a little closer.

Linsky parked and eased himself out of the car. The night was quiet. The stone-crushing plant shut down at seven every evening and sat brooding and silent until dawn. Linsky glanced in its direction and walked towards the house. The front door opened before he got near it. Warm light spilled out and he saw that Vladimir himself had come down to welcome him, which meant that Chenko had to be there too, upstairs, which meant that the Zec had assembled all his top boys, which meant that the Zec was worried.

Linsky took a breath, but he walked inside without a moment's hesitation. After all, what could be done to him that hadn't been done to him before? It was different for Vladimir and Chenko, but for men with Linsky's age and experience nothing was entirely unimaginable any more.

Vladimir said nothing. Just closed the door again and followed Linsky upstairs. It was a three-storey house. The ground floor was used for nothing at all, except surveillance. All the rooms were completely empty, except one that had four TV screens on a long table, showing wide-angle views north, east, south and west. Sokolov would be in there, watching them. Or Raskin. They alternated twelve-hour shifts. The second floor of the house had a kitchen, a dining room, a living room, and an office. The third floor had bedrooms and bathrooms. The second floor was where all the business was done. Linsky could hear the Zec's voice from the living room, calling him. He went straight in without knocking. The Zec was in an armchair with a glass of tea clamped between his palms. Chenko was sprawled on a sofa. Vladimir pushed in behind Linsky and sat down next to Chenko. Linsky stood still and waited.

'Sit, Grigor,' the Zec said. 'Nobody's upset at you. It was the boy's failure.'

Linsky nodded and sat down in an armchair, a

little closer to the Zec than Chenko was. That maintained the hierarchy in the proper order. The Zec was eighty, and Linsky himself was more than sixty. Chenko and Vladimir were both in their forties, important men for sure, but comparative youngsters. They didn't have the history that the Zec and Linsky shared. Not even close.

'Tea?' the Zec asked, in Russian.

'Please,' Linsky said.

'Chenko,' the Zec said. 'Bring Grigor a glass of tea.'

Linsky smiled inside. Chenko's being made to serve him tea was a statement of the greatest importance. And he noted that Chenko did it with no unwillingness. He just got up out of his slouch and went out to the kitchen and came back in with a glass of tea on a small silver tray. Chenko was a very small man, short, wiry, no bulk at all. He had coarse black hair that stuck up in all directions, even though he kept it cropped short. Vladimir was different. Vladimir was very tall and heavy and blond. Unbelievably strong. It was entirely possible that Vladimir had German genes somewhere in his background. Perhaps his grandmother had picked them up, back in 1941, like germs.

'We've been talking,' the Zec said.

'And?' Linsky said.

'We have to confront the fact that we made a mistake. Just one, but it could prove irksome.'

'The cone,' Linsky said.

'Obviously Barr isn't on tape placing it,' the Zec said.

'Obviously.'

222

'But will it be a problem?'

'Your opinion?' Linsky asked, politely.

'Significance is in the eye of the beholder,' the Zec said. 'The detective Emerson and the DA Rodin won't care about it. It's a minor detail, one they won't feel inclined to pursue. Why would they? They're not looking to trip themselves up. And no case is ever a hundred per cent perfect. They know that. So they'll write it off as an inexplicable loose end. They might even convince themselves that Barr used a different vehicle.'

'But?'

'But it's still a loose end. If the soldier tugs on it, something might unravel.'

'The evidence against Barr is indisputable.'

The Zec nodded. 'That's true.'

'So won't that be enough for them?'

'Certainly it would have been. But it's possible that Barr no longer exists. Not in the sense that he's a legal entity accessible to their jurisprudence. He has permanent retrograde amnesia. It's possible that Rodin won't be able to put him on trial. If so, Rodin will be very frustrated about that. He'll be expected to seek a consolation prize. And if the consolation prize were eventually to assume a higher profile than Barr himself, how could Rodin turn it down?'

Linsky sipped his tea. It was hot and sweet.

'All this from a videotape?' he said.

'It depends entirely on the soldier,' the Zec said. 'It depends on his tenacity and his imagination.'

'He was a military cop,' Chenko said, in English. 'Did you know that?'

223

Linsky glanced at Chenko. Chenko rarely spoke English in the house. He had a perfect American accent, and sometimes Linsky thought he was ashamed of it.

'That doesn't necessarily impress me,' Linsky said, in Russian.

'Or me,' the Zec said. 'But it's a factor we must weigh in the balance.'

'Silencing him now would draw attention,' Linsky said. 'Wouldn't it?'

'It would depend on how it was done.'

'How many ways are there?'

'We could use the redheaded girl again,' the Zec said.

'She would be no use against the soldier. He's a giant, and almost certainly extensively trained in self-defence.'

'But he already has an established issue with her. Several people know she tried to set him up for a beating. Perhaps she could be found severely injured. If she was, the soldier would be the obvious prime suspect. We could let the police department silence him for us.'

'She would know who attacked her,' Vladimir said. 'She would know it wasn't the soldier.'

The Zec nodded appreciatively. Linsky watched him. He was accustomed to the Zec's methods. The Zec liked to tease solutions out of people, like Socrates of old.

'Then perhaps she should be left unable to tell anyone anything,' the Zec said.

'Dead?'

'We've always found that the safest way, haven't we?'

'But it's possible she has many enemies,' Vladimir said. 'Not just him. Maybe she's a big time prick-teaser.'

'Then we should firm up the link. Possibly she should be found somewhere suggestive. Maybe he invited her out to renew their acquaintance.'

'In his hotel?'

'No, outside his hotel, I think. But close by. Where she can be discovered by someone other than the soldier himself. Someone who can call the police while the soldier is still asleep. That way he's a sitting duck.'

'Why would her body be outside his hotel?'

'Evidently he hit her and she staggered away and collapsed before she got very far.'

'The Metropole Palace,' Linsky said. 'That's where he is.'

'When?' Chenko asked.

'Whenever you like,' the Zec said.

The Astros beat the Cardinals 10–7 after a limp defensive performance by both franchises. Plenty of cheap hits, plenty of errors. A bad way to win, and a worse way to lose. Reacher had stopped paying attention halfway through. He had started thinking about Eileen Hutton instead. She was part of his mosaic. He had seen her once in the States before the Gulf, just briefly across a crowded courtroom, just long enough to register her head-turning quality, and he had assumed he would never see her again, which he figured was a pity. But then she had shown up in Saudi as part of the long ponderous Desert Shield build-up. Reacher had been there pretty much from the

225

start, as a recently demoted captain. The first stage of any clean-sheet foreign deployment always resembled gang warfare between the MPs and the troops they were sent out with, but after six weeks or so the situation usually settled down some, and Desert Shield wasn't any different. After six weeks there was a structure in place, and in terms of military law enforcement a structure demanded in-country personnel all the way up from jailers to judges, and Hutton had shown up as one of the prosecutors they shipped in. Reacher had assumed it was volunteer duty for her, which he was happy about, because that made it likely she was unmarried.

She was unmarried. First time their paths crossed, he checked her left hand and saw no ring. Then he checked her collar and saw a major's oak leaves. That would make it a challenge, he figured, for a recently demoted captain. Then he checked her eyes and saw that the challenge would be worth it. Her eyes were blue and full of intelligence and mischief. And promise, he figured. And adventure. He had just turned thirty-one years old, and he was up for anything.

The desert heat helped. Most of the time the temperature was above a hundred and twenty degrees and apart from regular gas-attack practices standard on-post dress devolved down to shorts and sleeveless undershirts. And in Reacher's experience the close proximity of hot and nearly naked men and women always led somewhere good. Better than serving out November in Minnesota, that was for damn sure.

The initial approach had promised to be tricky,

given the disparity in rank. And when it came to it he fumbled it slightly, and was saved only because she was just as up for it as he was, and wasn't afraid to let it show. After that it had been as smooth as silk, three long months. Good times. Then new orders had come through, like they always did eventually. He hadn't even said goodbye to her. Didn't get the chance. Never saw her again, either.

I'll see her again tomorrow, he thought.

He stayed in the bar until ESPN started recycling the highlights it had already shown once. Then he settled up his tab and stepped out to the sidewalk, into the yellow glare of the street lights. He decided he wouldn't go back to the Metropole Palace. He decided it was time for a change. No real reason. Just his normal restless instinct. *Keep moving. Never stay in one place too long.* And the Metropole was a gloomy old pile. Unpleasant, even by his undemanding standards. He decided to try the motor court instead. The one he had seen on his way to the auto parts store. The one next to the barbershop. *Any Style $7.* Maybe he could get a haircut before Hutton blew into town.

Chenko left the Zec's house at midnight. He took Vladimir with him. If the redhead was to be beaten to death, then Vladimir would have to do it. It had to look right, forensically. Chenko was too small to inflict the kind of battering that an enraged six foot five, two hundred and fifty pound ex-soldier might be provoked to. But Vladimir was a different matter. Vladimir might well be able to do the job with a single blow, which might be convincing on the postmortem slab. A refusal, an objection, a sexual taunt, a big man might lash out once in frustration, a little harder than he intended.

They were both familiar with the girl. They had met her before, because of her connection to Jeb Oliver. They had even all worked together once. They knew where she lived, which was in a rented garden apartment that nestled on a barren patch of land in the shadow of the state highway, where it first rose on its stilts, south and west of downtown. And they knew that she lived there alone.

Reacher walked a long aimless three-block circle before approaching the motor court. He kept his own footsteps light and listened hard for the gritty crunch of a shadow behind him. He heard nothing. Saw nothing. He was alone.

The motor court was practically an antique. At one time it must have been the latest thing and consequently fairly upmarket. But since then the relentless march of time and fashion had left it behind. It was well maintained but not updated. It was exactly the kind of place he liked.

He roused the clerk and paid cash for one night only. He used the name Don Heffner, who had played second base and hit .261 during the Yankees' lean year of 1934. The clerk gave him a big brass key and pointed him down the row to room number eight. The room was faded and a little damp. The counterpane on the bed and the drapes at the window looked original. So did the bathroom. But everything worked and the door locked tight.

He took a short shower and folded his pants and his shirt very carefully and put them flat under the mattress. That was as close as ever he got to ironing. They would look OK in the morning. He would shave and shower very carefully and go to the barbershop after breakfast. He didn't want to devalue whatever memories Hutton might have retained. Assuming she had retained any at all.

Chenko parked east of the highway and he and Vladimir walked under it and approached the girl's apartment building from the back, unseen. They kept close to the wall and walked round to her door. Chenko told Vladimir to keep out of sight. Then he knocked gently. There was no response, which wasn't entirely unexpected. It was late, and she was probably already in bed. So Chenko knocked again, a little louder. And again, as loud as he dared. He saw a light come on in a window. Heard the quiet shuffle of feet inside. Heard her voice, through the crack where the door met the jamb.

'Who's there?' she asked.

'It's me,' he said.

'What do you want?'

'We need to talk.'

'I was asleep.'

'I'm sorry.'

'It's awful late.'

'I know,' Chenko said. 'But it's very urgent.'

There was a pause.

'Wait a minute,' she said.

Chenko heard her shuffle back towards her bedroom. Then silence. Then she came back. The door opened. She was standing there, clutching a robe around her.

'What?' she said.

'You need to come with us,' Chenko said.

Vladimir stepped out of the shadow.

'Why is *he* here?' Sandy asked.

'He's helping me tonight,' Chenko said.

'What do you want?'

'You need to go out.'

'Like this? I can't.'

'I agree,' Chenko said. 'You need to get dressed. Like for a date.'

'A date?'

'You need to look really good.'

'But I'll have to shower. Do my hair.'

'We have time.'

'A date with who?'

'You just have to be seen. Like you were ready for a date.'

'At this time of night? The whole town is asleep.'

'Not the whole town. We're awake, for instance.'

'How much do I get?'

'Two hundred,' Chenko said. 'Because it's so late.'

'How long will it take?'

'Just a minute. You just have to be seen walking somewhere.'

'I don't know.'

'Two hundred for a minute's work isn't bad.'

'It isn't a minute's work. It'll take me an hour to get ready.'

230

'Two-fifty, then,' Chenko said.
'OK,' Sandy said.

Chenko and Vladimir waited in her living room, listening through the thin walls, hearing the shower running, hearing the hair dryer, the held breaths as she put on her make-up, the elastic snap of undergarments, the whisper of fabric on skin. Chenko saw that Vladimir was restless and sweating. Not because of the task ahead. But because there was a woman in a state of undress in a nearby room. Vladimir was unreliable, in certain situations. Chenko was glad he was there to supervise. If he hadn't been, the plan would have derailed for sure.

Sandy walked into the living room after an hour looking, as the Americans would say, like a million dollars. She was wearing a filmy black blouse that was nearly transparent. Underneath it was a black bra that moulded her breasts into twin mounds of implausible roundness. She had on tight black pants that ended just below the knee. Pedal pushers? Capri pants? Chenko wasn't sure of the name. She was wearing black high-heeled shoes. With her pale skin and her red hair and her green eyes she looked like a picture in a magazine.

Pity, Chenko thought.

'My money?' Sandy asked.

'Afterwards,' Chenko said. 'When we bring you back.'

'Let me see it.'

'It's in the car.'

'So let's go look at it,' Sandy said.

231

They walked in single file. Chenko led the way. Sandy came next. Vladimir brought up the rear. They walked under the highway. The car was right there ahead of them. It was cold and misted over. There was no money in it. None at all. Chenko knew that. So he stopped six feet short and turned around. Nodded to Vladimir.

'Now,' he said.

Vladimir reached forward with his right hand and put it on Sandy's right shoulder from behind. He used it to turn her upper body sideways and then he crashed his left fist into her right temple, a little above and in front of her ear. It was a colossal blow. Explosive. Her head snapped violently sideways and round and her legs gave way and she fell to the ground vertically like an empty suit of clothes slipping off a hanger.

Chenko squatted down next to her. Waited a moment for the body to settle and then felt the neck for a pulse. There wasn't one.

'You broke her neck,' he said.

Vladimir nodded.

'It's about placement,' he said. 'The main vector is mostly sideways, obviously, but you try for a little rotation, too. So it's not so much a break. It's more like a wrenching action. Like a hangman's noose.'

'Is your hand OK?'

'It will be tender tomorrow.'

'Good work.'

'I try my best.'

They unlocked the car and raised the rear armrest and laid the body across the back seat. There was just enough space, side to side. She

232

had been a small girl. Not tall. Then they got in the front together and drove off. They looped well to the east and came up on the Metropole Palace from behind. They avoided the bay where the garbage was piled and found a side alley. They stopped outside a fire exit. Vladimir slid out and opened the rear door. Pulled the body out by the shoulders and left it where it fell. Then he got back in. Chenko drove on and paused after five yards and turned in his seat. The body was lying in a heap against the alley's far wall. Directly opposite the fire door. It looked like a plausible scenario. She had fled the soldier's room in shame and panic, chosen not to wait for the elevator, and run down the fire stairs and out into the night. Maybe she had stumbled at that point and aggravated an injury already done to her. Maybe she had tripped and fallen against the wall, and the shock had dislodged an already wrenched vertebra.

Chenko turned back and faced front and drove on, not fast, not slow, not drawing attention, not standing out, eight miles north and west, all the way back to the Zec's house.

EIGHT

Reacher woke himself up at seven in the morning and went out to check for a tail and to look for a drugstore. He walked a zigzag half-mile and saw nobody behind him. He found a drugstore two blocks east of the motor court and bought black coffee in a cardboard cup, a pack of throwaway razors, a can of shaving foam, and a new tube of toothpaste. He carried his purchases back by a roundabout route and put his clothes back under the mattress and sat on the bed and drank the coffee. Then he showered and shaved, using his full twenty-two minute routine. He washed his hair twice. Then he dressed again and went out for breakfast to the only place he could find, which was the drive-through he had seen the day before. It had a small counter inside. He had more coffee and an English muffin filled with a round piece of ham and something that might have once been egg, first dried and powdered and then reconstituted. His threshold of culinary acceptability was very low, but right then he felt he might be pushing at the bottom edge of his personal envelope.

He followed the muffin with a piece of lemon pie, for a sugar hit. It was better than the muffin, so he had a second piece, with a second cup of coffee. Then he walked south to the barbershop. He pulled the door and sat down in the chair at eight thirty exactly.

By which time the homicide investigation outside the Metropole Palace was already three hours old. The body in the alley had been discovered at half past five in the morning by a cleaner coming in to work. The cleaner was a middle-aged man from Honduras. He didn't touch the body. Didn't check for vital signs. The way it was lying there told him all he needed to know. The slack emptiness of death is recognizable anywhere. The guy just rushed inside and told the night porter. Then he went home again, because he had no green card and didn't want to be around a police investigation. The night porter dialled 911 from the desk phone and then went out through the fire door to take a look. Came back inside thirty seconds later, not having enjoyed it.

Two patrol cars and an ambulance showed up within eight minutes. Paramedics confirmed the DOA and the ambulance went away again. The patrolmen blocked off the alley and the fire exit and then took a statement from the night porter. He said he had stepped out for some air and discovered the body himself, to protect the illegal from Honduras. It was close to true. Certainly the patrolmen had no reason to doubt his word. They just stood back and waited for Emerson.

Emerson got there by six twenty-five. He

brought his number two, a woman called Donna Bianca, and the city ME, and Bellantonio himself to run the crime scene. Technical work occupied the first thirty minutes. Measurement, photography, the accumulation of trace evidence. Then Emerson got the OK and stepped close to the body and ran into his first major problem. The girl had no purse and no ID. Nobody had the slightest idea who she was.

Ann Yanni showed up behind the Metropole at seven fifteen. She had an NBC crew with her, consisting of a cameraman and a sound guy with a microphone on a long boom. The microphone had a grey fur windsock on it and the boom was ten feet long. The guy put his hips against the police tape and extended his arms as far as he could and heard Emerson's voice in his headphones. Emerson was talking to Bianca about prostitution.

The ME had checked the girl's arms and thighs and between her toes and found no needle tracks. So she hadn't been there to score. So maybe she was hooking. Who else would come out the side door of a downtown hotel in the middle of the night, dressed like that? She was young and she still had her looks. Therefore she wouldn't have been cheap. Therefore she would have been carrying a big purse full of twenties that had just come out of some businessman's ATM. She had run into somebody waiting for her. Either somebody waiting for her specifically, or somebody waiting on the off chance for someone like her. Whoever, he had snatched her purse and hit her in the head, a little harder than necessary.

A nineteen- or twenty-year-old who wasn't an addict wouldn't necessarily have been finger-printed, unless she had a vice conviction somewhere. Emerson wasn't willing to count on that, therefore he didn't expect to discover her identity through the databases. He expected to discover it inside the hotel, either from the night porter who had pimped her in and out, or through the john who had called her.

'Nobody leaves,' he said to Bianca. 'We'll talk to all the guests and all the staff one by one. So find a room somewhere. And tell all units to be on the lookout for a guy with more new twenties than he should have.'

'A big guy,' Bianca said.

Emerson nodded. 'A real big guy. That was some punch.'

The ME took the body away to the morgue and Donna Bianca commandeered the hotel bar and the interviews were two-thirds through by eight thirty in the morning.

The barber was a competent old guy who had probably been cutting the same style for close to fifty years. He went for what the military would have called a whitewall. He left an inch and a half on the top and used his clippers to shave the bottom and the sides up towards it. Then he flipped the clippers over and squared off the side-burns and cleaned the fuzz off the neck. It was a style Reacher was familiar with. He had worn it most of his life, except for periods when he had been too lazy to care, and a couple of six-month stretches when he had favoured an all-over number-one buzz cut.

The barber did the thing with the hand mirror, to show Reacher the back.

'Happy?' he asked.

Reacher nodded. It looked OK, except that there was a half-inch margin all round where his skin was dead white. He had had longer hair in Miami and the tan hadn't penetrated. The barber brushed the clippings off his collar and removed the towel. Reacher gave him his seven bucks and tipped him a dollar. Then he walked round the block. Nobody followed him. He unlocked his room and washed his face and shaved under his sideburns again. There was a new half-inch of stubble there. The barber's clippers had been a little blunt.

The Metropole interviews were finished by nine twenty and they gave Emerson absolutely nothing at all. The night porter swore blind that he knew nothing about the girl. There were only eleven guests and none of them was promising. Emerson was an experienced and talented detective and he knew that people sometimes tell the truth. And he knew that accepting the truth was as important a part of a detective's professional arsenal as rejecting lies. So he conferred with Donna Bianca and together they concluded they had just wasted the best part of three hours on a faulty hunch.

Then a guy named Gary called, from the auto parts store.

*   *   *

238

Gary had got to work at eight and had found himself *really* short-staffed. There was still no sign of Jeb Oliver and Sandy didn't show, either. At first he had been annoyed. He had called her apartment and got no reply. *On her way*, he had assumed. *Late*. But she never showed. Thereafter he called every thirty minutes. By nine thirty the annoyance had given way to worry and he started thinking about auto wrecks. So he called the cops for information. The desk guy told him there had been no traffic accidents that morning. Then there was a pregnant pause and the desk guy seemed to consider another possibility and asked for a name and a description. Gary said Alexandra Dupree, known as Sandy, nineteen years old, white, petite, green and red. Ten seconds after that Gary was speaking to a detective called Emerson on a cell phone.

Gary agreed to close the store for the day and Emerson sent a patrol car to pick him up. First stop was the morgue. Gary identified the body and was white and badly shaken when he arrived in Emerson's office. Donna Bianca calmed him down and Emerson watched him carefully. Statistics show that women get killed by husbands, boyfriends, brothers, employers, and workmates, in descending order of likelihood, well before passing strangers show up on the list of possible suspects. And sometimes a boyfriend and a workmate can be the same guy. But Emerson knew that Gary was in the clear. He was too shaken. No way could a person fake that kind of sudden shock and surprise over something he had already known about for eight or ten hours.

So Emerson started in, gently, with all the usual cop questions. Last time you saw her? Know anything about her private life? Family? Boyfriends? Ex-boyfriends? Weird phone calls? Did she have any enemies? Problems? Money troubles?

And then, inevitably: Anything unusual over the last couple of days?

And so by ten fifteen Emerson knew all about the stranger who had come to the store the day before. Very tall, heavily built, tan, aggressive, demanding, wearing olive green pants and an olive green flannel shirt. He had spent two mysterious sessions with Sandy in the back office, and had borrowed her car, and had demanded Jeb Oliver's address with menaces, and Jeb Oliver was missing, too.

Emerson left Gary with Donna Bianca and went out to the corridor and used his cell to call Alex Rodin in his office.

'Your lucky day,' he said. 'We've got a nine-teen-year-old female homicide victim. Someone broke her neck.'

'How does that make me lucky?'

'Her last unexplained contact was yesterday, at her place of work, with a guy that sounds a whole lot like our pal Jack Reacher.'

'Really?'

'We got a pretty good description from her boss. And her neck was busted by a single blow to the side of the head, which ain't easy unless you're built like Reacher is.'

240

'Who was the girl?'

'A redhead from the auto parts store out towards the highway. There's also a boy missing from the same store.'

'Where did this thing happen?'

'Outside the Metropole Palace Hotel.'

'Is that where Reacher is staying?'

'Not according to the register.'

'So is he a suspect or not?'

'Right now he looks pretty damn good for it.'

'So when are you going to bring him in?'

'As soon as I find him.'

'I'll call Helen,' Alex Rodin said. 'She'll know where he is.'

Rodin lied to his daughter. He told her that Bellantonio needed to see Reacher to correct a possible misunderstanding about part of the prosecution's evidence.

'What part?' Helen asked.

'Just something they discussed. Probably nothing important, but I'm playing this very cautiously. Don't want to hand you grounds for an appeal.'

The traffic cone, Helen thought.

'He's on his way to the airport,' she said.

'Why?'

'To say hello to Eileen Hutton.'

'They know each other?'

'Apparently.'

'That's unethical.'

'To know each other?'

'To influence her testimony.'

'I'm sure he won't do that.'

'When will he be back?'

'After lunch, I think.'

'OK,' Rodin said. 'It'll keep.'

But it didn't keep, of course. Emerson left for the airport immediately. He had met Reacher twice face to face and could pick him out of a crowd. Donna Bianca went with him. They went in together through a restricted area and found a security office that looked out over the whole arrivals hall through one-way glass. They scanned the waiting faces carefully. No sign of Reacher. *Not here yet*. So they settled down to wait.

NINE

Reacher didn't go to the airport. He knew better. Senior military personnel spend a lot of time flying small aircraft, either fixed wing or rotary, and they don't like it. Outside of combat more military personnel die in plane crashes than from any other single cause. Therefore given a choice a smart brigadier general like Eileen Hutton wouldn't ride a puddle jumper down from Indianapolis. She would be happy enough with a big jet out of Washington National, but she wouldn't contemplate a twin-prop for the final leg of her journey. No way. She would rent a car instead.

So Reacher walked south and east to the library. Asked the subdued woman at the desk where the Yellow Pages were stored. He went where she pointed and hauled the book out onto a table. Opened it to *H* for Hotels. Started looking. Almost certainly some JAG Corps office grunt had done the equivalent thing the previous day, but remotely, probably on-line. Hutton would have told him to book her a room. He would have been anxious to please, so he would have turned first to the street map and found the courthouse and the road in from the north. Then he would have chosen a decent place convenient for both. Somewhere with parking, for the rental car. Probably a chain, with an established government rate accessible by a code number.

The Marriott Suites, Reacher thought. *That's where she'll be headed.* Off the highway, south towards town, an obvious left turn east, and there it was, three blocks north of the courthouse, an easy walk, breakfast included. The office grunt had probably printed out driving directions from the Internet and clipped them to her itinerary. Anxious to please. Hutton had that effect on people.

He memorized the Marriott's number and put the book away. Then he walked out to the lobby and dialled the pay phone.

'I want to confirm a reservation,' he said.

'Name?'

'Hutton.'

'Yes, we've got that. Tonight only, a suite.'

'Thank you,' Reacher said, and put the phone down.

She would take an early flight out of D.C. After two decades in uniform she would be up at five, in a cab at six, boarding at seven. She would be in Indianapolis by nine, latest. Out of the Hertz lot by nine thirty. It was a two and a half hour drive. She would arrive at noon. In about an hour.

He stepped out of the lobby and looped through the plaza and headed north and east through a thin crowd of people, past the far side of the recruiting office, past the back of the court-house. He found the Marriott easily enough and took a corner table in its coffee shop and settled down to wait.

Helen Rodin called Rosemary Barr at work. She wasn't there. The receptionist sounded a little embarrassed about it. So Helen tried Rosemary's home number, and got her after the second ring.

'Did they let you go?' she asked.

'Unpaid leave,' Rosemary said. 'I volunteered for it. Everyone was acting awkward around me.'

'That's awful.'

'It's human nature. I need to make a plan. I might have to move.'

'I need a list of your brother's friends,' Helen said.

'He doesn't have any. The true test of friend-ship is adversity, isn't it? And nobody's visited him. Nobody's even tried. Nobody's called me to ask how he is.'

'I meant before,' Helen said. 'I need to know who he saw, who he hung out with, who knew him well. Especially anyone new.'

'There wasn't anyone new,' Rosemary said. 'Not that I'm aware of.'

'Are you sure?'

'Pretty sure.'

'What about old?'

'Have you got a big piece of paper?'

'I've got a whole yellow pad.'

'Well, you aren't going to need it. A match-book cover would do it. James is a very self-sufficient person.'

'He must have buddies.'

'A couple, I guess,' Rosemary said. 'There's a guy called Mike from the neighbourhood. They talk about lawns and baseball, you know, guy stuff.'

Mike, Helen wrote. *Guy stuff*. 'Anyone else?'

There was a long pause.

'Someone called Charlie,' Rosemary said.

'Tell me about Charlie,' Helen said.

'I don't know much about him. I never really met him.'

'How long has James known him?'

'Years.'

'Including the time you lived there?'

'He never came around when I was in. I only ever saw him once. He was leaving as I was coming in. I said, who was that? James said, that was Charlie, like he was an old pal.'

'What does he look like?'

'He's small. He's got weird hair. Like a black toilet brush.'

'Is he local?'

'I guess so.'

'What was their point of contact?'

Another long pause.

'Guns,' Rosemary said. 'They shared an interest.'

Charlie, Helen wrote. *Guns*.

Donna Bianca spent some time on her cell phone and mapped out the flight schedules between D.C. and Indianapolis. She knew the onward connecting flights then left on the hour and took thirty-five minutes. She figured a person with a

246

courthouse appointment at four o'clock wouldn't aim to arrive on anything later than the two thirty-five. Which meant leaving Indianapolis at two, which meant getting in there at about one thirty, latest, to allow for the walk between gates. Which meant leaving Washington National at eleven thirty or twelve, latest. Which wasn't possible. The last direct flight from National to Indianapolis was at nine thirty. There was a morning cluster and an evening cluster. Nothing in between.

'She'll come in on the twelve thirty-five,' she said.

Emerson checked his watch. *Quarter to twelve.*

'Which means Reacher will be here soon,' he said.

At ten to twelve a courier arrived at Helen Rodin's building with six large cardboard cartons containing the defence's copies of the prosecution's evidence. The discovery process, mandated by the rules of due process. By the Bill of Rights, as interpreted. The courier called from the lobby and Helen told him to come on up. He had to make two trips with his hand cart. He stacked the boxes in the empty secretarial pen. Helen signed for them and he left. Then she opened them. There was a mass of paperwork and dozens of photographs. And eleven new VHS cassettes. They had labels with numbers neatly printed on them that referred to a notarized sheet that described them as faithful and complete copies of the parking garage's security tapes, made by an independent third-party contractor. Helen took them all out and stacked them separately. She would have to take them home and use her own VCR to look at them. She didn't have a VCR in the office. Or a television set.

There was a television set in the Marriott's coffee shop. It was mounted high in the corner, on a black articulated bracket bolted to the wall. The sound was off. Reacher watched an advertisement that featured a young woman in a filmy summer dress romping through a field of wild flowers. He wasn't sure what product was being advertised. The dress, maybe, or make-up, or shampoo, or allergy medicine. Then a news banner popped up. *Noon Report*. Reacher checked his watch. Twelve exactly. He glanced towards the reception desk in the lobby. He had a clear view. No sign of Hutton. Not yet. So he glanced back at the television. Ann Yanni was on. She seemed to be live on location, downtown, out on the street. *In front of the Metropole Palace Hotel*. She talked silently but earnestly for a moment and then the picture cut to tape of dawn twilight. An alley. Police barriers. A shapeless form under a white sheet. Then the picture cut again. To a driver's licence photograph. Pale skin. Green eyes. Red hair. Just under the chin a caption was superimposed: Alexandra Dupree.
Alexandra. Sandy.
Now they've gone too far, Reacher thought.
He shivered.
Way too far.
He stared at the screen. Sandy's face was still there. Then the picture cut again, back to tape of the early hours, to a head-and-shoulders shot

248

of Emerson. A recorded interview. Yanni had her microphone shoved up under Emerson's nose. He was talking. Yanni pulled the microphone back and asked a question. Emerson talked some more. His eyes were flat and empty and tired and hooded against the bright light on the camera. Even without the sound Reacher knew what he was saying. He was promising a full and complete investigation. *We'll get this guy*, he was saying.

'I saw you from the desk,' a voice said.

Then it said, 'And I thought to myself, don't I know that guy?'

Reacher looked away from the TV.

Eileen Hutton was standing right there in front of him.

Her hair was shorter. She had no tan. There were fine lines around her eyes. But otherwise she looked just the same as she had fourteen years ago. And just as good. Medium height, slim, poised. Groomed. Fragrant. Feminine as hell. She hadn't put on a pound. She was wearing civvies. Khaki chino pants, a white T, a blue oxford shirt open over it. Penny loafers, no socks, no make-up, no jewellery.

No wedding band.

'Remember me?' she said.

Reacher nodded.

'Hello, Hutton,' he said. 'I remember you. Of course I do. And it's good to see you again.'

She had a purse and a key card in her hand. A rolling carry-on with a long handle at her feet.

'It's good to see you again too,' she said. 'But please tell me it's a coincidence that you're here. Please tell me that.'

249

Feminine as hell, except she was still a woman in a man's world, and you could still see the steel if you knew where to look. Which was into her eyes. They ran like a stock ticker, warm, warm, welcome, welcome, with a periodic bright flash: *Mess with me and I'll rip your lungs out.*

'Sit down,' Reacher said. 'Let's have lunch.'

'Lunch?'

'It's what people do at lunch time.'

'You were expecting me. You've been waiting for me.'

Reacher nodded. Glanced back up at the TV set. Sandy's driver's licence picture was on the screen again. Hutton followed his gaze.

'Is that the dead girl?' she asked. 'I heard it on the radio, driving down. Sounds like a person should get combat pay, coming here.'

'What did the radio say? There's no sound in here.'

'Homicide. Late last night. Local girl got her neck broken. A single blow to the right temple. In an alley outside a hotel. Not this one, I hope.'

'No,' Reacher said. 'It wasn't this one.'

'Brutal.'

'I guess it was.'

Eileen Hutton sat down at the table. Not across from him. In the chair next to him. Just like Sandy, at the sports bar.

'You look great,' he said. 'You really do.'

She said nothing.

'It's good to see you,' he said again.

'Likewise,' she said.

'No, I mean it.'

'I mean it too. Believe me, if we were at some

250

Beltway cocktail party I would be getting all misty and nostalgic with the best of them. I might still, as soon as I find out you're not here for the reason I think you're here.'

'What reason would that be?'

'To keep your promise.'

'You remember that?'

'Of course I do. You talked about it all one night.'

'And you're here because the Department of the Army got a subpoena.'

Hutton nodded. 'From some idiot prosecutor.'

'Rodin,' Reacher said.

'That's the guy.'

'My fault,' Reacher said.

'Christ,' Hutton said. 'What did you tell him?'

'Nothing,' Reacher said. 'I didn't tell him anything. But he told me something. He told me my name was on the defence's witness list.'

'The *defence* list?'

Reacher nodded. 'That surprised me, obviously. So I was confused. So I asked him if my name had come from some old Pentagon file.'

'Not in this lifetime,' Hutton said.

'As I found out,' Reacher said. 'But still, I had said the magic words. I had mentioned the Pentagon. The type of guy he is, I knew he would go fishing. He's very insecure. He likes his cases armour-plated. So I'm sorry.'

'You should be. I get to spend two days in the back of beyond and I get to perjure myself from here to breakfast time.'

'You don't need to do that. You can claim national security.'

Hutton shook her head. 'We talked about it,

251

long and hard. We decided to stay away from anything that draws attention. That Palestinian thing was very thin. If that unravels, everything unravels. So I'm here to swear blind that James Barr was GI Joe.'

'You OK with that?'

'You know the army. None of us is a virgin any more. It's about the mission, and the mission is to keep a lid on the KC thing.'

'Why did they delegate you?'

'Two birds with one stone. No good to them to send someone else and still have me out there knowing the truth. This way, I can't talk about it ever again, anywhere. Not without effectively confessing to perjury one time in Indiana. They're not dumb.'

'I'm surprised they still care. It's practically ancient history.'

'How long have you been out?'

'Seven years.'

'And clearly you don't have a subscription to the *Army Times*.'

'What?'

'Or maybe you never knew.'

'Never knew what?'

'Where it went back then, up the chain of command.'

'Division, I supposed. But maybe not all the way to the top.'

'It stopped on a certain colonel's desk. He was the one who nixed it.'

'And?'

'His name was Petersen.'

'And?'

'Colonel Petersen is now Lieutenant General Petersen. Three stars. Congressional liaison. About to get his fourth star. About to be named Vice Chief of Staff of the Army.'

That could complicate things, Reacher thought.

'Embarrassing,' he said.

'You bet your ass embarrassing,' Hutton said. 'So believe me, this is one lid that is going to stay on. You need to bear that in mind. Whatever you want to do about your promise, you can't talk about what happened. Any more than I can. They would find a way to get to you.'

'Neither of us needs to talk about it. It's a done deal.'

'I'm very glad to hear it.'

'I think.'

'You think?'

'Ask me how they really got my name.'

'How did they really get your name?'

'From James Barr himself.'

'I don't believe it.'

'I didn't believe it either. But I do now.'

'Why?'

'We should have lunch. We really need to talk. Because I think there's someone else out there who knows.'

Emerson and Bianca called it quits at twelve fifty. Reacher never showed. The feeder flight came in on time. Nobody who could have been a female brigadier general from the Pentagon got off. They waited until the arrivals hall emptied out and went quiet. Then they got in their car and drove back to town.

253

Reacher and Hutton had lunch. A waitress came over, happy to get some business out of her corner table at last. The menu was coffee-shop basic. Reacher ordered a grilled cheese sandwich and coffee. Hutton went with chicken Caesar and tea. They ate and talked. Reacher ran through the details of the case. Then he ran through his theory. The perverse choice of location, the presumed coercion. He told Hutton about Niebuhr's theory of the new and persuasive friend. Told her that Barr claimed he had no new friends, and very few old ones.

'Can't be a new friend anyway,' Hutton said. 'Because this is a multi-layered set-up. There's the contemporaneous evidence, and the historical parallels. Second level of a parking garage fourteen years ago in KC, second level of a parking garage here and now. Virtually the same rifle. Boat tail sniper ammunition. And the desert boots. I never saw them before Desert Shield. They're suggestive. Whoever scripted this for him knew all about his past. Which means it isn't a new friend. It can't be. It would take years and years before Barr would feel like sharing anything about KC.'

Reacher nodded. 'But obviously he did, eventually. Which is why I said there's someone else out there who knows.'

'We need to find that person,' Hutton said. 'The mission is to keep the lid on this thing.'

'Not my mission. I don't care if this Petersen guy gets his fourth star.'

'But you do care that a quarter-million veterans

don't get their reputations trashed. The scandal would taint all of them. And they were good people.'

Reacher said nothing.

'It's easy enough,' Hutton said. 'If James Barr doesn't have many friends, you don't have a very big pool to search through. One of them has to be the guy.'

Reacher said nothing.

'Two birds with one stone,' Hutton said. 'You get to the puppet master and the army gets to relax.'

'So why doesn't the army do it for me?'

'We can't afford to draw attention.'

'I've got operational problems,' Reacher said.

'No jurisdiction?'

'Worse than that. I'm about to get arrested.'

'For what?'

'For killing that girl behind the hotel.'

'What?'

'The puppet master doesn't like me being here. He already tried something on Monday night, with that same girl as bait. So I went to see her yesterday, twice. And now they killed her and I'm sure I'm her last unexplained contact.'

'Have you got an alibi?'

'Depends on the exact timing, but probably not. I'm sure the cops are already looking for me.'

'Problem,' Hutton said.

'Only temporary,' Reacher said. 'Science is on my side. If her neck was broken by a single blow to her right temple, then her head rotated a little, counterclockwise, which means the punch was thrown by a left-hander. And I'm right-handed. If

I had hit her in the right temple I would have knocked her out for sure, but I wouldn't have broken her neck. I would have had to do that separately, afterwards.'

'You sure?'

Reacher nodded. 'I used to do this stuff for a living, remember.'

'But will they believe you? Or will they figure you're big enough to have done it with your weak hand?'

'I'm not going to risk finding out.'

'You're going to run?'

'No, I'm going to stick around. But I'm going to have to stay out of their way. Which will slow me down some. A lot, in fact. Which is why I said I've got operational problems.'

'Can I help?'

Reacher smiled.

'It's good to see you, Hutton,' he said. 'It really is.'

'How can I help?'

'My guess is there'll be a cop called Emerson waiting for you after you're done with your deposition. He'll ask you about me. Just play dumb. Just say I never showed up, you didn't see me, you don't know where I am, all that kind of stuff.'

She was quiet for a spell.

'You're upset,' she said. 'I can tell.'

He nodded. Rubbed his face, like he was washing without water.

'I don't care much about James Barr,' he said. 'If someone wanted to set him up so he took the punishment he should have taken fourteen years ago, that was OK with me. But this thing with the girl is different. It's way out of line. She was just a sweet dumb kid. She meant no harm.'

Hutton was quiet for a moment longer.

'Are you sure about the threat to Barr's sister?' she asked.

'I don't see any other leverage.'

'But there's no sign of a threat. As a prosecutor I couldn't see entering it as a separate charge.'

'Why else would Barr have done what he did?'

Hutton didn't answer.

'Will I see you later?' she asked.

'I've got a room not far away,' he said. 'I'll be around.'

'OK,' she said.

'Unless I'm already in jail.'

The waitress came back and they ordered dessert. Reacher asked for more coffee and Hutton got more tea. They kept on talking. Random subjects, random questions. They had fourteen years to catch up on.

Helen Rodin searched through the six cartons of evidence and found a crisp photocopy of a sheet of paper that had been found next to James Barr's telephone. It was as close as he had got to a personal phone book. It had three numbers on it, written in neat and careful handwriting. Two were for his sister Rosemary, one at her condo and the other at work. The third number was for Mike. The neighbourhood guy. Nothing for anyone called Charlie.

Helen dialled Mike's number. It rang six times

and cut to an answering machine. She left her office number and asked for a return call on a matter of great importance.

Emerson spent an hour with a sketch artist and came up with a pretty good likeness of Jack Reacher's face. The drawing was then scanned into a computer and colourized. Dirty-blond hair, ice blue eyes, medium-to-dark tan. Emerson then typed the name, and estimated the height at six-five, the weight at two-fifty, the age between thirty-five and forty-five. He put the police department's phone number on the bottom line. Then he e-mailed it all over the place and set the printer to churn out two hundred colour copies. He told every prowl car driver to take a sheaf and give one to every hotel clerk and barman in town. Then he added: every restaurant, diner, lunch counter and sandwich shop, too.

James Barr's friend Mike called Helen Rodin back at three o'clock in the afternoon. She asked for his address and got him to agree to a face-to-face interview. He said he was home for the rest of the day. So she called a cab and headed out. Mike lived on James Barr's street, twenty minutes from downtown. Barr's house was visible from Mike's front yard. Both houses were similar. All the houses on the street were similar. They were 1950s ranches, long and low. Helen guessed they had all started out identical. But a half-century's worth of adding on and reroofing and re-siding and ongoing landscaping had made them diverge in appearance. Some looked upmarket and some still looked basic. Barr's place looked worn. Mike's place looked manicured.

Mike himself was a tired fifty-something who worked the morning shift at a paint wholesaler. His wife arrived home while Helen was still introducing herself. She was also a tired fifty-something. Her name was Tammy, which didn't suit her. She was a part-time dental nurse. She worked two mornings a week for a downtown dentist. She ushered Helen and Mike into the living room and then went away to make coffee. Helen and Mike sat down and started out with an awkward initial silence that lasted minutes.

'So what can I tell you?' Mike asked, eventually.

'You were Mr Barr's friend,' Helen said.

Mike glanced at the living room door. It was open.

'Just a neighbour,' he said.

'His sister called you a friend.'

'We were neighbourly. Some folks might call that friendly.'

'Did you spend time together?'

'We would chat a little if he walked by with his dog.'

'About what kind of thing?'

'Our yards,' Mike said. 'If he was decorating he would ask me about paint. I asked him who fixed his driveway. Things like that.'

'Baseball?'

Mike nodded. 'We would talk about that.'

Tammy came in with three cups of coffee on a tray. There was cream and sugar and a small plate of cookies with them, and three paper napkins.

She put the tray on a low table and sat down next to her husband.

'Help yourself,' she said.

'Thank you,' Helen said. 'Thank you very much.'

They all served themselves and there was silence in the room.

'Were you ever in Mr Barr's house?' Helen asked.

Mike glanced at his wife.

'Once or twice,' he said.

'They weren't friends,' Tammy said.

'Was it a surprise?' Helen asked. 'That he did what he did?'

'Yes,' Tammy said. 'It was.'

'So you don't need to feel bad about mixing with him before. It wasn't something that anyone could have predicted. These things are always a surprise. Neighbours never know.'

'You're trying to get him off.'

'Actually I'm not,' Helen said. 'But there's a new theory that he didn't act alone. I'm just trying to make sure that the other man gets punished too.'

'It wasn't Mike,' Tammy said.

'I don't think it was,' Helen said. 'Really. Not for a moment. Not now that I've met him. But whoever the other man is, you or Mike might know him or have heard about him or even seen him coming and going.'

'Barr didn't really have friends,' Mike said.

'Nobody?'

'Not that he spoke about to me. He lived with his sister until she moved out. I guess that was enough for him.'

'Does the name Charlie mean anything to you?'
Mike just shook his head.

'What did Mr Barr do when he had a job?'

'I don't know,' Mike said. 'He hasn't worked for years.'

'I've seen a man over there,' Tammy said.

'When?'

'Now and then. Occasionally. He comes and goes. All times of the day and night, like a friend would.'

'For how long?'

'Ever since we moved here. I spend more time at home than Mike does. So I notice more.'

'When was the last time you saw this man?'

'Last week, I think. A couple of times.'

'Friday?'

'No, earlier. Tuesday and Wednesday, maybe.'

'What does he look like?'

'He's small. He's got funny hair. Black, like hog bristles.'

Charlie, Helen thought.

Eileen Hutton walked three fast blocks south from the Marriott and arrived at the courthouse at one minute to four exactly. Alex Rodin's secretary came down to escort her up to the third floor. Depositions were taken in a large conference room because most witnesses brought their own lawyers and court reporters with them. But Hutton was on her own. She sat down alone on one long side of a large table and smiled as a microphone was placed in front of her and a video camera was focused on her face. Then Rodin came in and introduced himself. He

261

brought a small team with him. An assistant, his secretary, a court reporter with her machine.

'Would you state your full name and title for the record?' he asked.

Hutton looked at the camera.

'Eileen Ann Hutton,' she said. 'Brigadier General, Judge Advocate General's Corps, United States Army.'

'I hope this won't take long,' Rodin said.

'It won't,' Hutton said.

And it didn't. Rodin was trawling in a sea he hadn't charted. He was like a man in a darkened room. All he could do was dart around randomly and hope he bumped into something. After six questions he realized he was never going to.

He asked, 'How would you characterize James Barr's military service?'

'Exemplary without being exceptional,' Hutton said.

He asked, 'Was he ever in trouble?'

'Not to my knowledge,' Hutton said.

He asked, 'Did he ever commit a crime?'

'Not to my knowledge,' Hutton said.

He asked, 'Are you aware of recent events in this city?'

'Yes, I am,' Hutton said.

He asked, 'Is there anything in James Barr's past that might shed light on the likelihood or otherwise of his having been involved in those events?'

'Not to my knowledge,' Hutton said.

Finally he asked, 'Is there any reason why the Pentagon might be more aware of James Barr than any other veteran?'

262

'Not to my knowledge,' Hutton said.

So at that point Alex Rodin gave up.

'OK,' he said. 'Thank you, General Hutton.'

Helen Rodin walked thirty yards and stood on the street for a moment outside James Barr's house. It had police tape across the entryway and a plywood sheet nailed over the broken front door. It looked forlorn and empty. There was nothing to see. So she used her cell phone to call a cab and had it take her to the county hospital. It was after four o'clock in the afternoon when she arrived and the sun was in the west. It lit up the white concrete building with pale shades of orange and pink.

She rode up to the sixth floor and signed in with the Board of Corrections and found the tired thirty-year-old doctor and asked him about James Barr's condition. The doctor didn't really answer. He wasn't very interested in James Barr's condition. That was clear. So Helen just walked past him and opened Barr's door.

Barr was awake. He was still handcuffed to the cot. His head was still clamped. His eyes were open and he was staring at the ceiling. His breathing was low and slow and the heart monitor was beeping less than once a second. His arms were trembling slightly and his handcuffs were rattling against the bed frame. Quiet, dull, metallic sounds.

'Who's there?' he said.

Helen stepped close and leaned into his field of view.

'Are they looking after you?' she asked.

'I have no complaints,' he said.

'Tell me about your friend Charlie.'

'Is he here?'

'No, he's not here.'

'Did Mike come?'

'I don't think they allow visitors. Just lawyers and family.'

Barr said nothing.

'Are those your only friends?' Helen said. 'Mike and Charlie?'

'I guess,' Barr said. 'And Mike's more of a neighbour.'

'What about Jeb Oliver?'

'Who?'

'He works at the auto parts store.'

'I don't know him.'

'Are you sure?'

Barr's eyes moved and his lips pursed, like a man searching his memory, trying to be helpful, desperate for approval.

'I'm sorry,' he said. 'I never heard of him.'

'Do you use drugs?'

'No,' Barr said. 'Never. I wouldn't do that.' He was quiet for a beat. 'Truth is I don't really do much of anything. I just live. That's why this whole thing makes no sense to me. I spent fourteen years in the world. Why would I throw it all away now?'

'Tell me about Charlie,' Helen said.

'We hang out,' Barr said. 'We do stuff.'

'With guns?'

'A little bit.'

'Where does Charlie live?'

'I don't know.'

'How long have you been friends?'

'Five years. Maybe six.'

'And you don't know where he lives?'

'He never told me.'

'He's been to your place.'

'So?'

'You never went to his place?'

'He came to mine instead.'

'Do you have his phone number?'

'He just shows up, here and there, now and then.'

'Are you close?'

'Close enough.'

'How close exactly?'

'We get along.'

'Well enough to tell him what happened fourteen years ago?'

Barr didn't answer. Just closed his eyes.

'Did you tell him?'

Barr said nothing.

'I think you told him,' Helen said.

Barr didn't confirm or deny it.

'I'm surprised that a man doesn't know where his friend lives. Especially a friend as close as I think Charlie is.'

'I didn't push it,' Barr said. 'I was lucky to have a friend at all. I didn't want to ruin it with questions.'

Eileen Hutton got up from Alex Rodin's deposition table and shook hands all round. Then she stepped out to the corridor and came face to face with a guy she assumed was the cop called Emerson. The one Reacher had warned her about.

265

He confirmed it by handing her a card with his name on it.

'Can we talk?' he asked.

'About what?' she asked back.

'About Jack Reacher,' Emerson said.

'What about him?'

'You know him, am I right?'

'I knew him fourteen years ago.'

'When did you last see him?'

'Fourteen years ago,' she said. 'We were in Kuwait together. Then he shipped out somewhere. Or I did. I can't remember.'

'You didn't see him today?'

'He's in Indiana?'

'He's in town. Right here, right now.'

'Small world.'

'How did you get here?'

'I flew into Indianapolis and rented a car.'

'Staying overnight?'

'Do I have a choice?'

'Where?'

'The Marriott.'

'Reacher killed a girl last night.'

'Are you sure?'

'He's our only suspect.'

'That would be very unlike him.'

'Call me if you see him. The station house number is on my card. And my direct extension. And my cell phone.'

'Why would I see him?'

'Like you said, it's a small world.'

A police black-and-white crawled north through the building rush hour traffic. Past the gun store.

Past the barbershop. *Any Style $7*. Then it eased right and turned into the motor court. The cop in the passenger seat got out and walked to the office. Gave the clerk a flyer. Laid it flat on the counter and swivelled it round and slid it across.

'Call us if this guy shows up, OK?' the cop said.

'He's already here,' the clerk said. 'But his name's Heffner, not Reacher. I put him in room eight, last night.'

The cop stood still. 'Is he in there now?'

'I don't know. He's come and gone a few times.'

'How long did he book for?'

'He paid one night. But he didn't give the key back yet.'

'So he's planning to be here again tonight.'

'I guess.'

'Unless he's already here.'

'Unless,' the clerk said.

The cop stepped back to the office door. Signalled his partner. His partner shut the motor down and locked the car and walked over.

'Room eight, false name,' the first cop said.

'In there now?' his partner asked.

'We don't know.'

'So let's find out.'

They took the clerk with them. They made him stand well back. They drew their weapons and knocked on room eight's door.

No response.

They knocked again.

No response.

'Got a master key?' the first cop asked.

The clerk handed him a key. The cop put it in the lock, gently, one-handed. Turned it slowly. Opened the door a half-inch and paused and then smashed it all the way open and stepped inside. His partner stepped in right behind him. Their guns traced left and right and up and down, fast and random and tense.

The room was empty.

Nothing in there at all, except a forlorn little sequence of bathroom items lined up on a shelf above the sink. A new pack of throwaway razors, open, one used. A new can of shaving foam, with dried bubbles round the nozzle. A new tube of toothpaste, twice squeezed.

'This guy travels light,' the first cop said.

'But he hasn't checked out,' his partner said. 'That's for sure. Which means he's coming back.'

TEN

Reacher was falling asleep on the bed in room 310 at the Marriott Suites. He was on his back, like a dead man. He and Hutton had talked so long in the coffee shop that she had almost been late for her appointment. She had checked her watch at five to four and had thrust her key card at him and asked him to dump her bag in her room. Then she had run straight out to the street. He guessed he was supposed to leave her card at the desk afterwards. But he didn't. He didn't have anywhere he needed to be. Not right then. So he just parked the bag and stayed inside.

He wasn't crazy about room 310, all things considered. It was on the third floor, which made the window a difficult escape route. Room eight at the motor court had been better. Much better. Ground floor, a tangled old neighbourhood, it gave a guy a sporting chance. Open the window, step out, look for an alley, or a door, or another window. That was good. This was bad. He was three floors up. A long climb. And he wasn't even sure if the Marriott's windows opened at all. Maybe they didn't. Maybe the main office lawyers had been worried about liability. Maybe they had foreseen a steady deluge of infants raining down on the parking lot blacktop. Or maybe it was a question of economies of scale. Maybe the cost of hinges and handles outweighed a little extra on the air conditioning bill. Whatever, it wasn't a great room to be in. Not by any measure. Not for the long term.

But it was OK for the short term. So he closed his eyes and drifted away. *Sleep when you can, because you never know when you're going to sleep again.* That was the old army rule.

Emerson's plan was pretty straightforward. He put Donna Bianca in room seven. Told the two patrolmen to stash their car three streets away and walk back and wait in room nine. He put a car two streets behind the motor court, and another four blocks north, where the auto dealers were, and another two blocks south. He told the clerk to stay awake and watch through the window and call Bianca in room seven as soon as he saw the guy he knew as Heffner walking in.

Eileen Hutton got back to the Marriott at four thirty. There was no key card waiting for her at the desk. No message. So she went up in the elevator and followed the arrows to room 310 and knocked on the door. There was a short pause and then the door opened and Reacher let her in.

'How's my room?' she asked.

'The bed's comfortable,' he said.

'I'm supposed to call Emerson if I see you,' she said.

270

'Are you going to?'

'No.'

'Perjury *and* harbouring a fugitive,' he said. 'All in one day.'

She dug in her purse and came out with Emerson's card. 'You're their only suspect. He gave me three separate phone numbers. They sound pretty serious.'

He took the card from her. Put it in his back pocket, with the cocktail napkin that had Helen Rodin's cell number on it. He was turning into a walking phone book.

'How was the thing with Rodin?' he asked.

'Straightforward,' she said.

He said nothing. She moved around, checking the suite. Bathroom, bedroom, living room, kitchenette. She took her bag and stood it neatly against a wall.

'Want to stay?' she said.

He shook his head.

'I can't,' he said.

'OK,' she said.

'But I could come back later, if you like.'

She paused a beat.

'OK,' she said. 'Come back later.'

Alex Rodin stepped back into his office and closed the door and called Emerson.

'Have you got him yet?' he asked.

'Just a matter of time,' Emerson said. 'We're looking for him all over. And we're watching his room. He's at the old motor court. Under a false name.'

'That's interesting,' Rodin said. 'It means he

271

might have used a false name at the Metropole too.'

'I'll check,' Emerson said. 'I'll show the clerk the picture.'

'We might really be able to nail him,' Rodin said. He clicked off, thinking about two new framed headlines for his office wall. First Barr, and then Reacher.

Reacher let himself out of Hutton's suite and used the stairs instead of the elevator. On the ground floor he turned away from the lobby and found a back corridor with a fire door at the end of it. He pushed the fire door open and held it ajar with his foot. Took Emerson's card out of his pocket and tore it in half lengthwise and folded the half with the name on it four times. He pressed the tongue into the fire door's lock with the ball of his thumb and wedged it there with the folded cardboard. He closed the door gently and pushed it flush with the frame with the flat of his hand. Then he walked away, past a Dumpster, through the staff lot, out to the street, heading north. The sidewalks were busy and the traffic lanes were starting to clog. He walked at a normal pace and used his height to scan the middle distance for patrol cars or cops on corners. The day was still warm. There was a weather system somewhere out there. Somewhere near. There was high pressure in the sky, clamping down, trapping the smell of damp earth and nitrogen fertilizer in the air.

He reached the raised highway and turned west in its shadow. The roadbed strode along on pillars forty feet high. Underneath it were untidy lots, some vacant and full of trash, some with old brick buildings with dark skylights in their roofs, some with new metal sheds housing body shops and spray paint operations. He passed the back of the black glass tower and stayed in the highway's shadow and turned south, ready to pass behind the library. He stopped suddenly and crouched and fiddled with his shoe. Like he had a stone. Glanced back under his arm and saw nobody behind him. No tail.

He moved on. After the library he was exposed for forty yards. The plaza was east of him. He stopped momentarily on a spot he judged was directly below where Helen Rodin had parked the day before and where James Barr should have parked on Friday. Forty feet lower down the view was different but the geometry was the same. He could see the wilted tributes propped against the pool's southern wall. They were small splashes of faded colour in the distance. Beyond them was the DMV's door. People were coming out in ones and twos. He checked his watch. Ten to five.

He moved on, in the open, and made it across to First Street's northernmost block. He looped one block south and three blocks east and came up on the parking garage from the west. He walked up the entrance ramp and found the security camera's lens. It was a small circle of dirty glass mounted on a plain black box that was bolted high up in the angle of two concrete beams. He waved at it. It was too high, ideally. It should have been lower, at licence plate level. But all the pillars below waist height were scuffed and scraped. A rainbow of different colours. Drivers were careless. Mounted lower, the camera would have lasted a day and a half. Maybe less.

He walked up the ramps to the second level. Headed north and east, to the far back corner. The garage was still and quiet, but full. The space that James Barr had used was occupied. No room for sentiment in the scramble for downtown parking. No room for reverence.

The border betwcen the old garage and the new construction was marked by a triple barrier of tape strung between pillars. There was standard yellow and black contractor's *Caution Do Not Enter* tape and above it and below it were new lengths of blue and white *Police Line Do Not Cross* tape. He used his forearm and stretched all three lines higher and just ducked underneath. No need to drop to one knee. No need to scuff a pair of jeans. No need to leave a mess of fibres. Not even for a guy six inches taller than Barr, and not even with a new line of tape six inches lower than the one Barr had encountered. *He was literally going out of his way to leave every last piece of evidence he could.*

Reacher walked on into the gloom. The new construction was rectangular in shape. Maybe forty yards south to north, maybe two hundred east to west. Which meant Reacher arrived at the new northeast corner after thirty-five paces. He stood six feet back from the perimeter wall and looked down and right. He had a perfectly good view. No need to press up against a pillar. No need to squirm around like a horse on its back in a summer meadow.

He stood there and watched. People were coming out of the government office in increasing numbers. There was quite a flow. Some paused and lit cigarettes as soon as they were out in the air. Others moved on directly west, some fast, some slow. All of them turned and tracked round the north end of the pool. None of them walked where Barr's victims had walked. The funeral tributes were a disincentive. A reminder. Therefore it was hard to judge what Friday's scene had looked like. Hard, but not impossible. Reacher watched the walking people and in his mind made them forgo their respectful right turns. He made them continue straight on. They would be slow entering the bottleneck. But not too slow. And they would be close. The combination of moderate speed and proximity would exaggerate the deflection angles. It would make the job harder. It was a basic principle of long gun use. A bird traversing the sky a hundred yards away was an easy target. The same bird at the same speed flying six feet in front of your face was an impossible target.

He pictured the people streaming right to left. He closed one eye and extended his arm and pointed his finger. *Click, click-click, click-click-click.* Six aimed shots. Four seconds. Fast. Tough geometry. Tension, exposure, vulnerability.

Six hits, including the deliberate miss.

Exceptional shooting.

They don't forget.

He dropped his arm to his side. It was cold in the gloom. He shivered. The air was clammy and damp and full of the smell of lime. It had been hot in Kuwait City. The air had been shimmering and full of the smell of baked dust and desert sand. Reacher had stood in the parking garage and sweated. The street below him had been blinding. Murderous. Like a blast furnace.

Hot in Kuwait City.

Four shots there.

Six shots here.

He stood and watched the people coming out the DMV door. There were plenty of them. Ten, twelve, fifteen, twenty. They turned and looped north and then turned again and walked west between the pool and the NBC peacock. They gave each other space. But if they had been in the bottleneck they would have bunched up tight.

Plenty of them.

Six shots, in four seconds.

He looked for anyone not moving. Didn't see anybody. No cops, no old men in boxy suits. He turned round and retraced his steps. Lifted the tape again and ducked under it and walked back down the ramps. Slipped out to the street and turned west, heading for the shadows under the highway. Heading for the library.

He crossed the forty yards of open ground and hugged the library's side wall and went in through a handicapped entrance. He had to walk close to the desk, but he wasn't worried about that. If Emerson started circulating wanted notices he would hit the post offices and bars and hotels first. It would be a long time before he started canvassing librarians.

He made it to the lobby OK and stepped over to the pay phones. Took the cocktail napkin out of his pocket and dialled Helen Rodin's cell. She picked up on the fifth ring. He pictured her rooting through her purse, squinting at the screen, fumbling with the buttons.

'Are you alone?' he asked.

'Reacher?'

'Yes,' he said. 'Are you alone?'

'Yes,' she said. 'But you're in trouble.'

'Who called you?'

'My father.'

'You believe him?'

'No.'

'I'm coming to see you.'

'There's a cop in the lobby.'

'I figured. I'll come in through the garage.'

He hung up and walked back past the desk and out the side entrance. Back under the highway. He stayed in its shelter until he was opposite the back of the black glass tower. Opposite the vehicle ramp. He checked left, checked right, and walked straight down. Past the NBC trucks, past the Mustang he figured for Ann Yanni's, to the elevator. He pressed the call button and waited. Checked his watch. Five thirty. Most people would be leaving the building. A down elevator was certain to stop at the lobby level. An up elevator, maybe not. He hoped.

The car arrived in the garage and let three people out. They walked away. Reacher stepped in. Pressed four. Stood back. The car rose one floor and stopped. In the lobby. The doors slid back like a theatre curtain. The cop was right there, four feet from the elevator, facing away. He had his feet apart and his hands on his hips. He was almost

277

close enough to touch. A man stepped into the elevator. He didn't speak. Just nodded a two-guys-in-an-elevator greeting. Reacher nodded back. The guy pressed seven. The doors stayed open. The cop watched the street. The new guy jiggled the button. The cop moved. He swiped his cap off his head and ran his fingers through his hair. The doors closed. The elevator moved up.

Reacher got out on four and walked through a small knot of people on their way home. Helen Rodin had her door open and ready. He stepped inside her suite and she closed up after him. She was wearing a short black skirt and a white blouse. She looked young. Like a schoolgirl. And she looked worried. Like a conflicted person.

'I should turn you in,' she said.

'But you won't,' Reacher said.

'No,' she said. 'I should, but I won't.'

'Truth is I liked that girl,' Reacher said. 'She was a sweet kid.'

'She set you up.'

'I wasn't offended.'

'Someone didn't like her.'

'We can't tell. Affection didn't come into it. She was disposable, that's all. A means to an end.'

'The puppet master really doesn't want you around.'

Reacher nodded. 'That's for damn sure. But he's shit out of luck there, because I'm not leaving now. He just guaranteed that for himself.'

'Is it safe to stay?'

'It's safe enough. But this thing with the girl is going to slow me down. So you're going to have to do most of the work.'

278

She led him into the inner office. She sat down at her desk. He stayed well away from the window. He sat on the floor and propped his back against the wall.

'I already started the work,' Helen said. 'I spoke to Rosemary and talked to Barr's neighbours. Then I went back to the hospital. I think we're looking for a guy called Charlie. Small guy, bristly black hair. Interested in guns. I got the impression he's kind of furtive. I think he's going to be hard to find.'

'How long has he been on the scene?'

'Five or six years, apparently. He's the only long-term friend anyone could name. And he's the only one Barr owns up to.'

Reacher nodded again. 'That works for me.'

'And Barr doesn't know Jeb Oliver and doesn't use drugs.'

'You believe him?'

'Yes, I do,' Helen said. 'Really. Right now I believe everything he says. It's like he spent fourteen years turning his life around and now he can't believe he went back. I think he's as upset about all this as anyone.'

'Except the victims.'

'Give him a break, Reacher. Something weird was going on.'

'Does this guy Charlie know about Kuwait City?'

'Barr wouldn't say. But I think he does.'

'Where does he live?'

'Barr doesn't know.'

'He doesn't *know*?'

'He just sees him around. He just shows up now

279

and then. Like I said, I think he's going to be hard to find.'

Reacher said nothing.

'Did you speak to Eileen Hutton?' Helen asked.

'She's no threat. The army is keeping the lid on.'

'Did you find the guy that was following you?'

'No,' Reacher said. 'I didn't see him again. They must have pulled him off.'

'So we're nowhere.'

'We're closer than we were. We can start to see a shape. We can see four guys, at least. One, the old guy in the suit. Two, this guy called Charlie. Three, someone big and very strong and left-handed.'

'Why him?'

'He killed the girl last night. The old guy is too old and it sounds like Charlie might be too small. And the physical evidence suggests a left-handed blow.'

'And number four is the puppet master.'

Reacher nodded again. 'In the shadows somewhere, making plans, pulling strings. We can assume he doesn't run around doing this kind of stuff himself.'

'But how can we get to him? If he's pulled the guy off your tail, we can assume he's pulled Charlie back, too. They're hunkering down.'

'There's another way. A big wide highway.'

'Where?'

'We missed something very obvious,' Reacher said. 'We spent all this time looking down the wrong end of the gun. All we've done is look at who fired it.'

280

'What should we have done?'

'We should have thought harder.'

'About what?'

'James Barr fired four times in Kuwait City. And he fired six times here.'

'OK,' Helen said. 'He fired two more shots here. So?'

'But he didn't,' Reacher said. 'Not really. Not if you think about it laterally. Truth is he fired four *fewer* shots here.'

'That's ridiculous. Six is two more than four. Not four *fewer*.'

'Kuwait City was very hot. Unbearable in the middle of the day. You had to be nuts to be out and about. The streets were empty most of the time.'

'So?'

'So in Kuwait City James Barr killed every live human he saw. One, two, three, four, game over. The street was deserted apart from our four guys. They were the only people dumb enough to be out in the heat. And Barr took them all. He ran the table. At the time it seemed logical to me. He wanted to see the pink mist. It struck me that maybe he might have been satisfied with seeing it once, but apparently he wasn't. So it made some kind of sense that if he didn't stop at one, he would go all the way until he ran out of targets. And he did. In Kuwait City, he ran out of targets.'

Helen Rodin said nothing.

'But he didn't run out of targets here,' Reacher said. 'There had to have been a dozen people in that bottleneck. Or fifteen. More than ten, anyway. And he had a ten-round magazine. But he

281

stopped shooting after six. Just stopped. He left four rounds in the gun. They're listed right there in Bellantonio's dog and pony show. And that's what I meant. He fired the most he could fire in Kuwait City, and four *less* than the most he could fire here. Which makes the psychology different here. He chose not to run the table here. Why?'

'Because he was hurrying?'

'He had an autoloader. The voice mail recording shows six shots in four seconds. Which means he could have fired ten in less than seven seconds. Three seconds wouldn't have made any kind of a difference to him.'

Helen said nothing.

'I asked him,' Reacher said. 'When I saw him in the hospital. I asked him how he would have done it, theoretically. Like a recon briefing. So he thought about it. He knows the area. He said he would have parked on the highway. Behind the library. He said he would have buzzed the window down and *emptied the mag.*'

Helen said nothing.

'But he didn't empty the mag,' Reacher said. 'He stopped shooting after six. Just stopped. Coldly and calmly. Which makes the whole dynamic different. This wasn't a crazy man sent out to terrorize the city on a dare. He wasn't pushed into it just for the fun of the carnage. This wasn't random, Helen. It wasn't psychotic. There was a specific, limited, coherent purpose behind it. Which reverses the focus. We should have seen it. We should have seen that this whole thing is about the victims, not the shooter. They weren't just unlucky people in the wrong place at the wrong time.'

'They were targets?' Helen said.

'Carefully chosen,' Reacher said. 'And as soon as they were safely down, Barr packed up and left. With four bullets remaining. A random psycho episode wouldn't have panned out like that. He'd have kept on pulling the trigger until he clicked on empty. So this wasn't a spree. It was an assassination.'

Silence in the office.

'We need to look at who the victims were,' Reacher said. 'And we need to look at who wanted them dead. That's what's going to lead us to where we need to be.'

Helen Rodin didn't move.

'And we need to do it real fast,' Reacher said. 'Because I don't have much time and we already wasted the best part of three days looking at everything ass-backward.'

The tired thirty-year-old doctor on the sixth floor of the county hospital was finishing up his afternoon rounds. He had left James Barr for last. Partly because he wasn't expecting any dramatic change in his condition, and partly because he didn't care anyway. Looking after sick thieves and swindlers was bad enough, but looking after a mass-murderer was absurd. Doubly absurd, because straight after Barr was on his feet he was going to be laid back down on a gurney and some other doctor was going to come in and kill him.

But ethical obligations are hard to ignore. As is habit. As is duty, and routine, and structure. So the doctor went into Barr's room and picked up his chart. Took out his pen. Glanced at the machines. Glanced at the patient. He was awake. His eyes were moving.

Alert, the doctor wrote.

'Happy?' he asked.

'Not really,' Barr said.

Responsive, the doctor wrote.

'Tough shit,' he said, and put his pen away.

Barr's right handcuff was rattling gently against the cot rail. His right hand itself was trembling and slightly cupped and the thumb and index finger were in constant motion, like he was trying to roll an imaginary ball of wax into a perfect sphere.

'Stop that,' the doctor said.

'Stop what?'

'Your hand.'

'I can't.'

'Is that new?'

'A year or two.'

'Not just since you woke up?'

'No.'

The doctor looked at the chart. *Age: Forty-one.*

'Do you drink?' he asked.

'Not really,' Barr said. 'A sip sometimes, to help me sleep.'

The doctor disbelieved him automatically and flipped through the chart to the tox screen and the liver function test. But the tox screen was clear and the liver function was healthy. *Not a drinker. Not an alcoholic. Not even close.*

'Have you seen your own physician recently?' he asked.

284

'I don't have insurance,' Barr said.

'Stiffness in your arms and legs?'

'A little.'

'Does your other hand do that too?'

'Sometimes.'

The doctor took out his pen again and scribbled on the bottom of the chart: *Observed tremor in right hand, not post-traumatic, primary diagnosis alcohol unlikely, stiffness in limbs present, possible early-onset PA?*

'What's wrong with me?' Barr asked.

'Shut up,' the doctor said. Then, duty done, he clipped the chart back on the foot of the bed and walked out of the room.

Helen Rodin searched through the evidence cartons and came out with the formal specification of charges against James Barr. Among many other technical violations of the law the State of Indiana had listed five counts of homicide in the first degree with aggravating circumstances, and as due process required had gone on to list the five alleged victims by name, sex, age, address, and occupation. Helen scanned the page, ran her fingers down the columns for address and occupation.

'I don't see any obvious connections,' she said.

'I didn't mean they were all targets,' Reacher said. 'Probably only one of them was. Two, at most. The others were window dressing. An assassination, disguised as a spree. That's my guess.'

'I'll get to work,' she said.

'I'll see you tomorrow,' he said.

He used the fire stairs instead of the elevator

and got back to the garage unseen. He hustled up the ramp and across the street and under the highway again. *The invisible man. Life in the shadows*. He smiled. He stopped.

He decided to go look for a pay phone.

He found one on the side wall of a small grocery called Martha's two blocks north of the cheap clothing store he had used. The booth faced a wide alley that was used as a narrow parking lot. There were six slanted spaces full of six cars. Beyond them, a high brick wall topped with broken glass. The alley turned ninety degrees behind the grocery. He guessed it turned again somewhere and let out on the next block south.

Safe enough, he thought.

He took Emerson's torn card out of his pocket. Chose the cell number. Dialled the phone. Leaned his shoulder against the wall and watched both ends of the alley at once and listened to the purr of the ring tone in his ear.

'Yes?' Emerson said.

'Guess who?' Reacher said.

'Reacher?'

'You named that tune in one.'

'Where are you?'

'I'm still in town.'

'Where?'

'Not far away.'

'You know we're looking for you, right?'

'I heard.'

'So you need to turn yourself in.'

'I don't think so.'

'Then we'll come find you,' Emerson said.

'Think you can?'

'It'll be easy.'

'You know a guy called Franklin?'

'Sure I do.'

'Ask him how easy it'll be.'

'That was different. You could have been any-where.'

'You got the motor court staked out?'

There was a pause. Emerson said nothing.

'Keep your people there,' Reacher said. 'Maybe I'll be back. Or on the other hand, maybe I won't.'

'We'll find you.'

'Not a chancc. You're not good enough.'

'Maybe we're tracing this call.'

'I'll save you the trouble. I'm outside a grocery called Martha's.'

'You should come in from the cold.'

'I'll trade,' Reacher said. 'Find out who placed the cone in the parking garage and then I'll think about coming in.'

'Barr placed the cone.'

'You know he didn't. His van isn't on the tapes.'

'So he used another vehicle.'

'He doesn't have another vehicle.'

'So he borrowed one.'

'From a friend?' Reacher said. 'Maybe. Or maybe the friend placed the cone for him. Either way, you find that friend, and I'll think about coming in to talk to you.'

'There are hundreds of cars on those tapes.'

'You've got the resources,' Reacher said.

'I don't trade,' Emerson said.

'I think his name is Charlie,' Reacher said. 'Small guy, wiry black hair.'

'I don't trade,' Emerson said again.

'I didn't kill the girl,' Reacher said.

'Says you.'

'I liked her.'

'You're breaking my heart.'

'And you know I didn't stay at the Metropole last night.'

'Which is why you dumped her there.'

'And I'm not left-handed.'

'I don't follow.'

'Tell Bellantonio to talk to your ME.'

'We'll find you,' Emerson said.

'You won't,' Reacher said. 'Nobody ever has before.'

Then he hung up and walked back to the street. Crossed the road and hiked half a block north and took cover behind a stack of unused concrete lane dividers in a vacant lot. He waited. Six minutes later two cruisers pulled up in front of Martha's grocery. Lights, but no sirens. Four cops spilled out. Two went in the store and two went to find the phone. Reacher watched them regroup on the sidewalk. Watched them search the alley and check round its corner. Watched them come back. Watched them admit defeat. He saw one of the four get on his radio for a short conversation full of defensive body language. Raised palms, shrugged shoulders. Then the conversation ended and Reacher slipped away east, heading back towards the Marriott.

*   *   *

The Zec had only a thumb and a single finger remaining on each hand. On the right was a stump of an index finger, blackened and gnarled by frostbite. He had once spent a week outdoors in the winter, wearing an old Red Army tunic, and the way its previous owner's water canteen had ridden on his belt had worn the fabric of the right pocket thinner than the left. On such trivial differences survival had hung. His left hand had been saved, and his right hand lost. He had felt his fingers die from the pinkie inward. He had taken his hand out of his pocket and let it freeze hard enough to go completely numb. Then he had chewed off the dead fingers before the gangrene could spread. He remembered dropping them to the ground, one by one, like small brown twigs.

His left hand retained the pinkie. The middle three fingers were missing. Two had been amputated by a sadist with garden shears. The Zec had removed the other himself, with a sharpened spoon, so as to be disqualified for labour in some machine shop or other. He couldn't recall the specifics, but he remembered a persuasive rumour that it was better to lose another finger than work on that particular detail. Something to do with the overseer.

Ruined hands. Just two of many souvenirs of another time, another place. He wasn't very aware of them any more, but they made modern life difficult. Cell phones had got so damn *small*. Linsky's number was ten digits long, and it was a pig to dial. The Zec never retained a phone long enough to make it worth storing a number. That would be madness.

Eventually he got the number entered and he concentrated hard and pressed the call button with his left-hand pinkie. Then he juggled the phone into his other palm and cupped it near his ear. He didn't need to hold it close. His hearing was still excellent, which was a miracle all by itself.

'Yes?' Linsky said.

'They can't find him,' the Zec said. 'I shouldn't have told you to break off our own surveillance. My mistake.'

'Where have they looked?'

'Here and there. He stayed last night at the motor court. They've got it staked out, but I'm sure he won't go back. They've got a man at the lawyer's office. Other than that, they're stumbling around in the dark.'

'What do you want me to do?'

'I want you to find him. Use Chenko and Vladimir. And I'll send Raskin to you. Work together. Find him tonight and then call me.'

Reacher stopped two blocks short of the Marriott. He knew what Emerson would be doing. He had *been* Emerson for thirteen years. Emerson would be running down a mental list. Likely haunts, known associates. Likely haunts at this time of day would include eating places. So Emerson would be sending cars to diners and restaurants and cafés, including the salad place that Helen Rodin liked and the sports bar. Then he would move on to known associates, which pretty much limited him to Helen Rodin herself. He would have the lobby cop ride up to the fourth floor and knock on the office door.

Then he would take a chance on Eileen Hutton.

So Reacher stopped two blocks short of the Marriott and looked round for a place to wait. He found one behind a shoe store. There was a three-sided corral made of head-high brick walls shielding a shoulder-high plastic garbage receptacle from public view. Reacher stepped in and found that if he leaned his shoulder on the trash can he could see a yard-wide sliver of the Marriott's main door. He wasn't uncomfortable. And it was the best-smelling garbage dump he had ever been in. The can smelled of fresh cardboard and new shoes. Better than the kind of place you find behind a fish store.

He figured if Emerson was efficient he would have to wait less than thirty minutes. *Very* efficient, less than twenty. Average, somewhere up around an hour. He leaned on the trash can and passed the time. It wasn't late but the streets were already quiet. There were very few people out and about. He watched, and waited. Then the smell of new leather from the discarded shoe boxes distracted him. It started him thinking about footwear. Maybe he should drop by the store sometime and pick out a brand new pair. He stuck his foot out and looked down. The boat shoes he had on were soft and light and the soles were thin. They had been fine for Miami. Not so good for his current situation. He could foresee a time when he would appreciate something heavier.

Then he looked down again. Rocked back and brought his feet together and took the same pace

291

forward. And stopped. He tried it again with his other foot, and stopped again, like a freeze-frame of a man walking. He stared down, with something in the back of his mind. Something from Bellantonio's evidence. Something among all those hundreds of printed pages.

Then he looked up again, because he sensed movement in the corner of his eye at the Marriott's door two blocks away. He saw a squad car's hood. It moved into his field of view and dipped once as it braked and stopped. Then two cops appeared, in uniform, walking forward. He glanced at his watch. Twenty-three minutes. He smiled. Emerson was good, but not unbelievable. The cops went in through the door. They would spend five minutes with the desk clerk. The clerk would give up Hutton's room number without a fight. Generally speaking hotel clerks from small heartland cities weren't ACLU activists. And guests were gone tomorrow, but the local PD was always there.

So the cops would go to Hutton's room. They would knock on her door. Hutton would let them in. She had nothing to hide. The cops would poke around and be on their way. Ten minutes, tops, beginning to end.

Reacher checked his watch again, and waited.

The cops were back out after eight minutes. They paused outside the doors, tiny figures far in the distance. One of them ducked his head to his collar and used his radio, calling in a negative progress report, listening for the next destination. The next likely haunt. The next known associate. Pure routine. *Have a fun evening, boys*, Reacher thought. *Because I'm going to. That's for damn sure*. He watched them drive off and waited another minute in case they were driving his way. Then he stepped out of the brick corral and headed for Eileen Hutton.

Grigor Linsky waited in his car in a fire lane in a supermarket parking lot, framed against a window that was entirely pasted over with a gigantic orange advertisement for ground beef at a very low price. *Old and spoiled*, Linsky thought. *Or full of listeria. The kind of thing the Zec and I would once have killed to eat.* And *killed* was the truth. Linsky had no illusions. None at all. The Zec and he were bad people made worse by experience. Their shared suffering had conferred no grace or nobility. Quite the reverse. Men in their situation inclined towards grace and nobility had died within hours. But the Zec and he had survived, like sewer rats, by abandoning inhibition, by fighting and clawing, by betraying those stronger than themselves, by dominating those weaker.

And they had learned. What works once works always.

Linsky watched in his mirror and saw Raskin's car coming towards him. It was a Lincoln Town Car, the old square style, black and dusty, listing like a holed battleship. It stopped nose to tail with him and Raskin got out. He looked exactly like what he was, which was a second-rate Moscow hoodlum. Square build, flat face, cheap leather jacket, dull eyes. Forty-some years old. A stupid man, in Linsky's opinion, but he had survived the Red Army's last hurrah in

Afghanistan, which had to count for something. Plenty of people smarter than Raskin hadn't come back whole, or come back at all. Which made Raskin a survivor, which was the quality that meant more than any other to the Zec.

Raskin opened the rear door and slid into the back seat behind Linsky. He didn't speak. Just handed over four copies of Emerson's wanted poster. A delivery from the Zec. How the Zec had got the posters, Linsky wasn't sure. But he could make a guess. The posters themselves were pretty good. The likeness was pretty accurate. It would serve its purpose.

'Thank you,' Linsky said politely.

Raskin didn't respond.

Chenko and Vladimir showed up two minutes later, in Chenko's Cadillac. Chenko was driving. Chenko always drove. He parked behind Raskin's Lincoln. Three large black cars, all in a line. Jack Reacher's funeral procession. Linsky smiled to himself. Chenko and Vladimir got out of their car and walked forward, one small and dark, the other big and fair. They got into Linsky's own Cadillac, Chenko in the front, Vladimir in the back next to Raskin, so that counting clockwise there was Linsky in the driver's seat, then Chenko, then Vladimir, then Raskin. The proper pecking order, instinctively obeyed. Linsky smiled again and handed out three copies of the poster. He kept one for himself, even though he didn't need it. He had seen Jack Reacher many times already.

'We're going to start over,' he said. 'Right from the beginning. We can assume the police will have missed something.'

Reacher pulled the fire door open and removed the cardboard plug from the lock and put it in his pocket. He stepped inside and let the door latch behind him. He followed the back corridor to the elevator and rode up to three. Knocked on Hutton's door. He had a line in his head, from Jack Nicholson playing a hard-ass Marine colonel in some movie about Navy lawyers: *Nothing beats a woman you have to salute in the morning.*

Hutton took her time opening the door. He guessed she had settled down somewhere after getting rid of the cops. She hadn't expected to be disturbed again so soon. But eventually the door opened and she was standing there. She was wearing a robe, fresh out of the shower. The light behind her haloed her hair. The corridor was dim and the room looked warm and inviting.

'You came back,' she said.

'Did you think I wouldn't?'

He stepped into the suite and she closed the door behind him.

'The cops were just here,' she said.

'I know,' he said. 'I watched them all the way.'

'Where were you?'

'In a garbage dump two blocks away.'

'You want to wash up?'

'It was a very clean garbage dump. Behind a shoe store.'

'You want to go out to dinner?'

'I'd prefer room service,' he said. 'I don't want to be walking around more than I have to.'

'OK,' she said. 'That makes sense. Room service it is.'

'But not just yet.'

'Should I get dressed?'

'Not just yet.'

She paused a beat.

'Why not?' she said.

'Unfinished business,' he said.

She said nothing.

'It's good to see you again,' he said.

'It's been less than three hours,' she said.

'I mean today,' he said. 'As a whole. After all this time.'

Then he stepped close and cupped her face in his hands. Pushed his fingertips into her hair like he used to and traced the contours of her cheekbones with his thumbs.

'Should we do this?' she said.

'Don't you want to?'

'It's been fourteen years,' she said.

'Like riding a bicycle,' he said.

'Think it will be the same?'

'It'll be better.'

'How much better?' she asked.

'We were always good,' he said. 'Weren't we? How much better could it get?'

She held still for a long moment. Then she put her hands behind his head. She pulled and he bent down and they kissed. Then again, harder. Then again, longer. Fourteen years melted away. Same taste, same feel. Same excitement. She pulled his shirt out of his pants and unbuttoned it from the bottom upward, urgently. When the last button was open she smoothed the flat of her hands over his chest, his shoulders, his back, down to his waistband, around to the front. His boat shoes came off easily. And his socks. He kicked his pants across the room and untied her belt. Her robe fell open.

'Damn, Hutton,' he said. 'You haven't changed a bit.'

'You either,' she said.

Then they headed for the bed, stumbling, fast and urgent, locked together like an awkward four-legged animal.

Grigor Linsky took the south side of town. He checked the salad place and then cruised down to the docks. Turned around and quartered the narrow streets, covering three sides of every block, pausing at the turns to scan the sidewalks on the fourth. The Cadillac idled along. The power steering hissed at every corner. It was slow, patient work. But it wasn't a large city. There was no bustle. No crowds. And nobody could hide for ever. That had been Grigor Linsky's experience.

Afterwards Hutton lay in Reacher's arms and used her fingertips to trace a long slow inventory of the body she had known so well. It had changed in fourteen years. He had said *you haven't changed a bit* and she had said *you either*, but she knew both of them had been generous. Nobody stays the same. The Reacher she had known in the desert had been younger and baked lean by the heat, as fluid and graceful as a greyhound. Now he was heavier, with knotted muscles as hard as old mahogany. The scars she remembered had smoothed out and faded and were replaced by newer marks. There were lines

297

in his forehead. Lines around his eyes. But his nose was still straight and unbroken. His front teeth were still there, like trophies. She slid her hand down to his and felt his knuckles. They were large and hard, like walnut shells matted with scar tissue. *Still a fighter*, she thought. *Still trading his hands for his nose and his teeth*. She moved up to his chest. He had a hole there, left of centre. Ruptured muscle, a crater big enough for the tip of her finger. A gunshot wound. Old, but new to her. Probably a .38.

'New York,' Reacher said. 'Years ago. Everyone asks.'

'Everyone?'

'Who sees it.'

Hutton snuggled in closer. 'How many people see it?'

He smiled. 'You know, on beaches, stuff like that.'

'And in bed?'

'Locker rooms,' he said.

'And in bed,' she said again.

'I'm not a monk,' he said.

'Did it hurt?'

'I don't remember. I was out for three weeks.'

'It's right over your heart.'

'It was a little revolver. Probably a weak load. He should have tried a head shot. That would have been better.'

'For him. Not for you.'

'I'm a lucky man. Always have been, always will be.'

'Maybe. But you should take better care.'

'I try my best.'

298

Chenko and Vladimir stayed together and took the north side of town. They kept well away from the motor court. The cops had that situation buttoned up, presumably. So their first stop was the sports bar. They went in and walked around. It was dark inside and not very busy. Maybe thirty guys. None of them matched the sketch. None of them was Reacher. Vladimir stayed near the door and Chenko checked the men's room. One stall had a closed door. Chenko waited until the toilet flushed and the guy came out. It wasn't Reacher. It was just a guy. So Chenko rejoined Vladimir and they got back in the car. Started quartering the streets, slowly, patiently, covering three sides of every block and pausing at the turns to scan the sidewalks on the fourth.

Hutton propped herself on an elbow and looked down at Reacher's face. His eyes were still the same. Set a little deeper, maybe, and a little more hooded. But they still shone blue like ice chips under an Arctic sun. Like a colour map of twin snow-melt lakes in a high mountain landscape. But their expression had changed. Fourteen years ago they had been rimmed red by the desert sandstorms and clouded with some kind of bitter cynicism. They had been army eyes. Cop eyes. She remembered the way they would swing slow and lazy across a room like deadly tracers curling in towards a target. Now they were clearer. Younger. More innocent. He was fourteen years older, but his gaze was like a child's again.

'You just had your hair cut,' she said.

'This morning,' he said. 'For you.'

'For me?'

'Yesterday I looked like a wild man. They told me you were coming. I didn't want you to think I was some kind of a bum.'

'Aren't you?'

'Some kind, I guess.'

'What kind?'

'The voluntary kind.'

'We should eat,' she said.

'Sounds like a plan,' he said.

'What do you want?'

'Whatever you get. We'll share. Order big portions.'

'You can choose your own if you want.'

He shook his head. 'A month from now some DoD clerk is going to go through your expenses. Better for you if he sees one meal rather than two.'

'Worried about my reputation?'

'I'm worried about your next promotion.'

'I won't get one. I'm terminal at brigadier general.'

'Not now this Petersen guy owes you a big one.'

'Can't deny two stars would be cool.'

'For me too,' Reacher said. 'I got screwed by plenty of two-stars. To think I screwed one myself would be fun.'

She made a face.

'Food,' Reacher said.

'I like salads,' she said.

'Someone's got to, I guess.'

'Don't you?'

'Get a chicken Caesar to start and a steak to

300

follow. You eat the rabbit food, I'll eat the steak. Then get some kind of a big dessert. And a big pot of coffee.'

'I like tea.'

'Can't do it,' Reacher said. 'There are some compromises I just can't make. Not even for the DoD.'

'But I'm thirsty.'

'They'll send ice water. They always do.'

'I outrank you.'

'You always did. You ever see me drink tea because of it?'

She shook her head and got out of bed. Padded naked across to the desk. Checked the menu and dialled the phone. Ordered chicken Caesar, a sixteen-ounce sirloin, and a big pie with ice cream. And a six-cup pot of coffee. Reacher smiled at her.

'Twenty minutes,' she said. 'Let's take a shower.'

Raskin took the heart of downtown. He was on foot with the sketch in his hand and a list in his head: restaurants, bars, diners, sandwich shops, groceries, hotels. He started at the Metropole Palace. The lobby, the bar. No luck. He moved on to a Chinese restaurant two blocks away. In and out, fast and discreet. He figured he was pretty good for this kind of work. He wasn't a very noticeable guy. Not memorable. Average height, average weight, unremarkable face. Just a hole in the air, which in some ways was a frustration, but in others was a major advantage. People looked at him, but they didn't really *see* him. Their eyes slid right on by.

Reacher wasn't in the Chinese place. Or the sub shop, or the Irish bar. So Raskin stopped on the sidewalk and decided to dodge north. He could check the lawyer's office and then head towards the Marriott. Because according to Linsky those places were where the women were. And in Raskin's experience guys who weren't just holcs in the air got to hang out with women more than the average.

Reacher got out of the shower and borrowed Hutton's toothbrush and toothpaste and comb. Then he towelled off and walked around and collected his clothes. Put them on and tucked them in. He was dressed and sitting on the bed when he heard the knock at the door.

'Room service,' a foreign voice called.

Hutton put her head out the bathroom door. She was dressed but halfway through drying her hair.

'You go,' Reacher said.

'Me?'

'You have to sign for it.'

'You can write my name.'

'Two hours from now the cops won't have found me and they'll come back here. Better that we don't have a guy downstairs who knows you're not alone.'

'You never relax, do you?'

'The less I relax the luckier I get.'

Hutton patted her hair into shape and headed for the door. Reacher heard the rattle of a cart and the clink of plates and the scratch of a pen. Then he heard the door close and he stepped through to the living room and found a wheeled table set up in the middle of the floor. The waiter had placed one chair behind it.

'One knife,' Hutton said. 'One fork. One spoon. We didn't think of that.'

'We'll take turns,' Reacher said. 'Kind of romantic.'

'I'll cut your steak up and you can use your fingers.'

'You could feed it to me. We should have ordered grapes.'

She smiled.

'Do you remember James Barr?' he asked.

'Too much water over the dam,' she said. 'But I reread his file yesterday.'

'How good a shooter was he?'

'Not the best we ever had, not the worst.'

'That's what I remember. I was just in the garage, taking a look. It was impressive shooting. Very impressive. I don't remember him being *that* good.'

'There's a lot of evidence there.'

He nodded. Said nothing.

'Maybe he's been practising hard,' she said. 'He was in five years but he's been out nearly three times as long. Maybe he was a late developer.'

'Maybe,' he said.

She looked at him. 'You're not staying, are you? You're planning on leaving right after dinner. Because of this thing with the cops. You think they'll come back to the room.'

'They will,' Reacher said. 'Count on it.'

'I don't have to let them in.'

'A place like this, the cops will do pretty much

what they want. And if they find me here, you're in trouble.'

'Not if you're innocent.'

'You've got no legitimate way of telling what I am. That's what they'll say.'

'I'm the lawyer here,' Hutton said.

'And I was a cop,' Reacher said. 'I know what they're like. They hate fugitives. Fugitives drive them nuts. They'll arrest you along with me and sort it all out next month. By which time your second star will be in the toilet.'

'So where are you going?'

'No idea. But I'll think of something.'

The street door at the bottom of the black glass tower was locked for the night. Raskin knocked on it, twice. The security guard at the lobby desk looked up. Raskin waved the sketch at him.

'Delivery,' he mouthed.

The guard got up and walked over and used a key from a bunch on a chain to unlock the door. Raskin stepped inside.

'Rodin,' he said. 'Fourth floor.'

The guard nodded. The law offices of Helen Rodin had received plenty of deliveries that day. Boxes, cartons, guys with hand trucks. One more was to be expected. No big surprise. He walked back to his desk without comment and Raskin walked over to the elevator. Got in and pressed four.

First thing he saw on the fourth floor was a city cop standing outside the lawyer's door. Raskin knew what that meant, immediately. It meant the lawyer's office was still a live possibility. Which meant Reacher wasn't in there at the present time and hadn't tried to get in there any time recently. So Raskin wheeled round like he was confused by the corridor layout and headed round a corner. Waited a moment and then headed back to the elevator. He folded the sketch and put it in his pocket. In the lobby he gave the guard a job-done type of wave and headed back out into the night. Turned left and headed north and east towards the Marriott Suites.

The six-cup pot of coffee was more than even Reacher could manage. He quit after five. Hutton didn't seem to mind. He guessed she thought five out of six justified his insistence.

'Come see me in Washington,' she said.

'I will,' he said. 'For sure. Next time I'm there.'

'Don't get caught.'

'I won't,' he said. 'Not by these guys.'

Then he just looked at her for a minute. Storing away the memory. Adding another fragment to his mosaic. He kissed her once on the lips and walked to the door. Let himself out into the corridor and headed for the stairs. On the ground floor he turned away from the lobby and used the fire door again. It swung shut and locked behind him and he took a deep breath and stepped out of the shadows and headed for the sidewalk.

Raskin saw him immediately. He was thirty yards away, walking fast, coming up on the Marriott from the rear. He saw a flash of glass in the street light. A fire door, opening. He saw a tall man stepping out. Standing still. Then the door jerked shut on a hydraulic closer and the tall man turned to watch it latch behind him and a stray beam of light was reflected off the moving glass and played briefly across his face. Just for a split second, like a hand-held flashlight swinging through a fast arc. Like a camera strobe. Not much. But enough for Raskin to be certain. The man who had come through the fire door was thc man in the sketch. Jack Reacher, for sure, no question. Right height, right weight, right face. Raskin had studied the details long and hard.

So he stopped dead and stepped backwards into the shadows. Watched, and waited. Saw Reacher glance right, glance left, and set out walking straight ahead, due west, fast and easy. Raskin stayed where he was and counted *one, two, three* in his head. Then he came out of the shadows and crossed the parking lot and stopped again and peered round the corner to the west. Reacher was twenty yards ahead. Still walking, still relaxed. Still unaware. Centre of the sidewalk, long strides, his arms swinging loose at his sides. He was a big guy. That was for sure. As big as Vladimir, easily.

Raskin counted to three again and let Reacher get forty yards ahead. Then he set out following. He kept his eyes fixed on the target and fumbled his cell phone out of his pocket. Speed-dialled Grigor Linsky's number. Reacher walked on, forty yards in the distance. Raskin put the phone to his ear.

'Yes?' Linsky said.

'I found him,' Raskin whispered.

'Where?'

'He's walking. West from the Marriott. He's about level with the courthouse now, three blocks to the north.'

'Where's he going?'

'Wait,' Raskin whispered. 'Hold on.'

Reacher stopped on a corner. Glanced left and turned right, towards the shadows under the raised highway. Still relaxed. Raskin watched him across waist-high trash in an empty lot.

'He's turned north,' he whispered.

'Towards?'

'I don't know. The sports bar, maybe.'

'OK,' Linsky said. 'We'll come north. We'll wait fifty yards up the street from the sports bar. Call me back in three minutes exactly. Meanwhile don't let him out of your sight.'

'OK,' Raskin said. He clicked his phone off but kept it up at his ear and took a short cut across the empty lot. Paused against a blank brick wall and peered round its corner. Reacher was still forty yards ahead, still in the centre of the sidewalk, arms swinging, still moving fast. A confident man, Raskin thought. Perhaps overconfident.

Linsky clicked off with Raskin and immediately dialled Chenko and Vladimir. Told them to rendezvous fifty yards north of the sports bar as fast as possible. Then he dialled the Zec.

'We found him,' he said.

'Where?'

'North part of downtown.'

'Who's on him?'

'Raskin. They're on the street, walking.'

The Zec was quiet for a moment.

307

'Wait until he settles somewhere,' he said. 'And then get Chenko to call the cops. He's got the accent. He can say he's a barman or a desk clerk or whatever.'

Raskin stayed forty yards back. He called Linsky again and kept the connection open. Reacher kept on walking, same stride, same pace. His clothes were dull and hard to see in the darkness. His neck and his hands were tan, but a little more visible. And he had a narrow stripe of pale skin round a fresh haircut, ghostly in the gloom. Raskin fixed his eyes on it. It was a white U-shaped glow, six feet off the ground, alternately rising and falling an inch with every step Reacher took. *Idiot*, Raskin thought. *He should have used boot polish. That's what we'd have done in Afghanistan.* Then he thought: *Not that we ever had boot polish. Or haircuts.*

Then he stopped because Reacher stopped forty yards ahead. Raskin stepped back into a shadow and Reacher glanced right and turned left, into the mouth of a cross street, out of sight behind a building.

'He's gone west again,' Raskin whispered into the phone.

'Still good for the sports bar?' Linsky asked.

'Or the motor court.'

'Either one works for us. Move up a little. Don't lose him now.'

Raskin sprinted ten paces and slowed at the turn. Pressed himself up against the corner of the building and peered round. And stared. *Problem.* Not with the view. The cross street was long and wide and straight and lit at the far end by bright lights on the four-lane that ran north to the state highway. So, he had an excellent view. The problem was that Reacher was no longer part of it. He had disappeared. Completely.

ELEVEN

Reacher had once read that boat shoes had been invented by a yachtsman looking for better grip on slippery decks. The guy had taken a regular smooth-soled athletic shoe and cut tiny sipes into the rubber with a straight razor. He had experimented and ended up with the cuts lateral and wavy and close together. They had done the trick, like a miniature tyre tread. A whole new industry had grown up. The style had migrated by association from yachts to slips to marinas to boardwalks to summer sidewalks. Now boat shoes were everywhere. Reacher didn't like them much. They were thin and light and insubstantial.

But they were quiet.

He had seen the guy in the leather coat as soon as he stepped out of the Marriott's fire door. It would have been hard not to. Thirty yards distant, shallow angle, decent illumination from vapour lights on poles all over the place. His glance had flicked left and he had seen him quite clearly. Seen him react. Seen him stop. Seen him thereby identify himself as an opponent. Reacher had set out walking straight ahead and had scrutinized

310

the after-image his night vision had retained. What kind of opponent was this guy? Reacher had closed his eyes and concentrated, two or three paces.

Generic Caucasian, medium height, medium weight, red face and fair hair tinted orange and yellow by the street lights.

Cop or not?

Not. Because of the jacket. It was a boxy square-shouldered double-breasted style made of chestnut-coloured leather. By day it would be a definite shade of red-brown. And it had a glossy patina. It was definitely shiny. Not American. Not even from the kind of fire-sale store that sells leather garments for forty-nine bucks. It was a foreign style. East European, just like the suit the twisted old guy had worn in the plaza. Not cheap. Just different. Russian, Bulgarian, Estonian, somewhere in there.

So, not a cop.

Reacher walked on. He kept his own footsteps quiet and focused on the sounds behind him, forty yards back. Shorter strides, thicker soles, the slap of leather, the faint crunch of grit, the thump of a rubber three-quarter heel. This wasn't Charlie. No way would anybody call this guy small. Not large, but definitely not small, either. And he didn't have black hair. And this wasn't the guy who had killed the girl. Not big enough. So, add one to the tally. Not four of them. Five of them. At least. Maybe more.

Plan?

Was this guy armed? Possibly, but only with a handgun. He hadn't been carrying anything longer.

311

And Reacher was sanguine about his chances as a moving target a hundred and twenty feet in front of a guy with a handgun. Handguns were across-the-room weapons, not down-the-street propositions. Average range for a successful engagement with a handgun was about twelve feet. He was ten times more distant. And he would hear the sound of the slide in the stillness. He would have time to react.

So, what was the plan? It was tempting to think about doubling back and taking the guy down. Just for fun. For retaliation. Reacher liked retaliation. *Get your retaliation in first*, was his credo. *Show them what they're dealing with*.

Maybe.

Or maybe not. Or maybe later.

He walked on. He kept his steps silent. He kept his pace steady. He let the guy behind him fall into the rhythm. Like hypnosis. Left, right, left, right. He forced everything out of his mind except the distant footsteps behind him. He zoomed in on them. Concentrated on them. They were there, faint but perceptible. *Crunch, crunch, crunch, crunch*. Left, right, left, right. Like hypnosis. He heard the sound of a cell phone being dialled. Just ten little electronic squawks, very quiet, almost inaudible, coming at him on the breeze in a random little sequence.

He took a random turn and walked on. Left, right, left, right. The streets were deserted. Downtown was dead after working hours were over. The city still had some way to go before it grew a vibrant urban community. That was for sure. He walked on. Heard faint sibilant whispering, forty yards behind him. The cell phone. *Who are you talking to, pal?* He walked on. Then he stopped on the next corner. Glanced right and turned left, into a wide straight cross street, behind the cover of a four-storey building.

Then he ran. Five paces, ten, fifteen, twenty, fast and silent, across the street to the right-hand sidewalk, past the first alley he saw, into the second. He crouched back in the shadows, in a blank grey double doorway. A fire exit, maybe from a theatre or a movie house. He lay down flat on his front. The guy had been used to a vertical target. Instinctively he would be looking six feet off the ground. A low shape on the floor would mean less to him.

Reacher waited. He heard footsteps on the opposite sidewalk. The guy had seen his quarry turn a tight radius from the left-hand sidewalk of one street onto the left-hand sidewalk of the next street. Therefore subconsciously he would concentrate on the left, not the right. His first thought would be to look for still vertical shapes in the alleys and the doorways on the left.

Reacher waited. The footsteps kept on coming. Close now. Then Reacher saw the guy. He was on the left-hand sidewalk. He was moving slow. He was looking indecisive. He was glancing ahead, glancing left, glancing ahead. He had a cell phone up at his ear. He stopped. Stood still. Looked back over his right shoulder, at the doorways and the alleys on the other side of the street. *Worth checking?*

Yes.

The guy moved sideways and backwards like a

crab, diagonally, facing the street ahead of him and searching the right-hand sidewalk all at the same time. He moved out of Reacher's field of view like a film running in reverse. Reacher stood up silently and moved deeper into the alley into total darkness at its far end. He found a fat vertical kitchen vent and slid round behind it. Crouched on his haunches and waited.

It was a long wait. Then the footsteps came back. On the sidewalk. Into the alley. Slow, soft, careful. The guy was on his toes. No sound from the heels. Just the scrape of leather soles on grit. They rustled gently and low-level echoes of the sound came back off the alley's walls. The guy came closer. And closer.

He came close enough to smell.

Cologne, sweat, leather. He stopped four feet from where Reacher was hidden and peered hopelessly into the darkness. Reacher thought: *Another step and you're history, pal. Just one more and it's game over for you.*

The guy turned round. Walked back to the street.

Reacher stood up and followed him, swift and silent. *Tables turned. Now* I'm *behind* you. *Time to hunt the hunters.*

Reacher was bigger than most human beings and in some ways quite clumsy, but he could be light on his feet when he needed to be and had always been good at covert pursuit. It was a skill born of long practice. Mostly it employed caution and anticipation. You had to know when your quarry was going to slow, stop, turn, check. And if you

314

didn't know, you had to err on the side of caution. Better to hide and fall ten extra yards behind than give yourself away.

The guy in the leather coat searched every alley and every doorway on both sides of the street. Not well, but adequately. He searched and he moved forward, prey to the mistake that all adequate people make: *I didn't screw up yet. He's still somewhere up ahead.* He spoke twice on his cell phone. Quietly, but with agitation obvious in the tenor of his whisper. Reacher slipped from shadow to shadow behind him, hanging well back because the bright lights at the end of the street were getting close. The guy's searches became faster and more cursory. Hopeless and panicked, all at the same time. He made it to within twenty feet of the next turn and stopped dead and stood still.

And gave up. Just quit. He stood in the middle of the sidewalk and listened to his phone and said something in reply and then dropped his arms to his sides and all the covert rigidity went out of his body. He slumped a little and walked straight ahead, fast and big and loud and obvious like a guy with no purpose in the world except getting directly from *A* to *B*. Reacher waited long enough to be certain it wasn't a trick. Then he followed, moving silently from shadow to shadow.

Raskin walked past the sports bar's door and headed up the street. He could see Linsky's car in the distance. And Chenko's. The two Cadillacs were parked nose to tail at the kerb, waiting for him. Waiting for the failure. Waiting for the hole in the air. *Well, here I am*, he thought.

But Linsky was civil about it. Mainly because to criticize one of the Zec's appointees was to criticize the Zec himself, and nobody would dare to do that.

'He probably took a wrong turn,' Linsky said. 'Maybe he didn't intend to be on that particular street at all. He probably doubled back through the alleys. Or else went into one of them to take a leak. Delayed himself and came out behind you.'

'Did you check behind you?' Vladimir asked.

'Of course I did,' Raskin lied.

'So what now?' Chenko asked.

'I'll call the Zec,' Linsky said.

'He'll be royally pissed,' Vladimir said. 'We nearly had the guy.'

Linsky dialled his phone. Relayed the bad news and listened to the response. Raskin watched his face. But Linsky's face was always unreadable. A skill born of long practice, and vital necessity. And it was a short call. A short response. Indecipherable. Just faint plastic sounds in the earpiece.

Linsky clicked off.

'We keep on looking,' he said. 'On a half-mile radius of where Raskin last saw him. The Zec is sending us Sokolov. He says we're sure of success with five of us.'

'We're sure of nothing,' Chenko said. 'Except a big pain in the ass and no sleep tonight.'

Linsky held out his phone. 'So call the Zec and tell him that.'

Chenko said nothing.

316

'Take the north, Chenko,' Linsky said to him. 'Vladimir, the south. Raskin, head back east. I'll take the west. Sokolov can fill in where we need him when he gets here.'

Raskin headed back east, the way he had come, as fast as he could. He saw the sense in the Zec's plan. He had last seen Reacher about fifteen minutes ago, and a furtive man moving cautiously couldn't cover more than half a mile in fifteen minutes. So elementary logic dictated where Reacher must be. He was somewhere inside a circle one mile across. They had found him once. They could find him again.

He made it all the way down the wide straight cross street and turned south towards the raised highway. Retracing his steps. He passed through the shadows under the highway and headed for the vacant lot on the next corner. Kept close to the wall. Made the turn.

Then the wall fell on him.

At least that was what it felt like. He was hit a staggering blow from behind and he fell to his knees and his vision went dark. Then he was hit again and his lights went out and he pitched forward on his face. Last thing he felt before he lost consciousness was a hand in his pocket, stealing his cell phone.

Reacher headed back under the highway spur with the cell phone warm in his hand. He leaned his shoulder against a concrete pillar as wide as a motel room and slid round it until his body was in the shadow and his hands were in the light

317

from a lamp on a pole far above him. He took out the torn card with Emerson's numbers on it and dialled his cell.

'Yes?' Emerson said.

'Guess who?' Reacher said.

'This isn't a game, Reacher.'

'Only because you're losing.'

Emerson said nothing.

'How easy am I to find?' Reacher asked.

No reply.

'Got a pen and paper?'

'Of course I do.'

'So listen up,' Reacher said. 'And take notes.' He recited the plate numbers from the two Cadillacs. 'My guess is one of those cars was in the garage before Friday, leaving the cone. You should trace the plates, check the tapes, ask some questions. You'll find some kind of an organization with at least six men. I heard some names. Raskin and Sokolov, who seem to be low-level guys. Then Chenko and Vladimir. Vladimir looks good for the guy who killed the girl. He's as big as a house. Then there's some kind of a lieutenant whose name I didn't get. He's about sixty and has an old spinal injury. He talked to his boss and referred to him as the Zec.'

'Those are Russian names.'

'You think?'

'Except Zec. What kind of a name is Zec?'

'It's not Zec. It's *the* Zec. It's a word. A word, being used as a name.'

'What does it mean?'

'Look it up. Read some history books.'

There was a pause. The sound of writing.

'You should come in,' Emerson said. 'Talk to me face to face.'

'Not yet,' Reacher said. 'Do your job and I'll think about it.'

'I am doing my job. I'm hunting a fugitive. You killed the girl. Not some guy whose name you claim you heard, as big as a house.'

'One more thing,' Reacher said. 'I think the guy called Chenko also goes by the name of Charlie and is James Barr's friend.'

'Why?'

'The description. Small guy, dark, with black hair that sticks up like a brush.'

'James Barr has got a Russian friend? Not according to our inquiries.'

'Like I said, do your job.'

'We're doing it. Nobody mentioned a Russian friend.'

'He sounds American. I think he was involved with what happened on Friday, which means maybe this whole crew was involved.'

'Involved how?'

'I don't know. But I plan to find out. I'll call you tomorrow.'

'You'll be in jail tomorrow.'

'Like I'm in jail now? Dream on, Emerson.'

'Where are you?'

'Close by,' Reacher said. 'Sleep well, detective.'

He clicked the phone off and put Emerson's number back in his pocket and took out Helen Rodin's. Dialled it and moved round the concrete pillar into deep shadow.

'Yes?' Helen Rodin said.

'This is Reacher.'

319

'Are you OK? The cop is right outside my door now.'

'Suits me,' Reacher said. 'Suits him too, I expect. He's probably getting forty bucks an hour for the overtime.'

'They put your face on the six o'clock news. It's a big story.'

'Don't worry about me.'

'Where are you?'

'Free and clear. Making progress. I saw Charlie. I gave Emerson his plate number. Are you making progress?'

'Not really. All I've got is five random names. No reason I can see why anybody told James Barr to shoot any one of them.'

'You need Franklin. You need research.'

'I can't afford Franklin.'

'I want you to find that address in Kentucky for me.'

'Kentucky?'

'Where James Barr went to shoot.'

Reacher heard her juggle the phone and flip through paper. Then she came back and read out an address. It meant nothing to Reacher. A road, a town, a state, a zip.

'What's Kentucky got to do with anything?' Helen asked.

Reacher heard a car on the street. Close by, to his left, fat tyres rolling slow. He slid round the pillar and looked. A PD prowl car, crawling, lights off. Two cops in the front, craning their necks, looking right, looking left.

'Got to go,' he said. He clicked the phone off and put it on the ground at the base of the pillar.

320

Emerson's caller ID would have trapped the number and any cell phone's physical location could be tracked by the recognition pulse that it sends to the network, once every fifteen seconds, regular as clockwork. So Reacher left the phone in the dirt and headed west, forty feet below the raised roadbed.

Ten minutes later he was opposite the back of the black glass tower, in the shadows under the highway, facing the vehicle ramp. There was an empty cop car parked on the kerb. It looked still and cold. Settled. Like it had been there for a spell. *The guy outside Helen's door*, Reacher thought. He crossed the street and walked down the ramp. Into the underground garage. The concrete was all painted dirty white and there were fluorescent tubes blazing every fifteen feet. There were pools of light and pools of darkness. Reacher felt like he was walking out of the wings across a succession of brightly lit stages. The ceiling was low. There were fat square pillars holding up the building. The service core was in the centre. The whole space was cold and silent and about forty yards deep and maybe three times as wide.

Forty yards deep.

Just like the new extension on First Street. Reacher stepped over and put his back against the front wall. Walked all the way across to the back wall. *Thirty-five paces.* He turned like a swimmer at the end of a lap and walked back. *Thirty-five paces.* He crossed diagonally to the far corner. The garage was dark back there. He threaded between two NBC vans and found the blue Ford Mustang he guessed belonged to Ann Yanni. It was clean and shiny. Recently waxed. It had small windows, because of the convertible top. A raked windshield. Tinted glass.

He tried the passenger door. Locked. He moved round the hood and tried the driver's door. The handle moved. Unlocked. He glanced around and opened the door.

No alarm.

He reached inside and touched the unlock button. There was a triple *thunk* as both door locks and the trunk lock unlatched. He closed the driver's door and stepped back to the trunk. The spare tyre was under the floor. Nested inside the wheel were the jack and a length of metal pipe that both worked the jack and undid the wheel nuts. He took the pipe out and closed the trunk. Stepped round to the passenger side and opened the door and got inside the car.

The interior smelled of perfume and coffee. He opened the glove box and found a stack of road maps and a small leather folder the size of a purse diary. Inside the folder were an insurance slip and an auto registration both made out to *Ms Janine Lorna Ann Yanni* at a local Indiana address. He put the folder away again and closed the glove box. Found the right levers and lowered his seat as far as it would go. He reclined the back all the way, which wasn't far. Then he moved the whole seat backwards to give himself as much legroom as he could get. He untucked his shirt and rested the pipe in his lap and lay back in the seat. Stretched. He had about three hours to wait. He tried to sleep. *Sleep when you can* was the old army rule.

First thing Emerson did was contact the phone company. He confirmed that the number his caller ID had caught was a cell phone. The service contract was written out to a business operating under the name *Specialized Services of Indiana*. Emerson tasked a first-year detective to track the business and told the phone company to track the phone. Initial progress was mixed. Specialized Services of Indiana dead-ended because it was owned by an offshore trust in Bermuda and had no local address. But the phone company reported that the cell phone was stationary and was showing up on three cells at once, which meant it had to be in the downtown area and would be easy to triangulate.

Rosemary Barr sweet-talked her way past the Board of Corrections desk on the sixth floor of the hospital and was granted an out-of-hours visit with her brother. But when she got to his room she found he was deeply asleep. Her sweet talk was wasted. She sat for thirty minutes but he didn't wake up. She watched the monitors. His heartbeat was strong and regular. His breathing was fine. He was still handcuffed and his head was still clamped but his body was perfectly still. She checked his chart, to make sure he was being properly cared for. She saw the doctor's scribbled note: *possible early-onset PA?* She had no idea what that meant, and in the middle of the evening she couldn't find anyone willing to explain it to her.

< star row>

*　　*　　*

The phone company marked the cell phone's location on a large scale city map and faxed it to Emerson. Emerson tore it out of the machine and spent five minutes trying to make sense of it. He was expecting to find the three arrows meeting at a hotel, or a bar, or a restaurant. Instead they met on a vacant lot under the raised highway. He had a brief image in his mind of Reacher sleeping rough in a cardboard box. Then he concluded that the phone was abandoned, which was confirmed ten minutes later by the patrol car he sent out to check.

And then just for formality's sake he fired up his computer and entered the plate numbers Reacher had given him. They came back as late-model Cadillac Devilles, both black, both registered to Specialized Services of Indiana. He wrote *dead end* on the sheet of paper and put it in a file.

Reacher woke up every time he heard the elevator motors start. The sound whined down the shaft through the cables and the moving cars rumbled. The first three times were false alarms. Just anonymous office people heading home after a long day at work. Every forty minutes or so they came down alone and walked wearily to their cars and drove away. Three times the tang of cold exhaust fumes drifted and three times the garage went quiet again and three times Reacher went back to sleep.

The fourth time, he stayed awake. He heard the elevator start and checked his watch. Eleven forty-five. *Showtime.* He waited and heard the elevator doors open. This time, it wasn't just another lone guy in a suit. It was a big crowd. Eight or ten people. Noisy. It was the whole cast and crew from the NBC affiliate's eleven o'clock news.

Reacher pressed himself down in the Mustang's passenger seat and hid the tyre iron underneath the tails of his shirt. It was cold against the skin of his stomach. He stared up at the fabric roof and waited.

A heavy guy in baggy jeans passed through the darkness within five feet of the Mustang's front fender. He had a ragged grey beard and was wearing a Grateful Dead T-shirt under a torn cotton cardigan. Not on-screen talent. Maybe a cameraman. He walked on towards a silver pick-up and climbed inside. Then came a man in a sharkskin suit and orange make-up. He had big hair and white teeth. Definitely on-screen talent, maybe weather, maybe sports. He passed by on the Mustang's other side and got into a white Ford Taurus. Then came three women together, young, casual dress, maybe the studio director and the floor manager and the vision mixer. They squeezed between the Mustang's trunk and a broadcast van. The car rocked three times as they nudged it. Then they split up and headed for their own separate rides.

Then came three more people.

Then came Ann Yanni.

Reacher didn't notice her individually until she put her hand on her car's door handle. She paused and called something out to one of the others. She got an answer, said something else, and then opened the door. She came in butt first, swivelling and ducking her head. She was wearing old jeans and a new silk blouse. It looked expensive. Reacher guessed she had been on camera, but at an anchor's desk, visible from the waist up only. Her hair was stiff with spray. She dumped herself in the seat and shut her door. Then she glanced to her right.

'Keep very quiet,' Reacher said to her. 'Or I'll shoot you.'

He jabbed the tyre iron at her, under his shirt. Half-inch wide, long and straight, it looked plausible. She stared at it in shock. Face to face two feet away she looked thinner and older than she looked on the television screen. There were fine lines all around her eyes, full of makeup. But she was very beautiful. She had impossibly perfect features, bold and vivid and larger than life, like most TV people. Her blouse had a formal collar but was open three buttons. Prim and sexy, all at the same time.

'Hands where I can see them,' Reacher said. 'In your lap.' He didn't want her to go for the horn. 'Keys on the console.' He didn't want her to hit the panic button. The new Fords he had driven had a little red button on the remote fob. He assumed it set off an alarm.

'Just sit tight,' he said. 'Nice and quiet. We'll be OK.'

He clicked the button on his side and locked the car.

'I know who you are,' she said.

'So do I,' he said.

He kept the tyre iron in place and waited.

Yanni sat still, hands in her lap, breathing hard, looking more and more scared as all around them her colleagues' cars started up. Blue haze drifted. People drove away, one by one. No backward glances. The end of a long day.

'Keep very quiet,' Reacher said again, as a reminder. 'Then we'll be OK.'

Yanni glanced left, glanced right. Tension in her body.

'Don't do it,' Reacher said. 'Don't do anything. Or I'll pull the trigger. Gut shot. Or thigh. You'll take twenty minutes to bleed out. Lots of pain.'

'What do you want?' Yanni asked.

'I want you to be quiet and sit still. Just for a few more minutes.'

She clamped her teeth and went quiet and sat still. The last car drove away. The white Taurus. The guy with the hair. The weather man, or the sportscaster. There was tyre squeal as he turned and engine noise as he gunned up the ramp. Then those sounds faded out and the garage went completely silent.

'What do you want?' Yanni asked again. Her voice was faint. Her eyes were huge. She was trembling. She was thinking rape, murder, torture, dismemberment.

Reacher turned on the dome light.

'I want you to win the Pulitzer Prize,' he said.

'What?'

'Or the Emmy or whatever it is you guys get.'

'What?'

'I want you to listen to a story,' he said.

'What story?'

'Watch,' Reacher said.

327

He lifted his shirt. Showed her the tyre iron resting against his stomach. She stared at it. Or at his shrapnel scar. Or both. He wasn't sure. He balanced the tyre iron in his palm. Held it up in the light.

'From your trunk,' he said. 'Not a gun.'

He clicked the button on the door and unlocked the car.

'You're free to go,' he said. 'Whenever you want.'

She put her hand on the handle.

'But if you go, I go,' Reacher said. 'You won't see me again. You'll miss the story. Someone else will get it.'

'We've been running your picture all night,' she said. 'And the cops have got wanted posters all over town. You killed the girl.'

Reacher shook his head. 'Actually I didn't, and that's part of the story.'

'What story?' she said again.

'Last Friday,' Reacher said. 'It wasn't what it seemed.'

'I'm going to get out of the car now,' Yanni said.

'No,' Reacher said. 'I'll get out. I apologize if I upset you. But I need your help and you need mine. So I'll get out. You lock the doors, start the car, keep your foot on the brake, and open your window an inch. We'll talk through the window. You can drive off any time you want.'

She said nothing. Just stared straight ahead as if she could make him vanish by not looking at him. He opened his door. Slid out and turned and laid the tyre iron gently on the seat. Then he closed the door and just stood there. He tucked his shirt in. He heard the *thunk* of her door locks. She started her engine. Her brake lights flared red. He saw her reach up and switch off the dome light. Her face disappeared into shadow. He heard the transmission move out of Park. Her reversing lights flashed white as she moved the selector through Reverse into Drive. Then her brake lights went out and the engine roared and she drove off in a fast wide circle through the empty garage. Her tyres squealed. Grippy rubber on smooth concrete. The squeals echoed. She lined up for the exit ramp and accelerated hard.

Then she jammed on the brakes.

The Mustang came to rest with its front wheels on the base of the ramp. Reacher walked towards it, crouching a little so he could see through the small rear window. No cell phone. She was just sitting there, staring straight ahead, hands on the wheel. The brake lights blazed red, so bright they hurt. The exhaust pipes burbled. White fumes kicked backwards. Drops of water dripped out and made tiny twin pools on the floor.

Reacher walked round to her window and stayed three feet away. She buzzed the glass down an inch and a half. He dropped into a crouch, so he could see her face.

'Why do I need your help?' she asked.

'Because Friday was over too soon for you,' he said. 'But you can get it back. There's another layer. It's a big story. You'll win prizes. You'll get a better job. CNN will beat a path to your door.'

'You think I'm that ambitious?'

'I think you're a journalist.'

'What does *that* mean?'

'That in the end journalists like stories. They like the truth.'

She paused, almost a whole minute. Stared straight ahead. The car ticked and clicked as it warmed up. Reacher could sense the idle speed straining against the brakes. Then he saw her glance down and move her arm and shove the selector into Park. The Mustang rolled back six inches and stopped. Reacher shuffled sideways to stay level with the window. Yanni turned her head and looked straight at him.

'So tell me the story,' she said. 'Tell me the truth.'

He told her the story, and the truth. He sat cross-legged on the concrete floor, so as to appear immobile and unthreatening. He left nothing out. He ran through all the events, all the inferences, all the theories, all the guesses. At the end he just stopped talking and waited for her reaction.

'Where were you when the girl was killed?' she asked.

'Asleep in the motor court.'

'Alone?'

'All night. Room eight. I slept very well.'

'No alibi.'

'You never have an alibi when you need one. That's a universal law of nature.'

She looked at him for a long moment.

'What do you want me to do?' she said.

'I want you to research the victims.'

She paused.

'We could do that,' she said. 'We have researchers.'

'Not good enough,' Reacher said. 'I want you to hire a guy called Franklin. Helen Rodin can tell you about him. She's in this building, two floors above you.'

'Why hasn't she hired this Franklin guy herself?'

'Because she can't afford him. You can. I assume you've got a budget. A week of Franklin's time probably costs less than one of your weather guy's haircuts.'

'And then what?'

'Then we put it all together.'

'How big is this?'

'Pulitzer-sized. Emmy-sized. New-job-sized.'

'How would you know? You're not in the business.'

'I was in the army. I would guess this is worth a Bronze Star. That's probably a rough equivalent. Better than a poke in the eye with a sharp stick.'

'I don't know,' she said. 'I should turn you in.'

'You can't,' he said. 'You pull out a phone and I'll take off up the ramp. They won't find me. They've been trying all day.'

'I don't really care about prizes,' she said.

'So do it for fun,' he said. 'Do it for professional satisfaction.'

He rocked sideways and took out the napkin with Helen Rodin's number on it. Held it edge-on at the crack of the window. Yanni took it from him, delicately, trying to avoid touching his fingers with hers.

'Call Helen,' Reacher said. 'Right now. She'll vouch for me.'

Yanni took a cell phone out of her purse and

turned it on. Watched the screen and waited until it was ready and then dialled the number. She passed the napkin back. Listened to the phone.

'Helen Rodin?' she said. Then she buzzed the window all the way up and Reacher didn't hear any of the conversation. He gambled that it was really Helen she was speaking to. It was possible that she had looked at the napkin and dialled another number entirely. Not 911, because she had dialled ten digits. But she might have called the cops' main desk. A reporter might know that number by heart.

But it was Helen on the line. Yanni buzzed the window down again and passed him her phone through the gap.

'Is this for real?' Helen asked him.

'I don't think she's decided yet,' Reacher said. 'But it might work out.'

'Is it a good idea?'

'She's got resources. And having the media watching our backs might help us.'

'Put her back on.'

Reacher passed the phone through the window. This time Yanni kept the glass down so that Reacher heard her end of the rest of the conversation. Initially she sounded sceptical, and then neutral, and then somewhat convinced. She arranged to meet on the fourth floor first thing in the morning. Then she clicked the phone off.

'There's a cop outside her door,' Reacher said.

'She told me that,' Yanni said. 'But they're looking for you, not me.'

'What exactly are you going to do?'

'I haven't decided yet.'

Reacher said nothing.

'I guess I need to understand where you're coming from first,' Yanni said. 'Obviously you don't care anything about James Barr himself. So is this all for the sister? Rosemary?'

Reacher watched her watching him. A woman, a journalist.

'Partly for Rosemary,' he said.

'But?'

'Mostly for the puppet master. He's sitting there thinking he's as smart as a whip. I don't like that. Never have. Makes me want to show him what smart really is.'

'Like a challenge?'

'He had the girl killed, Yanni. She was just a dumb sweet kid looking for a little fun. He pushed open the wrong door there. So he deserves to have something come out at him. That's the challenge.'

'You hardly knew her.'

'That doesn't make her any less innocent.'

'OK.'

'OK what?'

'NBC will spring for Franklin. Then we'll see where that takes us.'

'Thanks,' Reacher said. 'I appreciate it.'

'You should.'

'I apologize again. For scaring you.'

'I nearly died of fright.'

'I'm very sorry.'

'Anything else?'

'Yes,' Reacher said. 'I need to borrow your car.'

'My *car*?'

333

'Your car.'

'What for?'

'To sleep in and then to go to Kentucky in.'

'What's in Kentucky?'

'Part of the puzzle.'

Yanni shook her head. 'This is nuts.'

'I'm a careful driver.'

'I'd be aiding and abetting a fugitive criminal.'

'I'm not a criminal,' Reacher said. 'A criminal is someone who has been convicted of a crime after a trial. Therefore I'm not a fugitive, either. I haven't been arrested or charged. I'm a suspect, that's all.'

'I can't lend you my car after running your picture all night.'

'You could say you didn't recognize me. It's a sketch, not a photograph. Maybe it isn't totally accurate.'

'Your hair is different.'

'There you go. I had it cut this morning.'

'But I would recognize your name. I wouldn't lend my car to a stranger without at least knowing his name, would I?'

'Maybe I gave you a false name. You met a guy with a different name who didn't look much like the sketch, that's all.'

'What name?'

'Joe Gordon,' Reacher said.

'Who's he?'

'Yankees' second baseman in 1940. They finished third. Not Joe's fault. He had a decent career. He played exactly one thousand games and had exactly one thousand hits.'

'You know a lot.'

'I'll know more tomorrow if you lend me your car.'

'How would I get home tonight?'

'I'll drive you.'

'Then you'll know where I live.'

'I already know where you live. I checked your registration. To make sure it was your car.'

Yanni said nothing.

'Don't worry,' Reacher said. 'If I wanted to hurt you, you'd already be hurt, don't you think?'

She said nothing.

'I'm a careful driver,' he said again. 'I'll get you home safe.'

'I'll call a cab,' she said. 'Better for you that way. The roads are quiet now and this is a distinctive car. The cops know it's mine. They stop me all the time. They claim I'm speeding but really they want an autograph or they want to look down my shirt.'

She used her phone again and told a driver to meet her inside the garage. Then she climbed out of the car and left the motor running.

'Go park in a dark corner,' she said. 'Safer for you if you don't leave before the morning rush.'

'Thanks,' Reacher said.

'And do it now,' she said. 'Your face has been all over the news and the cab driver will have been watching. At least I hope he was watching. I need the ratings.'

'Thanks,' Reacher said again.

Ann Yanni walked away and stood at the bottom of the ramp like she was waiting for a bus. Reacher slid into her seat and racked it back and reversed the car deep into the garage. Then he swung it round and parked nose-in in a distant corner. He shut it down and watched in the mirror. Five minutes later a green-and-white Crown Vic rolled down the ramp and Ann Yanni climbed into the back. The cab turned and drove out to the street and the garage went quiet.

Reacher stayed in Ann Yanni's Mustang but he didn't stay in the garage under the black glass tower. Too risky. If Yanni had a change of heart he would be a sitting duck. He could picture her getting hit by cold feet or a crisis of conscience and picking up the phone and calling Emerson. *He's fast asleep in my car in the corner of the garage at work. Right now.* So three minutes after her cab left he started up again and drove out and round to the garage on First Street. It was empty. He went up to the second level and parked in the space that James Barr had used. He didn't put money in the meter. Just pulled out Yanni's stack of road maps and planned his route and then pushed back on the wheel and reclined the seat and went back to sleep.

He woke himself up five hours later, before dawn, and set out on the drive south to Kentucky. He saw three cop cars before he passed the city limits. But they didn't pay him any attention. They were too busy hunting Jack Reacher to waste time harassing a cute news anchor.

TWELVE

Dawn happened somewhere way over in the east about an hour into the drive. The sky changed from black to grey to purple and then low orange sunlight came up over the horizon. Reacher switched his headlights off. He didn't like to run with lights after daybreak. Just a subliminal thing, for the State Troopers camped out on the shoulders. Lights after dawn suggested all kinds of things, like fast through-the-night escapes from trouble hundreds of miles behind. The Mustang was already provocative enough. It was loud and aggressive and it was the kind of car that gets stolen a lot.

But the troopers that Reacher saw stayed put on the shoulder. He kept the car at a nothing-to-hide seventy miles an hour and touched the CD button on the dash. Got a blast of mid-period Sheryl Crow in return, which hc didn't mind at all. He stayed with it. *Every day is a winding road*, Sheryl told him. *I know*, he thought. *Tell me about it.*

*   *   *

He crossed the Ohio river on a long iron trestle with the sun low on his left. For a moment it turned the slow water into molten gold. Light reflected up at him from below the horizontal and made the inside of the car unnaturally bright. The trestle spars flashed past like a stroboscope. The effect was disconcerting. He closed his left eye and entered Kentucky squinting.

He kept south on a county road and waited for the Blackford river. According to Ann Yanni's maps it was a tributary that flowed on a southeast to northwest diagonal into the Ohio. Near its source it formed a perfect equilateral triangle about three miles on a side with two rural routes. And according to Helen Rodin's information James Barr's favoured firing range was somewhere inside that triangle.

But it turned out that the firing range *was* the triangle. Three miles out Reacher saw a wire fence on the left shoulder of the road that started directly after he crossed the Blackford on a bridge. The fence ran all the way to the next intersection and had *Keep Out Live Gunfire* signs on every fourth post. Then it turned a sixty-degree angle and ran three more miles north and east. Reacher followed it and where it met the Blackford again he found a gate and a gravel clearing and a complex of low huts. The gate was chained. It was hung with a hand-painted sign that read: *Open 8 a.m. until dark.*

He checked his watch. He was a half-hour too early. On the other side of the road was an aluminium coach diner fronted by a gravel lot. He pulled in and stopped the Mustang right by the diner's door. He was hungry. The Marriott's room-service steak seemed like a long time ago.

He ate a long slow breakfast at a window table and watched the scene across the street. By eight o'clock there were three pickup trucks waiting to get into the range. At five after eight a guy showed up in a black diesel Humvee and mimed an apology for being late and unchained the gate. He stood aside and let his customers in ahead of him. Then he climbed back in his Humvee and followed them. He went through the same apologetic routine with the main hut door and then all four guys went inside and disappeared from view. Reacher called for another cup of coffee. He figured he would let the guy deal with the early rush and then stroll over when he had a moment to talk. And the coffee was good. Too good to pass up. It was fresh, hot, and very strong.

By eight twenty he started to hear rifles firing. Dull percussive sounds, robbed of their power and impact by distance and wind and berms of earth. He figured the guns were about two hundred yards away, firing west. The shots came slow and steady, the sound of serious shooters aiming for the inner rings. Then he heard a string of lighter pops, from a handgun. He listened to the familiar sounds for a spell and then left two bucks on the table and paid a twelve-dollar check at the register. Went outside and got back in the Mustang and drove through the lot and bumped up over the camber of the road and straight in through the range's open gate.

He found the Humvee guy behind a waist-high

counter in the main hut. Up close he was older than he had looked from a distance. More than fifty, less than sixty, sparse grey hair, lined skin, but ramrod straight. He had a weathered neck wider than his head and the sort of eyes that pegged him as an ex-Marine noncom even without the tattoos on his forearms and the souvenirs on the wall behind him. The tattoos were old and faded and the souvenirs were mostly pennants and unit patches. But the centrepiece of the display was a yellowing paper target framed under glass. It had a tight group of five .300 holes inside the inner ring and a sixth just clipping it.

'Help you?' the guy said. He was looking past Reacher's shoulder, out the window, at the Mustang.

'I'm here to solve all your problems,' Reacher said.

'Really?'

'No, not really. I just want to ask you some questions.'

The guy paused. 'About James Barr?'

'Good guess.'

'No.'

'No?'

'I don't speak to reporters.'

'I'm not a reporter.'

'That's a five-litre Mustang out there, with a couple of options on it. So it ain't a cop car or a rental. And it's got Indiana plates. And it's got an NBC sticker in the windshield. Therefore my guess is you're a reporter fixing to gin up a television story about how James Barr used my place to train and prepare.'

340

'Did he?'

'I told you, I'm not talking.'

'But Barr came here, right?'

'I'm not talking,' the guy said again. No malice in his voice. Just determination. No hostility. Just self-assurance. He wasn't talking. End of story. The hut went quiet. Nothing to hear except the distant gunfire and a low rattling hum from another room. A refrigerator, maybe.

'I'm not a reporter,' Reacher said again. 'I borrowed a reporter's car, that's all. To get down here.'

'So what are you?'

'Just a guy who knew James Barr way back. I want to know about his friend Charlie. I think his friend Charlie led him astray.'

The guy didn't say: *What friend?* He didn't ask: *Who's Charlie?* He just shook his head and said, 'Can't help you.'

Reacher switched his gaze to the framed target. 'Is that yours?' he asked.

'Everything you see here is mine.'

'What range was it?' he asked.

'Why?'

'Because I'm thinking that if it was six hundred yards, you're pretty good. If it was eight hundred, you're very good. If it was a thousand, you're unbelievable.'

'You shoot?' the guy asked.

'I used to,' Reacher said.

'Military?'

'Once upon a time.'

The guy turned round and lifted the frame off its hook. Laid it gently on the counter and turned

341

it round for inspection. There was a handwritten inscription in faded ink across the bottom of the paper: *1978 U.S. Marine Corps 1000 Yard Invitational. Gunny Samuel Cash, third place.* Then there were three signatures from three adjudicators.

'You're Sergeant Cash?' Reacher said.

'Retired and scuffling,' the guy said.

'Me too.'

'But not from the Corps.'

'You can tell that just by looking?'

'Easily.'

'Army,' Reacher said. 'But my dad was a Marine.'

Cash nodded. 'Makes you half-human.'

Reacher traced his fingertip over the glass, above the bullet holes. A fine group of five, and a sixth that had drifted just a hair.

'Good shooting,' he said.

'I'd be lucky to do that at half the range today.'

'Me too,' Reacher said. 'Time marches on.'

'You saying you could have done it back in the day?'

Reacher didn't answer. Truth was he had actually won the Marine Corps 1000 Yard Invitational, exactly ten years after Cash had scraped third place. He had placed all his rounds through the precise centre of the target, in a ragged hole a man could put his thumb through. He had displayed the shiny cup on one office shelf after another through twelve busy months. It had been an exceptional year. He had been at some kind of peak, physically, mentally, every way there was. That year, he couldn't miss, literally or metaphorically. But he hadn't defended his title the following year, even though the MP hierarchy had wanted him to. Later, looking back, he understood how that decision marked two things: the beginning of his long slow divorce from the army, and the beginning of restlessness. The beginning of always moving on and never looking back. The beginning of never wanting to do the same thing twice.

'Thousand yards is a long way,' Gunny Cash said. 'Truth is since I left the Corps I haven't met a man who could even put a mark on the paper.'

'I might have been able to clip the edge,' Reacher said.

Cash took the frame off the counter and turned and hung it back on its hook. He used the ball of his right thumb to level it.

'I don't have a thousand-yard range here,' he said. 'It would be a waste of ammunition and it would make the customers feel bad about themselves. But I've got a nice three-hundred that's not being used this morning. You could try it. A guy who could clip the paper at a thousand should be able to do pretty well at three hundred.'

Reacher said nothing.

'Don't you think?' Cash said.

'I guess,' Reacher said.

Cash opened a drawer and took out a new paper target. 'What's your name?'

'Bobby Richardson,' Reacher said. *Robert Clinton Richardson, hit .301 in 1959, 141 hits in 134 games, but the Yanks still only finished third.*

Cash took a roller ball pen from his shirt

343

pocket and wrote *R. Richardson, 300 yards*, and the date, and the time, on the paper.

'Record keeper,' Reacher said.

'Habit,' Cash said. Then he drew an *X* inside the inner ring. It was about half an inch tall and because of the slant of his handwriting a little less than half an inch wide. He left the paper on the counter and walked away into the room with the refrigerator noise. Came back out a minute later carrying a rifle. It was a Remington M24, with a Leupold Ultra scope and a front bipod. A standard-issue Marine sniper's weapon. It looked to be well used but in excellent condition. Cash placed it sideways on the counter. Detached the magazine and showed Reacher that it was empty. Operated the bolt and showed Reacher that the chamber was empty, too. Reflex, routine, caution, professional courtesy.

'Mine,' he said. 'Zeroed for three hundred yards exactly. By me myself, personally.'

'Good enough,' Reacher said. Which it was. An ex-Marine who in 1978 had been the third-best shooter in the world could be trusted on such matters.

'One shot,' Cash said. He took a single cartridge from his pocket. Held it up. It was a .300 Winchester round. Match grade. He stood it upright on the *X* on the paper target. It hid it entirely. Then he smiled. Reacher smiled back. He understood the challenge. He understood it perfectly. *Hit the X and I'll talk to you about James Barr.*

At least it's not hand-to-hand combat, Reacher thought.

'Let's go,' he said.

344

*　　*　　*

Outside the air was still and it was neither hot nor cold. Perfect shooting weather. No shivering, no risk of thermals or currents or shimmer. No wind. Cash carried the rifle and the target and Reacher carried the cartridge in the palm of his hand. They climbed into Cash's Humvee together and Cash fired it up with a loud diesel clatter.

'You like this thing?' Reacher asked, over the noise.

'Not really,' Cash said. 'I'd be happier with a sedan. But it's a question of image. Customers like it.'

The landscape was all low hills, covered in grass and stunted trees. Someone had used a bulldozer to carve wide straight paths through it. The paths were hundreds of yards apart and hundreds of yards long, and all of them were parallel. Each path was a separate rifle range. Each range was isolated from the others by natural hills and backed by high berms made from the earth scraped up by the bulldozer. The whole place looked like a half-built golf course. It was part green, part raw, all covered with red earth gashes. White-painted rocks and boulders delineated tracks through it, some for vehicles, some for foot traffic.

'My family owned this land for ever,' Cash said. 'The range was my idea. I thought I could be like a golf pro, or tennis. You know those guys, they've been on the tour, they retire, they set up teaching afterwards.'

'Did it work?' Reacher asked.

'Not really,' Cash said. 'People come here to

345

shoot, but to get a guy to admit he doesn't really know how is like pulling teeth.'

Reacher saw three pickup trucks parked at separate shooting stations. The guys who had been waiting at eight o'clock were well into their morning sessions. They were all prone on coconut mats, firing, pausing, sighting, firing again.

'It's a living,' Cash said, in answer to a question Reacher hadn't asked. Then he pulled the Humvee off the main track and drove three hundred yards down the length of an empty range. He got out and clipped the paper target to a frame and got back in and K-turned the truck and headed back. He parked it neatly and shut it down.

'Good luck,' he said.

Reacher sat still for a moment. He was more nervous than he should have been. He breathed in and held it and felt the thrill of caffeine in his veins. Just a tiny microscopic tremble. Four fast cups of strong coffee were not an ideal preparation for accurate long-distance shooting.

But it was only three hundred yards. Three hundred yards, with a good rifle, no heat, no cold, still air. More or less the same thing as pressing the muzzle into the centre of the target and pulling the trigger. He could do it with his eyes closed. There was no fundamental problem with the marksmanship. The problem was with the stakes. He wanted the puppet master more than he had wanted the Marines' cup all those years before. A lot more. He didn't know why. But that was the problem.

He breathed out. It was only three hundred yards. Not six. Not eight. Not a thousand. No big deal.

He slid out of the Humvee and took the rifle off the back seat. Carried it across rough earth to the coconut mat. Placed it gently with its bipod feet a yard back from the edge. Bent down and loaded it. Stepped back behind it and lined himself up and crouched, knelt, lay full length. He snuggled the stock into his shoulder. Eased his neck left and right and looked around. It felt like he was alone in the middle of nowhere. He ducked his head. Closed his left eye and moved his right eye to the scope. Draped his left hand over the barrel and pressed down and back. Now he had a tripod mount. The bipod, and his shoulder. Solid. He spread his legs and turned his feet out so they were flat on the mat. Drew his left leg up a little and dug the sole of his shoe into the mat's fibres so the dead weight of the limb anchored his position. He relaxed and let himself sprawl. He knew he must look like a guy who had been shot, instead of a guy preparing to shoot.

He gazed through the scope. Saw the hyper-vivid image of great optics. He acquired the target. It looked close enough to touch. He laid the reticle where the two strokes of the X met. Squeezed the slack out of the trigger. Relaxed. Breathed out. He could feel his heart. It felt like it was loose in his chest. The caffeine was buzzing in his veins. The reticle was dancing over the X. It was hopping and jerking, left and right, up and down, in a tiny random circle.

He closed his right eye. Willed his heart to stop. Breathed out and kept his lungs empty, one second, two. Then again, in, out, hold. He pulled all his energy downward, into his gut. Let his shoulders slacken. Let his muscles relax. Let himself settle. He opened his eye again and saw that the reticle was still. He stared at the target. Feeling it. *Wanting* it. He pulled the trigger. The gun kicked and roared and the muzzle blast blew a cloud of dust out of the coconut mat and obscured his view. He lifted his head and coughed once and ducked back to the scope.

Bull's eye.

The *X* was gone. There was a neat hole drilled through the centre of it, leaving only four tiny ballpoint ticks visible, one at the top and one at the bottom of each stroke. He coughed again and pushed back and stood up. Cash dropped down in his place and used the scope to check the result.

'Good shooting,' he said.

'Good rifle,' Reacher said.

Cash operated the bolt and the spent case fell out on the mat. He got to his knees and picked it up and put it in his pocket. Then he stood up and carried the rifle back towards the Humvee.

'So do I qualify?' Reacher called after him.

'For what?'

'For talking to.'

Cash turned round. 'You think this was a test?'

'I sincerely hope it was.'

'You might not want to hear what I've got to say.'

'Try me,' Reacher said.

Cash nodded. 'We'll talk in the office.'

They detoured up the length of the range for Cash to retrieve the target. Then they turned and drove back to the huts. They passed the pickup guys. They were still blasting away. Cash parked and they went inside and Cash filed Reacher's target in a drawer, under R for Richardson. Then he danced his fingers forward to B for Barr and pulled out a thick sheaf of paper.

'You looking to show your old buddy didn't do it?' he asked.

'He wasn't my buddy,' Reacher said. 'I knew him once, is all.'

'And?'

'I don't remember him being that great a shooter.'

'TV news said it was pretty short range.'

'With moving targets and deflection angles.'

'TV said the evidence is pretty clear.'

'It is,' Reacher said. 'I've seen it.'

'Check these out,' Cash said.

He dealt the filed targets like a deck of cards, all along the length of the counter. Then he butted them edge-to-edge and squared them off to make room for more. Then he started a second row, directly underneath the first. In the end he had thirty-two sheets of paper displayed, two long rows of repetitive concentric circles, all of them marked *J. Barr, 300 yards*, with times and dates stretching back three years.

'Read them and weep,' Cash said.

Every single target showed an expert score.

Reacher stared at them, one after the other. Each inner ring was tightly packed with clean, crisp holes. Tight clusters, big and obvious. Thirty-two targets, ten rounds each, three hundred and twenty rounds, all of them dead-on maximum scores.

'This is everything he did?' Reacher asked.

Cash nodded. 'Like you said, I'm a record keeper.'

'What gun?'

'His own Super Match. Great rifle.'

'Did the cops call you?'

'Guy called Emerson. He was pretty decent about it. Because I've got to think about my own ass, because Barr trained here. I don't want to damage my professional reputation. I've put in a lot of work here, and this place could get a bad name.'

Reacher scanned the targets, one more time. Remembered telling Helen Rodin: *They don't forget.*

'What about his buddy Charlie?' he asked.

'Charlie was hopeless by comparison.'

Cash butted James Barr's targets into a pile and put them back in the *B* slot. Then he opened another drawer and ran his fingers back to *S* and took out another sheaf of paper.

'Charlie Smith,' he said. 'He was military too, by the look of him. But Uncle Sam's money didn't buy anything long-term there.'

He went through the same routine, laying out Charlie's targets in two long rows. Thirty-two of them.

'They always showed up together?' Reacher asked.

'Like peanut butter and jelly,' Cash said.

'Separate ranges?'

'Separate planets,' Cash said.

Reacher nodded. In terms of numerical score Charlie's targets were much worse than James Barr's. *Way* worse. They were the product of a very poor shooter. One had just four hits, all of them outside the outer ring, one each in the quadrants in the corners. Across all thirty-two targets he had just eight hits inside the inner ring. One was a dead-on bull's eye. Dumb luck, maybe, or wind or drift or a random thermal. Seven were very close to clipping the black. Apart from that, Charlie was all over the place. Most of his rounds must have missed altogether. Percentage-wise most of his hits happened in the white between the two outer rings. Low, low scores. But his hits weren't precisely random. There was a weird kind of consistency there. He was aiming, but he was missing. Maybe some kind of bad astigmatism in his eyes.

'What type of a guy was he?' Reacher asked.

'Charlie?' Cash said. 'Charlie was a blank slate. Couldn't read him at all. If he had been a better shot, he'd have come close to frightening me.'

'Small guy, right?'

'Tiny. Weird hair.'

'Did they talk to you much?'

'Not really. They were just two guys down from Indiana, getting off on shooting guns. I get a lot of that here.'

'Did you watch them shoot?'

Cash shook his head. 'I learned never to watch anybody. People take it as a criticism. I let them come to me, but nobody ever does.'

'Barr bought his ammo here, right?'

'Lake City. Expensive.'

'His gun wasn't cheap, either.'

'He was worth it.'

'What gun did Charlie use?'

'The same thing. Like a matched pair. In his case it was a comedy. Like a fat guy who buys a carbon fibre racing bike.'

'You got separate handgun ranges here?'

'One indoor. People use it if it rains. Otherwise I let them blast away outside, anywhere they want. I don't care much for handguns. No art to them.'

Reacher nodded and Cash swept Charlie's targets into a pile, careful to keep them in correct date order. Then he stacked them together and put them back in the *S* drawer.

'Smith is a common name,' Reacher said. 'Actually I think it's the most common name in America.'

'It was genuine,' Cash said. 'I see a driver's licence before anyone gets membership.'

'Where was he from originally?'

'Accent? Somewhere way north.'

'Can I take one of James Barr's targets?'

'What the hell for?'

'For a souvenir,' Reacher said.

Cash said nothing.

'It won't go anywhere,' Reacher said. 'I'm not going to sell it on the Internet.'

Cash said nothing.

'Barr's not coming back,' Reacher said. 'That's for damn sure. And if you really want to cover your ass you should dump them all anyway.'

Cash shrugged and turned back to the file drawer.

'The most recent one,' Reacher said. 'That would be best.'

Cash thumbed through the stack and pulled a sheet. Handed it across the counter. Reacher took it and folded it carefully and put it in his shirt pocket.

'Good luck with your buddy,' Cash said.

'He's not my buddy,' Reacher said. 'But thanks for your help.'

'You're welcome,' Cash said. 'Because I know who you are. I recognized you when you got behind the gun. I never forget the shape of a prone position. You won the Invitational ten years after I was in it. I was watching, from the crowd. Your real name is Reacher.'

Reacher nodded.

'Polite of you,' Cash said. 'Not to mention it after I told you how I only came in third.'

'You had tougher competition,' Reacher said. 'Ten years later it was all a bunch of deadbeats.'

He stopped at the last gas station in Kentucky and filled Yanni's tank. Then he called Helen Rodin from a pay phone.

'Is the cop still there?' he asked.

'Two of them,' she said. 'One in the lobby, one at my door.'

'Did Franklin start yet?'

'First thing this morning.'

'Any progress?'

'Nothing. They were five very ordinary people.'

'Where is Franklin's office?'

She gave him an address. Reacher checked his watch. 'I'll meet you there at four o'clock.'

'How was Kentucky?'

'Confusing,' he said.

* * *

353

He recrossed the Ohio on the same trestle bridge with Sheryl Crow telling him all over again about how every day was a winding road. He cranked up the volume and turned left and headed west. Ann Yanni's maps showed a highway cloverleaf forty miles ahead. He could turn north there and a couple of hours later he could scoot past the whole city, forty feet in the air. It seemed like a better idea than trying the surface streets. He figured Emerson would be getting seriously frustrated. And then seriously enraged, at some point during the day. Reacher would have been. Reacher had been Emerson for thirteen years, and in this kind of a situation he would have been kicking ass big time, blanketing the streets with uniforms, trying everything.

He found the cloverleaf and joined the highway going north. He killed the CD when it started over again and settled in for the cruise. The Mustang felt pretty good at seventy miles an hour. It rumbled along, lots of power, no finesse at all. Reacher figured if he could put that drive-train in some battered old sedan body, then that would be his kind of car.

Bellantonio had been at work in his crime lab since seven o'clock in the morning. He had fingerprinted the cell phone found abandoned under the highway and come up with nothing worth a damn. Then he had copied the call log. The last number dialled was Helen Rodin's cell. Last but one was Emerson's cell. Clearly Reacher had made both of those calls. Then came a long string of calls to several different cell phones

354

registered to Specialized Services of Indiana. Maybe Reacher had made those too, or maybe he hadn't. No way of knowing. Bellantonio wrote it all up, but he knew Emerson wouldn't do anything with it. The only viable pressure point was the call to Helen Rodin, and no way could Emerson start hassling a defence lawyer about a conversation with a witness, suspect or not. That would be a waste of breath.

So he moved on to the garage tapes. He had four days' worth, ninety-six hours, nearly three thousand separate vehicle movements. His staff had logged them all. Only three of them were Cadillacs. Indiana was the same as most heartland states. People bought pickup trucks as a first preference, then SUVs, then coupés, then convertibles. Regular sedans claimed a tiny market share, and most of them were Toyotas or Hondas or mid-size domestics. Full-size turnpike cruisers were very rare, and premium brands rarest of all.

The first Cadillac on tape was a bone-white Eldorado. A two-door coupé, several years old. It had parked before ten in the morning on the Wednesday and stayed parked for five hours. The second Cadillac on tape was a new STS, maybe red or grey, possibly light blue. Hard to be sure, with the murky monochrome picture. Whatever, it had parked soon after lunch on the Thursday and stayed there for two hours.

The third Cadillac was a black Deville. It was caught on tape entering the garage just after six o'clock in the morning on the Friday. *Black Friday*, as Bellantonio was calling it. At six o'clock in the morning the garage would have been more or less completely empty. The tape showed the Deville sweeping up the ramp, fast and confident. It showed it leaving again after just four minutes.

Long enough to place the cone.

The driver wasn't really visible in either sequence. There was just a grey blur behind the windshield. Maybe it was Barr, maybe it wasn't. Bellantonio wrote it all up for Emerson. He made a mental note to check through again to determine if four minutes was the shortest stay on the tapes. He suspected it was, easily.

Then he scanned the forensic sweep through Alexandra Dupree's garden apartment. He had assigned a junior guy to do it, because it wasn't the crime scene. There was nothing of interest there. Nothing at all. Except the fingerprint evidence. The apartment was a mess of prints, like all apartments are. Most of them were the girl's, but there were four other sets. Three of them were unidentifiable.

The fourth set of prints belonged to James Barr.

James Barr had been in Alexandra Dupree's apartment. In the living room, in the kitchen, in the bathroom. No doubt about it. Clear prints, perfect matches. Unmistakable.

Bellantonio wrote it up for Emerson.

Then he read a report just in from the medical examiner. Alexandra Dupree had been killed by a single massive blow to the right temple, delivered by a left-handed assailant. She had fallen onto a gravel surface that contained organic matter including grass and dirt. But she

356

had been found in an alley paved with limestone. Therefore her body had been moved at least a short distance between death and discovery. Other physiological evidence confirmed it.

Bellantonio took a new sheet of memo paper and addressed two questions to Emerson: *Is Reacher left-handed? Did he have access to a vehicle?*

The Zec spent the morning hours deciding what to do with Raskin. Raskin had failed three separate times. First, with the initial tail, then by getting attacked from behind, and finally by letting his cell phone get stolen. The Zec didn't like failure. He didn't like it at all. At first he considered just pulling Raskin off the street and restricting him to duty in the video room on the ground floor of the house. But why would he want to depend on a failure to monitor his security?

Then Linsky called. They had been searching fourteen straight hours and had found no sign of the soldier.

'We should go after the lawyer now,' Linsky said. 'After all, nothing can happen without her. She's the focal point. She's the one making the moves here.'

'That raises the stakes,' the Zec said.

'They're already pretty high.'

'Maybe the soldier's gone for good.'

'Maybe he is,' Linsky said. 'But what matters is what he left behind. In the lawyer's head.'

'I'll think about it,' the Zec said. 'I'll get back to you.'

'Should we keep on looking?'

'Tired?'

Linsky was exhausted and his spine was killing him.

'No,' he lied. 'I'm not tired.'

'So keep on looking,' the Zec said. 'But send Raskin back to me.'

Reacher slowed to fifty where the highway first rose on its stilts. He stayed in the centre lane and let the spur that ran behind the library pass by on his right. He kept on north for two more miles, and came off at the cloverleaf that met the four-lane with the auto dealers and the parts store. He went east on the county road and then turned north again, on Jeb Oliver's rural route. After a minute he was deep in the silent countryside. The irrigation booms were turning slowly and the sun was making rainbows in the droplets.

The heartland. Where the secrets are.

He coasted to a stop next to the Olivers' mailbox. No way was the Mustang going to make it down the driveway. The centre hump would have ripped all the parts off the bottom. The suspension, the exhaust system, the axle, the diff, whatever else was down there. Ann Yanni wouldn't have been pleased at all. So he slid out and left the car where it was, low and crouched and winking blue in the sun. He picked his way down the track, feeling every rock and stone through his thin soles. Jeb Oliver's red Dodge hadn't been moved. It was sitting right there, lightly dusted with brown dirt and streaked with dried dew. The old farmhouse was quiet. The barn was closed and locked.

Reacher ignored the front door. He walked round the side of the house to the back porch. Jeb's mother was right there on her glider. She was dressed the same but this time she had no bottle. Just a manic stare out of eyes as big as saucers. She had one foot hooked up under her and was using the other to scoot the chair about twice as fast as she had before.

'Hello,' she said.

'Jeb not back yet?' Reacher said.

She just shook her head. Reacher heard all the sounds he had heard before. The irrigation hiss, the squeak of the glider, the creak of the porch board.

'Got a gun?' he asked.

'I don't hold with them,' she said.

'Got a phone?' he asked.

'Disconnected,' she said. 'I owe them money. But I don't need them. Jeb lets me use his cell if I need it.'

'Good,' Reacher said.

'How the hell is that good? Jeb's not here.'

'That's exactly what's good about it. I'm going to break into your barn and I don't want you calling the cops while I'm doing it. Or shooting me.'

'That's Jeb's barn. You can't go in there.'

'I don't see how you can stop me.'

He turned his back on her and continued down the track. It curved a little and led directly to the barn's double doors. The doors like the barn itself were built of old planks alternately baked and

359

rotted by a hundred summers and a hundred winters. Reacher touched them with his knuckles and felt a dry hollowness. The lock was brand new. It was a U-shaped bicycle lock like the ones city messengers used. One leg of the U ran through two black steel hasps that were bolted through the planks of the doors. Reacher touched the lock. Shook it. Heavy steel, warm from the sun. It was a pretty solid arrangement. No way of cutting it, no way of breaking it.

But a lock was only as strong as what it was fixed to.

Reacher grabbed the straight end of the lock at the bottom of the U. Pulled on it, gently, and then harder. The doors sagged towards him and stopped. He put the flat of his palm against the wood and pushed them back. Held them closed with a straight left arm and yanked on the lock with his right. The bolts gave a little, but not much. Reacher figured that Jeb must have used washers on the back, under the nuts. Maybe big wide ones. They were spreading the load.

He thought: *OK, more load.*

He held the straight part of the lock with both hands and leaned back like a waterskier. Pulled hard and smashed his heel into the wood under the hasps. His legs were longer than his arms, so he was cramped and the kick didn't carry much power. But it carried enough. The old wood splintered a little and something gave half an inch. He regrouped and tried it again. Something gave a little more. Then a plank in the left-hand door split completely and two bolts pulled out. Reacher put his left hand flat on the door and got his right-hand fingers hooked in the gap with a backhand grip. He took a breath and counted to three and jerked hard. The last bolt fell out and the whole lock assembly hit the ground and the doors sagged all the way open. Reacher stepped away and folded the doors back flush with the walls and let the sunlight in.

He guessed he was expecting to see a meth lab, maybe with workbenches and beakers and scales and propane burners and piles of new baggies ready to receive the product. Or else a big stash, ready for onward distribution.

He saw none of that.

Bright light leaked in through long vertical gaps between warped planks. The barn was maybe forty feet by twenty inside. It had a bare earth floor, swept and compacted. It was completely empty except for a well-used pickup truck parked in the exact centre of the space.

The truck was a Chevy Silverado, several years old. It was light brown, like fired clay. It was a working vehicle. It had been built down to a plain specification. A base model. Vinyl seats, steel wheels, undramatic tyres. The load bed was clean but scratched and dented. It had no licence plates. The doors were locked and there was no sign of a key anywhere.

'What's that?'

Reacher turned and saw Jeb Oliver's mother behind him. She had her hand tight on the door jamb, like she was unwilling to cross the threshold.

'It's a truck,' Reacher said.

'I can see that.'

'Is it Jeb's?'

'I never saw it before.'

'What did he drive before that big red thing?'

'Not this.'

Reacher stepped closer to the truck and peered in through the driver's side window. Manual shift. Dirt and grime. High mileage. But no trash. The truck had been someone's faithful servant, used but not abused.

'I never saw it before,' the woman said again.

It looked like it had been there for a long time. It was settled on soft tyres. It didn't smell of oil or gasoline. It was cold, inert, filmed with dust. Reacher got on his knees and checked underneath. Nothing to see. Just a frame, caked with old dirt, clipped by rocks and gravel.

'How long has this thing been in here?' he asked, from the floor.

'I don't know.'

'When did he put the lock on the door?'

'Maybe two months ago.'

Reacher stood up again.

'What did you expect to find?' the woman asked him.

Reacher turned to face her and looked at her eyes. The pupils were huge.

'More of what you had for breakfast,' he said.

She smiled. 'You thought Jeb was cooking in here?'

'Wasn't he?'

'His stepfather brings it by.'

'You married?'

'Not any more. But he still brings it by.'

'Jeb was using on Monday night,' Reacher said.

The woman smiled again. 'A mother can share

362

with her kid. Can't she? What else is a mother for?'

Reacher turned away and looked at the truck one more time. 'Why would he keep an old truck locked in here and a new truck out in the weather?'

'Beats me,' the woman said. 'Jeb always does things his own way.'

Reacher backed out of the barn and walked each door closed. Then he used the balls of his thumbs to press the bolts back into their splintered holes. The weight of the lock dragged them all halfway out again. He got it looking as neat as he could, and then he left it alone and walked away.

'Is Jeb ever coming back?' the woman called after him.

Reacher didn't answer.

The Mustang was facing north, so Reacher drove north. He put the CD player on loud and kept going ten miles down an arrow-straight road, aiming for a horizon that never arrived.

Raskin dug his own grave with a Caterpillar backhoe. It was the same machine that had been used to level the Zec's land. It had a twenty-inch entrenching shovel with four steel teeth on it. The shovel took long slow bites of the soft earth and laid them aside. The engine roared and slowed, roared and slowed, and pulsed clouds of diesel exhaust filled the Indiana sky.

Raskin had been born during the Soviet, and he had seen a lot. Afghanistan, Chechnya, unthinkable upheaval in Moscow. A guy in his position could have been dead many times over, and that fact combined with his natural Russian fatalism made him utterly indifferent to his fate.

'*Ukase*,' the Zec had said. *An order from an absolute authority.*

'*Nichevo*,' Raskin had said in reply. *Think nothing of it.*

So he worked the backhoe. He chose a spot concealed from the stone-crushers' view by the bulk of the house. He dug a neat trench, twenty inches wide, six feet long, six feet deep. He piled the excavated earth to his right, to the east, like a high barrier between himself and home. When he was finished he backed the machine away from the hole and shut it down. Climbed down from the cab and waited. There was no escape. No point in running. If he ran, they would find him anyway, and then he wouldn't need a grave. They would use garbage bags, five or six of them. They would use wire ties to seal the several parts of him into cold black plastic. They would put bricks in with his flesh and throw the bags in the river.

He had seen it happen before.

In the distance the Zec came out of his house. A short wide man, ancient, stooped, walking at a moderate speed, exuding power and energy. He picked his way across the uneven ground, glancing down, glancing forward. Fifty yards, a hundred. He came close to Raskin and stopped. He put his ruined hand in his pocket and came out with a small revolver, his thumb and the stump of his index finger pincered through the trigger guard. He held it out, and Raskin took it from him.

'*Ukase*,' the Zec said.

'*Nichevo*,' Raskin replied. A short, amiable, self-deprecating sound, like *de rien* in French, like *de nada* in Spanish, like *prego* in Italian. *Please. I'm yours to command.*

'Thank you,' the Zec said.

Raskin stepped away to the narrow end of the trench. Opened the revolver's cylinder and saw a single cartridge. Closed the cylinder again and turned it until it was lined up right. Then he pulled the hammer back and put the barrel in his mouth. He turned round, so that he was facing the Zec and his back was to the trench. He shuffled backwards until his heels were on the edge of the hole. He stood still and straight and balanced and composed, like an Olympic diver preparing for a difficult backward pike off the high board.

He closed his eyes.

He pulled the trigger.

For a mile around black crows rose noisily into the air. Blood and brain and bone arced through the sunlight in a perfect parabola. Raskin's body fell backwards and landed stretched out and flat in the bottom of the trench. The crows settled back to earth and the faint noise of the distant stone-crushing machines rolled back in and sounded like silence. Then the Zec clambered up into the Caterpillar's cab and started the engine. The levers all had knobs as big as pool balls, which made them easy to manipulate with his palms.

*   *   *

Reacher stopped fifteen miles north of the city and parked the Mustang on a big V-shaped gravel turnout made where the corners of two huge circular fields met. There were fields everywhere, north, south, east and west, one after the other in endless ranks and files. Each one had its own irrigation boom. Each boom was turning at the same slow, patient pace.

He shut the engine down and slid out of the seat. He stood and stretched and yawned. The air was full of mist from the booms. Up close the booms were like massive industrial machines. Like alien spaceships, recently landed. There was a central vertical standpipe in the middle of each field, like a tall metal chimney. The boom arm came off it horizontally and bled water out of a hundred spaced nozzles all along its length. At the outer end the arm had a vertical leg supporting its weight. At the bottom of the leg was a wheel with a rubber tyre. The wheel was as big as a plane's landing gear. It rolled round a worn track, endlessly.

Reacher watched and waited until the wheel in the nearest field came close. He walked over and stepped alongside it. Kept pace with it. The tyre came almost to his waist. The boom itself was way over his head. He kept the wheel on his right and tracked it through its long clockwise circle. He was walking through fine mist. It was cold. The boom hissed loudly. The wheel climbed gentle rises and rolled into low depressions. It was a long, long circle. The boom was maybe a hundred and fifty feet long, which made the perimeter track more than three hundred yards. *Pi* times diameter. Area was *pi* times the radius squared, which would therefore be more than seventy-eight hundred square yards. More than one and a half acres. Which meant that the wasted corners added up to a little less than twenty-two hundred square yards. More than twenty-one per cent. More than five hundred square yards in each corner. Like the shapes in the corners of a target. The Mustang was parked on one of the corners, proportionally the same size as a bullet hole.

Like one of Charlie's bullet holes, in the corners of the paper.

Reacher arrived back where he had started, a little wet, his boat shoes muddy. He stepped away from the circle and stood still on the gravel, facing west. On the far horizon a cloud of crows rose suddenly and then settled. Reacher got back in the car and turned the ignition on. Found the clamps on the header rail and the switch on the dash and lowered the roof. He checked his watch. He had two hours until his rendezvous at Franklin's office. So he lay back in the seat and let the sun dry his clothes. He took the folded target out of his pocket and looked at it for a long time. He sniffed it. Held it up to the sun and let the light shine through the crisp round holes. Then he put it away again, in his pocket. He stared upward and saw nothing but sky. He closed his eyes against the glare and started to think about ego and motive, and illusion and reality, and guilt and innocence, and the true nature of randomness.

THIRTEEN

Emerson read through Bellantonio's reports. Saw that Reacher had called Helen Rodin. He wasn't surprised. It was probably just one of many calls. Lawyers and busybodies, working hard to rewrite history. No big shock there. Then he read Bellantonio's twin questions: *Is Reacher left-handed? Did he have access to a vehicle?*

Answers: *Probably*, and *Probably*. Southpaws weren't rare. Line up twenty people, and four or five of them would be left-handed. And Reacher had access to a vehicle *now*, that was for damn sure. He wasn't in town, and he hadn't left on a bus. Therefore he had a vehicle, and probably had had one all along.

Then Emerson read the final sheet: James Barr had been in Alexandra Dupree's apartment. What the hell was *that* about?

According to Ann Yanni's road maps Franklin's office was dead-centre in a tangle of streets right in the heart of the city. Not an ideal destination. Not by any means. Construction, the start of rush hour, slow traffic on surface streets. Reacher was

368

going to be putting a lot of trust in the tint in the Ford Motor Company's glass. That was for sure.

He started the motor and put the roof back up. Then he eased off the turnout and headed south. He repassed the Oliver place after twelve minutes, turned west on the county road, and then south again on the four-lane into town.

Emerson went back to Bellantonio's cell phone report. *Reacher had called Helen Rodin.* They had business. They had matters to discuss. He would go back to her, sooner or later. *Or she would go to him.* He picked up the phone. Spoke to his despatcher.

'Put an unmarked car on Helen Rodin's office,' he said. 'If she leaves the building, have her followed.'

Reacher drove past the motor court. He stayed low in the seat and glanced sideways. No sign of any activity. No obvious surveillance. He passed the barbershop, and the gun store. Traffic slowed him as he approached the raised highway. Then it slowed him more, to walking speed. His face was feet away from the pedestrians on his right. Feet away from the stalled drivers on his left. Four lanes of traffic, the two inbound lanes moving slow, the two outbound lanes static.

He wanted to get away from the sidewalk. He put his turn signal on and forced his way into the next lane. The driver behind his shoulder wasn't happy. *Don't sweat it*, Reacher thought. *I learned to drive in a deuce-and-a-half. Time was when I would have rolled right over you.*

The left-hand lane was moving a little faster. Reacher crept past cars on his right. Glanced ahead. There was a police cruiser three cars in front. In the right-hand lane. There was a green light in the distance. Traffic in the left-hand lane was approaching it slowly. Traffic in the right-hand lane was approaching it slower still. Each successive car reached the painted line and paused a moment and then jumped the gap. Nobody wanted to block the box. Now Reacher was two cars behind the cop. He hung back. The irritated guy behind him honked. Reacher inched forward. Now he was one car behind the cop.

The light went orange.

The car in front of Reacher sprinted.

The light went red.

The cop stopped on the line and Reacher stopped directly alongside him.

He put his elbow on the console and cupped his head in his hand. Spread his fingers wide and covered as much of his face as he could. Stared straight head, up under the header rail, looking at the light, willing it to change.

Helen Rodin rode down two floors in the elevator and met Ann Yanni in the NBC reception area. NBC was paying for Franklin's time, so it was only fair that Yanni should be at the conference. They rode down to the garage together and got into Helen's Saturn. Came up the ramp and out into the sunshine. Helen glanced right and made a left. Didn't register the grey Impala that moved off the kerb twenty yards behind her.

*   *   *

The light stayed red an awful long time. Then it went green and the guy behind Reacher honked and the cop turned to look. Reacher took off through his field of vision and didn't look back. He filtered into a left-turn lane and the cop car swept past on his right. Reacher watched it jam up again ahead. He didn't want to go through the side-by-side thing again so he stuck with the left turn. Found himself back in the street with Martha's grocery on it. It was clogged with slow traffic. He shifted on the seat and checked his pants pocket. Sifted through the coins by feel. Found a quarter. Debated with himself, twenty yards, thirty, forty.

Yes.

He pulled into Martha's tiny lot. Left the engine running and slid out of the seat and danced round the hood to the pay phone on the wall. He put his quarter in the slot and took out Emerson's torn card. Chose the station house number and dialled.

'Help you?' the desk guy said.

'Police?' Reacher asked.

'Go ahead, sir.'

Reacher kept his voice fast and light, rushed and low. 'That guy on the wanted poster? The thing you guys were passing around?'

'Yes, sir?'

'He's right here, right now.'

'Where?'

'In my drive-through, the one on the four-lane north of town next to the tyre store. He's inside right now, at the counter, eating.'

'You sure it's the guy?'

371

'Looks just like the picture.'

'Does he have a car?'

'Big red Dodge pickup.'

'Sir, what's your name?'

'Tony Lazzeri,' Reacher said. *Anthony Michael Lazzeri, batted .273 in 118 appearances at second base in 1935. Second-place finish.* Reacher figured he would need to move around the diamond soon. The Yankees hadn't had enough second basemen, or enough non-championship years.

'We're on our way, sir,' the desk cop said.

Reacher hung up and slid back into the Mustang. Sat still until he heard the first sirens battling north.

Helen Rodin was halfway down Second Street when she caught a commotion in her mirror. A grey Impala sedan lurched out of the lane three cars behind her and pulled a crazy U-turn through the traffic and took off back the way it had come.

'Asshole,' she said.

Ann Yanni twisted in her seat.

'Cop car,' she said. 'You can tell by the antennas.'

Reacher made it to Franklin's place about ten minutes late. It was a two-storey brick building. The lower floor looked like some kind of a light industrial unit, abandoned. It had steel shutters over its doors and windows. But the upstairs windows had venetian blinds with lights behind them. There was an outside staircase leading to an upper door. The door had a white plastic plate on it: *Franklin Investigations*. There was a parking apron at street level, just a patch of blacktop one car deep and about six wide. Helen Rodin's green Saturn was there, and a blue Honda Civic, and a black Chevy Suburban so long that it was over-hanging the sidewalk by a foot. The Suburban was Franklin's, Reacher guessed. The Honda was Rosemary Barr's, maybe.

He drove past the place without slowing and circled the block. Saw nothing he didn't want to see. So he slotted the Mustang next to the Saturn and got out and locked it. Ran up the staircase and went in the door without knocking. He found himself in a short hallway with a kitchenette to his right and what he guessed was a bathroom to his left. Up ahead he could hear voices in a large room. He went in and found Franklin at a desk, Helen Rodin and Rosemary Barr in two chairs huddled in conversation, and Ann Yanni looking out the window at her car. All four turned as he came in.

'Do you know any medical terminology?' Helen asked him.

'Like what?'

'PA,' she said. 'A doctor wrote it. Some kind of an abbreviation.'

Reacher glanced at her. Then at Rosemary Barr.

'Let me guess,' he said. 'The hospital diagnosed James Barr. Probably a mild case.'

'Early onset,' Rosemary said. 'Whatever it is.'

'How did you know?' Helen asked.

'Intuition,' Reacher said.

'What is it?'

'Later,' Reacher said. 'Let's do this in order.' He turned to Franklin. 'Tell me what you know about the victims.'

'Five random people,' Franklin said. 'No connection between any of them. No real connection with anything at all. Certainly no connection to James Barr. I think you were absolutely right. He didn't shoot them for any reason of his own.'

'No, I was absolutely wrong,' Reacher said. 'Thing is, James Barr didn't shoot them at all.'

Grigor Linsky stepped back into a shadowed doorway and dialled his phone.

'I followed a hunch,' he said.

'Which was?' the Zec asked.

'With the cops at the lawyer's office, I figured the soldier wouldn't be able to go see her. But obviously they still have business. So I thought maybe she would go to him. And she did. I followed her. They're together in the private detective's office right now. With the sister. And that woman from the television news.'

'Are the others with you?'

'We've got the whole block covered. East, west, north and south.'

'Sit tight,' the Zec said. 'I'll get back to you.'

Helen Rodin said, 'You want to explain that statement?'

'The evidence is rock solid,' Franklin said.

Ann Yanni smiled. *A story.*

Rosemary Barr just stared.

'You bought your brother a radio,' Reacher

374

said to her. 'A Bose. For the ballgames. He told me that. Did you ever buy him anything else?'

'Like what?'

'Like clothes.'

'Sometimes,' she said.

'Pants?'

'Sometimes,' she said.

'What size?'

'Size?' she repeated, blankly.

'What size pants does your brother wear?'

'Thirty-four waist, thirty-four leg.'

'Exactly,' Reacher said. 'He's relatively tall.'

'How does this help us?' Helen asked.

'You know anything about numbers games?' Reacher asked her. 'Old-fashioned illegal numbers, state lotteries, the Powerball, things like that?'

'What about them?'

'What's the hardest part of them?'

'Winning,' Ann Yanni said.

Reacher smiled. 'From the players' point of view, sure. But the hardest part for the organizers is picking truly random numbers. True randomness is very hard for humans to achieve. In the old days numbers runners used the business pages in the newspapers. They would agree in advance, maybe the second page of the stock prices, maybe the second column, the last two figures in the first six prices quoted. Or the last six, or the middle six, or whatever. That came close to true randomness. Now the big lotteries use complicated machines. But you can find mathematicians who can prove the results aren't truly random. Because humans built the machines.'

'How does *this* help us?' Helen said.

375

'Just a train of thought,' Reacher said. 'I sat all afternoon in Ms Yanni's car, enjoying the sun, thinking about how hard it is to achieve true randomness.'

'Your train is on the wrong track,' Franklin said. 'James Barr shot five people. The evidence is crushing.'

'You were a cop,' Reacher said. 'You put yourself in danger. Stake-outs, take-downs, high-pressure situations, moments of extreme stress. What's the first thing you did afterwards?'

Franklin glanced at the women.

'Went to the bathroom,' he said.

'Correct,' Reacher said. 'Me too. But James Barr didn't. Bellantonio's report from Barr's house shows cement dust in the garage, the kitchen, the living room, the bedroom, and the basement. But not in the bathroom. So he got home, but he didn't take a leak until after he changed and showered? And how could he shower anyway without going into the bathroom?'

'Maybe he stopped on the way.'

'He was never there.'

'He was *there*, Reacher. What about the evidence?'

'There's no evidence that says he was there.'

'Are you nuts?'

'There's evidence that says his van was there, and his shoes, and his pants, and his coat, and his gun, and his ammo, and his quarter, but there's nothing that says *he* was there.'

'Someone *impersonated* him?' Ann Yanni asked.

'Down to the last detail,' Reacher said. 'Drove

376

his car, wore his shoes and his clothes, used his gun.'

'This is fantasy,' Franklin said.

'It explains the raincoat,' Reacher said. 'A big roomy garment that covered everything except the denim jeans? Why else wear a raincoat on a warm dry day?'

'Who?' Rosemary asked.

'Watch,' Reacher said.

He stood still, and then he took a single pace forward.

'My pants are thirty-seven-inch legs,' he said. 'I crossed the new part of the garage in thirty-five strides. James Barr has a thirty-four-inch leg, which means he should have done it in about thirty-eight strides. But Bellantonio's footprint count shows *forty*-eight strides.'

'A very short person,' Helen said.

'Charlie,' Rosemary said.

'I thought so, too,' Reacher said. 'But then I went to Kentucky. Initially because I wanted to confirm something else. I got around to thinking that maybe James Barr just wasn't good enough. I looked at the scene. It was tough shooting. And fourteen years ago he was good, but he wasn't great. And when I saw him in the hospital the skin on his right shoulder was unmarked. And to shoot as well as he apparently did, a guy's got to practise. And a guy who practises builds up bruising on his shoulder. Like a callus. He didn't have it. So I figured a guy who started out average could only have gotten worse with time. Especially if he wasn't practising much. That's logical, right? Maybe he'd gotten to the point

377

where he *couldn't* have done the thing on Friday. Through a simple lack of ability. That's what I was thinking. So I went down to Kentucky to find out for sure how much worse he'd gotten.'

'And?' Helen asked.

'He'd gotten *better*,' Reacher said. '*Way* better. Not worse. Look at this.' He took the target out of his shirt pocket and unfolded it. 'This is the latest of thirty-two sessions over the last three years. And this is much better than he was shooting when he was in the army fourteen years ago. Which is weird, right? He's fired only three hundred and twenty rounds in the last three years, and he's great? Whereas he was firing two thousand a week back when he was only average?'

'So what does this mean?'

'He went down there with Charlie, every time. And the guy who runs the range is a Marine champion. And a real anal pack rat. He files all the used targets. Which means that Barr had at least two witnesses to what he was scoring, every time.'

'I'd *want* witnesses,' Franklin said. 'If I was shooting like that.'

'It's not possible to get better by not practising,' Reacher said. 'I think the truth is he had actually gotten really bad. And I think his ego couldn't take it. Any shooter is competitive. He knew he was lousy now, and he couldn't face it, and he wanted to cover it up. He wanted to show off.'

Franklin pointed at the target. 'Doesn't look lousy to me.'

'This is faked,' Reacher said. 'You're going to give this to Bellantonio and Bellantonio is going to prove it to you.'

'Faked how?'

'I'll bet this was done with a handgun. Nine-millimetre, from point-blank range. If Bellantonio measures the holes, my guess is he'll find they're forty-six thousands of an inch bigger than .308 holes. And if he tests the paper, he'll find gunpowder residue on it. Because my guess is James Barr took a stroll down the range and made these holes from an inch away, not three hundred yards. Every time.'

'That's a stretch.'

'It's simple metaphysics. Barr was *never* this good. And it's fair to assume he must have gotten worse. If he'd gotten a little worse, he'd have owned up to it. But he didn't own up to it, so we can assume he'd gotten a *lot* worse. Bad enough to be seriously embarrassed about it. Maybe bad enough that he couldn't hit the paper at all.'

Nobody spoke.

'It's a theory that proves itself,' Reacher said. 'To fake the score because of embarrassment proves he couldn't shoot well any more. If he couldn't shoot well any more, he didn't do the thing on Friday.'

'You're just guessing,' Franklin said.

Reacher nodded. 'I was. But I'm not now. Now I know for sure. I fired a round down in Kentucky. The guy made me, like a rite of passage. I was full of caffeine. I was twitching like crazy. Now I know James Barr will have been way worse.'

'Why?' Rosemary asked.

'Because he has Parkinson's Disease,' Reacher said to her. 'PA means Paralysis Agitans, and Paralysis Agitans is what doctors call Parkinson's Disease. Your brother is getting sick, I'm afraid. Shaking and twitching. And no way on earth can you fire a rifle accurately with Parkinson's Disease. My opinion, not only didn't he do the thing on Friday, he *couldn't possibly* have done it.'

Rosemary went quiet. *Good news and bad news.* She glanced at the window. Looked at the floor. She was dressed like a widow. Black silk blouse, black pencil skirt, black nylons, black patent leather shoes with a low heel.

'Maybe that's why he was so angry all the time,' she said. 'Maybe he felt it coming on. Felt helpless and out of control. His body started to let him down. He would have hated that. Anyone would.'

Then she looked straight at Reacher.

'I told you he was innocent,' she said.

'Ma'am, I apologize unreservedly,' Reacher said. 'You were right. He reformed. He kept to his bargain. He deserves credit. And I'm sorry he's sick.'

'Now you've got to help him. You promised.'

'I am helping him. Since Monday night I haven't done anything else.'

'This is crazy,' Franklin said.

'No, it's exactly the same as it always was,' Reacher said. 'It's someone setting James Barr up for the fall. But instead of actually making him do it, they just made it look like he did it. That's the only practical difference here.'

'But is it possible?' Ann Yanni asked.

'Why not? Think it through. *Walk* it through.'

Ann Yanni walked it through. She rehearsed little movements, slowly, thoughtfully, like an actress. 'He dresses in Barr's clothes, and shoes, and maybe finds a quarter in a jar. Or in a pocket somewhere. He wears gloves, so as not to mess up Barr's fingerprints. He's already taken the traffic cone from Barr's garage, maybe the day before. He gets the rifle from the basement. It's already been loaded, by Barr himself, previously. He drives to town in Barr's minivan. He leaves all the clues. Covers himself in cement dust. Comes back to the house and puts everything away and leaves. Fast, not even taking the time to use the bathroom. Then James Barr comes home some time later and walks into a trap he doesn't even know is there.'

'That's exactly how I see it,' Reacher said.

'But where was Barr at the time?' Helen said.

'Out,' Reacher said.

'That's a nice coincidence,' Franklin said.

'I don't think it was,' Reacher said. 'I think they arranged something to get him out of the way. He remembers going out somewhere, previously. Then being optimistic, like something good was about to happen. I think they set him up with someone. I think they engineered a chance meeting that led somewhere. I think he had a date on Friday.'

'With who?'

'The redhead, maybe. They turned her loose on me. Maybe they turned her loose on him, too. He dressed well on Friday. The report shows his wallet was in a decent pair of pants.'

'So who really did it?' Helen asked.

'Someone cold as ice,' Reacher said. 'Someone who didn't even need to use the bathroom afterwards.'

'Charlie,' Rosemary said. 'Got to be. Has to be. He's small. He's weird. He knew the house. He knew where everything was. The dog knew him.'

'He was a terrible shooter too,' Reacher said. 'That's the other reason why I went to Kentucky. I wanted to test that theory.'

'So who was it?'

'Charlie,' Reacher said. 'His evidence was faked as well. But in a different way. The holes in his targets were all over the place. Except they weren't *really* all over the place. The distribution wasn't entirely random. He was trying to disguise how good he actually was. He was aiming at arbitrary points on the paper, and he was hitting those points, every time, dead on, believe me. Once in a while he would get bored, and he'd put one through the inner ring. Or he'd pick on a quadrant outside the outer ring and put a round straight through it. One time he drilled all four corners. The point is, it doesn't really matter what you aim at, as long as you hit it. It's only convention that makes us aim at the ten-ring. It's just as good practice to aim at some other spot. Even a spot off the paper, like a tree. That's what Charlie was doing. He was a tremendous shot, training hard, but trying to look like he was missing all the time. But like I said, true randomness is impossible for a human to achieve. There are always patterns.'

'Why would he do that?' Helen asked.

'For an alibi.'

'Making people think he couldn't shoot?'

Reacher nodded. 'He noticed that the range master was saving the used targets. He's an ice-cold pro who thinks about every wrinkle ahead of time.'

'Who is he?' Franklin asked.

'His real name is Chenko and he hangs with a bunch of Russians. He's probably a Red Army veteran. Probably one of their snipers. And they're real good. They always have been.'

'How do we get to him?'

'Through the victim.'

'Square one. The victims are all dead ends. You'll have to come up with something better than that.'

'His boss calls himself the Zec.'

'What kind of a name is that?'

'It's a word, not a name. Old-time Soviet slang. A zec was a labour camp inmate. In the Gulag in Siberia.'

'Those camps are ancient history.'

'Which makes the Zec a very old man. But a very tough old man. Probably way tougher than we can imagine.'

The Zec was tired after his stint with the backhoe. But he was used to being tired. He had been tired for sixty-three years. He had been tired since the day the recruiter came to his village, in the early fall of 1942. His village was four thousand miles from anywhere, and the recruiter was a type of Moscow Russian nobody had ever seen before. He was brisk, and self-assured, and confident. He permitted no argument. No discussion. All males between the ages of sixteen and fifty were to come with him.

The Zec was seventeen at that point. Initially he was overlooked, because he was in prison. He had slept with an older man's wife, and then beaten the guy badly when he complained about it. The beaten guy claimed exemption from the draft because of his physical condition, and then he told the recruiter about his assailant in prison. The recruiter was anxious to make his numbers, so the Zec was hauled out of his cell and told to line up with the others in the village square. He did so quite happily. He assumed he was being given a ride to freedom. He assumed there would be a hundred opportunities just to walk away.

He was wrong.

The recruits were locked into a truck, and then a train, for a journey that lasted five weeks. Formal induction into the Red Army happened along the way. Uniforms were issued, thick woollen garments, and a coat, and a pair of felt-lined boots, and a pay book. But no actual pay. No weapons. And no training, either, beyond a brief stop in a snow-covered rail yard where a commissar brayed over and over again at the locked train through a huge metal megaphone. The guy repeated a simple twenty-word speech, which the Zec remembered ever after: *The fate of the world is being decided at Stalingrad, where you will fight to the last for the Motherland.*

The five-week journey ended on the eastern bank of the Volga, where the recruits were unloaded like cattle and forced to run straight for a small assemblage of old river ferries and pleasure cruisers. Half a mile away on the opposite bank was a vision from hell. A city, larger than anything the Zec had ever seen before, was in ruins, belching smoke and fire. The river was burning and exploding with mortar shells. The sky was full of planes which lined up and fell into dives, dropping bombs, firing guns. There were corpses everywhere, and body parts, and screaming wounded.

The Zec was forced onto a small boat that had a gaily coloured striped sunshade. It was crammed tight with soldiers. Nobody had room to move. Nobody had a weapon. The boat lurched out into the freezing current and aeroplanes fell on it like flies on shit. The crossing lasted fifteen minutes and at the end of it the Zec was slimy with his neighbours' blood.

He was forced off onto a narrow wooden pier and made to line up single file and then made to run towards the city, past a staging post where the second phase of his military training took place: two quartermasters were doling out loaded rifles and spare ammunition clips in an endless alternate sequence and chanting what later struck the Zec as a poem, or a song, or a hymn to complete and utter insanity, over and over again without pausing:

The one with the rifle shoots
The one without follows him
When the one with the rifle is killed
The one who is following picks up the rifle
   and shoots.

385

The Zec was handed an ammunition clip. No rifle. He was shoved forward, and blindly followed the back of the man ahead. He turned a corner. Passed in front of a Red Army machine gun nest. At first he thought the front line must therefore be very close. But then a commissar with a flag and another huge megaphone roared at him: *No retreat! If you turn back even one step we will shoot you down!* So the Zec ran helplessly onward and turned another corner and stepped into a hail of German bullets. He stopped, half turned, and was hit three times in the arms and legs. He was bowled over and came to rest lying on the shattered remains of a brick wall and within minutes was buried under a mounting pile of corpses.

He came to forty-eight hours later in an improvised hospital and made his first acquaintance with Soviet military justice: harsh, ponderous, ideological, but running strictly in accordance with its own arcane rules. The matter at issue was caused by his having half turned: were his wounds inflicted by the Motherland's enemy, or had he been retreating towards his own side's guns? Because of the physical ambiguity he was spared execution and sentenced to a penal battalion instead. Thus began a process of survival that had so far lasted sixty-three years.

A process he intended to continue.

He dialled Grigor Linsky's number.

'We can assume the soldier is talking,' he said. 'Whatever he knows, they all know now. Therefore it's time to get ourselves an insurance policy.'

Franklin said, 'We're really no further ahead. Are we? No way is Emerson going to accept a damn thing unless we give him more than we've got right now.'

'So work the victim list,' Reacher said.

'That could take for ever. Five lives, five life histories.'

'So let's focus.'

'Great. Terrific. Just tell me which one you want me to focus on.'

Reacher nodded. Recalled Helen Rodin's description of what she had heard. The first shot, and then a tiny pause, and then the next two. Then another pause, a little longer, but really only a split second, and then the last three. He closed his eyes. In his mind he pictured Bellantonio's audio graph from the cell phone voice mail. Pictured his own mute simulation, in the gloom of the new parking garage, his right arm extended like a rifle: *click, click-click, click-click-click*.

'Not the first one,' he said. 'Not the first cold shot. No guarantee of hitting anything with that. Therefore the first victim was meaningless. Part of the window dressing. Not the last three, either. That was bang-bang-bang. The deliberate miss, and more window dressing. The job was already done by then.'

'So, the second or the third. Or both of them.'

Click, click-click.

Reacher opened his eyes.

'The third,' he said. 'There's a rhythm there. The first cold shot, then a lead-in, and then the money shot. The target. Then a break. His eye is lagging in the scope. He's making sure the target is down. It is. So then the last three.'

'Who was the third?' Helen asked.

'The woman,' Franklin said.

Linsky called Chenko, and then Vladimir, and then Sokolov. He explained the mission and pulled them all in tighter. Franklin's office had no back entrance. There was just the exposed staircase. The target's car was right there on the apron. Easy.

Reacher said, 'Tell me about the woman.'

Franklin shuffled his notes. Put them in a new order of priority.

'Her name was Oline Archer,' he said. 'Caucasian female, married, no children, thirty-seven years old, lived west of here in the outer suburbs.'

'Employed in the DMV building,' Reacher said. 'If she was the specific target, Charlie had to know where she was and when she would be coming out.'

Franklin nodded. 'Employed by the DMV itself. Been there a year and a half.'

'Doing what exactly?'

'Clerical supervisor. Doing whatever they do in there.'

'So was it work-related?' Ann Yanni asked.

'Too long of a counter delay?' Franklin said. 'A bad photo on a driver's licence? I doubt it. I checked the national databases. DMV clerks don't get killed by customers. That just doesn't happen.'

'So what about her personal life?' Helen Rodin asked.

'Nothing jumped out at me,' Franklin said. 'She was just an ordinary woman. But I'll keep digging. I'll go down a few levels. Got to be something there.'

'Do it fast,' Rosemary Barr said. 'For my brother's sake. We have to get him out.'

'We need medical opinions for that,' Ann Yanni said. 'Regular doctors now, not psychiatrists.'

'Will NBC pay?' Helen Rodin asked.

'If it's likely to work.'

'It should,' Rosemary said. 'I mean, shouldn't it? Parkinson's is a real thing, isn't it? Either he's got it or he hasn't.'

'It might work at trial,' Reacher said. 'A plausible reason why James Barr couldn't have done it, plus a plausible narrative about someone else doing it? That's usually how you create reasonable doubt.'

'Plausible is a big word,' Franklin said. 'And reasonable doubt is a risky concept. Better to get Alex Rodin to drop the charges altogether. Which means convincing Emerson first.'

'I can't talk to either one of them,' Reacher said.

'I can,' Helen said.

'I can,' Franklin said.

'And I sure as hell can,' Ann Yanni said. 'We all can, apart from you.'

'But you might not want to,' Reacher said.

'Why not?' Helen asked.

'You're not going to like this part very much.'

'Why not?' Helen asked again.

'Think,' Reacher said. 'Work backwards. The thing with Sandy being killed, and the thing in the sports bar Monday night, why did those two things happen?'

'To tie you up. To prevent you hurting the case.'

'Correct. Two attempts, same aim, same goal, same perpetrator.'

'Obviously.'

'And the thing Monday night started with me being followed from my hotel. Sandy and Jeb Oliver and his other pals were cruising around, standing by, waiting until someone called them and told them where I ended up. So really it started with me being followed *to* my hotel. Much earlier in the day.'

'We've been through all of this.'

'But how did the puppet master get my name? How did he even know I was in town? How did he know there was a guy here who was a potential problem?'

'Someone told him.'

'Who knew, early in the day on Monday?'

Helen paused a beat.

'My father,' she said. 'Since early on Monday morning. And then Emerson, presumably. Shortly afterwards. They'll have talked about the case. They'll have communicated immediately if there was a danger that the wheels were coming off.'

'Correct,' Reacher said. 'Then one of those two guys called the puppet master. Well before lunch on Monday.'

Helen said nothing.

'Unless one of those two guys *is* the puppet master,' Reacher said.

'The Zec is the puppet master. You said so yourself.'

'I said he's Charlie's boss. That's all. We've got no way of knowing whether he's actually at the top of the tree.'

'You're right,' Helen said. 'I don't like this line of thinking at all.'

'Someone communicated,' Reacher said. 'That's for damn sure. Either your father or Emerson. My name was on the street two hours after I got off the bus. So one of them is bent and the other one won't help us either because he already likes the case exactly the way it is.'

The room went quiet.

'I need to get back to work,' Ann Yanni said.

Nobody spoke.

'Call me if there's news,' Yanni said.

The room stayed quiet. Reacher said nothing. Ann Yanni crossed the room. Stopped next to him.

'Keys,' she said.

He dug in his pocket and handed them over.

'Thanks for the loan,' he said. 'Nice car.'

Linsky watched the Mustang leave. It went north. Loud engine, loud exhaust. It was audible for a whole block. Then the street went quiet again and Linsky dialled his phone.

'The television woman is out of there,' he said.

'The private detective will stay at work,' the Zec said.

'So what if the others leave together?'

'I hope they don't.'

'What if they do?'

'Take them all.'

Rosemary Barr asked, 'Is there a cure? For Parkinson's Disease?'

'No,' Reacher said. 'No cure, no prevention. But it can be slowed down. There are drugs for it. Physiotherapy helps. And sleep. The symptoms disappear when a person is asleep.'

'Maybe that's why he wanted the pills. To escape.'

'He shouldn't try to escape too much. Social contact is good.'

'I should go to the hospital,' Rosemary said.

'Explain to him,' Reacher said. 'Tell him what really happened on Friday.'

Rosemary nodded. Crossed the room and went out the door. A minute later Reacher heard her car start up and drive away.

Franklin went out to the kitchenette to make coffee. Reacher and Helen Rodin were left alone in the office together. Reacher sat down in the chair that Rosemary Barr had used. Helen stepped to the window and looked down at the street below. She kept her back to the room. She was dressed the same as Rosemary Barr. Black shirt, black skirt, black patent leather shoes. But she didn't look like a widow. She looked like something from New York or Paris. Her heels were higher and her legs were long and bare and tan.

'These guys we're talking about are Russians,' she said.

Reacher said nothing.

'My father is an American,' she said.

'An American called Aleksei Alekseivitch,' Reacher said.

'Our family came here before World War One. There's no possible connection. How could there be? These people we're talking about are low-life Soviets.'

'What did your father do before he was the DA?'

'He was an assistant DA.'

'Before that?'

'He always worked there.'

'Tell me about his coffee service.'

'What about it?'

'He uses china cups and a silver tray. The county didn't buy them for him.'

'So?'

'Tell me about his suits.'

'His suits?'

'On Monday he was wearing a thousand-dollar suit. You don't see many public servants wearing thousand-dollar suits.'

'He's got expensive tastes.'

'How does he afford them?'

'I don't want to talk about this.'

'One more question.'

Helen said nothing.

'Did he pressure you not to take the case?'

Helen said nothing. Looked left. Looked right. Then she turned round. 'He said losing might be winning.'

'Concern for your career?'

'I thought so. I still think so. He's an honest man.'

Reacher nodded. 'There's a fifty per cent chance you're right.'

Franklin came back in with the coffee, which was a thin own-brand brew in three non-matching pottery mugs, two of them chipped, on a cork bar tray, with an open carton of half-and-half and a yellow box of sugar and a single pressed-steel spoon. He put the tray on the desk and Helen Rodin stared at it, like it was making Reacher's point for him: *This is how coffee is served in an office.*

'David Chapman knew your name on Monday,' she said. 'James Barr's first lawyer. He's known about you since Saturday.'

'But he didn't know I ever showed up,' Reacher said. 'I assume nobody told him.'

'I knew your name,' Franklin said. 'Maybe I should be in the mix too.'

'But you knew the real reason I was here,' Reacher said. 'You wouldn't have had me attacked. You'd have had me subpoenaed.'

Nobody spoke.

'I was wrong about Jeb Oliver,' Reacher said. 'He isn't a dope dealer. There was nothing in his barn except an old pickup truck.'

'I'm glad you can be wrong about something,' Helen said.

'Jeb Oliver isn't Russian,' Franklin said.

'Apple pie,' Reacher said.

'Therefore these guys can work with Americans. That's what I'm saying. It could be Emerson. Doesn't have to be the DA.'

'Fifty per cent chance,' Reacher said. 'I'm not accusing anybody yet.'

'If you're right in the first place.'

'The bad guys were all over me very fast.'

'Doesn't sound like either Emerson or the DA to me, and I know them both.'

'You can say his name,' Helen said. 'His name is Alex Rodin.'

'I don't think it's either one of them,' Franklin said.

'I'm going back to work,' Helen said.

'Give me a ride?' Reacher asked. 'Let me out under the highway?'

'No,' Helen said. 'I really don't feel like doing that.'

She picked up her purse and her briefcase and walked out of the office alone.

Reacher sat still and listened to the sounds out on the street. He heard a car door opening and closing. An engine starting. A car driving away. He sipped his coffee and said, 'I guess I upset her.'

Franklin nodded. 'I guess you did.'

'These guys have got someone on the inside. That's clear, right? That's a fact. So we should be able to discuss it.'

'A cop makes more sense than a DA.'

'I don't agree. A cop controls his own cases only. Ultimately a prosecutor controls everything.'

'I'd prefer it that way. I *was* a cop.'

'So was I,' Reacher said.

'And I have to say, Alex Rodin kills a lot of cases. People say it's caution, but it could be something else.'

'You should analyse what kind of cases he kills.'

'Like I don't have enough to do already.'

Reacher nodded. Put his mug down. Stood up.

'Start with Oline Archer,' he said. 'The victim. She's what's important now.'

Then he stepped to the window and checked the street. Saw nothing. So he nodded to Franklin and walked down the hallway and out the door to the top of the outside staircase.

He paused on the top step and stretched in the warmth. Rolled his shoulders, flexed his hands, took a deep breath of air. He was cramped from driving and sitting all day. And oppressed by hiding out. It felt good just to stand still and do nothing, high up and exposed. Out in the open, in the daylight. Below him to his left the cars were gone except for the black Suburban. The street was quiet. He glanced to his right. There was traffic building up on the north-south drag. To his left, there was less. He figured he would dodge west first. But a long way west, because the police station must be near. He would need to loop round it. Then he would head north. North of downtown was a warren. North of downtown was where he felt best.

He started down the stairs. As he stepped off onto the sidewalk at the bottom he heard a footfall fifteen feet behind him. A side-step. Thin soles on limestone grit. Quiet. Then the unmistakable *crunch-crunch* of a pump-action shotgun racking a round.

Then a voice.

It said: 'Stop right there.'

An American accent. Quiet, but distinct. *From somewhere way north*. Reacher stopped. Stood still and stared straight ahead at a blank brick wall across the street.

The voice said: 'Step to your right.'

Reacher stepped to his right. A long sideways shuffle.

The voice said: 'Now turn around real slow.'

Reacher turned around, real slow. He kept his hands away from his body, palms out. Saw a small figure fifteen feet away. The same guy he had seen the night before, from the shadows. Not more than five-four, not more than a hundred and thirty pounds, slight, pale, with cropped black hair that stuck up crazily. Chenko. Or, Charlie. In his right hand, rock-steady, was a sawn-off with a pistol grip. In his left hand was some kind of a black thing.

'Catch,' Charlie said.

He tossed the black thing underhand. Reacher watched it tumble and sparkle through the air straight at him and his subconscious said: *Not a grenade*. So he caught it. Two-handed. It was a shoe. A woman's patent-leather dress shoe, black, with a heel. It was still slightly warm.

'Now toss it back,' Charlie said. 'Just like I did.'

Reacher paused. *Whose shoe was it?* He stared down at it.

Low heel.

Rosemary Barr's?

'Toss it back,' Charlie called. 'Nice and slow.'

Assess and evaluate. Reacher was unarmed. He was holding a shoe. Not a stone, not a rock.

The shoe was lightweight and unaerodynamic. It wouldn't do anyone any harm. It would stall and flutter in the air and Charlie would just swat it away.

'Toss it back,' Charlie said again.

Reacher did nothing. He could tear the heel off and throw it like a dart. Like a missile. But Charlie would shoot him while he was drawing his arm back and winding up. Charlie was fifteen feet away, poised, balanced, unblinking, with the gun rock-steady in his hand. Too close to miss, too far to get to.

'Last chance,' Charlie said.

Reacher soft-tossed the shoe back. A long, looping underhand throw. Charlie caught it one-handed and it was like the scene had rewound right back to the beginning.

'She's in summer school,' Charlie said. 'Think about it like that. She's going to get acquainted with the facts of life. She's going to work on her testimony. About how her brother planned in advance. About how he let slip what he was going to do. She's going to be a great witness. She's going to make the case. You understand that, right?'

Reacher said nothing.

'So the game is over now,' Charlie said.

Reacher said nothing.

'Take two steps backwards,' Charlie said.

Reacher took two steps backwards. They put him right on the kerb. Now Charlie was twenty feet away. He was still holding the shoe. He was smiling.

'Turn around,' he said.

'You going to shoot me?' Reacher asked.

'Maybe.'

'You should.'

'Why?'

'Because if you don't, I'm going to find you and I'm going to make you sorry.'

'Big talk.'

'Not just talk.'

'So maybe I'll shoot you.'

'You should.'

'Turn around,' Charlie said.

Reacher turned around.

'Now stand still,' Charlie said.

Reacher stood still. Faced the street. He kept his eyes open. Stared down at the blacktop. It was laid over ancient cobblestones. It was full of small humps in a regular pattern. He started counting them, to fill what might be the last seconds of his life. He strained to hear sounds behind him. Listened for the whisper of clothing as Charlie's arm extended. Listened for the quiet metallic click as the trigger moved through its first tenth of an inch. Would Charlie shoot? Common sense said no. Homicides were always investigated.

But these people were crazy. And there was a fifty per cent chance they owned a local cop. Or that *he* owned *them*.

Silence. Reacher strained to hear sounds behind him.

But he heard nothing. Nothing happened. Nothing at all. One minute. Two. Then a hundred yards away to the east he heard a siren. Just two brief electronic blips from a cop car forcing a path through traffic.

'Stand still,' Charlie said again.

Reacher stood still. Ten seconds. Twenty. Thirty. Then two police cruisers turned into the street simultaneously. One from the east and one from the west. They were both moving fast. Their engines roared. Their tyres howled. Their sounds beat against the brick. They jammed to a stop. Doors opened. Cops spilled out. Reacher turned his head. Charlie wasn't there any more.

FOURTEEN

The arrest was fast and efficient. It went down the usual way. Guns, shouting, handcuffs, Miranda. Reacher stayed silent throughout. He knew better than to speak. He had been a cop for thirteen years and he knew the kind of trouble that talking can get a guy into. And the kind of delay it can cause. Say something, and the cops have to stop to write it down. And Reacher couldn't afford for anyone to stop. Not right then.

The trip to the station house was mercifully short. Not more than four blocks. Reacher guessed it made sense that an ex-cop like Franklin would pick an office location in the neighbourhood he was accustomed to. He used the drive time to work on a strategy. He figured he would be taken straight to Emerson, which gave him a fifty per cent chance of being put in a room with a bad guy.

Or with a good guy.

But he ended up a hundred per cent sure he was in a room with a bad guy because Emerson and Alex Rodin were both there together. Reacher was hauled out of the squad car and hustled straight to

Emerson's office. Emerson was behind the desk. Rodin was in front of it.

Can't say a word, Reacher thought. *But this has got to be real fast.*

Then he thought: *Which one? Rodin? Or Emerson?* Rodin was wearing a suit. Blue, summer weight, expensive, maybe the same one as on Monday. Emerson was in shirtsleeves. Playing with a pen. Bouncing it off his blotter, one end, then the other.

Get on with it, Reacher thought.

'You weren't so hard to find,' Emerson said.

Reacher said nothing. He was still handcuffed.

'Tell us about the night the girl was killed,' Rodin said.

Reacher said nothing.

'Tell us how it felt,' Emerson said. 'When her neck snapped.'

Reacher said nothing.

'The jury's going to hate you,' Rodin said.

Reacher said, 'Phone call.'

'You want to lawyer up?' Emerson said.

Reacher said nothing.

'Who's your lawyer?' Rodin asked.

'Your daughter,' Reacher said.

'Want us to call her?' Emerson asked.

'Maybe. Or maybe Rosemary Barr instead.'

He watched their eyes.

'The sister?' Rodin said.

'You want us to call the *sister*?' Emerson said.

One of you knows she ain't going to answer, Reacher thought.

Which one?

Nothing in their eyes.

'Call Ann Yanni,' he said.

'From the TV?' Rodin said. 'Why her?'

'I get a phone call,' Reacher said. 'I don't have to explain anything. I say who, you dial the number.'

'She'll be getting ready to go on the air. The local news is at six o'clock.'

'So we'll wait,' Reacher said. 'I've got all the time in the world.'

Which one of you knows that isn't true?

They waited, but it turned out the wait wasn't long. Emerson placed the call to NBC and told Ann Yanni's assistant that the police department had arrested Jack Reacher and that Reacher was requesting Yanni's presence, reason unknown. It was a bizarre message. But Yanni was in Emerson's office less than thirty minutes later. She was a journalist on the scent of a story. She knew that network tomorrow was better than local today.

'How can I help?' she asked.

She had presence. She was a star in her market. And she was media. Both Emerson and Rodin looked a little intimidated. Not by her as an individual. But by what she represented.

'I'm sorry,' Reacher said to her. 'I know you won't want to, and I know I said I would never tell, but under the circumstances you're going to have to confirm an alibi for me. No choice, I'm afraid.'

He glanced at her. Saw her following his words. Saw confusion cross her face. She had no reaction. He kept his eyes on hers. No reaction.

403

Help me out here, girl.

One second.

Two seconds.

No reaction.

Reacher held his breath. *Get with the damn programme, Yanni. One more second and it's all going to fall apart.*

No reaction.

Then she nodded. She caught on. Reacher breathed out. *Good call.* Professional skill. She was a person accustomed to hearing breaking news in her earpiece and repeating it live on air half a second later like she had known about it all her life.

'What alibi?' Emerson said.

Yanni glanced at him. Then at Rodin.

'I thought this was about Jack Reacher,' she said.

'It is,' Emerson said.

'But this is Joe Gordon,' she said. 'At least, that's what he told me.'

'He told you his name was Gordon?'

'When I met him.'

'Which was when?'

'Two days ago.'

'You've been running his picture on your show.'

'That was *his* picture? It looked nothing like him. The hair was totally different. No similarity at all.'

'What alibi?' Emerson said again.

'For when?' Yanni asked.

'The night the girl was killed. That's what we're talking about here.'

Yanni said nothing.

Rodin said, 'Ma'am, if you know something, you need to tell us now.'

'I'd rather not,' Yanni said.

Reacher smiled to himself. The way she said it absolutely guaranteed that Emerson and Rodin were a minute away from begging to hear the story. She was standing there, blushing on command all the way up to her temples, her back straight, her blouse open three buttons. She was a hell of an actress. Reacher figured maybe all news anchors were.

'It's a question of evidence,' Emerson said.

'Obviously,' Yanni said. 'But can't you just take my word?'

'For what?'

'That he didn't do it.'

'We need details,' Rodin said.

'I have to think of my reputation,' Yanni said.

'Your statement won't be made public if we drop the charges.'

'Can you guarantee dropping the charges?'

'Not before we hear your statement,' Emerson said.

'So it's a catch-22,' Yanni said.

'I'm afraid it is.'

Don't push too far, Reacher thought. *We don't have time*.

Yanni sighed. Looked down at the floor. Looked up, straight into Emerson's eyes, furious, embarrassed, magnificent.

'We spent that night together,' she said.

'You and Reacher?'

'Me and Joe Gordon.'

Emerson pointed. 'This man?'

Yanni nodded. 'That man.'

'All night?'

'Yes.'

'From when to when?'

'From about eleven forty. When the news was over. Until I got paged the next morning when you guys found thc body.'

'Where were you?'

Reacher closed his eyes. Recalled the conversation the night before in the parking garage. The car window, open an inch and a half. *Had he told her?*

'The motor court,' Yanni said. 'His room.'

'The clerk didn't say he saw you.'

'Of course the clerk didn't see me. I have to think about things like that.'

'Which room?'

Had he told her?

'Room eight,' Yanni said.

'He didn't leave the room during the night?'

'No, he didn't.'

'Not at all?'

'No.'

'How can you be sure?'

Yanni looked away. 'Because we didn't actually sleep a wink.'

The office went quiet.

'Can you offer any corroboration?' Emerson asked.

'Like what?' Yanni asked back.

'Distinguishing marks? That I can't see right now but that someone who had been in your position would have seen?'

406

'Oh, please.'

'It's the last question,' Emerson said.

Yanni said nothing. Reacher recalled switching on the Mustang's dome light and lifting his shirt to reveal the tyre iron. He moved his cuffed hands and laid them across his waistband.

'Anything?' Emerson said.

'It's important,' Rodin said.

'He has a scar,' Yanni said. 'Low down on his stomach. A horrible big thing.'

Emerson and Rodin both turned and looked at Reacher. Reacher got to his feet. Grabbed a fold of fabric in both hands and pulled his shirt out of his pants. Lifted it.

'OK,' Emerson said.

'What *was* that?' Rodin asked.

'Part of a Marine sergeant's jawbone,' Reacher said. 'The medics figured it must have weighed about four ounces. It was travelling at five thousand feet per second away from the epicentre of a trinitrotoluene explosion. Just surfing along on the pressure wave, until it hit me.'

He dropped his shirt back down. Didn't try to tuck it in. The handcuffs would have made it difficult.

'Satisfied now?' he asked. 'Have you embarrassed the lady enough?'

Emerson and Rodin looked at each other. *One of you knows for sure I'm innocent*, Reacher thought. *And I don't care what the other one thinks.*

'Ms Yanni will have to put it in writing,' Emerson said.

'You type it, I'll sign it,' Yanni said.

Rodin looked straight at Reacher. 'Can *you* offer corroboration?'

'Like what?'

'Something along the lines of your scar. But relating to Ms Yanni.'

Reacher nodded. 'Yes, I could. But I won't. And if you ask again I'll knock your teeth down your throat.'

Silence in the office. Emerson dug in his pocket and found a handcuff key. Turned suddenly and tossed it underarm through the air. Reacher's hands were cuffed but he was careful to lead with his right. He caught the key in his right palm, and smiled.

'Bellantonio been talking to you?' he said.

'Why did you give Ms Yanni a false name?' Emerson asked.

'Maybe I didn't,' Reacher said. 'Maybe Gordon is my real name.'

He tossed the key back and stepped over and held his wrists out and waited for Emerson to unlock the cuffs.

The Zec took the phone call two minutes later. A familiar voice, low and hurried.

'It didn't work,' it said. 'He had an alibi.'

'For real?'

'Probably not. But we're not going to go there.'

'So what next?'

'Just sit tight. He can't be more than one step away now. In which case he'll be coming for you soon. So be locked and loaded and ready for him.'

* * *

408

'They didn't fight very hard,' Ann Yanni said. 'Did they?' She started the Mustang's engine before Reacher even got his door closed.

'I didn't expect them to,' he said. 'The innocent one knows the case was weak. And the guilty one knows putting me back on the street takes me off the board about as fast as putting me in a cell right now.'

'Why?'

'Because they've got Rosemary Barr and they know I'll go find her. So they'll be waiting for me, ready to rock and roll. I'll be dead before morning. That's the new plan. Cheaper than jail.'

They drove straight back to Franklin's office and ran up the outside staircase and found Franklin sitting at his desk. The lights were off and his face was bathed in the glow from his computer screen. He was staring at it blankly, like it was telling him nothing. Reacher broke the news about Rosemary Barr. Franklin went very still and glanced at the door. Then the window.

'We were right here,' he said.

Reacher nodded. 'Three of us. You, me, and Helen.'

'I didn't hear anything.'

'Me either,' Reacher said. 'They're really good.'

'What are they going to do to her?'

'They're going to make her give evidence against her brother. Some kind of a made-up story.'

'Will they hurt her?'

'That depends on how fast she caves.'

'She's not going to cave,' Yanni said. 'Not in a

million years. Don't you see that? She's totally dedicated to clearing her brother's name.'

'Then they're going to hurt her.'

'Where is she?' Franklin said. 'Best guess?'

'Wherever they are,' Reacher said. 'But I don't know where that is.'

She was in the upstairs living room, taped to a chair. The Zec was staring at her. He was fascinated by women. Once he had gone twenty-seven years without seeing one. The penal battalion he had joined in 1943 had had a few, but they were a small minority and they died fast. And then after the Great Patriotic War had been won his nightmare progress through the Gulag had begun. In 1949 he had seen a woman peasant near the White Sea Canal. She was a stooped and bulky old crone two hundred yards away in a beet field. Then nothing, until in 1976 he saw a nurse riding a troika sled through the frozen wastes of Siberia. He was a quarryman then. He had come up out of the hole with a hundred other zecs and was walking home in a long ragged column down a long straight road. The nurse's sled was approaching on another road that ran at right angles. The land was flat and featureless and covered with snow. The zecs could see for ever. They stood and watched the nurse drive a whole mile. Then they turned their heads as one as she passed through the crossroads and watched her through another mile. The guards denied them food that night as punishment for the unauthorized halt. Four men died, but the Zec didn't.

'Are you comfortable?' he asked.

Rosemary Barr said nothing. The one called Chenko had returned her shoe. He had crouched in front of her and fitted it to her foot like a store clerk. Then he had backed away and sat down next to the one called Vladimir on the sofa. The one called Sokolov had stayed downstairs in a room full of surveillance equipment. The one called Linsky was pacing the room, white with pain. He had something wrong with his back.

'When the Zec speaks, you should answer,' the one called Vladimir said.

Rosemary looked away. She was afraid of Vladimir. More so than the others. Vladimir was huge, and he gave off an air of depravity, like a smell.

'Does she understand her position?' Linsky asked. The Zec smiled at him, and Linsky smiled back. It was a private joke between them. Any claim to rights or humane treatment in the camps was always met with a question: *Do you understand your position?* The question was always followed by a statement: *You don't* have *a position. You are* nothing *to the Motherland*. The first time Linsky had heard the question he had been about to reply, but the Zec had hauled him away. By that point the Zec had eighteen years under his belt, and the intervention was uncharacteristic. But clearly he had felt something for the raw youngster. He had taken the kid under his wing. They had been together ever since, through a long succession of locations neither of them could name. Many books had been written about the Gulag, and documents

411

had been discovered, and maps had been made, but the irony was that those who had participated had no idea where they had been. Nobody had told them. A camp was a camp, with wire, huts, endless forest, endless tundra, endless work. What difference did a name make?

Linsky had been a soldier and a thief. In the west of Europe or in America he would have served time, two years here, three years there, but during the Soviet stealing was an ideological transgression. It showed an uneducated and antisocial preference for private property. Such a preference was answered with a swift and permanent removal from civilized society. In Linsky's case the removal had lasted from 1963 until civilized society had collapsed and Gorbachev had emptied the Gulag.

'She understands her position,' the Zec said. 'And next comes acceptance.'

Franklin called Helen Rodin. Ten minutes later she was back in his office. She was still mad at Reacher. That was clear. But she was too worried about Rosemary Barr to make a big deal out of it. Franklin stayed at his desk, one eye on his computer screen. Helen and Ann Yanni sat together at a table. Reacher stared out the window. The sky was darkening.

'We should call someone,' Helen said.

'Like who?' Reacher asked.

'My father. He's the good guy.'

Reacher turned round. 'Suppose he is. What do we tell him? That we've got a missing person? He'll just call the cops, because what else can he do? And if Emerson's the bad guy, the cops will sit on it. Even if Emerson's the good guy the cops will sit on it just the same. Missing adults don't get anyone very excited. Too many of them.'

'But she's integral to the case.'

'The case is about her brother. So the cops will figure it's only natural she ran away. Her brother is a notorious criminal and she couldn't stand the shame.'

'But you saw her get kidnapped. You could tell them.'

'I saw a shoe. That's all I can tell anybody. And I've got no credibility here. I've been playing silly games for two days.'

'So what do we do?'

Reacher turned back to the window.

'We take care of it ourselves,' he said.

'How?'

'All we need is a location. We work through the woman who was shot, we get names, we get some kind of a context, we get a place. Then we go there.'

'When?' Yanni asked.

'Twelve hours,' Reacher said. 'Before dawn. They'll be working on some kind of a timetable. They want to take care of me first, and then they want to start in on Rosemary Barr. We need to get to her before they run out of patience.'

'But that means you'll be showing up exactly when they're expecting you.'

Reacher said nothing.

'It's like walking into a trap,' Yanni said.

Reacher didn't answer that. Yanni turned to Franklin and said, 'Tell us more about the woman who was shot.'

413

'There's nothing more to tell,' Franklin said. 'I've been through everything forwards and backwards. She was very ordinary.'

'Family?'

'All of them are back east. Where she came from.'

'Friends?'

'Two, basically. A co-worker and a neighbour. Neither of them is interesting. Neither of them is a Russian, for instance.'

Yanni turned back to Reacher. 'So maybe you're wrong. Maybe the third shot wasn't the money shot.'

'It must have been,' Reacher said. 'Or why would he pause after it? He was double-checking he had a hit.'

'He paused after the sixth, too. For good.'

'He wouldn't wait that long. It could have gone completely out of control by then. People could have been jumping all over each other.'

'But they weren't.'

'He couldn't have predicted that.'

'I agree,' Franklin said. 'A thing like that, you don't do it with your first or your last shot.'

Then his eyes lost focus. He stared at the wall, like he wasn't seeing it.

'Wait,' he said.

He glanced at his screen.

'Something I forgot,' he said.

'What?' Reacher asked.

'What you said about Rosemary Barr. Missing persons.'

He turned back to his mouse and his keyboard and started clicking and typing. Then he hit his

414

enter key and sat forward intently, like proximity would speed the process.

'Last chance,' he said.

Reacher knew from television commercials that computers operated at all kinds of gigahertz, which he assumed was pretty fast. But even so, Franklin's screen stayed blank for a long, long time. There was a little graphic in the corner. It was rotating slowly. It implied a thorough and patient search through an infinite amount of data. It spun for minutes. Then it stopped. There was an electrostatic crackle from the monitor and the screen wiped down and redrew into a densely printed document. Plain computer font. Reacher couldn't read it from where he was.

The office went quiet.

Franklin looked up.

'OK,' he said. 'There you go. At last. Finally something that isn't ordinary. Finally we catch a break.'

'What?' Yanni said.

'Oline Archer reported her husband missing two months ago.'

FIFTEEN

Franklin pushed his chair back to make space and the others all crowded round the screen together. Reacher and Helen Rodin ended up shoulder to shoulder. No more animosity. Just the thrill of pursuit.

Most of the document was taken up with coded headers and source information. Letters, numbers, times, origins. The substantive message was short. Two months previously Mrs Oline Anne Archer had made a missing persons report concerning her husband. His name was Edward Stratton Archer. He had left the marital home for work early on a routine Monday and had not returned by end of business on the Wednesday, which was when the report was made.

'Is he still missing?' Helen asked.

'Yes,' Franklin said. He pointed to a letter *A* buried in the code at the top of the screen. 'It's still active.'

'So let's go talk to Oline's friends,' Reacher said. 'We need some background here.'

'Now?' Franklin said.

'We've only got twelve hours,' Reacher said. 'No time to waste.'

Franklin wrote down names and addresses for Oline Archer's co-worker and neighbour. He handed the paper to Ann Yanni, because she was paying his bill.

'I'll stay here,' he said. 'I'll see if the husband shows up in the databases. This could be a coincidence. Maybe he's got a wife in every state. Wouldn't be the first time.'

'I don't believe in coincidences,' Reacher said. 'So don't waste your time. Find a phone number for me instead. A guy called Cash. Former Marine. He owns the range where James Barr went to shoot. Down in Kentucky. Call him for me.'

'Message?'

'Give him my name. Tell him to get his ass in his Humvee. Tell him to drive up here, tonight. Tell him there's a whole new Invitational going on.'

'Invitational?'

'He'll understand. Tell him to bring his M24. With a night scope. And whatever else he's got lying around.'

Reacher followed Ann Yanni and Helen Rodin down the stairs. They got into Helen's Saturn, the women in the front and Reacher in the back. Reacher figured they would all have preferred the Mustang, but it only had two seats.

'Where first?' Helen asked.

'Which is closer?' Reacher asked back.

'The co-worker.'

'OK, her first.'

417

Traffic was slow. Roads were torn up and construction traffic was lumbering in and out of work zones. Reacher glanced between his watch and the windows. Daylight was fading. Evening was coming. *Time ticking away.*

The co-worker lived in a plain heartland suburb east of town. It was filled with a grid of straight residential streets. The streets were lined on both sides by modest ranch houses. The houses had small lots, flags on poles, hoops over the garage doors, satellite dishes on brick chimneys. Some of the sidewalk trees had faded yellow ribbons tied round them. Reacher guessed they symbolized solidarity with troops serving overseas. Which conflict, he wasn't sure. What the point was, he had no idea. He had served overseas for most of thirteen years and had never met anyone who cared what was tied to trees back home. As long as someone sent pay cheques and food and water and bullets and wives stayed faithful, then most guys were happy enough.

The sun was going down behind them and Helen was driving slowly with her head ducked forward so she could see the house numbers early. She spotted the one she wanted and pulled into a driveway and parked behind a small sedan. It was new. Reacher recognized the brand name from his walk up the four-lane: *America's Best Warranty!*

The co-worker herself was a tired and harassed woman of about thirty-five. She opened her door and stepped out to the stoop and pulled the door shut behind her to block out the noise from

418

what sounded like a dozen kids running riot inside. She recognized Ann Yanni immediately. Even glanced beyond her, looking for a camera crew.

'Yes?' she said.

'We need to talk about Oline Archer,' Helen Rodin said.

The woman said nothing. She looked conflicted, like she knew she was supposed to think it was tasteless to talk about victims of tragedy to journalists. But apparently Ann Yanni's celebrity status overcame her reluctance.

'OK,' she said. 'What do you want to know? Oline was a lovely person and all of us at the office miss her terribly.'

The nature of randomness, Reacher thought. Random slayings always involved people described as lovely afterwards. Nobody ever said *she was a rat-faced fink and I'm glad she's dead. Whoever it was did us all a favour*. That never happened.

'We need to know something about her husband,' Helen said.

'I never met her husband,' the woman said.

'Did Oline talk about him?'

'A little, I guess. Now and then. His name is Ted, I think.'

'What does he do?'

'He's in business. I'm not sure what kind of business.'

'Did Oline say anything about him being missing?'

'Missing?'

'Oline reported him missing two months ago.'

419

'I know she seemed very worried. I think he was having problems with his business. In fact I think he'd been having problems for a year or two. That's why Oline went back to work.'

'She didn't always work?'

'Oh, no, ma'am. I think she did way back, and then she gave it up. But she had to come back. Because of circumstances. Whatever the opposite of rags to riches is.'

'Riches to rags,' Reacher said.

'Yes, like that,' the woman said. 'She needed her job, financially. I think she was embarrassed about it.'

'But she didn't give you details?' Ann Yanni asked.

'She was a very private person,' the woman said.

'It's important.'

'She would get kind of distracted. That wasn't like her. About a week before she was killed she was gone most of one afternoon. That wasn't like her either.'

'Do you know what she was doing?'

'No, I really don't.'

'Anything you remember about her husband would help us.'

The woman shook her head. 'His name is Ted. That's all I can say for sure.'

'OK, thanks,' Helen said.

She turned and headed back to her car. Yanni and Reacher followed her. The woman on the stoop stared after them, disappointed, like she had failed an audition.

* * *

420

Ann Yanni said, 'Strike one. But don't worry. It always happens that way. Sometimes I think we should just skip the first person on the list. They never know anything.'

Reacher was uncomfortable in the back of the car. His pants pocket had got underneath him and a coin was digging edge-on into his thigh. He squirmed round and pulled it out. It was a quarter, new and shiny. He looked at it for a minute and then he put it in the other pocket.

'I agree,' he said. 'We should have skipped her. My fault. Stands to reason a co-worker wouldn't know much. People are cagey around co-workers. Especially rich people fallen on hard times.'

'The neighbour will know more,' Yanni said.

'We hope,' Helen said.

They were caught in cross-town traffic. They were headed from the eastern suburbs to the western, and it was a slow, slow ride. Reacher was glancing between his watch and the windows again. The sun was low on the horizon ahead of them. Behind them it was already twilight.

Time ticking away.

Rosemary Barr moved in her chair and struggled against the tape binding her wrists.

'We know it was Charlie who did it,' she said.

'Charlie?' the Zec repeated.

'My brother's so-called *friend*.'

'Chenko,' the Zec said. 'His name is Chenko. And yes, he did it. Tactically it was his plan. He did well. Of course, his physique helped. He was able to wear his own shoes inside your brother's. He had to roll the pants and the raincoat sleeves.'

421

'But we *know*,' Rosemary said.

'But *who* knows? And what exactly do they bring to the party?'

'Helen Rodin knows.'

'You'll dismiss her as your lawyer. You'll terminate the representation. She'll be unable to repeat anything she learned while your relationship was privileged. Linsky, am I right?'

Linsky nodded. He was six feet away, on the sofa, propped at an odd angle to rest his back.

'That's the law,' he said. 'Here in America.'

'Franklin knows,' Rosemary said. 'And Ann Yanni.'

'Hearsay,' the Zec said. 'Theories, speculation, and innuendo. Those two have no persuasive evidence. And no credibility, either. Private detectives and television journalists are exactly the kind of people who peddle ridiculous and alternative explanations for events like these. It's to be expected. Its absence would be unusual. Apparently a president was killed in this country more than forty years ago and people like them still claim that the real truth has not yet been uncovered.'

Rosemary said nothing.

'Your deposition will be definitive,' the Zec said. 'You'll go to Rodin and you'll give sworn testimony about how your brother plotted and planned. About how he *told* you what he was intending. In detail. The time, the place, everything. You'll say that to your sincere and everlasting regret you didn't take him seriously. Then some poor excuse for a public defender will take one look at your evidence and plead your brother guilty and the whole thing will be over.'

'I won't do it,' Rosemary said.

The Zec looked straight at her.

'You will do it,' he said. 'I promise you that. Twenty-four hours from now you'll be *begging* to do it. You'll be insane with fear that we might change our minds and not *let* you do it.'

The room went quiet. Rosemary glanced at the Zec as if she had something to say. Then she glanced away. But the Zec answered her anyway. He had heard her message loud and clear.

'No, we won't be there with you at the deposition,' he said. 'But we *will* know what you tell them. Within minutes. And don't think about a little detour to the bus depot. For one thing, we'll have your brother killed. For another, there's no country in the world we can't find you in.'

Rosemary said nothing.

'Anyway,' the Zec said. 'Let's not argue. It's unproductive. And pointless. You'll tell them what we tell you to tell them. You will, you know. You'll see. You'll be desperate to. You'll be wishing we had arranged an earlier appointment for you. At the courthouse. You'll spend the waiting time on your knees pleading for a chance to show us how word-perfect you are. That's how it usually happens. We're very good at what we do. We learned at the feet of masters.'

'My brother has Parkinson's Disease,' Rosemary said.

'Diagnosed when?' the Zec asked, because he knew the answer.

'It's been developing.'

The Zec shook his head. 'Too subjective to be helpful. Who's to say it's not a similar condition brought on suddenly by his recent injury? If not, then who's to say such a condition is a true handicap anyway? When shooting from such a close range? If the public defender brings in an expert, then Rodin will bring in three. He'll find doctors who will swear that Little Annie Oakley was racked with Parkinson's Disease from the very day she was born.'

'Reacher knows,' Rosemary said.

'The soldier? The soldier will be dead by morning. Dead, or a runaway.'

'He won't run away.'

'Therefore he'll be dead. He'll come for you tonight. We'll be ready for him.'

Rosemary said nothing.

'Men have come for us before in the night,' the Zec said. 'Many times, in many places. And yet we're still here. *Da*, Linsky?'

Linsky nodded again.

'We're still here,' he said.

'When will he come?' the Zec asked.

'I don't know,' Rosemary said.

'Four o'clock in the morning,' Linsky said. 'He's an American. They're trained that four o'clock in the morning is the best time for a surprise attack.'

'Direction?'

'From the north would make the most sense. The stone-crushing plant would conceal his staging area and leave him only two hundred yards of open ground to cover. But I think he'll double-bluff us there. He'll avoid the north, because he knows it's best.'

'Not from the west,' the Zec said.

Linsky shook his head. 'I agree. Not down the driveway. Too straight and open. He'll come from the south or the east.'

'Put Vladimir in with Sokolov,' the Zec said to him. 'Tell them to watch the south and the east very carefully. But tell them to keep an eye out north and west, too. All four directions must be monitored continuously, just in case. Then put Chenko in the upstairs hallway with his rifle. He can be ready to deploy to whichever window is appropriate. With Chenko, one shot will be enough.'

Then he turned to Rosemary Barr.

'Meanwhile we'll put you somewhere safe,' he said. 'Your tutorials will start as soon as the soldier is buried.'

The outer western suburbs were bedroom communities for people who worked in the city, so the traffic stayed bad all the way out. The houses were much grander than in the east. They were all two-storey, all varied, all well maintained. They all had big lots and pools and ambitious evergreen landscaping. With the last of the sunset behind them they looked like pictures in a brochure.

'Tight-ass middle class,' Reacher said.

'What we all aspire to,' Yanni said.

'They won't want to talk,' Reacher said. 'Not their style.'

'They'll talk,' Yanni said. 'Everyone talks to me.'

They drove past the Archer place, slowly. There was a cast-metal sign on thin chains under the mailbox: *Ted and Oline Archer*. Beyond it across a broad open lawn the house looked closed-up and dark and silent. It was a big Tudor place. Dull brown beams, cream stucco. Three-car garage. *Nobody home*, Reacher thought.

The neighbour they were looking for lived across the street and one lot to the north. Hers was a place about the same size as the Archers' but done in an Italianate style. Stone accents, little crenellated towers, dark green sun awnings on the south-facing ground floor windows. The evening light was fading away to darkness and lamps were coming on behind draped windows. The whole street looked warm and rested and quiet and very satisfied with itself. Reacher said, 'They sleep safely in their beds because rough men stand ready in the night to visit violence on those who would do them harm.'

'You know George Orwell?' Yanni asked.

'I went to college,' Reacher said. 'West Point is technically a college.'

Yanni said, 'The existing social order is a swindle and its cherished beliefs mostly delusions.'

'It is not possible for any thinking person to live in such a society as our own without wanting to change it,' Reacher said.

'I'm sure these are perfectly nice people,' Helen said.

'But will they talk to us?'

'They'll talk,' Yanni said. 'Everyone talks.'

Helen pulled into a long limestone driveway and parked about twenty feet behind an imported

426

SUV that had big chrome wheels. The front door of the house was made of ancient grey weathered oak with iron banding that had nail heads as big as golf balls. It felt like you could step through it straight into the Renaissance.

'Property is theft,' Reacher said.

'Proudhon,' Yanni said. 'Property is desirable, is a positive good in the world.'

'Abraham Lincoln,' Reacher said. 'In his first State of the Union.'

There was an iron knocker shaped like a quoit in a lion's mouth. Helen lifted it and used it to thump on the door. Then she found a discreet electric bell push and pressed that, too. They heard no answering sound inside the house. Heavy door, thick walls. She tried again with the bell and before she got her finger off the button the door sucked back off copper weatherproofing strips and opened like a vault. A guy was standing there with his hand on the inside handle.

'Yes?' he said. He was somewhere in his forties, solid, prosperous, probably a golf club member, maybe an Elk, maybe a Rotarian. He was wearing corduroy pants and a patterned sweater. He was the kind of guy who gets home and immediately changes clothes as a matter of routine.

'Is your wife at home?' Helen asked. 'We'd like to speak with her about Oline Archer.'

'About Oline?' the guy said. He was looking at Ann Yanni.

'I'm a lawyer,' Helen said.

'What is there to be said about Oline?'

'Maybe more than you think,' Yanni said.

427

'You're not a lawyer.'

'I'm here as a journalist,' Yanni said. 'But not on a human interest story. Nothing tacky. There might have been a miscarriage of justice. That's the issue here.'

'A miscarriage in what way?'

'They might have arrested the wrong man for the shootings. That's why I'm here. That's why we're all here.'

Reacher watched the guy. He was standing there, holding the door, trying to decide. In the end he just sighed and stepped back.

'You better come in,' he said.

Everyone talks.

He led the way through a muted yellow hallway to a living room. It was spacious and immaculate. Velvet furniture, little mahogany tables, a stone fireplace. No television. There was probably a separate room for that. A den, or a home theatre. Or perhaps they didn't watch television. Reacher saw Ann Yanni calculating the odds.

'I'll get my wife,' the guy said.

He came back a minute later with a handsome woman a little younger than himself. She was wearing pressed jeans and a sweatshirt the same yellow as the hallway walls. Penny loafers on her feet. No socks. She had hair that had been expensively styled to look casual and windswept. She was medium height and lean in a way that spoke of diet books and serious time in aerobics classes.

'What's this about?' she asked.

'Ted Archer,' Helen said.

'Ted? I thought you told my husband it was about Oline.'

'We think there may be a connection. Between his situation and hers.'

'How could there be a connection? Surely what happened to Oline was completely out of the blue.'

'Maybe it wasn't.'

'I don't understand.'

'We suspect that Oline might have been a specific target, kind of hidden behind the confusion of the other four victims.'

'Wouldn't that be a matter for the police?'

Helen paused. 'At the moment the police seem satisfied with what they've got.'

The woman glanced at her husband.

'Then I'm not sure we should talk about it,' he said.

'At all?' Yanni asked. 'Or just to me?'

'I'm not sure if we would want to be on television.'

Reacher smiled to himself. *The other side of the tracks.*

'This is deep background only,' Yanni said. 'It's entirely up to you whether your names are used.'

The woman sat down on a sofa and her husband sat next to her, very close. Reacher smiled to himself again. They had subconsciously adopted the standard couple-on-a-sofa pose that television interviews used all the time. Two faces close together, ideally framed for a tight camera shot. Yanni took her cue and sat in an armchair facing them, perched right on the edge, leaning forward, her elbows on her knees, a frank and open expression on her face. Helen took another chair. Reacher stepped away to the window. Used

429

a finger to move the drapes aside. It was full dark outside.

Time ticking away.

'Tell us about Ted Archer,' Yanni said. 'Please.' A simple request, only six words, but her tone said: *I think you two are the most interesting people in the world and I would love to be your friend.* For a moment Reacher thought Yanni had missed her way. She would have been a great cop.

'Ted had business problems,' the woman said.

'Is that why he disappeared?' Yanni asked.

The woman shrugged. 'That was Oline's initial assumption.'

'But?'

'Ultimately she rejected that explanation. And I think she was right to. Ted wasn't that kind of a man. And his problems weren't those kind of problems. The fact is he was getting screwed rotten and he was mad as hell about it and he was fighting. And people who fight don't just walk away. I mean, do they?'

'How was he getting screwed?'

The woman glanced at her husband. He leaned forward. *Boy stuff.* 'His principal customer stopped buying from him. Which happens. Power in the marketplace ebbs and flows. So Ted offered to renegotiate. Offered to drop his price. No dice. So he offered to drop it more. He told me he got to the point where he was giving it away. Still no dice. They just wouldn't buy.'

'What do you think was happening?' Yanni asked. *Keep talking, sir.*

'Corruption,' the guy said. 'Under-the-table inducements. It was completely obvious. One of

430

Ted's competitors was offering kickbacks. No way for an honest man to compete with that.'

'When did this start?'

'About two years ago. It was a major problem for them. Financially they went downhill very fast. No cash flow. Ted sold his car. Oline had to go out to work. The DMV thing was all she could find. They made her supervisor after about a month.' He smiled a thin smile, proud of his class. 'Another year, she'd have been running the place. She'd have been Commissioner.'

'What was Ted doing about it? How was he fighting?'

'He was trying to find out which competitor it was.'

'Did he find out?'

'We don't know. He was trying for a long time, and then he went missing.'

'Didn't Oline include this in her report?'

The guy sat back and his wife leaned forward again. Shook her head. 'Oline didn't want to. Not back then. It was all unproven. All speculation. She didn't want to throw accusations around. And it wasn't definitely connected. I guess the way we're telling it now it sounds more obvious than it was at the time. I mean, Ted wasn't Sherlock Holmes or anything. He wasn't on the case twenty-four/seven. He was still doing normal stuff. He was just talking to people when he could, you know, asking questions, comparing notes, comparing prices, trying to put it all together. It was a two-year period. Occasional conversations, phone calls, enquiries, things like that. It didn't seem dangerous, certainly.'

'Did Oline *ever* go to anyone with this? Later, maybe?'

The woman nodded. 'She stewed for two months after he disappeared. We talked. She was up and down with it. Eventually she decided there had to be a connection. I agreed with her. She didn't know what to do. I told her she should call the police.'

'And did she?'

'She didn't call. She went personally. She felt they would take her more seriously face to face. Not that they did, apparently. Nothing happened. It was like dropping a stone down a well and never hearing the splash.'

'When did she go?'

'A week before the thing in the plaza last Friday.'

Nobody spoke. Then, kindly, gently, Ann Yanni asked the obvious question: 'You didn't suspect a connection?'

The woman shook her head. 'Why would we? It seemed to be a total coincidence. The shootings were random, weren't they? You said so yourself. On the television news. We heard you say it. Five random victims, in the wrong place at the wrong time.'

Nobody spoke.

Reacher turned away from the window.

'What business was Ted Archer in?' he asked.

'I'm sorry, I assumed you knew,' the husband said. 'He owns a quarry. Huge place about forty miles north of here. Cement, concrete, crushed stone. Vertically integrated, very efficient.'

'And who was the customer who backed off?'

'The city,' the guy said.

432

'Big customer.'

'As big as they come. All this construction going on right now is manna from heaven for people in that business. The city sold ninety million in tax-free municipals just to cover the first year. Add in the inevitable overruns and it's a nine-figure bonanza for somebody.'

'What car did Ted sell?'

'A Mercedes Benz.'

'Then what did he drive?'

'He used a truck from work.'

'Did you see it?'

'Every day for two years.'

'What was it?'

'A pickup. A Chevy, I think.'

'An old brown Silverado? Plain steel wheels?'

The guy stared. 'How did you know that?'

'One more question,' Reacher said. 'For your wife.'

She looked at him.

'After Oline went to the cops, did she tell you who it was she talked to? Was it a detective called Emerson?'

The woman was already shaking her head. 'I told Oline if she didn't want to call she should go to the station house, but she said it was too far, because she never got that long of a lunch hour. She said she'd go to the DA instead. His office is much closer to the DMV. And Oline was like that anyway. She preferred to go straight to the top. So she took it to Alex Rodin himself.'

Helen Rodin was completely silent on the drive back to town. So silent she quivered and vibrated

433

and shook with it. Her lips were clamped and her cheeks were sucked in and her eyes were wide open. Her silence made it impossible for Reacher or Yanni to speak. It was like all the air had been sucked out of the car and all that was left was a black hole of silence so loud it hurt.

She drove like a robot, competently, not fast, not slow, displaying a mechanical compliance with lane markers and stop lights and yield signs. She parked on the apron below Franklin's office and left the motor running and said, 'You two go on ahead. I just can't do this.'

Ann Yanni got out and walked over to the staircase. Reacher stayed in the car and leaned forward over the seat.

'It'll be OK,' he said.

'It won't.'

'Helen, pull the keys and get your ass upstairs. You're an officer of the court and you've got a client in trouble.' Then he opened his door and climbed out of the car and by the time he had walked round the trunk she was waiting for him at the foot of the stairs.

Franklin was in front of his computer, as always. He told Reacher that Cash was on his way up from Kentucky, no questions asked. Told him that Ted Archer hadn't shown up anywhere else in the databases. Then he noticed the silence and the tension.

'What's up?' he asked.

'We're one step away,' Reacher said. 'Ted Archer was in the concrete business and he was frozen out of all these new city construction

434

contracts by a competitor who was offering bribes. He tried to prove it and must have been getting very close to succeeding because the competitor offed him.'

'Can you prove that?'

'Only by inference. We'll never find his body without digging up First Street again. But I know where his truck is. It's in Jeb Oliver's barn.'

'Why there?'

'They use Oliver for things they can't do themselves. For when they don't want to show their faces, or for when they can't. Presumably Archer knew them and wouldn't have gone near them. But Oliver was just a local kid. Maybe he staged a flat tyre or hitched a ride. Archer would have walked right into it. Then the bad guys hid the body and Oliver hid the truck.'

'Oline Archer didn't suspect anything?'

'She did eventually,' Reacher said. 'She sat on it two months and then presumably she pieced together enough to make some kind of sense out of it. Then she started to go public with it and all kinds of private alarm bells must have gone off because a week later she was dead. Staged the way it was because to have a missing husband and then a murdered wife two months later would have raised too many flags. But as long as it looked random it was going to be seen as coincidental.'

'Who had Oline taken it to? Emerson?'

Reacher said nothing.

'She took it to my father,' Helen Rodin said.

There was silence for a long moment.

'So what now?' Franklin said.

'You need to hit that keyboard again,' Reacher said. 'Whoever got the city contracts has pretty much defined himself as the bad guy here. So we need to know who he is. And where he's based.'

'Public record,' Franklin said.

'So check it.'

Franklin turned away in the silence and started his fingers pattering over the keys. He pointed and clicked for a minute. Then he came up with the answer.

'Specialized Services of Indiana,' he said. 'They own all the current city contracts for cement, concrete, and crushed stone. Many, many millions of dollars.'

'Where are they?'

'That was the good news.'

'What's the bad?'

'There's no paperwork. They're a trust registered in Bermuda. They don't have to file anything.'

'What kind of a system is that?'

Franklin didn't answer.

'A Bermuda trust needs a local lawyer,' Helen said. Her voice was low, quiet, resigned. Reacher recalled the plate outside A. A. Rodin's office: the name, followed by the letters that denoted the law degree.

Franklin clicked his way through two more screens.

'There's a phone number,' he said. 'That's all we've got.'

'What is it?' Helen asked.

Franklin read it out.

'That's not my father's number,' Helen said.

Franklin clicked his way into a reverse directory.

Typed in the number and the screen changed and gave him a name and a business address.

'John Mistrov,' he said.

'Russian name,' Reacher said.

'I guess so.'

'Do you know him?'

'Vaguely. He's a wills and trusts guy. One-man band. I've never worked for him.'

Reacher checked his watch. 'Can you find a home address?'

Franklin went into a regular directory. Typed in the name and came up with a domestic listing.

'Should I call him?' he said.

Reacher shook his head. 'We'll pay him a visit. Face to face works better, when time is short.'

Vladimir made his way down to the ground-floor surveillance room. Sokolov was in a rolling chair in front of the long table that carried the four television monitors. From left to right they were labelled North, East, South, and West, which made sense if a person viewed the world from a clockwise perspective. Sokolov was scooting his chair slowly down the line, examining each picture, moving on, returning from West to North with a powerful push off the wall. All four screens were misty and green, because it was dark outside and the thermal imaging had kicked in. Occasionally a bright dot could be seen moving fast in the distance. An animal. Nocturnal. Fox, skunk, raccoon, or a pet cat or a lost dog far from home. The North monitor showed a glow from the crushing plant. It would fade, as the idle machines cooled. Apart from that all the backgrounds were a deep olive colour, because there was nothing out there except for miles of fields constantly misted with cold water from the always-turning irrigation booms.

Vladimir pulled up a second wheeled chair and sat down on Sokolov's left. He would watch north and east. Sokolov would concentrate on the south and west. That way they each had responsibility for one likely direction and one unlikely. It was a fair distribution of labour.

Upstairs in the third-floor hallway Chenko loaded his own Super Match. Ten rounds, Lake City .308s. One thing Americans did right was ammunition. He opened all the bedroom doors to speed his access north, south, east or west, as required. He walked to a window and turned his night scope on. Set it for seventy-five yards. He figured he would get the call when the soldier was about a hundred and fifty yards out. That was about the practical limit for the cameras. He would step to the right window and acquire the target when it was still more than a hundred yards distant. He would track its progress. He would let it come to him. When it was seventy-five yards out, he would kill it.

He raised the rifle. Checked the image. It was bright and clear. He watched a fox cross the open ground east to west. *Good hunting, my little friend*. He walked back to the hallway and propped the gun against the wall and sat down in a straight-backed chair to wait.

Helen Rodin insisted on staying behind in Franklin's office. So Reacher and Yanni went out alone, in the Mustang. The streets were dark and quiet. Yanni drove. She knew her way around. The address they were looking for was a loft building carved out of an old warehouse halfway between the river wharf and the railhead. Yanni said it was a part of the new urban strategy. *Soho comes to the heartland*. She said she had thought about buying in the same building.

Then she said, 'We should put Helen on suicide watch.'

'She'll be OK,' Reacher said.

'You think?'

'I'm pretty sure.'

'What if it was your old man?'

Reacher didn't answer that. Yanni slowed as the bulk of a large brick building loomed through the darkness.

'You can ask first,' Reacher said. 'If he doesn't answer, I'll ask second.'

'He'll answer,' Yanni said. 'They all answer.'

But John Mistrov didn't. He was a thin guy of about forty-five. He was dressed like a post-divorce midlife crisis victim. Acid-rinsed too-tight jeans, black T-shirt, no shoes. They found him all alone in a big white loft apartment eating Chinese food from paper cartons. Initially he was very pleased to see Ann Yanni. Maybe hanging out with celebrities was a part of the lifestyle glamour that the new development had promised. But his early enthusiasm faded fast. It disappeared completely when Yanni ran through her suspicions and then insisted on knowing the names behind the trust.

'I can't tell you,' he said. 'Surely you understand

439

there are confidentiality issues here. Surely you understand that.'

'I *understand* that serious crimes have been committed,' Yanni said. 'That's what I *understand*. And you need to understand that too. You need to choose up sides, right now, *fast*, before this thing goes public.'

'No comment,' the guy said.

'There's no downside here,' Yanni said, gently. 'These names we want, they'll all be in jail tomorrow. No comebacks.'

'No comment,' the guy said again.

'You want to go down with them?' Yanni asked. Sharply. 'Like an accessory? Or do you want to get out from under? It's your choice. But one way or the other you're going to be on the news tomorrow night. Either doing the perp walk or standing there looking good, like oh my *God*, I had no *idea*, I was only too happy to help.'

'No comment,' the guy said for the third time.

Loud, clear, and smug.

Yanni gave up. Shrugged, and glanced at Reacher. Reacher checked his watch. *Time ticking away*. He stepped up close.

'You got medical insurance?' he asked.

The guy nodded.

'Dental plan?'

The guy nodded again.

Reacher hit him in the mouth. Right-handed, short swing, hard blow.

'Get *that* fixed,' he said.

The guy rocked back a step and doubled over and then came up coughing with blood all over

440

his chin. Cut lips, loose teeth all rimed with red.

'Names,' Reacher said. 'Now. Or I'll take you apart a piece at a time.'

The guy hesitated. *Mistake*. Reacher hit him again. Then the guy came up with names, six of them, and descriptions, and an address, all from a position flat on the floor and all in a voice thick and bubbly with mouthfuls of blood.

Reacher glanced at Yanni.

'They all answer,' he said.

In the dark in the Mustang on the way back Ann Yanni said, 'He'll call and warn them.'

'He won't,' Reacher said. 'He just betrayed them. So my guess is he'll be going on a long vacation tomorrow.'

'You hope.'

'Doesn't matter anyway. They already know I'm coming for them. Another warning wouldn't make a difference.'

'You have a very direct style. One they don't mention in Journalism 101.'

'I could teach you. It's about surprise, really. If you can surprise them you don't have to hit them very hard.'

Yanni dictated to Franklin the names that John Mistrov had given up. Four of them corresponded with names Reacher had already heard: Charlie Smith, Konstantin Raskin, Vladimir Shumilov, and Pavel Sokolov. The fifth was Grigor Linsky, which Reacher figured had to be the damaged man in the boxy suit, because the sixth name had been given simply as Zec Chelovek.

'I thought you said Zec was a word,' Franklin said.

'It is,' Reacher said. 'And so is Chelovek. It's a transliteration of their word for human being. Zec Chelovek means prisoner-human-being. Like Prisoner Man.'

'The others aren't using code names.'

'Neither is the Zec, probably. Maybe that's all he's got left. Maybe he forgot his real name. Maybe we all would, in the Gulag.'

'You sound sorry for him,' Yanni said.

'I'm not sorry for him,' Reacher said. 'I'm just trying to understand him.'

'No mention of my father,' Helen said.

Reacher nodded. 'The Zec is the puppet master. He's at the top of the tree.'

'Which means my father is just an employee.'

'Don't worry about that now. Focus on Rosemary.'

Franklin used an on-line map and figured out that the address John Mistrov had spilled related to a stone-crushing plant built next to a quarry eight miles north and west of the city. Then he searched the tax rolls and confirmed that Specialized Services of Indiana was its registered owner. Then he searched the rolls all over again and found that the only other real estate registered to the trust was a house on the lot adjacent to the stone-crushing plant. Yanni said she knew the area.

'Anything else out there?' Reacher asked her.

She shook her head. 'Nothing but farmland for miles.'

'OK,' Reacher said. 'There you go. That's where Rosemary is.'

He checked his watch. Ten o'clock in the evening.

'So what now?' Yanni said.

'Now we wait,' Reacher said.

'For what?'

'For Cash to get here from Kentucky. And then we wait some more.'

'For what?'

Reacher smiled.

'For the dead of night,' he said.

They waited. Franklin made coffee. Yanni told TV stories, about people she had known, about things she had seen, about governors' girlfriends, politicians' wives' lovers, rigged ballots, crooked unions, about acres of marijuana growing behind circular screens of tall corn on the edges of Indiana fields. Then Franklin talked about his years as a cop. Then Reacher talked about his years since the army, the wandering, the exploring, his rootless invisible life.

Helen Rodin said nothing at all.

At eleven o'clock exactly they heard the rattle of a big diesel engine beating off the brick outside. Reacher stepped to the window and saw Cash's Humvee nosing onto the parking apron. *Too noisy*, he thought. *We can't use it.*

Or, maybe we can.

'The Marines are here,' he said.

They heard Cash's feet on the outside stairs. Heard his knock on the door. Reacher went out to the hallway to open up. Cash came in, brisk, solid, reassuring. He was dressed all in black. Black canvas pants, black canvas windbreaker.

Reacher introduced him all round. Yanni, Franklin, Helen Rodin. Everyone shook hands and Cash took a seat. Inside twenty minutes he was up to speed and totally on board.

'They blanked a nineteen-year-old girl?' he said.

'You'd have liked her,' Reacher said.

'Do we have a plan?'

'We're about to make one,' Reacher said. Yanni went out to her car for the maps. Franklin cleared away the coffee cups and made space on the table. Yanni chose the right map. Spread it out flat.

'It's like a giant chessboard out there,' she said. 'Every square is a field a hundred yards across. There are roads laid out in a grid, north to south, west to east, about twenty fields apart.' Then she pointed. Slim finger, painted nail. 'But right *here* we've got two roads that meet and southeast of the corner they make we've got an empty space three fields wide and five fields high. No agriculture there. The northern part is the stone-crushing plant and the house is south of it. I've seen it and it stands about two hundred yards off the road, all alone in the middle of absolutely nothing. No landscaping, no vegetation. But no fence, either.'

'Flat?' Reacher asked.

'As a pool table,' Yanni said.

'Dark out there,' Cash said.

'As the Earl of Hell's waistcoat,' Reacher said. 'And I guess if there's no fence it means they're using cameras. With some kind of thermal imaging at night. Some kind of infrared.'

'How fast can you run two hundred yards?' Cash asked.

'Me?' Reacher said. 'Slow enough they could mail-order a rifle to shoot me with.'

'What's the best approach?'

'Walk in from the north,' Reacher said. 'Without a doubt. We could get into the stone place straight off the road and just hike through it. Then we could lie up as long as we wanted. Good concealment until the last minute.'

'Can't walk in from anywhere if they've got thermal cameras.'

'We'll worry about that later.'

'OK, but they'll anticipate the north.'

Reacher nodded. 'We'll pass on the north. Too obvious.'

'South or east would be next best. Because presumably the driveway comes in from the west. Probably too straight and too open.'

'They'll be thinking the same thing.'

'Makes us both right.'

'I kind of like the driveway,' Reacher said. 'What will it be? Paved?'

'Crushed limestone,' Yanni said. 'They've got plenty to spare.'

'Noisy,' Cash said.

'It'll have retained a little daytime heat,' Reacher said. 'It'll be warmer than the dirt. It'll put a stripe of colour down their thermal picture. If the contrast isn't great it'll give a shadow zone either side.'

'Are you kidding?' Cash said. 'You're going to be forty or fifty degrees hotter than ambient temperature. You're going to show up like a road flare.'

445

'They're going to be paying attention south and east.'

'Not exclusively.'

'You got a better idea?'

'What about a full frontal assault? With vehicles?'

Reacher smiled. 'If it abso*lutely* posi*tively* has to be destroyed by morning, call the United States Marine Corps.'

'Roger that,' Cash said.

'Too dangerous,' Reacher said. 'We can't give them a second's warning and we can't turn the place into a free-fire zone. We've got Rosemary to think about.'

Nobody spoke.

'I like the driveway,' Reacher said again.

Cash glanced at Helen Rodin.

'We could just call in the cops,' he said. 'You know, if it's the DA who's the bad guy here. A couple of SWAT teams could do it.'

'Same problem,' Reacher said. 'Rosemary would be dead before they got near the door.'

'Cut the power lines? Kill the cameras?'

'Same problem. It's an announcement ahead of time.'

'Your call.'

'The driveway,' Reacher said. 'I like the driveway.'

'But what about the cameras?'

'I'll think of something,' Reacher said. He stepped over to the table. Stared down at the map. Then he turned back to Cash. 'Does your truck have a CD player?'

Cash nodded. 'Part of the comfort package.'

446

'Do you mind if Franklin drives it?'

'Franklin can *have* it. I'd prefer a sedan.'

'OK, your Humvee is our approach vehicle. Franklin can drive us there, let us out, and then get straight back here.'

'Us?' Yanni said. 'Are we all going?'

'You bet your ass,' Reacher said. 'Four of us there, with Franklin back here as the comms centre.'

'Good,' Yanni said.

'We need cell phones,' Reacher said.

'I've got one,' Yanni said.

'Me too,' Cash said.

'Me too,' Helen said.

'I don't,' Reacher said.

Franklin took a small Nokia out of his pocket.

'Take mine,' he said.

Reacher took it. 'Can you set up a conference call? Four cell phones and your desk phone? As soon as you get back here?'

Franklin nodded. 'Give me your numbers.'

'And turn the ringers off,' Reacher said.

'When are we doing this?' Cash asked.

'Four o'clock in the morning is my favourite time,' Reacher said. 'But they'll be expecting that. We learned it from them. Four in the morning is when the KGB went knocking on doors. Least resistance. It's a biorhythm thing. So we'll surprise them. We'll do it at two thirty.'

'If you surprise them you don't have to hit them very hard?' Yanni said.

Reacher shook his head. 'In this situation if we surprise them they won't hit *me* very hard.'

'Where am I going to be?' Cash asked.

447

'Southwest corner of the gravel plant,' Reacher said. 'Looking south and east at the house. You can cover the west and the north sides simultaneously. With your rifle.'

'OK.'

'What did you bring for me?'

Cash dug in the pocket of his windbreaker and came out with a knife in a sheath. He tossed it across the room. Reacher caught it. It was a standard-issue Navy Seal SRK. Their survival–rescue knife. Carbon steel, black epoxy, seven-inch blade. Not new.

'This is it?' Reacher said.

'All I've got,' Cash said. 'The only weapons I own are my rifle and that knife.'

'You're kidding.'

'I'm a businessman, not a psycho.'

'Christ's sake, Gunny, I'll be taking a knife to a gunfight? Isn't it supposed to be the other way around?'

'All I've got,' Cash said again.

'Great.'

'You can take a gun from the first one you cut. Face it, if you don't get close enough to cut one of them you aren't going to win anyway.'

Reacher said nothing.

They waited. Midnight. Twelve thirty. Yanni fiddled with her cell phone and made a call. Reacher ran through the plan, one more time. First in his head, then out loud, until everyone was clear. Details, dispositions, refinements, adjustments.

'But we might still change everything,' he said.

448

'When we get there. No substitute for seeing the actual terrain.'

They waited. One o'clock. One thirty. Reacher started to allow himself to think about the end-game. About what would come after the victory. He turned to Franklin.

'Who is Emerson's number two?' he asked.

'A woman called Donna Bianca,' Franklin said.

'Is she any good?'

'She's his number two.'

'She'll need to be there. Afterwards. It's going to be a real three-ring circus. Too much for one pair of hands. I want you to bring Emerson and Donna Bianca out there. And Alex Rodin, of course. After we win.'

'They'll be in bed.'

'So wake them up.'

'*If* we win,' Franklin said.

At one forty-five people started to get restless. Helen Rodin stepped over and squatted down next to Reacher. She picked up the knife. Looked at it. Put it back down.

'Why are you doing this?' she asked.

'Because I can. And because of the girl.'

'You'll get yourself killed.'

'Unlikely,' Reacher said. 'These are old men and idiots. I've survived worse.'

'You're just saying that.'

'If I get in OK I'll be safe enough. Room to room isn't hard. People get very scared with a prowler loose in the house. They hate it.'

'But you won't get in OK. They'll see you coming.'

Reacher dug in his left-hand pocket and came out with the shiny new quarter that had bothered him in the car. Handed it to her.

'For you,' he said.

She looked at it. 'Something to remember you by?'

'Something to remember tonight by.'

Then he checked his watch. Stood up.

'Let's do it,' he said.

SIXTEEN

They stood for a moment in the shadows and the silence on the parking apron below Franklin's lighted windows. Then Yanni went to get the Sheryl Crow CD from her Mustang. She gave it to Cash. Cash unlocked the Humvee and leaned inside and put it in the player. Then he gave the keys to Franklin. Franklin climbed into the driver's seat. Cash got in next to him with his M24 across his knees. Reacher and Helen Rodin and Ann Yanni squeezed together in the back.

'Turn the heater up,' Reacher said.

Cash leaned to his left and dialled in maximum temperature. Franklin started the engine. Backed out into the street. Swung the wheel and took off west. Then he turned north. The engine was loud and the ride was rough. The heater kicked in and the fan blew hard. The interior grew warm, and then hot. They turned west, turned north, turned west, turned north, lining up with the grid that would run through the fields. The drive was a series of long droning cruises punctuated by sharp right-angle corners. Then they made the final turn. Franklin sat up straight behind the wheel and accelerated hard.

'This is it,' Yanni said. 'Dead ahead, about three miles to go.'

'Start the music,' Reacher said. 'Track eight.'

Cash hit the button.

Every day is a winding road.

'Louder,' Reacher said.

Cash turned it up. Franklin drove on, sixty miles an hour.

'Two miles,' Yanni called. Then: 'One mile.'

Franklin drove on. Reacher stared out the window to his right. Watched the fields flash past in the darkness. Random scatter from the headlights lit them up. The irrigation booms were turning so slowly they looked stationary. Mist filled the air.

'High beams,' Reacher called.

Franklin flicked them on.

'Music all the way up,' Reacher called.

Cash twisted the knob to maximum.

EVERY DAY IS A WINDING ROAD.

'Half a mile,' Yanni yelled.

'Windows,' Reacher shouted.

Four thumbs hit four buttons and all four windows dropped an inch. Hot air and loud music sucked out into the night. Reacher stared right and saw the dark outline of the house flash past, isolated, distant, square, solid, substantial, dimly lit from inside. Flat land all round it. The limestone driveway, pale, very long, as straight as an arrow.

Franklin kept his foot hard down.

'Stop sign in four hundred yards,' Yanni yelled.

'Stand by,' Reacher shouted. 'Show time.'

'One hundred yards,' Yanni yelled.

'Doors,' Reacher shouted.

Three doors opened an inch. Franklin braked hard. Stopped dead on the line. Reacher and Yanni and Helen and Cash spilled out. Franklin didn't hesitate. He took off again like it was just a normal dead-of-night stop sign. Reacher and Yanni and Cash and Helen dusted themselves down and stood close together on the crown of the road and stared north until the glow of the lights and the sound of the engine and the thump of the music were lost in the distance and the darkness.

Sokolov had picked up the Humvee's heat signature on both the south and west monitors when it was still about half a mile shy of the house. Hard not to. A big powerful vehicle, travelling fast, trailing long plumes of hot air from open windows, what was to miss? On the screen it looked like a bottle rocket flying sideways. Then he heard it too, physically, through the walls. Big engine, loud music. Vladimir glanced his way.

'Passerby?' he asked.

'Let's see,' Sokolov said.

It didn't slow down. It hurtled straight past the house and kept on going north. On the screen it trailed heat like a re-entry capsule. Through the walls they heard the music Doppler-shift like an ambulance's siren as it went by.

'Passerby,' Sokolov said.

'Some asshole,' Vladimir said.

Upstairs on the third floor Chenko heard it too.

He stepped through an empty bedroom to a west-facing window and looked out. Saw a big black shape doing about sixty miles an hour, high-beam headlights, bright tail lights, music thumping and thudding so loud he could hear the door panels flexing from two hundred yards away. It roared past. Didn't slow down. He opened the window and leaned out and craned his neck and watched the bubble of light track north into the distance. It went behind the skeletal tangle of machinery in the stone-crushing plant. But it was still visible as a moving glow in the air. After a quarter-mile the glow changed colour. Red now, not white. Brake lights, flaring for the stop sign. The glow paused for a second. Then the red colour died and the glow turned back to white and took off again, fast.

The Zec called up from the floor below: 'Was that him?'

'No,' Chenko called back. 'Just some rich kid out for a drive.'

Reacher led the way through the dark, four people single file on the edge of the blacktop with the gravel plant's high wire fence on their left and huge circular fields across the road on their right. After the roar of the diesel and the thump of the music the silence felt absolute. There was nothing to hear except the hiss of irrigation water. Reacher raised his hand and stopped them where the fence turned a right-angle and ran away east. The corner post was double thickness and braced with angled spars. Grass and weeds from the shoulder were clumped up high. He stepped forward and checked the view. He was on a perfect diagonal from the northwest corner of the house. He had an equal forty-five degree line of sight to the north façade and the west. Because of the diagonal the distance was about three hundred yards. Visibility was very poor. There was a glimmer of cloudy moonlight, but beyond that there was nothing at all.

He stepped back. Pointed at Cash, pointed at the base of the corner post.

'This is your position,' he whispered. 'Check it out.'

Cash moved forward and knelt down in the weeds. Six feet away he was invisible. He switched on his night scope and raised his rifle. Tracked it slowly left and right, up and down.

'Three storeys plus a basement,' he whispered. 'High-pitched shingle roof, plank siding, many windows, one door visible to the west. No cover *at all* in any direction. They bulldozed everything flat, all around. Nothing's growing. You're going to look like a beetle on a bed sheet out there.'

'Cameras?'

The rifle tracked a steady line from left to right. 'Under the eaves. One on the north side, one on the west. We can assume the same on the sides we can't see.'

'How big are they?'

'How big do you want them to be?'

'Big enough for you to hit.'

'Funny man. If they were spy cameras built into cigarette lighters I could hit them from here.'

'OK, so listen up,' Reacher whispered. 'This is how we're going to do it. I'm going to get to my starting position. Then we're all going to wait for Franklin to get back and put the comms net on the air. Then I'm going to make a move. If I don't feel good I'm going to call in fire on those cameras. I say the word, I want you to take them out. Two shots, bang, bang. That'll slow them down, maybe ten or twenty seconds.'

'Negative,' Cash said. 'I won't direct live rounds into a wooden structure we know contains a noncombatant hostage.'

'She'll be in the basement,' Reacher said.

'Or the attic.'

'You'd be firing at the eaves.'

'Exactly. She's in the attic, she hears gunfire, she hits the deck, that's exactly where I'm aiming. One man's ceiling is another man's floor.'

'Spare me,' Reacher said. 'Take the risk.'

'Negative. Won't do it.'

'Christ, Gunny, you are one uptight Marine, you know that?'

Cash didn't speak. Reacher stepped forward again and peered round the corner of the fence. Took a long hard look and pulled back.

'OK,' he said. 'New plan. Just watch the west windows. You see muzzle flash, you put suppressing fire into the room it's coming out of. We can assume the hostage won't be in the same room as the sniper.'

Cash said nothing.

'Will you do that at least?' Reacher asked.

'You might be in the house already.'

'I'll take my chances. Voluntary assumption of risk, OK? Helen can witness my consent. She's a lawyer.'

Cash said nothing.

'No wonder you came in third,' Reacher said. 'You need to lighten up.'

'OK,' Cash said. 'I see hostile gunfire, I'll return it.'

'Hostile is about the only kind you're going to see, don't you think? Since you only gave me a damn knife?'

'Army,' Cash said. 'Always bitching about something.'

'What do I do?' Helen asked.

'New plan,' Reacher said. He touched the fence with his palm. 'Keep low, follow the fence around the corner, stop opposite the house. Stay down. They won't pick you up there. It's too far. Listen to your phone. If I need a distraction I'll ask you to run a little ways towards the house and then back again. A zigzag, or a circle. Out and back. Real fast. Just enough to put a blip on their screen. No danger. By the time they move a rifle around you'll be back at the fence.'

She nodded. Didn't speak.

'And me?' Ann Yanni asked.

'You stay with Cash. You're the ethics police. He gets cold feet about helping me out, you kick his ass, OK?'

Nobody spoke.

'All set?' Reacher asked.

'Set,' they said, one after the other.

Reacher walked away into the darkness on the other side of the road.

He kept on walking, off the blacktop, across the shoulder, across the stony margin of the field, onward, right into the field, all the way into the middle of the soaking crop. He waited until the irrigation boom rolled slowly round and caught up with him. Then he turned ninety degrees and walked south with it, directly underneath it, keeping pace, letting the ceaseless water rain down and soak his hair and his skin and his clothes. The boom pulled away as it followed its circular path and Reacher kept straight on at a tangent and walked into the next field. Waited once again for the boom to find him and then walked on under it, matching its speed, raising his arms high and wide to catch as much drenching as he could. Then that boom swung away and left him and he walked on to find the next one. And the next, and the next. When at last he was opposite the driveway entrance he simply walked in a circle, under the last boom, waiting for his cell phone to vibrate, like a man caught in a monsoon.

Cash's cell phone vibrated against his hip and he pulled it out and clicked it on. Heard Franklin's voice, quiet and cautious in his ear.

'Check in, please,' it said.

Cash heard Helen say: 'Here.'

Yanni said, 'Here,' from three feet behind him.

Cash said, 'Here.'

Then he heard Reacher say: 'Here.'

Franklin said, 'OK, you're all loud and clear, and the ball is in your court.'

Cash heard Reacher say: 'Gunny, check the house.'

Cash lifted the rifle and swept left to right. 'No change.'

Reacher said: 'I'm on my way.'

Then there was nothing but silence. Ten seconds. Twenty. Thirty. A whole minute. Two minutes.

Cash heard Reacher ask: 'Gunny, do you see me?'

Cash lifted the rifle again and swept the length of the driveway from its mouth all the way to the house. 'Negative. I don't see you. Where are you?'

'About thirty yards in.'

Cash moved the rifle. Estimated thirty yards from the road and stared through the scope. Saw nothing. Nothing at all. 'Good work, soldier. Keep going.'

Yanni crawled forward. Whispered in Cash's ear. 'Why don't you see him?'

'Because he's nuts.'

'No, explain it to me. You've got a night scope, right?'

'The best money can buy,' Cash said. 'And it works off heat, just like their cameras.' Then he pointed away to his right. 'But my guess is Reacher walked through the fields. Soaked himself in water. It's coming straight up from the aquifer, stone cold. So right now he's close to ambient temperature. I can't see him, they can't see him.'

'Smart,' Yanni said.

'Brave,' Cash said. 'But ultimately dumb. Because he's drying out every step of the way. And getting warmer.'

459

Reacher walked through the dark in the dirt ten feet south of the driveway. Not fast, not slow. His shoes were soaked and they were sticking to the mud. Almost coming off. He was so cold he was shivering violently. Which was bad. Shivering is a physiological reaction designed to warm a cold body fast. And he didn't want to bc warm. Not yet.

Vladimir had got a rhythm going. He stared at the east monitor for four seconds, then the north for three. *East, two, three, four, north, two, three. East, two, three, four, north, two, three.* He didn't move his chair. Just leaned a little one way, then the other. Beside him Sokolov had a similar thing going south and west. Slightly different intervals. Not perfectly synchronized. But just as good, Vladimir guessed. Maybe even better. Sokolov had spent a lot of time on surveillance.

Reacher walked on. Not fast, not slow. On the map the driveway had looked to be about two hundred yards long. On the ground it felt like an airport runway. Straight as a die. Wide. And long, long, long. He had been walking for ever. And he was less than halfway to the house. He walked on. Just kept on going. Looking ahead every step of the way, watching the darkened windows far away in front of him.

He realized his hair wasn't dripping any more.

He touched one hand with the other. Dry. Not warm, but no longer cold.

He walked on. He was tempted to run.

Running would get him there faster. But running would heat him up. He was approaching the point of no return. He was right out there in no-man's-land. And he wasn't shivering. He raised his phone.

'Helen,' he whispered. 'I need a diversion.'

Helen took off her heels and left them neatly side by side at the base of the fence. For an absurd moment she felt like a person who piles all her clothes on the beach before she walks into the sea to drown. Then she put her palms down on the dirt like a sprinter in the blocks and took off forward. Just ran crazily, twenty feet, thirty, forty, and then she stopped dead and stood still facing the house with her arms out wide like a target. *Shoot me*, she thought. *Please shoot me.* Then she got scared that maybe she really meant it and she turned and ran back in a wide zigzag loop. Threw herself down and crawled along the fence again until she found her shoes.

Vladimir saw her on the north monitor. Nothing recognizable. Just a brief flare that because of the phosphor technology was smeared and a little time-lagged. But he bent his head close anyway and stared at the after-image. One second, two. Sokolov sensed the interruption to his rhythm and glanced over. Three seconds, four.

'Fox?' Vladimir said.

'I didn't see it,' Sokolov said. 'But probably.'

'It ran away again.'

'OK, then.' Sokolov turned back to his own pair of monitors. Glanced at the west view,

461

checked the south, and settled into his regular cadence again.

Cash had a cadence of his own. He was inching his night scope along at what he guessed was the speed of a walking man. But every five seconds he would sweep it suddenly forward and back in case his estimate was off. During one of those rapid traverses he picked up on what looked like a pale green shadow.

'Reacher, I can see you,' he whispered. 'You're visible, soldier.'

Reacher's voice came back: 'What scope have you got on that thing?'

'Litton,' Cash said.

'Expensive, right?'

'Thirty-seven hundred dollars.'

'Got to be better than a lousy thermal camera.'

Cash didn't reply.

Reacher said: 'Well, I'm hoping so, anyway.'

He walked on. Probably the most unnatural thing a human can force himself to do, to walk slowly and surely towards a building that probably has a rifle in it pointing directly at his centre mass. If Chenko had any sense at all he would wait, and wait, and wait, until his target was pretty close. And Chenko seemed to have plenty of sense. Fifty yards would be good. Or thirty-five, like Chenko's range out of the parking garage. Chenko was pretty good at thirty-five yards. That had been made very clear.

He walked on. Took the knife out of his pocket and unsheathed it and held it right-handed, low and easy. Transferred the phone to his left and held it near his ear. Heard Cash say: 'You're totally visible now, soldier. You're shining like the north star. It's like you're on fire.'

Forty yards to go.

Thirty-nine.

Thirty-eight.

'Helen?' he said. 'Do it again.'

He heard her voice: 'OK.'

He walked on. Held his breath.

Thirty-five yards.

Thirty-four.

Thirty-three.

He breathed out. He walked on, doggedly. Thirty yards to go. He heard panting in his ear. Helen, running. He heard Yanni ask, off-mike: 'How close is he?' Heard Cash answer: 'Not close enough.'

Vladimir leaned forward and said, 'There it is again.' He put his fingertip on the screen, as if touch might tell him something. Sokolov glanced across. Sokolov had spent many more hours with the screens than Vladimir. Primarily surveillance had been his job. His, and Raskin's.

'That's no fox,' he said. 'It's way too big.'

He watched for five more seconds. The image was weaving left and right at the very limit of the camera's range. Recognizable size, recognizable shape, inexplicable motion. He stood up and walked to the door. Braced his hands on the frame and leaned out into the hallway.

'Chenko!' he called. 'North!'

Behind his back on the west screen a shape as

463

big as his thumb grew larger. It looked like a painting-by-numbers figure done in fluorescent colours. Lime green on the outside, then a band of chrome yellow, with a core of hot red.

Chenko walked through an empty bedroom and opened the window as high as it would go. Then he backed away into the darkness. That way he was invisible from below and invulnerable except to a shot taken from the third storey of an adjacent building, and there were no adjacent buildings. He switched on his night scope and raised his rifle. Quartered the open ground two hundred yards out, up and down, left and right.

He saw a woman.

She was running crazily, barefoot, darting left and right, out and back, like she was dancing or playing a phantom game of soccer. Chenko thought: *What?* He squeezed the slack out of his trigger and tried to anticipate her next pirouette. Tried to guess where her chest would be a third of a second after he fired. He waited. Then she stopped moving. She stood completely still, facing the house, arms out wide like a target.

Chenko pulled the trigger.

Then he understood. He stepped back to the hallway.

'Decoy!' he screamed. 'Decoy!'

Cash saw the muzzle flash and called 'Shot fired' and jumped his scope to the north window. The lower pane was raised, the upper pane was fixed. No point in putting a round through the opening. The upward trajectory would guarantee a miss.

So he fired at the glass. He figured if he could get a hail of jagged shards going, then that might ruin somebody's night.

Sokolov was watching the crazy heat image on Vladimir's screen when he heard Chenko's shot and his shouted warning. He glanced back at the door and turned to the south monitor. Nothing there. Then he heard return fire and shattering glass upstairs. He pushed back from the table and stepped to the door.

'Are you OK?' he called.

'Decoy,' Chenko called back. 'Has to be.'

Sokolov turned and checked all four screens, very carefully.

'No,' he called. 'Negative. Definitely nothing incoming.'

Reacher touched the front wall of the house. Old plank siding, painted many times. He was ten feet south of the driveway, ten feet south of the front door, near a window that looked into a dark empty room. The window was a tall rectangle with a lower pane that slid upward behind the upper pane. Maybe the upper pane slid down over the lower pane, too. Reacher didn't know the name for the style. He had rarely lived in houses and had never owned one. *Sash? Double-hung?* He wasn't sure. The house was much older than it had looked from a distance. Maybe a hundred years. Hundred-year-old house, hundred-year-old window. But did the window still have a hundred-year-old catch? He pressed his cheek against the lower pane and squinted upward.

He couldn't see. Too dark.

Then he heard the shooting. Two rounds, one close, one not, shattering glass.

Then he heard Cash in his ear: 'Helen? You OK?'

He heard no reply.

Cash asked again: 'Helen? Helen?'

No reply.

Reacher put the phone in his pocket. Worked the blade of his knife up into the gap where the bottom of the upper casement overlapped the top of the lower casement. He moved the blade right to left, slowly, carefully, feeling for a catch. He found one, dead centre. Tapped it, gently. It felt like a heavy brass tongue. It would pivot through ninety degrees, in and out of a socket.

But which way?

He pushed it, right to left. *Solid*. He pulled the knife out and worked it back in an inch left of centre. Slid it back, until he found the tongue again. Pushed it, left to right.

It moved.

He pushed it hard, and knocked it right out of its socket.

Easy.

He lifted the lower pane high and rolled over the sill into the room.

Cash eased forward and swung his rifle through ninety degrees until it was sighted due east along the fence. He stared through the scope. Saw nothing. He moved back into cover. Raised his phone.

466

'Helen?' he whispered.

No response.

Reacher moved through the empty room to the door. It was closed. He put his ear against it. Listened hard. Heard nothing. He turned the handle, slowly, carefully. Opened the door, very slowly. Leaned out. Checked the hallway.

Empty.

There was light from an open doorway fifteen feet ahead on his left. He paused. Lifted one foot at a time and wiped the soles of his shoes on his pants. Wiped his palms. He took a single step. Tested the floor. No sound. He moved ahead, slowly, silently. *Boat shoes. Good for something.* He kept close to the wall, where the floor would be strongest. He stopped a yard shy of the lighted doorway. Took a breath. Moved on.

Stopped in the doorway.

He was looking at two guys from behind. They were seated side by side with their backs to him at a long table. Staring at TV monitors. At ghostly green images of darkness. On the left, Vladimir. On the right, a guy he hadn't seen before. *Sokolov? Must be.* To Sokolov's right, a yard away from him, a handgun rested on the very end of the table. A Smith and Wesson Model 60. The first stainless steel revolver produced anywhere in the world. Two and a half inch barrel. A five-shooter.

Reacher took a long silent step into the room. Paused. Held his breath. Reversed the knife in his hand. Held the blade an inch from its end between the ball of his thumb and the knuckle of

467

his first finger. Raised his arm. Cocked it behind his head. Snapped it forward.

Threw the knife.

It buried itself two inches deep in the back of Sokolov's neck.

Vladimir glanced right, towards the sound. Reacher was already moving. Vladimir glanced back. Saw him. Pushed himself away from the table and half rose. Reacher watched him calculate the distance between himself and the gun. Saw him decide to go for it. Reacher stepped into his charge and ducked under his swinging left hook and buried his shoulder in his chest and wrapped both arms round his back and jacked him bodily off his feet. Just lifted him up and turned him away from the table.

And then squeezed.

Best route to a silent kill against a guy as big as Vladimir was simply to crush him to death. No hitting, no shooting, no banging around. As long as his arms and his legs couldn't connect with anything solid there would be no noise. No shouting, no screaming. Just a long laboured barely audible tubercular sound as the last breath he had taken came back out, never to be replaced.

Reacher held Vladimir a foot off the ground and squeezed with all his strength. He crushed Vladimir's chest in a bear hug so vicious and sustained and powerful that no human could have survived it. Vladimir wasn't expecting it. He thought this was some kind of preamble. Not the main event. When he figured it out, he went crazy with panic. He rained desperate blows down on

Reacher's back and flailed with his feet at his shins. *Stupid*, Reacher thought. *You're just burning oxygen. And you ain't getting more, pal. Better believe it.* He tightened his grip. Crushed harder. And harder. And then harder, in a remorseless subliminal rhythm that said *more*, and *more*, and *more*. His teeth ground together. His heart pounded. His muscles swelled as big and hard as river rocks and started burning. He could feel Vladimir's ribcage moving, clicking, separating, cracking, crushing. And his last living breath leaking out of his starving lungs.

Sokolov moved.

Reacher staggered under Vladimir's weight. Turned clumsily on one leg. Kicked out and caught the hilt of the knife with his heel. Sokolov stopped moving. Vladimir stopped moving. Reacher kept the pressure full on for another whole minute. Then he eased off slowly and bent down and laid the body gently on the floor. Squatted down. Breathed hard. Checked for a pulse.

No pulse.

He stood up and pulled Cash's knife out of Sokolov's neck and used it to cut Vladimir's throat, ear to ear. *For Sandy*, he thought. Then he turned back and cut Sokolov's throat, too. *Just in case.* Blood soaked the tabletop and dripped to the floor. It didn't spurt. It just leaked. Sokolov's heart had already stopped pumping. He squatted down again and cleaned the blade on Vladimir's shirt, one side, then the other. He pulled the phone out of his pocket. Heard Cash say: '*Helen?*'

He whispered: 'What's up?'

Cash answered, 'We took an incoming round. I can't raise Helen.'

'Yanni, move left,' Reacher said. 'Find her. Franklin, you there?'

Franklin said, 'Here.'

'Stand by to call the medics,' Reacher said.

Cash asked, 'Where are you?'

'In the house,' Reacher said.

'Opposition?'

'Unsuccessful,' Reacher said. 'Where did the shot come from?'

'Third-floor window, north. Which makes sense, tactically. They've got the sniper up there. They can direct him based on what they see from the cameras.'

'Not any more,' Reacher said. He put the phone back in his pocket. Picked up the gun. Checked the cylinder. It was fully loaded. Five Smith and Wesson .38 Specials. He moved out to the hallway with the knife in his right hand and the gun in his left. Went looking for the basement door.

Cash heard Yanni talking to herself as she moved away to his left. Low voice, but clear, like a running commentary. She was saying: 'I'm moving east now, keeping low, staying tight against the fence in the darkness. I'm looking for Helen Rodin. We know they fired at her. Now she's not answering her phone. We're hoping she's OK, but we're worried that she isn't.'

Cash listened until he couldn't hear her any more. He shook his head in bemusement. Then he ducked his eye to the scope and watched the house.

470

Rosemary Barr wasn't in the basement. It took Reacher less than a minute to be completely certain of that. It was a wide open space, musty, dimly lit, uninterrupted and totally empty except for the foundations of three brick chimneys.

Reacher paused at the circuit-breaker box. He was tempted to throw the switch. But Chenko had a night sight, and he didn't. So he just crept back up the stairs.

Yanni found Helen Rodin's shoes literally by stumbling over them. They were placed neatly side by side at the base of the fence. High heels, black patent, gleaming slightly in the ragged moonlight. Yanni kicked them accidentally and heard the sound of empty footwear. She bent and picked them up. Hung them on the fence by their heels.

'Helen?' she whispered. '*Helen?* Where are you?'

Then she heard a voice: 'Here.'

'Where?'

'*Here*. Keep going.'

Yanni walked on. Found a black shape rolled tight against the base of the fence.

'I dropped my phone,' Helen said. 'Can't find it.'

'Are you OK?'

'He missed me. I was leaping around like a mad woman. But the bullet came real close. It scared me. I just dropped my phone and ran.'

Helen sat up. Yanni squatted next to her.

'Look,' Helen said. She was holding something

471

in the palm of her hand. Something bright. A coin. A quarter, new and shiny.

'What is it?' Yanni said.

'A quarter,' Helen said.

'So what?'

'Reacher gave it to me.'

Helen was smiling. Yanni could see the white of her teeth in the moonlight.

Reacher crept down the hallway. Opened doors and searched rooms to the left and right as he went. They were all empty. All unused. He paused at the bottom of the stairs. Backed away into an empty twelve-by-twenty space that might once have been a parlour. Crouched and laid the knife on the floor and pulled out his phone.

'Gunny?' he whispered.

Cash answered: 'You back with us?'

'Phone was in my pocket.'

'Yanni found Helen. She's OK.'

'Good. The basement and the ground floor are clear. I think you were right after all. Rosemary must be in the attic.'

'You going upstairs now?'

'I guess I'll have to.'

'Body count?'

'Two down so far.'

'Lots more upstairs, then.'

'I'll be careful.'

'Roger that.'

Reacher put the phone back in his pocket and retrieved the knife from the floor. Stood up and crept out to the hallway. The staircase was at the back of the house. It was wide, dog-legged,

472

and shallow-pitched. Quite grand. There was a wide landing halfway up where the dog-leg reversed direction. He went up the first half-flight backwards. It made more sense that way. He wanted to know right away if there was someone in the second-floor hallway looking down over the banister. He kept close to the wall. If stairs creaked at all, they creaked most in the middle of a tread. He went slowly, feeling with his heels, putting them down gently and deliberately. And quietly. *Boat shoes. Good for something.* After five up-and-back steps his head was about level with the second-storey floor. He raised the gun. Took another step. Now he could see the whole of the hallway. It was empty. It was a quiet carpeted space lit by a single low-wattage bulb. Nothing to see, except six closed doors, three on a side. He breathed out and made it to the half-landing. Shuffled left and crept up the second part of the dog-leg going forward. Stepped off the staircase. Into the hallway.

Now what?

Six closed doors. *Who was where?* He moved slowly towards the front of the house. Listened at the first door. Heard nothing. He moved on. Heard nothing at the second door. Moved on again but before he reached the third door he heard sounds from the floor above. Sounds that were coming down *through* the floor. Sounds that he didn't understand. Sliding, scraping, crunching noises, repeated rhythmically, with a single light footfall at the end of every sequence. *Slide, scrape, crunch, tap. Slide, scrape, crunch, tap.* He stared up at the ceiling. Then the third

473

door opened and Grigor Linsky stepped out into the hallway right in front of him. And froze.

He was wearing his familiar double-breasted suit. Grey colour, boxy shoulders, cuffed pants. Reacher stabbed him in the throat. Instantly, right-handed, instinctively. He buried the blade and jerked it left. *Sever the windpipe. Keep him quiet.* He stepped aside to avoid the fountain of blood. Caught him under the arms from behind and dragged him back into the room he had come out of. It was a kitchen. Linsky had been making tea. Reacher turned out the light under the kettle. Put the gun and the knife on the counter. Bent down and clamped Linsky's head between his hands and twisted it left and jerked it right. Broke his neck. The *snap* was loud enough to worry about. It was a very quiet house. Reacher retrieved the gun and the knife and listened at the door. Heard nothing except *slide, scrape, crunch, tap. Slide, scrape, crunch, tap*. He stepped back into the hallway. Then he knew.

Glass.

Cash had returned fire through Chenko's favoured northern vantage point and like all good snipers had sought maximum damage from his one shot. And in turn like all good snipers Chenko was keeping his physical environment operational. *He was cleaning up the broken glass*. He had a twenty-five per cent chance of being directed back to that particular window and he wanted his passage through the room clear.

Slide, scrape, crunch, tap. He was using the side of his foot to sweep the glass aside. Into a pile. Then he was stepping forward to sweep the

474

next arc. He would want a clear two-foot walkway through the room. No danger of slipping or sliding.

How far had he got?

Reacher crept to the next staircase. It was identical to the last one. Wide, shallow, doglegged. He walked up backwards, listening hard. *Slide, scrape, crunch, tap.* He crossed the half-landing. Kept on going, forward. The third-floor hallway had the same layout as the one below, but it wasn't carpeted. Just bare boards. There was an upright chair in the centre of the corridor. All the doors were open. North was to the right. Reacher could feel night air coming in. He stayed close to the wall. Crept onward. The noises got louder. He flattened against the wall. Took a breath. Pivoted slowly and stepped to his left. Into a doorway.

Chenko was twelve feet from him. Facing away. Facing the window. The lower pane had been pushed up behind the upper pane. Both panes had been blown out. The room was cold. The floor was covered in glass. Chenko was clearing a path from the door towards the window. He had about three feet left to go. His rifle was upright against the wall, six feet from him. He was stooped, looking down, concentrating hard on his task. It was an important task. Skidding on a pebble of glass could cost him precious time in a firefight. Chenko had discipline.

And ten seconds to live.

Reacher put the knife in his pocket. Freed his right hand. Flexed it. Stepped forward. Just walked slow and silent down the path that Chenko had cleared. Four quiet paces. Chenko sensed it. He straightened. Reacher caught him round the neck from behind. One-handed. He gripped hard. Took one more long fast stride and stiff-armed Chenko forward with it and threw him out the open window, head first.

'I warned you,' he whispered into the darkness below. 'You should have put me down when you had the chance.' Then he took out his phone.

'Gunny?' he whispered.

'Here.'

'Third-floor window, where you returned fire. You see it?'

'I see it.'

'A guy just fell out. If he gets up again, shoot him.'

Then he put the phone away and went looking for the attic door.

He found Rosemary Barr completely unharmed, sitting upright on the attic floor. Her feet were taped, her wrists were taped, her mouth was taped. Reacher put his finger to his lips. She nodded. He cut her free with the bloodstained knife and helped her stand. She was unsteady for a moment. Then she shook herself and gave a kind of nod. Then a smile. Reacher guessed that whatever fear she had felt and whatever reaction she was feeling right then had both been neutralized by some kind of a steely determination to help her brother. If she survived, he would survive. That belief had kept her going.

'Have they gone?' she whispered.

'All except Raskin and the Zec,' Reacher whispered back.

'No, Raskin killed himself. I heard them talking. The Zec made him do it. Because he let you steal his cell phone.'

'Where's the Zec likely to be?'

'He's in the living room most of the time. Second floor.'

'Which door?'

'Last on the left.'

'OK, stay here,' Reacher whispered. 'I'll round him up and I'll be right back.'

'I can't stay here. You have to get me out.'

He paused. 'OK, but you've got to be real quiet. And don't look left or right.'

'Why not?'

'Dead people.'

'I'm glad,' she said.

Reacher held her arm down the stairs to the third-floor hallway. Then he went ahead alone to the second. All quiet. The last door on the left was still closed. He waved her down. They made the turn together and headed to the first floor. To the front of the house. To the room he had entered through. He helped her over the sill and out the window, to the dirt below. He pointed.

'Follow the driveway to the road,' he said. 'Turn right. I'll tell the others you're coming. There's a guy in black with a rifle. He's one of ours.'

She stood still for a second. Then she bent down and took off her low-heeled shoes and held them in her hands and started running like hell, due west, through the dirt, towards the road. Reacher took out his phone.

477

'Gunny?' he whispered.

'Here.'

'Rosemary Barr is heading your way.'

'Outstanding.'

'Round up the others and meet her halfway. There's no more operational night vision. Then stand by. I'll get back to you.'

'Roger that.'

Reacher put the phone away. Backtracked through the silent house, on his way to find the Zec.

SEVENTEEN

In the end, it came down to waiting. Wait, and good things come to you. And bad things. Reacher crept back to the second floor. The last door on the left was still closed. He ducked into the kitchen. Linsky was on the floor, on his back in a pool of blood. Reacher relit the flame under the kettle. Then he stepped out to the hallway. Walked quietly to the front of the house and leaned on the wall beyond the last door on the left.

And waited.

The kettle boiled after five minutes. The whistle started low and quiet, and then the note and the volume rose to full blast. Within ten seconds the second floor of the house was full of an insane shrieking. Ten seconds after that, the door on Reacher's right opened. A small man stepped out. Reacher let him take a pace forward and then spun him round and jammed the Smith 60 hard in the base of his throat.

And stared.

The Zec. He was a wide, ancient, twisted, stooped, battered old man. A wraith. Barely human. He was covered in livid scars and patches of discoloured skin. His face was lined and drooping and seething with rage and hatred and cruelty. He was unarmed. His ruined hands didn't seem capable of holding a weapon. Reacher forced him down the hallway. Into the kitchen, backwards. To the stove. The noise from the kettle was unbearable. Reacher used his left hand and killed the flame. Then he hauled the Zec back towards the living room. The kettle's whistle died away, like an air raid siren winding down. The house went quiet again.

'It's over,' Reacher said. 'You lost.'

'It's never over,' the Zec replied. Hoarse voice, low, guttural.

'Guess again,' Reacher said. He kept the Smith hard against the Zec's throat. Too low and too close for him to see it. He eased the hammer back. Slowly, carefully. Deliberately. Loudly. *Click-click-click-crunch*. An unmistakable sound.

'I'm eighty years old,' the Zec said.

'I don't care if you're a hundred,' Reacher said. 'You're still going down.'

'Idiot,' the Zec said back. 'I meant I've survived things worse than you. Since long before you were born.'

'Nobody's worse than me.'

'Don't flatter yourself. You're nothing.'

'You think?' Reacher said. 'You were alive this morning and you won't be tomorrow. After eighty years. That makes me something, don't you think?'

No answer.

'It's over,' Reacher said. 'Believe me. Long and winding road, OK, I understand all of that, but this is the end of it. Had to happen sometime.'

No response.

'You know when my birthday is?' Reacher asked.

'Obviously not.'

'It's in October. You know what day?'

'Of course not.'

'You're going to find out the hard way. I'm counting in my head. When I reach my birthday, I'm going to pull the trigger.'

He started counting in his head. *First, second.* He watched the Zec's eyes. *Fifth, sixth, seventh, eighth.* No response. *Tenth, eleventh, twelfth.*

'What do you want?' the Zec said.

Negotiation time.

'I want to talk,' Reacher said.

'Talk?'

'The twelfth,' Reacher said. 'That's how long you lasted. Then you gave it up. You know why? Because you want to survive. It's the deepest instinct you've got. Obviously. Otherwise how would you have gotten as old as you are? It's probably a deeper instinct than I could ever understand. A reflex, a habit, roll the dice, stay alive, make the next move, take the next chance. It's in your DNA. It's *what you are.*'

'So?'

'So now we've got ourselves a competition. What you are, against what I am.'

'And what are you?'

'I'm the guy who just threw Chenko out a third-floor window. After crushing Vladimir to death with my bare hands. Because I didn't like what they did to innocent people. So now you've got to pit *your* strong desire to survive against *my*

481

strong desire to shoot you in the head and piss in the bullet hole.'

No response.

'One shot,' Reacher said. 'In the head. Lights out. That's your choice. Another day, another roll of the dice. Or not. As the case may be.'

He saw calculation in the Zec's eyes. Assessment, evaluation, speculation.

'I could throw you down the stairs,' he said. 'You could crawl over and take a look at Vladimir. I cut his throat afterwards. Just for fun. That's who *I* am. So don't think I don't mean what I say. I'll do it and I'll sleep like a baby the rest of my life.'

'What do you want?' the Zec asked again.

'Help with a problem.'

'What problem?'

'There's an innocent man I need to get out of the prison ward. So I need you to tell the truth to a detective called Emerson. The truth, the whole truth, and nothing but the truth. I need you to finger Chenko for the shooting, and Vladimir for the girl, and whoever it was for Ted Archer. And whatever else you've done. The whole nine yards. Including how you and Linsky set it all up.'

A flicker in the Zec's eyes. 'Pointless. I'd get the death penalty.'

'Yes, you would,' Reacher said. 'That's for damn sure. But you'd still be alive tomorrow. And the next day, and the next. The appeals process lasts for ever here. Ten years, sometimes. You might get lucky. There might be a mistrial, there might be a jailbreak, you might get a pardon, there might be a revolution, or an earthquake.'

'Unlikely.'

482

'Very,' Reacher said. 'But isn't that who you are? A guy who will take the tiniest slim fragment of a chance to live another minute, as opposed to no chance at all?'

No response.

'You already answered me once,' Reacher said. 'When you quit the birthday game on the twelfth of October. That was pretty fast. There are thirty-one days in October. Law of averages said you'd be OK until the fifteenth or the sixteenth. A gambler would have waited for the twentieth. But you didn't get past the twelfth. Not because you're a coward. Nobody could accuse you of that. But because you're a survivor. That's who you are. Now what I want is some practical confirmation.'

No response.

'Thirteenth,' Reacher said. 'Fourteenth, fifteenth, sixteenth.'

'OK,' the Zec said. 'You win. I'll talk to the detective.'

Reacher pinned him against the hallway wall with the Smith. Took out his phone. 'Gunny?'

'Here.'

'Come on in, all of you. I'll open the door. And Franklin? Wake those guys up, like we talked about before.'

The phone went dead. Franklin had killed the comms net to make his calls.

Reacher tied the Zec's wrists and ankles with wire torn from table lamps and left him on the living room floor. Then he went downstairs. Glanced into the surveillance room. Vladimir was on his back in a lake of blood. His eyes were open. So was his throat. Reacher could see bone. Sokolov was slumped face-down on the table. His blood was all over the place. Some of it must have seeped into the wiring, because the south monitor had shorted out. The other three pictures were still there, green and ghostly. On the west monitor four figures were visible on the driveway. Yellow haloes, red cores. Close together, moving fast. Reacher turned the lights off and closed up the room. Walked on down the hallway and opened the front door.

Yanni came in first. Then Cash. Then Rosemary. Then Helen. She was barefoot and carrying her shoes in her hand. She was covered in mud. She stopped in the doorway and hugged Reacher hard. Held him for a long moment and then moved on.

'What's that smell?' Yanni asked.

'Blood,' Cash said. 'And other organic fluids of various kinds.'

'Are they all dead?'

'All but one,' Reacher said.

He led the way upstairs. Stopped Rosemary outside the living room.

'The Zec is in there,' he said. 'You OK about seeing him?'

She nodded.

'I want to see him,' she said. 'I want to ask him a question.'

She stepped into the living room. The Zec was on the floor, where Reacher had left him. Rosemary stood over him, quiet, dignified, not gloating. Just curious.

'Why?' she said. 'I mean, to an extent I understand what you thought you had to do. From your warped perspective. But why didn't you just use Chenko from the highway? Why did you have to bring my brother down?'

The Zec didn't answer. He just stared into space, seeing something, but probably not Rosemary Barr.

'Psychology,' Reacher said.

'His?'

'Ours. The public's.'

'How?'

'There had to be a story,' Reacher said. 'No, there *was* a story, and he had to control what the story was about. If he gave up a shooter, then the story would be about the shooter. No shooter, the story would have been about the victims. And if the story had been about the victims, too many questions would have been asked.'

'So he sacrificed James.'

'That's what he does. There's a long list.'

'Why?'

'One death is a tragedy, a million is a statistic.'

'Joseph Stalin,' Yanni said.

Reacher kicked the Zec aside and pulled the sofa away from the window about four feet. Grabbed the Zec's collar and hauled him up and dumped him on one end. Got him sitting up straight against the arm.

'Our star witness,' he said.

He told Cash to perch on the window sill behind the sofa. Told Yanni to go find three dining chairs. Pushed armchairs against the side walls. Yanni came back three separate times dragging chairs behind her. Reacher put them in a line facing the sofa. He ended up with a square arrangement, sofa, dining chairs, armchairs off to the sides.

His clothes were nearly dry. Just a little dampness where the seams were thick. He ran his fingers through his hair. Patted it down. Checked his watch. Nearly four in the morning. *Least resistance. A biorhythm thing.*

'Now we wait,' he said.

They waited less than thirty minutes. Then they heard cars on the road far away in the distance. Tyres on the blacktop, engine noise, exhaust pipes. The sounds grew louder. The cars slowed. They crunched onto the limestone driveway. There were four of them. Reacher went downstairs and opened the door. Saw Franklin's black Suburban. Saw Emerson sliding out of a grey Crown Vic. Saw a compact woman with short dark hair getting out of a blue Ford Taurus. Donna Bianca, he assumed. He saw Alex Rodin climbing out of a silver BMW. Rodin locked it with his remote. He was the only one who did.

Reacher stood aside and let them gather in the hallway. Then he led them upstairs. He put Alex Rodin and Donna Bianca and Emerson in the dining chairs, left to right. He put Franklin in an armchair next to Yanni. Rosemary Barr and Helen Rodin were in armchairs on the other side of the room. Helen was looking at her father. He was looking at her. Cash was on the window sill. Reacher stepped away and leaned up in the doorway.

'Start talking,' Reacher said.

The Zec stayed silent.

486

'I can send these guys away again,' Reacher said. 'Just as easily as I brought them here. Then I'll start counting again. At the seventeenth.'

The Zec sighed. Started talking. Slowly at first, and then faster. He told a long story. So much length and so much complexity that it got confusing. He spilled details of earlier unconnected crimes. Then he got to the bidding process for the city contracts. He named the official he had suborned. It wasn't just about money. There had been girls, too, supplied in small groups in a Caribbean villa. Some of them very young. He talked about Ted Archer's fury, his two-year search, his close approach to the truth. He described the ambush, one Monday morning. Jeb Oliver had been used. The red Dodge Ram had been his payoff. Then the Zec paused, decided, moved on. He described the fast decision to get rid of Oline Archer two months later, when she became dangerous. He described Chenko's subterfuge, the hasty but thorough planning, the way they lured James Barr out of the way with a promise of a date with Sandy Dupree. He described the end of Jeb Oliver's usefulness. He told them where to find his body. He told them about Vladimir killing Sandy in an effort to stop Reacher in his tracks. Altogether he talked for more than thirty minutes, hands tied behind him, and then he stopped suddenly and Reacher saw calculation in his eyes. He was already thinking about the next move. The next roll of the dice. *A mistrial. A jailbreak. A ten-year appeals process.*

The room went quiet.

Donna Bianca said, 'Unbelievable.'

Reacher said, 'Keep talking.'

The Zec just looked at him.

'Something you left out,' Reacher said. 'You need to tell us about your inside man. That's what we're all waiting for.'

The Zec switched his gaze. He looked at Emerson. Then at Donna Bianca. Then at Alex Rodin. Right to left, along the line. Then he glanced back at Reacher.

'You're a survivor,' Reacher said. 'But you're not an idiot. There won't be a mistrial. There won't be a jailbreak. You're eighty years old and you won't survive a ten-year appeals process. You know all that. But still you agreed to talk. Why?'

The Zec said nothing.

'Because you knew sooner or later you'd be talking to a friend. Someone you own. Someone you bought and paid for. Am I right?'

The Zec nodded, slowly.

'Someone right here, right now, in fact.'

The Zec nodded again.

'One thing always bothered me,' Reacher said. 'From the start. At first I didn't know if I was right or if I was letting my ego get in the way. I went back and forth with it. Finally I decided I was right. The thing is, when I was in the service I was a hell of a good investigator. I was maybe the best they ever had. I would have put myself up against anyone. And you know what?'

'What?' Helen Rodin asked.

'I would never have thought of emptying that parking meter. Not in a million years. It would never have occurred to me to do that. So I was facing a question. Was Emerson a better

488

investigator than me? Or did he *know* that quarter was there?'

Nobody spoke.

'Emerson is not better than I was,' Reacher said. 'That's just not possible. That's what I decided.' Then he turned to the Zec. 'The coin was one clue too many. You see that now? It was unnatural. Was it Chenko's idea?'

The Zec nodded.

'You should have overruled him,' Reacher said. He turned to Emerson. 'Or *you* should have left it there. It wasn't like you needed it to make the case.'

'This is bullshit,' Emerson said.

Reacher shook his head. 'A lot of things clicked into place after that. I read the 911 transcripts and the squad car call log. Right at the start you were awful quick to make up your mind. You had a bunch of incoherent panic calls but within twenty seconds you were on the radio telling your guys that this was a lone nutcase with an automatic rifle. There was no basis for that conclusion. Six shots fired, ragged sequence, it could have been six kids with a handgun each, firing once. But you knew it wasn't.'

'Bullshit,' Emerson said again.

Reacher shook his head again. 'Final proof was when I was negotiating with your boss here. I said he'd have to tell the truth to a detective called Emerson. I could have said the cops generically, or Alex Rodin the DA. But I didn't. I said your name specifically, and a little light came on in his eyes. He sparred around for a minute more, for form's sake, but basically he agreed real fast because he figured he'd be OK as long as you were in charge.'

Silence. Then Cash said, 'But Oline Archer went to Alex Rodin here. *He* buried it. That's what you found out.'

Reacher shook his head again. 'We found out that Oline went to the DA's *office*. I went there myself, first thing after I got to town. And you know what? Alex here has got himself a couple of real dragon ladies working the door. They know he doesn't like walk-ins. Dollars to doughnuts they sent Oline on her way. That's a matter for the police, they'll have told her. Her co-worker said she was gone most of the afternoon. My guess is the dragon ladies sent her trekking all across town to the station house, where she sat down with Emerson here.'

Silence in the room.

The Zec struggled on the sofa. 'Emerson, *do* something, for Christ's sake.'

'Nothing he can do,' Reacher said. 'I'm not dumb. I think ahead. I'm sure he's got a Glock under his arm, but he's got me behind him with a .38 and a knife, and he's got Cash facing him with a sniper rifle hidden behind the sofa, and what can he do anyway? I guess he could try to kill us all and say there was some kind of a big massacre here, but how would that help him with NBC?'

Emerson stared at him.

'NBC?' Cash repeated.

'I saw Yanni fiddling with her phone earlier. I'm assuming she's transmitting all of this back to the studios.'

Yanni pulled out her Nokia.

'Open channel,' she said. 'Digital audio recording on three separate hard discs, plus two analogue tapes as backup. They've all been running since well before we got in the Humvee.'

Cash stared at her. 'That's why you asked me that dumb question about the night scope. That's why you were talking to yourself like a sports announcer.'

'She's a journalist,' Reacher said. 'She's going to win an Emmy.'

Nobody spoke. Everyone was suddenly self-conscious.

'Detective Bianca,' Reacher said loudly. 'You were just promoted head of the Serious Crimes Squad. How does it feel?'

Yanni made a face. Reacher stepped forward and leaned over the back of Emerson's chair and slid his hand under his coat. Came back out with a Glock nine. Handed it to Bianca.

'You've got arrests to make,' he said.

Then the Zec smiled, and Chenko walked into the room.

Chenko was covered in mud and his right arm was broken, or his shoulder, or his collar bone, or maybe all three. His wrist was jammed into his shirt like a sling. But there was nothing wrong with his left arm. Nothing at all. Reacher turned round to face him and saw the sawn-off rock-steady in his left hand. He thought, irrelevantly: *Where did he get that from? His car? Were the cars parked to the east?*

Chenko glanced at Bianca.

'Put the gun down, lady,' he said.

Bianca laid Emerson's Glock on the floor. No sound as it touched the carpet.

'Thank you,' Chenko said.

Nobody spoke.

'I guess I was out for a little while,' Chenko said. 'But I got to tell you, I feel a whole hell of a lot better now.'

'We survive,' the Zec said, from across the room. 'That's what we do.'

Reacher didn't look back at him. He looked at Chenko's gun instead. It had been a Benelli Nova Pump. The stock had been cut off behind the pistol grip. The barrel had been hacked off ahead of the slide. Twelve-gauge. Four-shot magazine. A handsome weapon, butchered.

'Emerson,' the Zec called. 'Come over here and untie me.'

Reacher heard Emerson stand up. He didn't look back at him. Just took a tiny pace forward and sideways, closer to Chenko. He was a foot taller and twice as wide.

'I need a knife here,' Emerson said.

'The soldier's got a knife,' Chenko said. 'I'm damn sure of that, based on what I saw happened to my buddies downstairs.'

Reacher moved a little closer to him. A big guy and a little guy directly face to face, separated by about three feet, most of which was occupied by the Benelli. Reacher's waist was level with Chenko's chest.

'Knife,' Emerson said.

'Come and get it,' Reacher said.

'Slide it across the floor.'

'No.'

'I'll shoot,' Chenko said. 'Twelve-gauge, in the gut.'

Reacher thought: *And then what? A pump-action shotgun ain't much use to a one-armed man.*

'So shoot,' he said.

He felt eyes on him. He knew everyone was looking at him. Staring at him. Silence buzzed in his ears. He was suddenly aware of the smells in the room. Dust in the carpet, worn furniture, fear, tension, damp night air blowing in from the open door downstairs and the busted window upstairs and carrying with it the odour of rich earth and fertilizer and budding new growth.

'Go ahead,' he said. 'Shoot.'

Chenko did nothing. Just stood there. Reacher stood there directly in front of him. He knew exactly how the room was laid out. He had arranged it. He pictured it in his mind. Chenko was in the doorway facing the window. Everyone else was facing the other way. Reacher himself right in front of Chenko, face to face, close enough to touch. Cash directly behind him, way back, behind the sofa, on the window sill, staring forward. Then the Zec on the sofa, looking the same way. Then Emerson in the middle of the floor, near the Zec, standing up, indecisive, watching. Then Yanni and Franklin and Helen and Rosemary Barr in the armchairs against the side walls, heads turned. Then Bianca and Alex Rodin on their dining chairs, twisted round at the waist, eyes wide.

Reacher knew where everyone was, and he knew what they were looking at.

'Shoot,' he said. 'Aim at my belt. That'll work. Go ahead.'

Chenko did nothing. Just stared up at him. Reacher was so close and so big he was all Chenko could see. It was just the two of them, like they were alone in the room.

'I'll help you out,' Reacher said. 'I'll count to three. Then you pull the trigger.'

Chenko just stood there.

'You understand?' Reacher said.

No reply.

'One,' Reacher said.

No reaction.

'Two,' Reacher said.

Then he stepped out of the way. Just took a long fast sideways shuffle to his right. Cash fired from behind the sofa at the spot where Reacher's belt had been a split second before and Chenko's chest blew apart.

Then Cash put his rifle back on the floor just as silently as he had picked it up.

Two night-shift squad cars came and took the Zec and Emerson away. Then four ambulances arrived for the casualties. Bianca asked Reacher what exactly had happened to the first three. Reacher told her he had absolutely no idea. None at all. He speculated that it might have been some kind of internal dispute. A falling-out among thieves, maybe? Bianca didn't push it. Rosemary Barr borrowed Franklin's cell phone and used it to call area hospitals, looking for a safe berth for her brother. Helen and Alex Rodin sat close together, talking. Gunny Cash sat in a chair and dozed. An old soldier's habit. *Sleep when you can*. Yanni stepped up close to Reacher and said, 'Rough men stand ready in the night.' Reacher found himself very aware of the live phone. He just smiled and said, 'I'm usually in bed by twelve o'clock.'

'Me too,' Yanni said. 'Alone. You remember my address?'

Reacher smiled again, and nodded. Then he went downstairs and stepped out to the front porch and walked a little way south across the dirt until he could see past the bulk of the house to the eastern sky. Dawn was coming. Black shaded to purple right on the horizon. He turned round and watched the last ambulance loading up. Vladimir's final ride, judging by the size of the shape under the sheet on the gurney. He emptied his pockets and left Emerson's torn business card, and Helen Rodin's cocktail napkin, and the motor court's big brass key, and the Smith 60, and Gunny Cash's Navy Seal SRK all in a neat little pile beside the front door. Then he asked the paramedics if he could ride with them to town. He figured he could walk east from the hospital and be at the bus depot before the sun was fully up. He could be in Indianapolis before lunch. Then he could buy a pair of shoes and be just about anywhere before the sun went down again.

THE AFFAIR

By Lee Child

A Jack Reacher thriller

'Child on top of his game. Could well be his best book yet'
Independent

March 1997. A woman has her throat cut behind a bar in Mississippi. Just down the road is a big army base. Is the murderer a local guy – or is he a soldier?

Jack Reacher, still a major in the military police, is sent in undercover. The county sherriff is a former U.S. Marine – and a stunningly beautiful woman. Her investigation is going nowhere. Is the Pentagon stonewalling her? Or doesn't she really want to find the killer?

Set just six months before the opening of *Killing Floor*, *The Affair* marks a turning point in Reacher's life. If he does what the army wants, will he be able to live with himself? And if he doesn't, will the army be able to live with him?

'Just when you thought it couldn't possibly get any better, Lee Child pulls Jack Reacher out of another hole and, bang, he produces nothing short of a thriller masterpiece . . . Here, we get what we've been waiting for . . . the story of how Reacher became Reacher'
Mirror

'A timely, reassuring wallow in the undiluted essence of Reacher'
Daily Telegraph

'Just finished *The Affair*. As always, hero Reacher grabs me on page one and never lets go'
Ken Follett

A WANTED MAN

By Lee Child

The new Jack Reacher thriller

When you're as big and rough as Jack Reacher – and you have a badly-set, freshly-busted nose, patched with silver duct tape – it isn't easy to hitch a ride. But Reacher has some unfinished business in Virginia, so he doesn't quit. And at last, he's picked up by three strangers – two men and a woman.

But within minutes it becomes clear they're all lying about everything – and then they run into a police roadblock on the highway. There has been an incident, and the cops are looking for the bad guys . . .

Will they get through because the three are innocent? Or because the three are now four? Is Reacher just a decoy?

With his signature Swiss-watch plotting and heart-thumping suspense, *A Wanted Man* shows Lee Child at his sublimely skilful best.

'The paradox of Reacher is that he is both a great big grizzly bear of a fighter . . . and a thinker, both Schwarzenegger and Socrates'
Independent

'Jack Reacher has long since earned his prominent place in the pantheon of cool, smart-talking American heroes'
New York Times

REACHER'S RULES

NEW: A handy guide to living life the Reacher Way

Foreword by Lee Child

My name is Jack Reacher.
No middle name, no address.
I've got a rule. People mess with me
at their own risk.

RULE 1
If in doubt, drink coffee.

RULE 2
Never volunteer for anything. Soldier's basic rule.

RULE 3
Don't break the furniture.

RULE 4
Only have one woman at a time.

RULE 5
Be on your feet and ready.

RULE 6
Show them what they're messing with.